"What do you think of the villa, Dr. Bradbury?"

"I like the tour guide." Oliver leaned an inch closer, backing Zoe against the wood frame of the door.

A kiss. That's all he wanted. One kiss. One long, wet, hot kiss just to ease the ache that already started way low in his gut. Way low. Everything in him wanted to touch her, to remember the silky feel of her skin, the pressure of her mouth, the warmth of her tongue.

That very tongue darted to wet her lips, her eyes locked on his, the message in them so, so clear.

Kiss me, Oliver.

His reply was silent, too. Just a whisper of warm breath into her mouth that almost instantly became more. A warm, tentative spark of a kiss that tightened every muscle in his body and completely flatlined his brain.

Their mouths melded as one, and against every will he dragged his hands out of his pockets just so he could cup her jaw and just hold her face like a precious jewel. "Do you interview all the nannies like this?" she murmured into the kiss.

"Just the mouthy ones. Do you give all the renters tongue?"

"Just the hot ones."

DISCARD

PRAISE FOR THE
BAREFOOT BAY SERIES

BAREFOOT IN THE RAIN

"In a love story with genuinely flawed yet sympathetic characters, set on a picturesque island off the coast of Florida, St. Claire focuses on the complexities of familial relationships, and the past hurts and experiences that can shape them. Honest, genuine, and occasionally gritty, this is a story that will resonate."

—RT Book Reviews

"I'm so glad I found the Barefoot Bay series. Not only are they well-written but [I] love connected books . . . You'll love it. You'll love it even more if you start with *Barefoot in the Sand*, but each book definitely stands on its own."

—Examiner.com

"[I] really enjoy the Barefoot Bay series and am anxiously awaiting the next in the series. I've come to love and adore these women and the resort they are building together."

—TheBookPushers.com

"This book stayed with me even when I had to put it down. It can challenge the reader and make her think, which is a quality I greatly enjoy in a book . . . I have to admire Ms. St. Claire for taking risks with this novel. They paid off."

—All About Romance (LikesBooks.com)

BAREFOOT IN THE SAND

"*Barefoot in the Sand*—the first in Roxanne St. Claire's new Barefoot Bay series—is an all-around knockout and soul-satisfying read. I loved everything about this book—the indomitable heroine, the hot hero, the lush tropical setting, and secondary characters I can't wait to read more about. Roxanne St. Claire writes with warmth and heart, and the community she's built in Barefoot Bay is one I want to revisit again and again and again."
—**Mariah Stewart,** *New York Times* **bestselling author of the** *Chesapeake Diaries*

"Lovely, lush, and layered—this story took my breath away. Rich, believable characters, multilayered plot, gorgeous setting, and a smokin' hot romance. One of the best books I've read all year."
—**Kristan Higgins,** *New York Times* **bestselling author, on** *Barefoot in the Sand*

"I enjoyed the typical mother/teen relationship Lacey had with Ashley—so comfortable and believable. Lacey is older than Clay, but the difference never matters. The chemistry between them is scorching hot. I adored her friends and I'm looking forward to their stories as well. *Barefoot in the Sand* is a wonderful story with plenty of heat, humor, and heart!"
—*USA Today's* **Happy Ever After blog**

ACCLAIM FOR ROXANNE ST. CLAIRE

Also by Roxanne St. Claire

THE BAREFOOT BAY QUARTET

Barefoot in the Rain

Barefoot in the Sand

THE GUARDIAN ANGELINOS

Face of Danger

Shiver of Fear

Edge of Sight

Barefoot in the Sun

roxanne
st. claire

FOREVER

NEW YORK   BOSTON

Copyright © 2013 by Roxanne St. Claire

Excerpt from *Barefoot by the Sea* copyright © 2013 by Roxanne St. Claire

Forever
Hachette Book Group
237 Park Avenue
New York, NY 10017

www.HachetteBookGroup.com

Printed in the United States of America

First Edition: April 2013

10 9 8 7 6 5 4 3 2 1

Forever is an imprint of Grand Central Publishing.
The Forever name and logo are trademarks of Hachette Book Group, Inc.

The Hachette Speakers Bureau provides a wide range of authors for speaking events. To find out more, go to www.hachettespeakersbureau.com or call (866) 376-6591.

The publisher is not responsible for Web sites (or their content) that are not owned by the publisher.

For Barbie Furtado
My beta reader, my cyber-daughter, my #1 Zoe fan—this one is most certainly for you.

Acknowledgments

Three cheers for the names who are not on the cover of this book but must share the credit and the love for all they do to bring my stories to life!

First of all, thank you to the readers who inspire me to pour my heart onto every page. Because of our social-networked world, I feel like I know so many of you! I love every letter, every Facebook comment, and every tweet. I'm eternally grateful to all of you who took a chance on visiting Barefoot Bay to fall in love—thank you!

On the research front, special thanks to Dr. Aris Sastre, who, at the time of writing, was chief resident of the Mayo Clinic in Jacksonville and who is also my beloved nephew-in-law. (Is there such a thing?) Aris is a brilliant and talented physician and is very generous with his time for Aunt Rocki's medical questions.

Additional research assistance came from Sgt. Adrian Youngblood of the Seminole County Sheriff's Office and Captain Jeff A. Thompson of Thompson Aire Hot Air Balloon Rides, both of whom answered questions and offered great insights. (If you want to float over Orlando, go to Thompson!)

My publishing team at Grand Central is superb at every turn in the process, starting with tireless Executive Editor Amy Pierpont, who leaves an indelible mark on every page of my books. Detail-oriented and sweet-as-pie assistant Lauren Plude keeps me in line and on time, and extremely generous Managing Editor Bob Castillo doles out patience and pages whenever I need them. And huge thanks to the art department for giving this book the cover of my dreams!

Also heartfelt thanks to literary agent Robin Rue, who is never more than a click or a call away with guidance, humor, balance, and sanity. (Not necessarily in that order.)

My writer girls, Kresley Cole, Leigh Duncan, Louisa Edwards, Kristen Painter, Lara Santiago, and Gena Showalter, are the *best* best friends. The support and encouragement they showed during the writing of this book was unparalleled in our long history as friends.

My beloved husband, Rich, and our two superstar teenagers, Dante and Mia, who (try to) leave me alone when I need to write and show me the love even when all I do is talk about the book. Those three (and the dogs!) humble and delight me.

And, finally, to my good and loving Father, who came through with words and wisdom exactly when I needed them most. I can't remember a book that had me asking for as much help as this one, and He answered every prayer.

Barefoot in the Sun

Prologue

Zoe reached into the backseat and pulled a faded black bandanna from her purse, snapping it like a lion tamer's whip inches from Oliver's face.

"Blindfold time," she announced, her eyes glistening like dew on fresh-cut grass.

He choked softly. "I won't be able to see."

"Ya think?" She gave his arm a playful punch, lingering on his muscle, which of course he flexed for her. "You know, Dr. Oliver Bradbury, for a Mensa-IQ summa-cum-laude chief resident of Mount Mercy Hospital who got himself into college at sixteen…" She nudged him. "You're not the sharpest scalpel in the sterilization tray. Turn and tie, them's my rules."

"As if you ever met a rule you couldn't chew up and spit out."

That made her laugh. "We are not getting out of the car and going past those trees until I'm one-hundred-percent certain you are blinded."

"I am." He leaned closer to her mouth. "By you."

"Sweet." She obliged, but the kiss was quick. "Now let me tie this."

"You think I'm kidding?" He tossed one final glance at her, then complied with her order. "You've wrecked my life, Zoe."

"Aw, thank you."

"Everything was all orderly and simple and straightforward and—"

"Boring."

"As hell," he agreed. "And now I'm letting you blindfold me and take me into the woods at the crack of dawn to do…God knows what, but I think I'm going to like it."

She was dead silent while she knotted the bandanna.

"I am going to like it, aren't I?"

More silence.

"Zoe?" He dragged out both syllables of her name, his voice lifting the long *e* in a playful question.

As she adjusted the material, her fingers caressed his cheeks, scratching the twenty-four-hour-shift shadow. "You'll like it if you're ready to face your fears."

He turned to her, and even though he couldn't see her, he could imagine the smile he'd been admiring and exploring for a month now, the smattering of freckles decorating a slightly upturned nose, and those honey-silk curls brushing her cheeks and begging to be tangled in his fingers. God, he loved her, even when he couldn't see her. And that, he admitted to himself, was the only thing that scared him.

"I'm not afraid of anything," he lied, mustering his macho. Not of anything in those woods, anyway.

"Not a thing?"

An image so old and dark that he could barely remember details flashed in his brain, but he instantly erased it. "My only fear is losing you," he told her, which was the absolute truth.

"Oh, you are freaking Shakespeare today. And you're lying. You're scared of heights and I know it."

He didn't like them, but...scared? "What makes you think that?"

"Ahem, first date? Skydeck of Sears Tower? Your excuses for not going up there were pathetic."

"Those weren't excuses. I wanted to get you home and in bed."

"Mmm." She leaned so close he could feel the warmth of her lips before they touched his. "Guess that worked."

He closed the space and took the kiss. "Could work again. Let's get out of here if you want to face some fears. I'll scare the clothes right off you."

She laughed. "We can do that later, but first..." Her voice trailed off.

"But first what? Survive your latest bout of crazy?"

"Yeah, you could say that."

He tried to imagine what in the rural area outside of Chicago could be life-threatening. "Are you going to make me climb a tree or something?"

"Umm...something."

"What something?"

"I'm going to tell you something."

A little jolt of joy kicked his chest, making him lift the edge of the bandanna for a one-eyed peek. "Hell, yeah."

She tugged the blindfold back over his eyes. "You don't know what I'm going to say."

Oh, yes he did. Three little words he'd been declaring and she'd been refusing to reciprocate.

"I'm going to tell you...something very important, very secret, and very..." For a second she hesitated, and he could hear her inhale a shaky breath. "Very revealing about me."

This time her vague answer made him grin. "'Bout damn time."

"Hope you're smiling like that after I tell you."

Of course he would be. *She loved him.* He'd be the happiest guy in the world. He might propose then and there. Who cares if they'd only known each other for a month? For the first time in his life he wasn't following the expected course, and nothing had ever felt better.

"Just say it, Zoe. Move your lips and say I..." He kissed her mouth. "Love." He nibbled her lower lip. "You." He sucked gently, making a squeak. "Your turn." *Come on, Zoe.*

"Or you could skip the preliminaries." She sucked his lip right back, way noisier and with more gusto, then shoved him to the door. "Go."

He let her lead him through the woods, along a trail he could see through the bottom of the blindfold, but he played her game and didn't cheat. They spent a good ten minutes crossing a grassy field, holding hands. With each step, he inhaled the scent of pine and honeysuckle and thought about what he'd say after she finally admitted she loved him.

Zoe, will you marry me? No, too straightforward.

Zoe, make me the happiest man on earth and marry me. She'd howl at the cliché.

Ever since the moment I saw you, I knew this was inevit—

"Stop." She froze them both in place. In the distance, he

heard voices, a cry of something that sounded like a mix of terror and joy. Where were they?

She pressed against his chest, sliding up on her tiptoes to reach his lips with hers. "Will you do this for me?"

Do what? It didn't matter. If this was her test, he'd pass. "Honey, I'd walk across fire for you and you know it."

"Then this ought to be a piece of cake. Oliver Bradbury, you are about to conquer your fears." She pulled off the blindfold. "And I'm about to face mine."

Yellow. The only thing he could see was a giant, rubbery, blinding mass of yellow spilled over the ground like a sea of sunflowers; it took a full five seconds for it all to compute. "No fucking way."

"Well, now, that's the attitude." She grabbed his hand and pulled him closer.

"A hot air balloon, Zoe? Are you nuts? I'm not getting on that thing." Not in a million years.

Rounding the basket, she stood on her tiptoes and peered in. "Oh, the crew did everything just like I asked. We only need to blow her up and take her high." She waved to a few people gathered near another balloon, this one partially inflated by a giant fan in front of it. "Climb in and meet the ground crew."

"The ground crew? How about the pilot?" At her smug smile he closed his eyes. No. Oh, Christ, no.

"I'm taking you up," she said, confirming his fear.

"You are." He gave a dubious look to the deflated balloon and tiny basket barely big enough to hold two people, let alone enough extra tanks to make sure they didn't run out of whatever it was that kept these things afloat.

"Want to see my license? I got it last week."

Last week?

Her laughter floated off into the breeze, like they were about to. Except they *weren't*.

"You want a lesson in how it works?" she asked. "Would that make you feel better? Those sandbags are—"

"I want a rain check." He stepped back, glancing up to a morning sky that promised no rain as a handy excuse. A brightly striped balloon ascended, already nearly a thousand feet in the air. Aw, fuck it *all*. "It's not happening, Zoe."

She angled her head and looked up at him. "And thirty seconds ago you were going to walk across fire for me."

"I still would. *On the ground.*"

For a long, quiet, seemingly endless moment, they looked at each other.

"How is it you can cut open a human chest and pluck out a heart and replace a stinking *artery* like a freaking car mechanic and you can't go up in the air in a machine brilliantly designed to fly safely?"

He took a slow breath. "First of all, I only did that during my cardiology rotation, but in surgery, I'm in control." He held up his two hands. "I operate these."

"Well, I operate this."

"No, Zoe, it's powered by wind and—chance."

She stepped closer, wrapping her arms around his waist, and gave him an irresistible smile. "Kind of like me, huh?"

He slid his hand into her hair and held her steady. "You're uplifting, not flighty. There's a difference."

She inched back, her eyes uncharacteristically serious, and maybe a little scared. Why would *she* be scared? "I want to tell you something, Oliver, and I want to be up there"—she pointed to the sky—"when I do."

"You can tell me right here, right now. Not two thousand feet in the air."

"Three."

Shit.

"I need to be sure you aren't going to leave."

He almost choked. "Leave? I'd never leave you. I'm attached to you. I changed my life for you, or did you forget?"

She shrugged. "Yes, you broke up with your girlfriend the day after we met. But"—she pointed a finger in his face—"you said yourself you didn't really love her."

Was this a test of whether or not he loved Zoe? Because if it was, Oliver wouldn't fail. But, damn it, he didn't want to take that ride. "This is crazy."

"*I'm* crazy," she assured him with a ridiculous amount of pride. "I'm a lunatic who loves to get up in the air and be completely untethered. And that's where I want to be with you when I tell you…something."

That something he needed to hear.

He searched her face, hating that he could already feel himself giving in. How did she do this to him? He couldn't say no to her. One kiss, one touch, one laugh, one time, and he was gone. "God, I love you."

"Is that a yes?" She tightened her grip. "Please say yes."

"I know what you're doing."

She tilted her head, that serious look darkening her eyes again. "Actually, I don't think you do."

"You're testing me. And you know damn well I have never met a test I didn't ace."

"I'm not testing you, Oliver. I'm testing me." She put her finger on his lips, holding his gaze. "And I want to do it on my turf."

"Which happens to be three thousand feet off the ground."

"Think of it as three thousand feet closer to the sun. Please?"

It was just enough to push him over an edge he knew he'd tumble over anyway.

He gave up the fight as a few guys—who looked as young and inexperienced as Zoe—came over to greet them. During the next half hour Zoe was in her element, and Oliver was in denial.

The fan blew the massive nylon balloon up to four stories high, until they were all dwarfed by its magnitude. When it was big enough, they attached what looked like really rickety burners, which blasted enough heat that the whole thing started to bounce a little—like Zoe in her strappy sandals and ruffled skirt that danced around her ankles.

"Let's go!" She grabbed his hand and they got into the basket, high-fived a few of their crew, and then there was more choreography of burners and sandbags and a great deal of waving and cries of "Good luck," which he hoped to hell they didn't need.

And then they were off, the ground drifting farther away, the gondola, as she called the basket, swinging like a heart-stopping pendulum, and the air thinner with each passing second.

Or maybe that was just Oliver having a tough time breathing.

He gripped the wicker rim, refusing to look down. Instead he watched Zoe fine-tune the burners and dance with the wind, as he tried to pretend he was paying attention and not mentally writing his last will and testament.

"Listen," she whispered as she twisted a valve. "Listen to that."

Silence. Complete and total silence.

"Nice," he admitted, relaxing a little as a slight breeze lifted them over a golf course and toward a lake, the residential developments of suburban Chicago fading into a quilt work of farms in rural Illinois about fifteen hundred feet below.

Wordlessly, Zoe and Oliver came together, folding into each other's arms like it was as natural as breathing.

"You okay?" she asked.

He nodded, lowering his face for a kiss. "Is this the part when we get to drink that champagne?" he asked, nodding toward the bottle that one of the ground crew had tossed in at the very last minute.

"Oh, that's not for us," she told him. "That's in case we land on someone's property. It's tradition for the balloon pilot to offer champagne to the people to thank them for letting them land there."

"In other words you don't have any idea where you're going to land."

"That, my darling, is the story of my life." She took a deep, deep breath and closed her eyes. "You ready?"

"For anything. Except jumping."

"Well, you might want to when I tell you this."

He searched her face, taking time to appreciate the fine bones and soft skin, the deep bow in her upper lip, the bottle-green eyes that tipped up at the sides and sparkled when she smiled. But it wasn't Zoe's external beauty that had wrapped around his heart and squeezed the life out of him. It was her spirit, her laugh, her willingness to give everything to every situation.

"Nothing you could tell me would make me want to jump," he said.

"All right." Her chest rose and fell with each strained breath. She eased out of his arms and steadied herself by holding on to the wicker edge, the rising sun silhouetting her. "My name's not really Zoe Tamarin."

He gave it a nanosecond of consideration. "Okay, what is it?"

"Bridget."

Bridget? "I like that name, but Zoe suits you so much better. So much more alive and wild than Bridget."

"Zoe means new life," she said softly, the words spoken almost as if she'd memorized them or she was quoting someone.

"Is that why you changed it?"

Her knuckles whitened on the basket rim. "I didn't change it. Pasha did."

Her aunt was even crazier than Zoe, that was for sure. "Don't tell me: a butterfly landed on her teacup and flapped out a new name in Morse code?"

She didn't laugh. Instead, she bit her lower lip and cast her eyes down. "I was in the Texas foster care system as a child."

"Really?" He tried to wrap his head around that. Why would she keep something so big from him? "You never told me."

"Because I never tell anyone."

On his belt loop the cell phone he was required to carry rang, jarring both of them.

"Whoops, I forgot to tell you that you're supposed to turn that off up here," she said. "FCC rules."

He glanced at the phone. "It's not a call, it's one of those new SMS messages the hospital put us on instead of pagers."

"Are you on call today?"

"No, but there's one patient who started a new treatment yesterday and I asked the shift nurse to shoot me a message on his status."

She nodded toward the phone when it rang again. "Then you'd better check it."

"Hold your thought." Pulling out the new hospital-issued flip-phone, he snapped up the cover.

Must talk. Very important!

He peered at the message, then the number, recognizing it instantly. Of course Adele would have access to every resident's number. And use it to stalk him. She wasn't going to let go of him that easily, was she? She'd been hounding him for four weeks, even though he'd broken up with her as civilly as he could and had stopped taking her calls.

He shook his head. "Not important." He focused on Zoe and this conversation, since everything the woman he loved said was far more important than messages from the one he did not. "Why were you in foster care if you have your Aunt Pasha?"

"She's not my aunt."

"Great-aunt," he corrected.

"Not that either. She was my next-door neighbor."

Now he really scowled. "And she adopted you?"

"She...took me." She gnawed at her lip and forced herself to meet his gaze, even though, he could tell, that wasn't easy. "She saved me. I was in trouble when I was ten years old, I was in..." She searched for a word, then shook her head in frustration. "Trouble. And I had to get away from the trouble. So Pasha, the next-door neighbor, took me and—"

"Wait." He didn't understand. "The neighbor took you? How?"

"She ran away with me. I needed help and she…" Zoe reached for his arm. "Pasha saved my life, Oliver. She kept me and changed our names and we moved constantly from town to town, and she got fake IDs made so we could manage and we stayed off the grid and under the radar." The words spilled out, each one a little harder to believe than the one before. "If you want to get technical about it, she kidnapped me."

The basket buffeted by a gust of wind, the balloon suddenly dropping at least five feet while Oliver's stomach felt like it plummeted another two hundred.

Zoe whipped around to adjust the valve.

"She *kidnapped* you?" How was that even possible? "And no one ever caught her?"

"Not yet."

The phone, still in his hand, rang again. While Zoe worked the valves and the balloon bounced, Oliver read the next message.

I'm serious, Oliver! This is an EMERGENCY!

He stared at the words but didn't really see them, his whole being waiting for Zoe to finish, his brain trying—and failing—to squeeze this new information into what he knew about her. She'd been *kidnapped*?

"That's why we move so much," she said, finally turning back to him, her cheeks pink from the wind. Or maybe that was shame. Which was crazy because she hadn't done anything wrong.

Except go along with the insanity, bouncing through life with her crazy aunt-neighbor with as little stability as this balloon.

"Zoe, you have to fix this problem. It's been, what? Fourteen years?"

"There's no statute of limitations on kidnapping," she said, her tone full of the authority of someone who'd done her research. "She could still go to jail."

"What about you?"

"Me? I didn't do anything, but I have to protect her."

"What you have to do is—is fix this." How could she not see that?

"Oliver, didn't you hear me? She could go to jail. There's nothing to *fix*."

Of course there was. "How about your life and your future?" Didn't she see that? He reached for her to make his point, the steps already clear to him even if the problem wasn't. "Zoe, you get a good lawyer and you work out a deal, maybe pay a fine or—"

"No!"

Her vehemence shocked him. "What are you going to do, hide your whole life?"

For a long, silent moment, she stood uncharacteristically still. As each second ticked by, her eyes filled. "I don't know, but I'm not going to do anything that's a risk to her. I'm not going to do anything official."

The phone rang again. "Damn it," he muttered. "Let me turn this off." He opened the cover to find the button, but the words on the screen assaulted him.

OLIVER I AM PREGNANT!

He snapped the phone closed with a crack, making Zoe startle.

"You're angry," she said.

"Not with you."

Adele was pregnant? Seriously? He couldn't even think

straight enough to do the math, but he didn't have to. They'd broken up four weeks ago. Adele could easily be pregnant.

Or she could be lying, just as easily.

Zoe backed away, her eyes already filled with tears. "I knew I shouldn't have told you. I've never told anyone, and this is why."

"No, no, Zoe. That's not—" His logical brain felt like it was short-circuiting. "First things first," he said, as much to himself as to her. "We get a lawyer and get her cleared."

Her jaw opened. "It isn't that easy, Oliver."

"You can't live your life like this, Zoe. You have to go to the authorities and—"

"Are you *nuts*?"

"Are you?" he fired back.

For a second she froze, staring at him. Then she turned back to the valves. "I'll take us down."

"Good," he said, taking out the phone to make sure he'd read Adele's message right. What would he do if she really was pregnant? He wouldn't abandon her, but he sure as hell wouldn't mar—

"Shit," she muttered, twisting a knob with a grunt.

"What? A problem?"

She whipped around to him, the balloon falling a little too fast. "Yes, Oliver. There is a problem."

"We're going to crash?"

"We just did," she said.

"Zoe, come on. Be smart about this. If Pasha—"

"No," she said sharply. "You be smart about it. Do you have any idea what it took to tell you that? Any idea at all how I guard that secret? I've never told my closest friends, my college roommates. I've never told anyone but you."

"I appreciate that, but—"

"No buts!" Tears splashed now, each one a little kick in his gut.

"Zoe, what did you think I'd say?"

"I thought you'd understand. I thought you'd step forward and tell me you love me anyway, despite my past. I really thought you'd be the one person I could trust."

"Did you think I'd say 'Oh, that's cool, no big deal—we'll live on the run the rest of our lives and that's fine?" He hated himself for taking his anger at Adele out on Zoe, but how could he walk away from a baby? He wouldn't, of course, he'd—

"I don't know what I was thinking. It was crazy to think I could ever…stay."

He reached for her, but she snapped out of his touch.

"Zoe, you can stay. You can do whatever you want. You have to clear up this problem." And so did he.

"Sure." She nodded, swiping her eyes. "I'm sorry."

"For what your aunt did when you were a kid? How can you be sorry about that?"

"I'm not sorry about that. She saved me, Oliver. I wasn't going to survive that situation and she knew it. She swooped in and risked *everything* for me. She gave up her life for me."

He didn't understand how making Zoe disappear and live the life of a tumbleweed made everything all right, but this wasn't the time to argue about that. His own life was falling apart faster than this balloon was heading for the ground. "Then what are you sorry for?"

Zoe manipulated the balloon, her hair flipping over her face. "For telling you. For being honest. For falling in—bed with you."

"You were going to say love, weren't you?" The phone rang again and he didn't even bother to look at this message. "Weren't you, Zoe?"

She flicked her hair off her face, doing something with the valves that made the basket drop and swing a little.

"Whoops!" She laughed playfully, that wind-chime giggle that he loved so much. Except there was something missing in the musical sound this time.

And just like that, her walls went up. He'd spent four weeks taking them down brick by brick, but now she was back to fun-loving, joke-making, carefree Zoe who kept everyone at a distance. Fuck. Could he be handling this any worse?

"We better get you home so you can take care of who-ever is so desperate to reach you, Doctor."

This was the wrong time, the wrong place. He'd fix this later. First he'd handle Adele, then he'd handle Zoe. "In a few weeks I'll have this all fixed."

She shot him a look. "'Cause that's what you do, right?"

Right. "I better get…to the hospital." Or to Adele's house. "And then we'll talk, Zoe."

"Not much to talk about now."

Like hell there wasn't. "Zoe, you have to attack the problem logically. You have to do the right thing, even though…" He glanced at the phone in his hand, his chest suddenly hollow and cold. "The right thing isn't easy."

She nodded, saying nothing as she worked to get them down. "I'll call the ground crew when we land and they'll pick us up," she said, all the joy and life that had taken them into the skies gone from her flat voice.

He pushed away the guilt. One problem at a time.

"We'll talk later?" he asked again.

"Oh, of course. We'll talk. I'll chat with my aunt and tell her what you think we should do. Then we can talk all you want."

Her voice had a strange note, almost like she was teasing. But he couldn't dig deeper into that now. Not with his phone exploding with bad news. "You promise?" he asked again.

But she didn't answer; she was too busy with the balloon instruments.

"Hold on, now," she finally said. "We're about to touch down. Prepare to crash." She winked at him. "Kidding." They hit with a solid thud, enough to knock him off balance and both of them into each other, and he held her as tightly as he could.

"Do you promise we'll talk later?" he pressed.

She made an X over her heart. "I promise."

Less than twelve hours later he stood in an abandoned house on the south side of Chicago, every sign that Zoe and Pasha Tamarin had ever rented it wiped away. Her promise had been broken, along with his heart. And he had no idea how to fix that.

Chapter One

Run, Zoe, run.

Stuff it, Zoe fired back at the voice in her head. Running wasn't an option this time.

It would be so much easier.

And, God, she loved her some easy. And there was nothing as easy as a mad dash when things got sketchy.

Well, things were about to zoom past sketchy and fly right into stupid. Or smart. Depending on how he reacted.

Zoe slid a glance across the wide boulevard that cut a swath through the exclusive business district of Naples, her gaze landing on a two-story Spanish hacienda–style building she'd spotted about six months ago on her last visit to Florida. Between her and that destination, heat shimmered off the road like burning coals.

I'd walk across fire for you.

The memory stabbed, and her finger lingered on the keys in the ignition. *Just turn it and run.*

The idea pounded as hard as the summer sun on this

beachside city, slamming down on her rented 4x4, melting her into the scorching leather seat.

No! She. Would. Not. Run. Not this time.

Zoe had been raised on the altar of "signs from the universe," and last night the universe had smacked her over the head with a billboard.

While all her closest friends had celebrated the birth of a baby who'd arrived with stunning drama during the Casa Blanca Resort & Spa grand-opening party, Zoe had played a part in a different drama.

Unlike everyone else in the room, Zoe knew the doctor who'd been pressed into emergency service to deliver Lacey and Clay Walker's baby. He wasn't just another guest at the event to her.

Calm and commanding, Oliver Bradbury had stepped into the role of lifesaver and baby-deliverer, unaffected by the chaos around him—until he saw Zoe, who had probably looked like a slack-jawed lunatic at that moment. But hadn't his dark eyes flashed? Hadn't he nearly stumbled over an order for everyone to leave the room?

Or maybe she'd imagined that. Either way, she'd followed that order and bolted down the hall, reeling. By the time the paramedics had whisked mother, son, and proud papa off to the hospital, the doctor had been on his way out. From the stretcher, holding her little bundle, Lacey had pronounced the man "an angel" and demanded to know his name.

Zoe stayed utterly silent, of course, admitting to no one that she knew far more than his name. Once, she'd known his heart.

She hadn't slept at all last night. She couldn't stop thinking about him and what he could do for her. It really was a sign from the universe, as her great-aunt, Pasha, would say.

All Zoe had to do was swallow her pride and beg. Maybe she had to make an offer he couldn't resist.

Except that among the few things Zoe knew about Dr. Oliver Bradbury was that he'd been married for nine years. Which meant he must have basically left her on their last date and gone straight back to his ex-girlfriend. Who could blame him, after finding out about Zoe and Pasha? Which woman held more appeal: the daughter of the hospital CEO who came with blue blood and big promises of a rich future or the girl who'd been kidnapped, lived underground, and never stuck around in any place long enough to risk attachment?

But you left him, Zoe, before you ever found out which woman held more appeal. You ran. Just like always.

Because he would have turned Pasha in!

The little war of the voices in her head reminded her why she was here and why, as much as she hated it, Oliver Bradbury was the one and only man who could help her right now.

She yanked the keys out of the ignition and jumped out of the big Jeep Rubicon. Heat singed through her wafer-thin sandals as her feet hit the pavement. Squaring her shoulders, she pinned her gaze on the charcoal glass doors and jaywalked to find out her destiny.

Would he or would he not?

He *had* to. He was the guy who always did the right thing. The logical thing. He couldn't have changed *that* much in nine years.

At the door, she took a shallow breath and ran her fingers over the elegant gold lettering that announced exactly what went on in this unassuming building tucked between an art gallery and a frozen-yogurt shop in the ritzy medical district of one of the world's wealthiest cities.

Dr. Oliver Bradbury.

Oncology.

Now that right there was one ugly word, one that should—

Both doors popped open, shoved from the inside, forcing Zoe to jump back or get smacked with glass. A woman strode out, stopping to blink into the sun and throw open a giant bag covered with a designer's initials. She whipped out a pair of sunglasses with the very same initials on the side.

But before she got them on, Zoe saw her face. It was one she'd seen the night before, milling about with the guests of the grand opening: Oliver's wife.

A phone followed the sunglasses, thrust under silky black hair that brushed her shoulders. "Thank Christ," she said, an amazing amount of sultry in the sarcasm. "I'm finally free and, honey, do I need a martini and massage."

Zoe snorted. "Who doesn't?"

The woman turned to Zoe, her eyes hidden by the sunglasses but her glare powerful nonetheless. Stark bones gave her angular face a hollow look, the aura of wealth and condescension clinging like a spritz of Chanel No. 5.

Zoe knew that face even before she'd spotted her walking out of Casa Blanca's lobby doors with Oliver after the baby was born. And even before that, she'd seen Adele Townshend Bradbury, thanks to a search engine powered by a few glasses of wine served at a self-pity party. Zoe took a little consolation in the fact that Oliver's wife didn't look quite as perfect without benefit of Photoshop. But damn close.

Zoe gave her a tight smile, knowing that Adele hadn't noticed Zoe the night before and surely had no idea who she was. "Excuse me," Zoe said, reaching for the door.

"Of course, dear." Adele stepped aside, switching the phone to the other ear. "No," she said into the phone as Zoe went inside. "That was no one. I'm listening."

No one. The door closed, blessedly shutting out the sun and the sound of the woman who'd married the only man Zoe had ever…No, that wasn't love. But then how would Zoe know? She certainly had no guidelines for what love was or wasn't. But they'd had something, and she was about to leverage whatever it was to get what she had to have.

Inside, cool air settled over Zoe as she took in the creamy white walls and icy marble floor. This was like no doctor's-office reception room she'd ever been in. No mess of magazines on a cheap coffee table for Dr. Bradbury. No impersonal glass panel that slid open and closed like a confessional, either. No worn leather chairs, cheesy art, or canned video presentation.

Nothing but old money and elegant sophistication.

So, *Mrs.* Bradbury must have decorated the offices.

"Can I help you?" The question came from a striking redhead with a tiny headset in her ear who was seated at a glass table that held nothing but a sleek tablet computer and a space-age-looking phone. Her smile matched the surroundings, cold and impersonal, exactly like her Arctic-blue eyes.

"I'm here…" Zoe's voice cracked. Great. Now she sounded like a teenage boy. She cleared her throat. "I'd like to see Dr. Bradbury."

The faintest frown pulled. "What time is your appointment?"

"He'll see me." Especially now that his *wife* had just left.

"I'm sorry." The woman angled her head, a practiced mix of pity and power in her expression. "You have to make an appointment, and that requires a referral, and, to be perfectly honest, Dr. Bradbury has absolutely no patient openings now. We can provide you with the names of—"

"He'll see me," she said, nodding to the phone. "Give it a try. That's Zoe. No *y*, just Z-o-e."

"I know how to spell."

"But do you know how to dial?"

The young woman held up her hand. "If you don't have an appointment, he will *not* see you. There are absolutely no exceptions to that rule."

"I'm the exception. Zoe Tamarin."

The woman didn't move, leveling her icy glare in a showdown. "Would you like the list of doctors I mentioned?"

"Not unless one of them is Oliver." At the woman's surprised look, Zoe added, "I'm a personal acquaintance."

The woman's gaze lingered on the thin tank top stuck to Zoe's sweat-dampened skin. The white cotton skirt that had seemed so whimsical when she'd picked it up at Old Navy suddenly felt like a cheap rag compared to the receptionist's silk and pearls.

Red gave a mirthless smile and shook her head as she stood, nearly six feet tall in four-inch heels. "I'm very sorry for your situation, but you need to leave, now."

"My situation?" She didn't even freaking *know* Zoe's situation. "Please call his assistant or whoever and tell him that Zoe Tamarin is waiting to see him."

The woman tapered her eyes but touched her earpiece. "Beth?"

Zoe let out a soft sigh of relief. As soon as Oliv—

"We need security in the lobby."

Zoe croaked out a cough. "Excuse me?"

The other woman completely ignored her. "Immediately," she said into the air. Then, to Zoe, "We get a lot of desperate people wanting to see Dr. Bradbury, and—"

"Well, I'm not one of them." Which was a complete lie, but she stepped forward anyway. "Just give him my damn name."

"I'm afraid I can't do that." She looked down at her tablet as if something more important had come up.

Zoe eyed the single door to the back, a nearly invisible slab of polished rosewood that blended right into the wall. But there was a slender silver knob that might not be locked. What the hell did she have to lose? With one more glance at Red, who was pointedly ignoring her now, Zoe lunged at the door.

"Hey!" the woman cried, but Zoe slammed down the handle and pushed.

The receptionist got her then, grabbing Zoe's arm to yank her back to the lobby. "You will leave the premises, ma'am. Right. This. Minute."

Zoe fought the fingers, wresting her body away with every ounce of strength she had, and suddenly the woman let go and Zoe stumbled toward the offices, tripping on the threshold strip, her hair falling over her face as her knees hit the floor.

"What in God's name is going on out here?"

Oliver. She didn't look up, but closed her eyes and let the sound of him reach all the way inside and touch her.

"*Zoe?*"

"You know her, Dr. Bradbury?"

"Imagine that," Zoe murmured, only slightly appeased by the little bit of horror in Red's voice. Finally, she lifted her face to meet his gaze.

But the sight of those bottomless dark chocolate eyes nearly flattened her again.

"Good God," he said, dropping to one knee and reaching out a hand. "What are you—here, get up." His hand enveloped hers, that strong, masculine, capable hand that healed and heated her with one stroke of his fingers. "What are you doing…"

She lifted an eyebrow as she stood to her full height, which was a few hairs shy of five-four; not as impressive as her adversary and only chest high with Oliver. But, oh, what a chest it was. In a zillion-dollar white shirt so soft and expensive she imagined it was hand-loomed purely to fit those incredible shoulders.

"Apparently it's easier to get into the Oval Office without an appointment."

He almost smiled, sparking a hint of burnished gold in his eyes. "You don't need an appointment to see me."

Zoe was dying to give a dose of "Take that, bitch" to the receptionist, but Oliver still held her hand and inched her a little closer, dizzying her with that clean, smart, crisp smell of capability—and Oliver. "You *do* want to see me?"

His whisper of uncertainty almost undid her.

"I do."

I do. I do. God, how she had once longed to say those words to him.

Instead she'd said other words, and those had sealed her fate in a completely different way.

Someone had said those words to him, though. Someone with dark hair and designer bags and the stink of wealth—and family. Big, powerful, undeniable, *real* family. The one thing Zoe could never offer him.

Damn Google and its endless pages of more information than tipsy ex-girlfriends ought to be able to get their hands on.

She lifted her chin and his expression flickered, zigzagging somewhere between amused and amazed as he studied her.

"Come into my office," he ordered with the sound of a man who didn't know the fine art of *suggestion*. Authority sat well on those broad shoulders.

"Would you like some coffee? Water?" he asked, ready to send the receptionist on the errand.

"After what it takes to get into this place? Grey Goose, straight up."

He nodded to Red. "Mr. Carlson is in room two. Have Beth tell him I'll be a few minutes longer."

Zoe blasted the woman with a fake smile. "Thank you so much for your help. Attila, was it?"

The other woman looked at Oliver, who bit his lip. "C'mon, Zoe. In here."

He led her down a hushed hallway, staying one step behind as they rounded a corner wordlessly. Her sandals were silent on plush carpet, but her heart thudded against her ribs loudly enough to reverberate through the halls of Dr. Bradbury's superplush, mega-exclusive, you-can't-have-an-appointment-without-a-referral-from-God practice.

His office was large, of course, and bright from a bank of windows, everything so much warmer than the reception area. Zoe took a sniff of cherry, leather, and that hint of success. It smelled like a man in this room, a strong, sub-stantial, still-so-stinkin'-hot-it-hurts man.

Her feet practically itched as she imagined whipping past him and dashing out the door she'd fought so hard to get through. *Sorry! Made a mistake!*

But she didn't move, a testament to how much she loved at least one person in this world. She kept her back to him, taking one last inhale and reviewing her game plan.

Which didn't exactly exist, since she'd left Barefoot Bay on a whim that morning, plan free. So now what? Plead? Demand? Barter? Whatever she did, she had to be strong and unyielding. She would not take no for an an-swer. She would not—

"Turn around."

Melt.

Oh, no. Falling into his arms would be much worse than running out the door as fast as—and hopefully with more grace than—she'd entered. Because once she felt those arms around her, all bets were off.

Slowly, she turned, meeting the gaze of a man who looked at her like he hadn't eaten in days and she was a hu-man cream puff.

While his eyes trailed over every inch of her, she took her own visual vacation, lingering on the things about him that had kept her awake so many, many nights. Not his classically handsome face, with all those angles of raw strength, and not his powerful shoulders or silky black hair. Zoe hadn't fallen for "the man with the teeth," as her Aunt Pasha had once described his movie-star smile, or the prominent nose that hinted at Roman or Greek ancestors, no doubt Julius Caesar himself.

No, Zoe loved the unexpected surprises of Oliver. Thick, bottlebrush, black lashes that feathered out to the side when he laughed at something she said. The muscle in his neck that flexed and tightened when he leaned in to kiss her. The tenor and depth of his voice when he whispered in her ear, the jolt of music when he said her name, the way his eyes shuttered before a kiss as if he were about to taste a fine French wine.

His eyes were open now, though, and slicing right through her. "How is the baby?"

For a minute she couldn't imagine what he was talking about. That was the thing about Oliver. He made Zoe forget her train of thought, her vows of secrecy, her common sense. He made her dream of things that couldn't be and remember things she was better off forgetting.

Things that were so, so good. Like the time they'd done it on the kitchen floor of his apartment. And the time he'd—

"I assume mother and child are thriving?"

Oh, *that* baby. The one he'd delivered last night. "He's perfect. Just, yeah. You left quickly and Lacey wanted to thank you."

"Is that why you're here?" A shadow of disappointment darkened his eyes, gone almost before she could grab hold of it.

Or you could grab that excuse instead and run with it, Zoe. Run fast and far.

Damn it, why did the only person who knew her secret have to be a doctor committed to saving lives, making it utterly impossible for her to run, hide, and pretend everything was fine?

Because everything *wasn't* fine, and he was the answer to the problem that kept her awake and in a low-grade panic more nights than not.

"Is it?" he asked again. "Are you the new family's thank-you committee of one?"

He was trying to be civil, even kind, and that gave her a little hope. Maybe their history was enough to get what she came for. Maybe she didn't have to make deals with the devil—although she would have. Right now, she'd do *anything*.

"It was no big deal," he said after a few too many seconds had passed. "I've done a few emergency deliveries in my career." Then he took a step closer, dipping his head almost imperceptibly, searching her face. "Zoe?"

"Oliver, you are one of two people in the world who knows the truth about me."

It was his turn to blink, silent.

"And once you said you'd do anything for me."

He still didn't respond.

"Do you remember saying that, Oliver?"

"Of course." He crossed his arms in a classic power stance. "What are you asking me, Zoe?"

She took a slow, steadying breath. "My great-aunt, Pasha, is sick. Really, really sick. You know that she…she can't exactly sally forth through the health-care system because she…" *Is a kidnapper.* "Can't."

He stared at her.

"I need you to treat her. And never report it."

His eyes narrowed as her demand sank in. "You're asking me to—"

"Do something illegal, yes. I know you are a big, important, successful doctor who shouldn't take risks that would possibly hurt your booming business, but I don't care, Oliver, because—"

"Stop." He was in front of her in one step, one hand on her shoulder, searing her bare skin, already too close.

"Will you?" she asked.

He was near enough for her to feel his warmth and the scent of air and woods, reminding her of the last time they'd kissed.

Go ahead, kiss him.

He dipped his head a tiny bit, not more than a millimeter closer, as if the voice in her head was loud enough for him to hear. "How could I do that?"

"Quietly," she said quickly. "Discreetly. Under the table, off the books, and away from the prying eyes of your witchy staff." She raised her chin, hating that he could feel her tremble. Let him think that quiver was because she wanted his help and not because every cell in her was screaming kiss, kiss, *kiss*.

Man, this might have been a bad idea. But she powered on. "That's how you could do it," she finished. "And you will. Because you…" *Loved me once.* "Always do what's right."

"I can't—"

"You *will*."

"Be this close to you and not—"

"I think you have a wife for that kind of thing," she said, wrangling out of his grip. "I need a doctor, and you happen to be in the area, in the right kind of practice, and conveniently the only medical professional who will agree to treat my aunt without reporting her to the authorities."

He searched her face, his expression impossible to read. But that didn't stop her from trying. And staring.

"That could jeopardize my practice," he finally said.

"How about jeopardizing her life? Doesn't that mean anything to you anymore? You used to care about people who were dying, Oliver."

He flinched so slightly she almost missed it. "I still do."

"Then help me!" She pushed his chest, fueled by frustration. He snagged her wrist and held it immobile.

"I'll do what I can," he said.

"What does that mean?" She shook off his fingers and he stepped back, sliding his hands into his trouser pockets as if to shackle himself.

His gaze dropped over her, as hot as his hands would be and sending just as many chills over her skin. "It means I'll do what I can within certain parameters."

"*Certain parameters*? So much for the Hippocratic oath."

He let his eyes go lower, lingering on her chest, amber turning to ebony as he watched it rise and fall.

"Not to mention your marriage vows."

He merely shook his head. "Those are broken."

"Well, goodie for you, hot stuff. But I need a doctor, not a quickie."

Ever so slightly, one brow lifted. "It was never quick with us, Zoe."

She narrowed her eyes. "You are married."

"I'm divorced. It was final last week."

"You were with her at the grand opening last night."

He shrugged. "Only as a favor. She'd been invited by some local socialite who backed out at the last minute and she didn't want to go alone."

Oh. *Oh.* "But I just saw her outside."

"She dropped…" He inched back, casting his eyes down for a second. "Something off."

A strange white heat rolled over her, along with the distinct and terrifying knowledge that the game had just changed. Oliver wasn't married. Which meant she could—no, she *wouldn't*. Never. Never, never, *never*.

Except…what exactly was Pasha's life worth to Zoe? Everything. Anything. Even *that*.

She bit her lip and took a step closer. "I need help, Oliver. And I can't get it anywhere else. I will do *whatever* you want."

"What are you suggesting, Zoe?"

"You want me to spell it out? Three simple letters, then: s-e—"

He stopped her with a raised hand, taking a deep, slow breath and a long, hungry gaze over her body again. Every hair on the back of her neck stood up, electrified. As he looked at her breasts, her nipples popped against the thin material. As he stared at her hips, she grew warm and achy right between her legs.

When he got to her knees, those bad boys would forget their job completely and she'd be on the floor, like that night in the kitchen. But he never made it down that far.

"No." He walked around his desk and sat in his over-sized chair. "Why don't you start by telling me what's wrong with her."

Holy hell. She'd offered herself as a human sacrifice and the son of a bitch turned her down.

Chapter Two

⟅

The rejection stung. Oliver could tell by the drop in Zoe's shoulders, the way her mouth fought not to open in surprise, and, of course, by the flinch of pain that turned her emerald eyes more of a flat jade green.

Still pretty—God, she was fucking gorgeous—but when he turned down her offer, the light went out of her face.

He'd hurt her. Fine. They were possibly on the road to even, then. Maybe when she was sitting on the empty floor of a deserted house crying like a damn three-year-old, maybe then they'd be approaching *even*.

"What are her symptoms, Zoe?" he asked, taking out a notepad to keep his itchy hands busy. Just so he didn't even think about how much he'd rather lean forward and thread his fingers through that mess of caramel-colored curls, all whimsical silk and sass that somehow never changed.

Corralling her cool, she dropped to the edge of a guest chair, pointing at the paper. "No notes. This is private. Off the record, completely. You may not make a file for her."

He angled his head. "You may believe the worst in me, but I honor patient confidentiality. Tell me what's the problem."

"So she can be your patient?"

"Tell me the problem."

On a soft sigh, she settled into the chair and tucked her legs under her, making the flowy skirt float over her legs and hide her feet like a lotus flower.

"First of all, I don't believe the worst in you, okay? We ended badly, I know, but—"

"Badly?" He fired the word at her, making her flinch. "You call that ending badly?"

She stared back. "Yeah, that was bad."

"Was it bad for you, Zoe?" He really needed to stop. She didn't have to know what he'd gone through all these years later.

"Bad enough," she said, far too cavalier for his tastes.

Really? Had she ached like he did? Had she wondered what the hell happened to him? Had she searched newspapers and bribed postal workers and haunted every hot air balloon field in the state of Illinois?

"It was pretty bad for me," he admitted, the words like stones in his mouth.

"I noticed," she said dryly. "So bad you got married five weeks later."

He should have seen that one coming. "Which is why, when I saw you in that lobby store in the Ritz a few years ago, the first words I said were 'I'm sorry.' Do you remember that?"

"I remember."

"You were buying condoms," he reminded her, a fact that had stuck in his craw for days.

"For a friend. Can we talk about my aunt?"

For a long moment he looked at her, his whole gut ripped right in half. Here was the one woman he had never forgotten—not for a fucking day in nine years—asking him to do something she had to know he couldn't do.

"Sure," he said. "Why don't we start with why you haven't had her name cleared."

"Why don't we not, because if I needed help with that I'd see a lawyer. Last time I checked, you're a doctor. An oncologist. And that's what I need."

At the little hitch in her voice, he put the past behind, instantly. "She has cancer?"

"We don't know for sure that it's cancer, but I've done a lot of Internet research—"

"You haven't talked to a professional?"

She blew out a breath. "Damn it, Oliver, you know the situation. I can't. But we did see this one guy who—it's a stretch, but I suppose you could call him a doctor."

He looked skyward. "Knowing your aunt, it was a psychic."

"Actually, he was a healer in Sedona." She sighed and gave an apologetic smile. "It was the best I could do. She doesn't want to see a doctor, for obvious reasons, and she still puts a lot of weight in those signs sent from the universe."

"Bad idea when the universe sends a tumor."

Her expression grew serious. "That's why I'm here, Oliver."

Of course it was. Not because she was sorry he had his heart kicked in and missed her every day and still jacked off just thinking about the way she—

No, he'd stopped doing *that* years ago. Well, months.

"Anyway," she continued. "This healer-doctor type made her swallow something awful—"

"Barium."

"Yeah, and this endo…thing."

"Endoscopy."

"Then he suggested a…" She closed her eyes. "Biopsy, but that Aunt Pasha refused because we would have had to go into a hospital or surgeon's office. That was a few weeks ago, and then we decided to come here so we could be in Barefoot Bay when Lacey's baby was born."

"And you decided to see me."

"Well, I honestly never thought of you."

"Not at all?" Damn it, he sounded pathetic.

"Well, other than the time I saw you at the Ritz and then, about six months ago, I was driving down this street with my friend Jocelyn, and I saw your sign on the door."

The words hit low and hard. She had been *here*. Driving down his street. "But you didn't come in."

"She wasn't sick then," she said, as if any other reason for visiting would be unfathomable. "But last night, when you came in to deliver Lacey's baby, I remembered you're an oncologist and thought maybe I should…try." Her voice cracked as she pushed herself up from the chair.

Zoe never stayed still for long; that hadn't changed any more than her hair or clothes or her magnetic aura. All still there, torturing him. "So I decided I need you."

Just like that. She needed him. In fact, she was willing to *give* herself to him, but not for the right reasons. And while that idea had incredible appeal, the motivation sucked. He'd had enough empty sex in his marriage, thank you very much.

"Tell me her symptoms," he ordered.

She rubbed her hands together, pacing as if the office couldn't contain her, already antsy from being in one room for ten minutes. "It started with heartburn, really bad, then she had trouble swallowing." As she paused and the light hit her face, he noticed the shadows under her eyes and a slightly swollen lip from a lot of gnawing. "She gets really hoarse at times and can barely talk. Then she started to lose weight. Like, a lot of it."

It wouldn't take years of oncology experience to diagnose this, he thought glumly. Especially if a holistic doctor suggested a biopsy after an endoscopy. "Was she a smoker?"

"She doesn't have lung cancer, he told us that. But, yes, she smoked and quit years ago, but…"

"How old is she?"

"Your guess is as good as mine, but I'd say eighty-ish."

His eyes widened. "You don't know how old your aunt is?"

"Great-aunt." She swallowed visibly and stared at him. "And we both know she's not really that, either. Let's say eighty for argument's sake."

So she probably had no access to family medical history. He stood, coming around the desk to the door.

"Where are you going?"

"I'm going to get some information for you on esophageal cancer, which is my guess. And some names of specialists who—"

She grabbed his arm. "I'm not going to a specialist, Oliver."

Closing his hand over her fingers, he pressed gently, fighting the desire to pull her into him and kiss all that desperation away. "I'm not the right doctor for someone

who hasn't had a single diagnosis yet. You need to understand something: I don't treat cancer with standard pro-
cedures. I work strictly in a cutting-edge and unorthodox
way, and many of my patients are undergoing experimental
treatments, many as volunteers to research programs being
done by a clinic I'm associated with. Believe me, cancer
patients don't come to me first. I'm a last-resort kind of
guy."

"Well, you're my *only* resort." She stepped back. "And
I've always been a big fan of unorthodox. I'll volunteer her
for anything. Where do we start? What do you need?"

He almost laughed at the open-endedness of that unan-
swerable question. He searched her face, still not quite
used to the impact of Zoe, so much brighter, bolder, and
better in the flesh than in his imagination. His gaze dropped
to her mouth, the bow over a hint of an overbite, the pout
of a lower lip that could suck the common sense right out
of a man's head.

Hell, just looking at her he felt everything below the belt
threaten to rise up and demand attention.

"I can read your expression, Oliver."

He hoped not. "What does it say?"

"Something pornographic."

"That's your mind, Zoe."

She shrugged, unfazed. "Whatever it takes to get some
of that unorthodox, experimental magic."

For a few seconds, he almost considered it. During that
flash of time, enough blood rushed south, a reaction he'd
had to Zoe from day one. Maybe he simply couldn't resist
her when he was thirty and willing to pay any price for the
pleasure of her body, but now he was old enough to know
that the price was too high for him.

"It's not magic," he said coolly. "It's medicine, and it's got as many risks as payoffs. There are a lot of things to consider, Zoe. I can't take a patient that hasn't been referred by a traditional doctor of—"

"She can't see another doctor and you know it."

"There's no way, not even a clinic or some kind of an emergency facility?"

She gave him a look of disbelief. "She doesn't even exist, for crying out loud."

Emotion rocked her whole body, making him want to reach out and steady her, but he didn't. Instead, he exhaled softly. "It wouldn't be proper medicine for me to treat her and—"

"Fuck proper medicine!" She grabbed both his arms and squeezed, desperation rolling off her. "Or fuck *me*, if that's what you want. I don't care."

That was the problem right there. She didn't care.

"Will that work?" She pressed against him, surely feeling the bulge in his pants.

He put his hands on her shoulders, ready to push her away, but her breasts felt so good against his chest that he hesitated. "No," he managed to say. "It will not work."

She slid her hands around his neck, sending every hair there to full attention. "Are you sure? 'Cause it kinda feels like it might work."

He lowered his head, giving in to the need to put his lips on her hair, her temple, her ear. He meant to just kiss her, but the words came tumbling out like they had a will of their own. "Why did you disappear?" he demanded in a harsh whisper.

Very slowly, she backed away, shaking her head. "You know why I had to leave."

Like hell he did. "Leave? You *evaporated*. It was like aliens abducted you. Clothes, furniture; there was goddamn food left in your refrigerator—"

"You wanted me to do something I couldn't, and since you're the guy who always follows the rules and does the right thing, I really worried that you'd turn us in and—"

"How could you think that? You knew me, Zoe. You…" *Loved me.* Or had she?

"I had to go," she said softly. "Pasha and I decided it wasn't worth the risk."

Love wasn't worth the risk. *He* wasn't worth the risk.

Wasn't that the lesson he'd learned that dark day, as a child, when he'd trudged up the stairs, climbed into the attic, and learned that love—even *unconditional* love—might not be enough in this life? Especially not for a woman who'd rather quit than fight.

"Listen to me." He reached for her face, cupping her cheeks, the shape of her jaw so familiar and fine in his hands. "Zoe, that—"

"Dr. Bradbury."

They both leaped apart at the sight and sound of his receptionist in the doorway. "Excuse me, but Beth's on the phone and couldn't come here to tell you, but Mr. Carlson is very distraught."

"I'll be right there, Johanna."

Her gaze flicked at Zoe. "Would you like me to show Miss, um, Tamarin out?"

"I'd like you to leave."

The receptionist gave him a shocked look, then backed away and closed the door. Oliver turned back to Zoe. "But I don't want you to leave. We have a lot to talk about."

"Like my aunt's treatment."

Would a promise to talk about that keep her here? With Zoe, who knew?

"Stay here and we'll talk after I'm finished with this patient." He stepped away, hoping that was enough. "I'll only be a few minutes."

He walked to the door, wishing like hell he could lock it from the outside. But that was the thing about Zoe, the original flight risk. He couldn't keep her. No one could. He couldn't let himself forget that.

Zoe damn near fell back on the desk when Oliver left, boneless and spent from being that close for that long to a man she'd really hoped she was *over*.

So not over.

But would he help Pasha or try to ship her off to some other doctor? Sighing, she walked around the desk and folded herself into his big doctor chair, imagining his long, strong body filling it again.

He isn't married.

The words inflated her heart like a shot of propane fumes, lifting her into hope-filled skies. *Hope-filled skies?*

Pathetic. And the only hope she needed was for Pasha. There were no hope-filled skies in a world without her aunt. And there was nothing but thunder and lightning in skies with Oliver. How could she forget that?

He'd shown his true colors, marrying his ex-girlfriend within *weeks* of the day Zoe had left. But then, Adele had no problem getting a marriage license. Whereas Zoe? Hell, Pasha damn near had to sell her soul to buy the fake paperwork to get Zoe into college.

She'd have done anything for Zoe, and that was why Zoe had to get Pasha medical help. Unorthodox and experimental? Perfect. Zoe didn't know much about medicine, but Pasha was old and frail. She'd never survive chemo and radiation, let alone the stress of going through some kind of health-care hell that didn't take a patient without *insurance,* let alone no real identity.

Puffing out a breath at the familiar cycle of worry she spent so much time treading along, Zoe let her gaze drift over the floor-to-ceiling bookshelf behind her, scanning the medical tomes and landing on a framed photo of a little boy. Was that Oliver?

Shooting forward, she picked up the frame, a weird heaviness in her arm as she brought the picture closer and studied the face of a boy who could only be Oliver's son.

No Internet search had ever mentioned a child. But then, he'd be the kind of man to take great care to keep his child out of the limelight, wouldn't he?

She tried to swallow, but a lump of longing and dismay squeezed her throat. *Oliver had a son.* She'd have given anything to have been the woman to give him a son.

She guessed the boy in the picture to be five or six, missing front teeth, the last of lingering baby chubbiness around his chin. But there was no question what gene pool this child had been dipped in.

He had Oliver's distinct intelligent gleam in his mahogany eyes, the same flat brows, and something about his lightly freckled cheeks hinted at a bone structure that would be strong and prominent once the right hormones and age kicked in.

It was a school picture, taken in a navy polo shirt with an insignia that read Cumberland Academy. A private school, of course.

Zoe had been homeschooled by Pasha.

The door opened and Zoe froze, not wanting to be caught ogling Oliver's child as he returned to continue their conversation. Knowing her head didn't even show over the back of the chair, she waited, completely still.

Maybe Oliver would think she'd left, and when he went out to find her she could replace the picture and he wouldn't—

A sniff broke the silence. And another, followed by a full-blown sob.

Zoe bit her lip to not react.

That wasn't Oliver. Probably one of his staffers having a breakdown because he'd yelled at her. Maybe it was Big Red. A splash of satisfaction warmed her gut. Bitch got what she—

"I hate this!" The voice was thin, broken, and frail. "I hate *him*." A smack against the leather sofa underscored the emotion.

That wasn't the receptionist or the secretary.

"It's so not fair!"

That was a kid. Zoe slowly turned the chair, making it squeak and getting a loud gasp in response. As she lifted her gaze from the picture, she met the very same face in three dimensions. Maybe a year or two older, eyes brimming with tears, a Chicago Bulls tank top draped over skinny shoulders that shuddered with the effort to stop crying.

"Who are you?" he asked, eyes popping in surprise.

"Fairy Godmother."

For a moment he tried to speak, but another shuddering sob came out as a half hiccup, half burp.

"Why the waterworks, kid?"

He swiped his eyes, a soft color rising to his cheeks. "Who are you, really?"

"Friend of…" She took a not-too-wild guess. "Your dad's?"

"Are you another nanny?"

Her heart slipped a little at the mix of hope and dread in his voice. "Have there been a few?"

"Like, nineteen in two weeks."

She almost smiled. "That's a lot."

"Okay, four. But since we got here and have to live in that stupid, ugly hotel, there's like a different one every day."

"What stupid, ugly hotel do you live in?"

"The Ritz-Carlton."

"Oh, yeah, the stupidest and ugliest of them all." Why did Oliver live in a hotel?

"I know, right?" He sniffed again. "I was glad all their dumb babysitters were busy and my mom had to bring me here all day."

She dropped off…something. His son was a something? "Yeah, 'cause what's better than hanging out at the cancer ward?"

He choked on a laugh he didn't want to have but couldn't help. "So, are you talking to my dad about the job?"

A job, not *that* job. "More or less. Are you looking for him?"

He shrugged, then shook his head. "I'm mad at him."

"I heard." She set the picture on the desk to lean forward, intrigued. "What'd he do?"

He sniffled one last time and wiped his nose, leaving it gleaming wet with teary snot. "I want a dog."

"Probably frowned upon at the Ritz."

He gave her a "Yeah, duh" look that only a kid his age could nail with such perfection. "No dogs at the Shitz-Carlton."

She tried not to laugh at the name, so out of place on his little lips. "You allowed to talk like that?"

"Who's gonna know?"

"Me."

"Who are you?"

"I told you—"

"There's no such thing as fairy godmothers."

She put her elbow on the desk and pointed to him. "Now that, kid, is where you're wrong. I've got one and she rocks."

"Does she have a wand?" he asked, the question rich with childish sarcasm.

"Several. And a crystal ball. And"—she leaned forward and shifted her eyes from side to side, as if a nosy nurse could pop up at any minute—"a man-eating plant."

His eyes widened, then he snorted with disbelief. "Do you play cards?"

She smiled at the non sequitur. "Like a freak. You like Egyptian Rat Screws?"

"Never heard of it , but I can play canasta and pinochle."

"Oooh, super fun." *Not.* "Where'd you learn that, from the shuffleboard crowd at the Shitz-Carlton?"

He fought a smile. "My grandma taught me."

"Ah, I see." Oliver's mother had passed away when he was very young, and he'd never talked much about his father. So Zoe guessed the boy was referring to his maternal grandmother. Yeah, people that rich would totally be the bridge and pinochle type.

"Can you teach me that Egyptian game?"

"I don't know. It's really complicated."

"I'm smart and I know a lot about Egyptians. They built the pyramids."

"Sorry, but there are no Egyptians in Egyptian Rat

Screws." She smiled. "There is a lot of cussing, however, and apparently you've got that covered."

He grinned and that did incredibly stupid things to her poor heart. *Oliver's son.* A heavy mix of envy and longing and regret rolled around her belly. "How old are you, anyway?"

"Eight. How old are you?"

"A hundred."

He rolled his eyes. "I'm not one of those kids."

"You don't say. I'm thirty-four. Five." *Eight?* Seriously? Wow, Oliver didn't waste any time, did he?

"I have a hundred-and-sixty-two IQ."

"Ouch, that's gotta hurt carrying that much smart around."

He tapped his head like it could handle the weight. "Not a problem. Want me to get cards? That lady in the front has a deck."

"Cruella?"

He laughed. "I saw that movie." Then his face dropped. "All those *dogs*."

Something inside her chest cracked. "Spotted ones that talk. Bet you liked them."

"Yeah." He pushed up and stood. "You gonna be here for a while?"

Was she? *Run, Zoe, run.* "Maybe."

"What's your name, anyway?"

Don't tell him. Don't get connected. Don't fall for Oliver's son. "Zoe. You?"

"Evan Townshend Bradbury."

"Wow, that's as big as your IQ. What do you want to be when you grow up, Evan Townshend Bradbury? A doctor like your dad?"

He squished his face and shook his head. "Cancer people make me sad."

"True that. So, not a doctor, then what? Lawyer? Investment banker? President? I assume you're thinking big."

"Meteorologist."

She drew back. "Never saw that coming. Like you want to be on TV and lie about the next day's weather?"

"No, I want to be a scientist and get inside a hurricane."

"Interesting career goal. Hurricanes can be nasty. My friend lost her house in one."

He lifted his brows and opened his mouth into a toothy "O" shape. "That is so cool. What happened to her? Did she die?"

She laughed at the onslaught of questions. "No, but her house got completely annihilated while she was in it."

He practically jumped out of his skin. "Get out! What did she do?"

"Survived. Thrived. Built this." She grabbed her handbag and opened it, snagging the Casa Blanca brochure she'd picked up at the party the night before. "Look." She spun it around for him to see. "This used to be this crappy old house on the beach and now look at it. It's a resort. I'm staying there."

"In that house?" He pointed to the largest of the villas, Bay Laurel.

"I wish. No, my friend puts me up in the not-so-fancy staff housing."

He looked up. "Do you work there?"

"Nah, they don't have what I do."

"What's that?"

"I fly hot air balloons."

His jaw practically hit the floor and he climbed out of his chair. "You are…" He shook his head, speechless.

She bit her lip to keep from laughing. "What?"

"Like, you are the coolest person I've ever met."

Well, there you go, Zoe. Nice. Your heart just got handed to you on a platter by Oliver's eight-year-old.

"Thanks."

"When's your birthday?" he asked suddenly.

Now there was a question she never answered without consulting her latest fake ID. "Why do you want to know?"

"I want to know your sign."

"You tell me first," she said.

"Oh, my birthday's October 28. I'm a Scorpio. What are you?"

She angled her head, considering so many possibilities. "Dubious. Do you know what that means?"

"Doubtful, from the Latin *dubito*, to doubt. What are you doubting?"

She cracked up. Could he be any more adorable, this little Einstein? "I'm doubting if you're for real."

"Well, I do have a—"

"Hundred-and-sixty-two IQ. I heard."

He grinned. "You want me to get the cards and you can teach me that game?"

Holding up both hands, she shrugged. "What the—"

"Hell," he finished for her, scampering to the door. What a piece of work that kid was. Dumped by his mother, ignored by his father. She could sure relate to that. And he seemed so much older than…

October 28. Eight years old.

For a second she dropped back in the chair, pulling up

an image of an unseasonably warm late March day nine years ago, when...

Using her fingers, she counted the months between March and October.

Seven months.

Ice water trickled through her veins, numbing her to her fingertips as realization hit.

Evan had already been conceived the day Zoe and Oliver took that balloon ride.

Or maybe Oliver wasn't—no. One look at Evan confirmed that he was Oliver's son. Conceived when they were dating?

Time to fly, Zoe.

But she couldn't run away from this; there was Pasha to consider. Pressing her fingers to her temples, she tried to think.

He wasn't going to help Pasha. He was going to do what Oliver always did: follow the rules, play by the book, and do the right thing. He'd send Pasha to another doctor, or a lawyer, or the police.

So why was she sitting around here ready to relive an old pain? Or, worse, start up a new one?

Run, Zoe, run.

She snatched her bag and darted around the desk, praying she could get out without seeing him. She made it down the hall, ignored the secretary, then shot out the door into the lobby—right smack into Evan Townshend Bradbury.

"I got the cards. Can we play that screw game?"

Behind him, the bitch with the red hair dropped her jaw and stood, sparks shooting from her eyes.

"This lady was just leaving, Evan."

The little boy's face fell, but Zoe refused to let that stop her. The last person she wanted to fall for was Oliver's son. Okay, the second-to-the-last person. "Yes, I was."

"Why?" he asked, his voice rising in a whine.

"Because that's what I do."

She dashed to the door and ran across the street to the safety of her getaway car.

Chapter Three

Oliver heard footsteps pounding down the hall, too fast, too loud, too…young to be Zoe. It was Evan, then, running amok in the office. He grunted under his breath as he flipped the last page of Eugene Carlson's chart.

"What?" the older man demanded. "Is there something you're not telling me, Dr. Bradbury? You see something?"

"Absolutely not." He shook his head clear, forced his focus where it belonged. "Your test results are excellent, Gene. You're one of IDEA's most astounding success stories."

The old gray eyes that met his filled with tears. "You sure gave that clinic of yours the right name. Might be an acronym for integrated something—"

"Integrated Diagnostics through Experimental Analysis," Oliver supplied.

"Whatever. The idea of IDEA is great. I don't know how to thank you, Dr. Bradbury. And, of course, Dr. Mahesh. A year ago I couldn't get out of bed, certain I'd been handed a death sentence. Yesterday I shot a seventy-nine. That's re-markable, young man, I don't care what you call it."

"I call it remission, Gene." Not a complete cure, but damn close. "And that's what the research and medical team there calls our goal." He added an easy smile. "And you know Raj isn't going to be happy until you break seventy-five."

Eugene laughed. "I'm just thrilled to be golfing. He's a competitor, your partner, that's for sure."

"We both are, and we're both enjoying a victory with your progress," Oliver told him. "Best we've ever seen on a leukemia patient." Oliver reached out his hand to shake Eugene's hand, anxious to get back to Zoe and finish the conversation but unwilling to rush this patient, especially after Eugene had waited to see him.

Instantly, the other man took a step forward and held out his arms. "Hey, give me one of those guy hugs."

Oliver complied, fighting a smile and that warm, wel-come sense of satisfaction in his chest. He'd made the right choice in leaving hospital administration for the far less stable world of research medicine, partnering with Raj Mahesh, working with an incredibly talented team of re-searchers, and getting back to the rewarding business of saving lives.

The move may have cost him his marriage, his high-profile position in Chicago's society, along with a steady—and monstrous—paycheck, but Gene Carlson's hug was worth the fee.

Another set of footsteps padded in the hall, almost as fast as Evan's and made by someone in sandals.

"I'll see you in three months, Gene," he said, trying not to rush out of the room even though his whole being wanted to make a mad dash to stop Zoe before she left.

But that would be like trying to stop the sun from rising. Trying to stop waves on the sand or a storm blowing in from the Gulf of Mexico. Nothing could stop the inevitable.

"By then I'll have a new granddaughter," Eugene said, dragging Oliver back to the moment.

"I'll expect pictures, then." Waiting a polite beat, he opened the door and headed into the hall as the door to the reception area clicked closed. He hustled forward, pulling the door open to nearly mow down his son.

"Evan, what are you doing out here? I told you to stay in the break room." He looked over the child's shoulder through the darkly tinted glass door in time to see a big white Jeep whip out of a parking spot, blond curls behind the steering wheel.

Not that he was surprised. But that didn't change the needle-jab of disappointment right to his chest. "Damn it," he murmured, an echo of a wound that had long ago stopped festering. Or so he'd thought.

Evan's face mirrored how Oliver imagined his own looked. Deflated. "You should have hired her to be my sitter, Dad."

Behind him, Johanna lifted a dubious brow. "I don't think she'd have made a suitable nanny, Dr. Bradbury."

Oliver sliced her with a cold look. "When I want your opinion, I'll ask for it."

"You want *my* opinion?" Evan asked. "I liked her. I thought she was funny."

"You talked to her?"

"Yeah. She's pretty, too."

No kidding. "Did you tell her you're my son?"

"Of course. Will she be back?"

Wasn't that the million-dollar question? "I don't know. She's…enigmatic." He opened the door to the offices and held it for his son. "Which means—"

"I know what that means." Evan slipped under Oliver's arm.

"From your Latin class?"

"Nah. Video games. So, she's gone for good? Because she was about to teach me a card game." He let out a sigh and mumbled, "Damn it."

"*Evan.*"

"You just said it."

"I'm thirty-nine years old. And don't tell me; she wanted you to play Egyptian Rat Screws?"

His whole face lit. "Yeah! How'd you know?"

Because he knew her. They'd turned her favorite fast-and-furious card game into *Strip* Egyptian Rat Screws with a bottle of tequila and a bag of limes one night.

"It must be fun," Evan said.

That night was. "How do you know?"

"'Cause you're smiling, Dad. And that hardly ever happens."

He led Evan into his office. "All right, Evan. I'm in the middle of my workday."

"You're always in the middle of your workday."

"Save the guilt trips for your mother." Who chose to unload Evan at the office the day before she left for a month in the south of France. "We don't have a choice today. No sitters, no nanny, no day off for me."

"Well, that blonde lady could have hung out with me. 'Cept she said it's no fun at a cancer ward."

"Sounds like something that blonde lady would say."

With that sexy, smart-ass mouth that would now haunt him for the rest of the day.

"She likes to swear, too."

"Nice of her to share that with you."

"I thought so."

He laughed softly. "Evan, do you want to play computer games or something, because I have to…" *Sit here and think about Zoe. And her mouth.* "Write up some reports."

Evan sighed, his narrow chest sinking. "No, Dad, I don't want to play computer games. And I don't want to sit in the break room. And I don't want to swim by myself at the Shitz-Carlton—"

"Evan." Damn, why did he have to have an eight-year-old going on sixteen? He didn't even want to *think* about sixteen. If he couldn't connect to the kid now, God only knew how bad it would be in eight more years.

"I hate it here."

"A fact you have made undeniably clear, son."

"Don't call me son." He pivoted and headed to the door.

"Evan!"

He stopped, and, for a split second, Oliver half feared he was about to get flipped off by a third-grader. But Evan didn't move; he kept his back to Oliver.

Oliver dug for the right words and came up with nothing. Why was it easier to talk to a cancer patient than his own preadolescent child?

"Look," Oliver said, thrashing around his brain for the right words to show some balance of compassion and discipline. "I know you're not happy about your mom and me splitting up."

Evan still didn't move, unless Oliver counted the rise and fall of his shoulders.

"And I know you'd rather be in Chicago where you have friends."

"And Grandma."

"And your grandmother. But you can't be there this summer, Evan. I live here and work here, and your mother's going to Europe tomorrow, so you've got to make the best of this today." And every day for the rest of the summer.

Slowly, Evan turned. "Can I just sit on the sofa while you work, Dad? I hate the break room."

Shit. What could he say to that? A few weeks ago, when Adele had announced she'd be coming to Naples with Evan and then leaving him while she traveled, Oliver had been happy—and scared. Maybe because his own father had been so distant and busy, Oliver wasn't ever sure how to handle a kid. Adele hadn't been much of a mom, either, making liberal use of nannies and her own mother, who could probably lay claim to really raising the boy.

But this was his chance to *bond*. However the hell that was done. "Sure. Please turn the sound off your game... thing."

"I'm not even going to turn it on," he promised. "I'm reading something."

As Oliver came around his desk, he frowned, instantly sensing something was different. Evan's picture had been moved. "Were you sitting at my desk?"

Evan looked up from a brightly colored brochure. "No, she was."

What did Zoe think about him having a son? Could she possibly know that... "What did you two talk about?"

Evan flipped the paper, mesmerized by whatever it was.

"Just, you know, stuff." He frowned and looked closer. "Whoa, look at that."

"What kind of stuff?" Like Evan's age? "Did you tell her you were here for the summer?"

"I think so."

"What else?"

He held out the paper. "This place looks really cool."

"What else did you talk about?" Oliver asked.

"Oh, stuff like her fairy godmother who has a man-eating plant. Wow, would you look at that." Evan flung the paper out. "She left this flyer thingie for a hotel, but it's not really a hotel. Look." Evan waved a pamphlet under Oliver's nose. "Casa Blanca. Sounds neat, huh?"

He took the paper, glancing at it. "I delivered a baby there last night." He flipped the page, studying the pristine beach and the understated elegance of the architecture.

"I'd rather live there than the Shitz—" Evan stopped in response to Oliver's stern look. "But they have houses, Dad. Not rooms." He pointed to a beautifully appointed villa overlooking the Gulf inlet known as Barefoot Bay. "That would almost be like, you know, normal."

He squashed the guilt. "It's another hotel, son, and what we need to do is buy a place." If he ever had time, or even the inclination. For the months he'd lived in Naples, the upscale hotel had been easier. Of course, he'd planned to buy something and be moved in when Evan came for his two weeks of summer that the custody agreement allowed. Then Adele announced her plans, and Evan came down six weeks sooner than expected.

Evan was still mooning over the brochure. "That place doesn't seem so fancy."

"It's fancy all right, but it's not gaudy." Although, to be

fair, he hadn't seen much of Casa Blanca the night before. After delivering the baby—after seeing Zoe—he'd wanted to get the hell out of there. Much to Adele's displeasure, he'd insisted on leaving, his efforts to make their split amicable no longer important.

"Well, I don't like gaudy," Evan said. "And that beach looks really cool."

If he hadn't gone there last night he wouldn't have seen Zoe, and she probably wouldn't have come in here today. But why had she left so suddenly?

He glanced up at Evan and suspected he knew exactly why. Damn it, he'd wanted to tell her himself—then and now. But both times she took off.

"Don't you think, Dad?"

He looked up, zoned out on the question. "Don't I think what?"

"That we could live in one of those houses instead of that stupid hotel?"

He pulled himself back to the moment and studied Evan's face, the earnest eyes so much like the ones that stared at him in the mirror every day, and the turned-down mouth, always so serious.

"Oh, I don't know."

"We could see her all the time then."

There was *that*.

"And I could find out why she ran away like that," Evan added. "Do you think it was because of me?"

The hurt in Evan's voice hit home. Oliver had blamed himself, too, for a while. Then he'd realized that Zoe was...Zoe. "No, Evan, she didn't leave because of..." But the truth was she *had* left because of Evan, at least indirectly. "Anything you said."

"I didn't tell her anything, except my IQ and how old I am." He looked down and kicked at the ground. "I know I'm not supposed to 'brag about my brains.'"

But his IQ wasn't the number that had sent Zoe running. She'd done the math and figured it all out.

Sighing, Oliver knew he had to do what he hadn't done last time: go after her. And this time he knew where to find her.

Zoe slept until almost noon the next day and woke to an eerily empty bungalow.

Where was Pasha? She didn't normally leave the little house without a note, but maybe she'd gone out to the greenhouse to talk to Tessa. Grabbing a mug of coffee on the way, Zoe stepped out to the tiny back patio of the bungalow, one of a half-dozen units that had been built for resort staff who would move in once Casa Blanca was fully up and, they hoped, booked, in the next few months. The little cul-de-sac of cottages was tucked behind all the villas, overlooking the gardens that Tessa Galloway had planted and nurtured since she'd taken over the job as Casa Blanca's gardener.

Zoe didn't see Pasha in the rows of veggies and leafy greens. Or on any of the paths, which meandered through the gardens and were lined with palm trees that stood stark against the midday sky. Beyond the gardens color splashed everywhere, from purple and red hibiscus flowers to the poinciana trees bursting with persimmon buds, but no sign of Pasha.

Despite the hurricane that had ripped through Mimosa Key's northern inlet nearly two years before, Barefoot Bay now thrummed with life again—plant and people life. Now that it was June, Casa Blanca had a few "beta" guests—travel agents and friendly bloggers—and Lacey had started to hire in anticipation of a trickle of summer guests. In a few months, it would be the first real "season" for the Northern snowbirds they hoped to attract to the small, upscale resort.

Zoe leaned against the railing, enjoying the salty Gulf breeze from an inlet she couldn't quite see this far away from the beach.

God, she loved Barefoot Bay. Of course she hadn't admitted that to anyone, even though her three best friends from college, Lacey, Tessa, and Jocelyn, were all living on this island now. Tessa had taken the staff bungalow right next door, and Jocelyn had moved in with Will on the southern end of Mimosa Key, living next door to her aging father.

If the girls even got a whiff of Zoe's desire to stay, they'd start a full-court press to permanently reunite the Fearsome Foursome of Tolbert Hall.

The sweet idea had been teasing her for weeks, and she'd been ready to whisper the possibility to Pasha, planning to start with a reminder that they'd been in Arizona three years, which was the longest they'd ever stayed anywhere except for the years Zoe had gone to college in Gainesville. She'd been hoping Pasha would get better and finally let go of her determination to run fast and far and often.

But that hope was dashed now, and not by Aunt Pasha. By Oliver.

Truth was, she couldn't live in a place that was one causeway drive away from Oliver. And his son.

The son conceived before they'd even met.

Blowing out a breath, she let all the disappointment that had been brewing since yesterday morning settle low in her belly. Pasha needed a doctor, and she'd let pride and jealousy steal the best possible solution.

Somehow, she had to go back to Oliver and try again.

Or did she?

The debate had raged for twenty-four hours now. Would he treat Pasha in secret? The man who obviously felt compelled to marry the woman he got pregnant, whether or not he loved her? Because Zoe might question a lot of things in her life, but not that. Oliver had loved her; she believed that. But he would always do the right thing in any situation—that was what made him tick.

So what was the right thing in this situation?

And, really, did he have to be hot, even these nine years later? Did he have to still emit some kind of crazy, sinful, senseless pheromones that attacked Zoe's sex-deprived brain like little hormone ninjas? Would Oliver fire up her girly bits if she hadn't sworn off sex after a string of excruciating few-night-stands almost four years ago? Probably.

Come on, Zoe. You practically inhaled the guy the night you met.

But we'd waited, she countered her mental adversary, also known as the voice. They'd waited—almost twenty-four whole hours. And in that time, Oliver said, he'd gone straight to his girlfriend, the daughter of Mount Mercy Hospital's CEO, and broken up with her.

But obviously not for good.

You left him!

What else could she do after he insisted they turn Pasha in? Pasha had had that panic bag packed and in the car in a flash. She'd given Zoe the choice to stay, but, really, there was no choice. She loved Pasha. And Oliver? Well, how would she know romantic love if it bit her in the nose? She'd never lived with a happily married couple. She didn't know the rules and regs, or where the lines were drawn with people who were in love—don't you tell your true love everything?

Zoe had, and look how that turned out. Oliver had practically jumped out of the balloon that day. So she ran. Honestly, both she and Oliver had to be accountable for the demise of that romance.

A trickle of sweat meandered down her back, the midday sun brutal already. She went inside to dress in the only suitable clothes for a day this hot: a bikini and thin cotton cover-up, which was good enough for finding Pasha, wherever she was.

A tendril of worry wrapped around her throat. Where *was* Pasha?

She hadn't even mentioned the visit to Oliver's office to her aunt because, well, she wasn't ready to leave Barefoot Bay and she knew what Pasha's response to Zoe's idea would be. Exit stage right.

And Zoe would go because she and Pasha were a team, partners, together forever.

She rinsed her cup and looked out into the gardens again.

There was no such thing as forever. Pasha was sick and this team would inevitably end. And the funny thing was, when that happened, Zoe would finally be free. There'd be no need to live "off the grid" once Pasha was gone.

So why was she fighting so hard to keep her alive? Because the only "love" Zoe had ever known, other than her three closest girlfriends, was given and taken by Pasha. Zoe might not have had normal parents to be role models of how good couples acted, but she had had Pasha to shower her with attention and affection for almost all of her life, ever since Bridget Lessington disappeared and Zoe Tamarin was born.

We'll call you Zoe. ...Zoe means "new life."

And twenty-four years later, she was still Zoe and they were still running. God, she was so, so tired of running. Of keeping everyone in the dark and at a distance. Of building walls made of sarcasm and apathy. Of skimming the surface with men because anything more would mean repeating what had happened with Oliver.

Tired, but scared of losing the only person who'd ever truly loved her, Zoe headed outside again to find Pasha.

She wandered through the gardens, marveling at Tessa's pungent herbs, sniffing tangy basil and sweet tomatoes as she made her way to the greenhouse where her friend spent every waking hour.

But the greenhouse was locked.

Worry ratcheted up a notch as Zoe scanned the grounds, her eyes landing on the barrel-tile roof of Clay and Lacey's home, perched on a rise of land between the gardens and the Gulf.

But where was Pasha? Had she collapsed somewhere? Out in the west field, hidden in the cornstalks? Zoe froze, torn between common sense and her wild imagination. Maybe—

"Hey, Aunt Zoe! Come and see my new brother!" Lacey's teenage daughter, Ashley, stood on the upstairs balcony, waving. "They just brought him home from the hospital! Everyone's here!"

"Pasha, too?"

"She's reading his little palm right this minute!"

Zoe puffed out a prayer of thanks and made her way to the house, not surprised that relief washed her skin with a chill despite the heat. She paused in a cluster of sea grass to gather her wits and push away all those thoughts of staying and regretting and running. Pasha was safe and, right now, that was all that mattered.

Although, damn it, she really didn't want to leave this time. "Look at this place," she mumbled to herself. Why did they always have to *leave*?

Because Pasha freaked the minute people asked questions or became too close or needed some official paper. But that wouldn't happen here, would it? Zoe looked around at the nearly complete resort. Casa Blanca was nothing less than heavenly. Clay Walker, Lacey's husband, had somehow managed to break the mold of the typical Florida resort, building a place that was clean, natural, and fitted into the foliage like Mother Nature herself had been on the architectural review board.

Stop ogling. You can't live here.

Zoe followed the path to the private drive to Lacey and Clay's two-story hacienda, which was already hugged by vibrant bougainvillea vines wrapped over the arched entryway.

A pang of something that could only be called the green monster twisted inside Zoe as tight as those flowery vines. Tessa may be envious of Lacey's baby, but Zoe longed for something different.

What would it be like to call a place like this home? To build a family. To put down roots. To come home every night, year after year after year, to...*home*?

Not in your lifetime, girlie. Well, certainly not in Pasha's lifetime.

The front door swung open before she reached it, and Jocelyn Bloom stood in the doorway, sporting a most uncharacteristic wet splotch on the shoulder of her always-pressed-to-perfection blouse.

Zoe pointed at the stain. "Will really ought to wipe his drool."

"Very funny." Jocelyn took a cursory swipe at the stain, remarkably unconcerned by it. A year ago she'd be changed into something fresh and already have this shirt cataloged in her closet under D for Dry Cleaners. "It's baby vomit."

Zoe sniffed. "Tessa probably wants to bottle and drink that."

Jocelyn gave her a look. "Don't start."

"What? We can't make jokes about each other's not-so-secret desires anymore?"

"Tessa's infertility issues aren't the butt of your crass jokes."

She rolled her eyes. "Everything's the butt of my crass jokes. Even Baby Pukes-A-Lot. Where is he, anyway?" She inched around Jocelyn to look into the house. "I heard Pasha's giving a reading."

"She is." Jocelyn laughed. "Oh, Zoe. He's so tiny and perfect. It makes you want to…" She squeezed her hands together and made a soft mewing sound that could only be hormonally driven.

"Woman, you got engaged two nights ago." Zoe nudged her. "No ovary bomb detonations yet."

Will Palmer stepped into the hallway, tall and tanned and looking at Jocelyn like he'd trudged through the desert and found an oasis. "Who's detonating?" he asked, still beaming like he had been the night the baby was born and he'd squeezed a "yes" out of Jocelyn.

"Don't rush her, Will," Zoe said. "She'll need months just for the list making."

"Not true," Jocelyn countered. "I've already promised him a quick and easy ceremony with no stress."

"And no waiting," Will added, capturing Jocelyn under his arm.

"You two are killing me." Zoe shouldered between them. "Let me at the kid, please."

"Get in line," Will said. "Pasha and Tessa aren't about to give him up. Lacey went to rest, and Clay's with her."

"Is Pasha feeling okay?" she asked.

Jocelyn shrugged. "She seems tired today. All the excitement, I guess."

"I guess," Zoe agreed. She hadn't told her friends about the initial diagnosis they'd gotten before they'd left Arizona. Pasha had sworn Zoe to secrecy—big shockeroo there—and the others didn't know Pasha well enough to notice the subtle signs of deterioration, weight loss, and easy exhaustion.

Of course, if Zoe told them, she'd have to have a damn good explanation for why they didn't just go to a doctor. And she'd have to do better than her usual joking and sarcasm. They loved Pasha, too. Especially Tessa, who, after her divorce, had lived with Pasha and Zoe for a few months and gotten close to the older woman.

But not close enough to know the truth.

How much longer could she keep her closest friends in the dark? Not only was Pasha's illness forcing Zoe to find medical care—a daunting task without insurance, let alone without legal identification—but it was entirely possible the jig was up for Zoe, too. At the very least, she might have to face Lacey, Jocelyn, and Tessa and admit they didn't even know her name.

A splash of hot, dark dread shot through her stomach at the thought.

"We're in the family room," Tessa called to Zoe. "Come and see your nephew."

"Brace yourself, Elijah!" Zoe called in a singsong voice. "Here comes the fun aunt!"

Zoe headed into the large, high-ceilinged great room to find Pasha in an overstuffed chair, baby in arms. It was like an artist's rendering of time passages: Pasha with her silver hair shooting in a few different directions, her skin hanging like crepe paper on bony cheeks, her arms holding the perfect, pink, baby bud of new life.

One ending the journey, the other just beginning.

"Zoe!" Pasha scolded, her voice even raspier than usual, her brown eyes misty. "Don't you know it's incredibly bad luck to cry the first time you see a baby?"

Without a quip handy, Zoe dropped to her knees in front of Pasha, swallowing the unexpected lump in her throat.

"This isn't the first time I've seen him," she said, reaching out to take the tiny bundle, the move revealing his tuft of reddish blonde wisps, the perfect combination of Lacey's strawberry and Clay's golden hair. "I was there the other night when Lacey spread her legs and gave new meaning to the term 'grand opening' party." He was ridiculously light. "Hey, little dude. Way to blow lunch on Joss. Didn't anyone tell you she doesn't like to get dirty?"

She ran a finger over his air-soft cheek and the dip in his

tiny chin, almost speechless at the perfection of his bowed lips and speck of a nose.

Tessa perched on the armrest of the sofa. "He throws up a lot," she said. "I think Lacey might have to watch the nitrates in her diet."

Zoe leaned close to inhale powder and warm baby. "That's Tessa, the healthy auntie who won't let you eat evil Froot Loops and Pop-Tarts. Don't worry, I will." She looked at Pasha. "What did his palms say?"

Pasha lifted her narrow shoulders in a casual shrug. "Longevity, health, happiness, three children, and a weakness for brunettes."

"Brunettes? We better work on that." Zoe frowned and wormed her finger into his fist to spread out his hand and see that info-rich palm. He squeezed tighter. "Does that mean he's going to hold on to his money or something?"

Tessa moved closer. "It means you're not a brunette. Give that child to me."

They held each other's eyes, smiling. "You've been holding him all day."

"How do you know?"

"Am I right?"

"So?" Tessa lifted a shoulder nonchalantly, no trace of the sadness Zoe had expected in her eyes as she held out greedy hands. "Come to Aunt Tess, Eli."

"Don't go, baby." Zoe turned, refusing to give him up. "She'll make you wear hemp diapers. Are we calling him Eli or Elijah?"

"I don't know what we're calling him," Jocelyn said, coming to the other side so that the three of them surrounded the baby.

"She changed her mind about the name?" Zoe couldn't

believe it. "He's been Elijah since the day we found out which team he played for."

Jocelyn shook her head. "Lacey is on a tear to find out that doctor's name. *You* wouldn't happen to know, would you, Zoe?"

"Me?" She felt her cheeks warm and directed all her attention to the baby, lifting his little body to her face, hoping he'd cover any unwanted blushing. "Oh, my goodness. Nothing smells like a baby, huh?"

Nobody answered.

Of course they'd all been in the room when Oliver had swept in; they'd all seen Zoe and Oliver react to each other. Had she said his name? Had he said hers? She didn't even remember. The moment had been like the slow motion of a car wreck—afterwards, the details are impossible to remember. The only thing that lingered was the shock of impact.

When she looked up, she met Jocelyn's gaze and gave her a look that she hoped, after fifteen years of friendship, could be interpreted correctly: *Shut the hell up or die.*

If Jocelyn even *mentioned* the name of the only human on earth who knew their secret in front of Pasha, Zoe would scream. She had to tell Pasha herself, and in her own way, about Oliver's arrival in their life.

"We are *not* naming him after the doctor." Surprising them all, Lacey stood in the kitchen, earning a cheer of greetings and "How are you feeling?" questions from everyone, which made little Elijah stir and shudder in Zoe's arms.

As Lacey came into the room to give Zoe a hug, Pasha asked, "Why not name the baby after this doctor? I think that would be a wonderful tribute to the hero who saved him."

Oh, Lord. "I wouldn't go so far as saying he *saved* the baby," Zoe said quickly.

"Zoe, I was crowning. God only knows what would have happened if he hadn't come."

"The paramedics were on the way," Zoe countered.

"Not fast enough. I can't imagine what would have happened if that doctor hadn't been there," Lacey insisted. "I was freaking out."

"You were in labor," Zoe said. "From what I saw, that'd freak anyone out."

"You're wrong, Zoe," Pasha said, her voice reed thin but still carrying the authority of age. "It would be extremely good karma to name the child after him."

"I don't know." Zoe fought to remain completely calm, and to keep the emotions welling up in her throat out of her voice. "There were no complications and he wasn't Superman, just some guy who's been through medical school. Anyone can deliver a baby; you don't have to be a god or..." Her voice trailed off as she realized that everyone was silent, and staring at her.

"Anyway," she mumbled, looking down at the baby. "Elijah Clay is a beautiful name and that's what his name is. Right, little man?"

"Right," Clay answered, following Lacey into the room wearing his own stained T-shirt. Elijah strikes again. "Plus I just talked to the doc and he told me he thinks we should stick to Elijah."

Zoe froze. "You talked to him?" Fortunately, three people asked the question at the same time, so no one heard Zoe's voice crack.

"Just hung up," Clay said, holding up a cell phone as if that proved it.

"What's his name?" Tessa asked.

"How did you find him?" Jocelyn wondered.

"I bet he wants to see the baby," Pasha said.

Zoe clamped her mouth shut as Clay reached for his son, taking him out of Zoe's arms with more assurance than she'd expect for a new papa. "He does want to see the baby. In fact, he and his son are on their way over here right now."

What? "Now?" Zoe asked.

"Oh, and since we don't want this boy to be called Ollie for short, we're sticking with Elijah."

"The doctor's name was Oliver?" Pasha asked.

Please don't say his last name. Please don't—

"Dr. Oliver Bradbury." Clay cuddled his son, the tiny baby lost in his daddy's broad chest.

Pasha took in the slightest breath, so tiny that no one noticed but Zoe, who instantly swooped in. "You are looking so wiped out, Aunt P. Let's get you home for an afternoon nap before…strangers invade the place."

But the color drained from Pasha's face, leaving her pale. *He's not a stranger.* Zoe could practically hear the other woman's thoughts.

"I'll take her home," Will offered quickly. "I've got my car and she shouldn't walk all the way back to the bungalows."

"I'll go with you," Zoe said.

"No." Pasha's command was harsh enough for the others to notice. She recovered quickly. "I want to nap, Zoe. You stay here. Please, you stay."

Unsure, Zoe tried to gauge what Pasha was thinking. "Are you sure?"

Pasha stood when Will offered his hand. "I've never

been more sure of anything," she said, her dark eyes slicing through Zoe with an incomprehensible message.

No way Zoe was staying here and facing Oliver in front of her friends. "I'm coming back with you," she said, standing up as Pasha hooked her arm into Will's and headed out.

Tessa grabbed the strap of Zoe's cover-up. "Hang on, Miss Z. You're not running away this time."

"Tessa, I want to go with her."

"She's fine." She kept a grip on Zoe long enough for Pasha to get on her way. "Do you think I'm blind and stupid?" Tessa whispered so softly only Zoe could hear her. "You could have lit up the whole resort with the electricity in that room last night. You need to face this guy down and get rid of whatever hold he has over you."

Just before Pasha disappeared around the corner, she turned and gave Zoe a long, incomprehensible look. Then she was gone.

"He doesn't have any hold over me," Zoe said softly.

Except he knew her darkest secret and he'd been the only man she'd ever loved. But all that mattered now was that he held the keys to the one thing she wanted most in the whole world: Pasha's life.

"Prove it," Tessa challenged.

"I will." She wasn't sure how, but she had to. Pasha's life depended on it.

Chapter Four

⟋‿⟍

This is fun, Dad."

"Is it?" Oliver tried to see Mimosa Key through his son's eyes. Thick with tropical foliage, dotted with colorful, mismatched cottages and old-school mom-and-pop retailers, the center of the island was no more than a tiny town built around one main intersection that boasted a convenience store as its main attraction. Lowbrow as it was, Oliver imagined the charm of the place was more appealing than the manicured perfection of Naples to an eight-year-old.

Frankly, it was more appealing to a thirty-nine-year-old, too, but that might have more to do with the charm of a current resident than the town itself.

"And Mom says you hate fun."

Oliver almost smiled. "So I've heard." But if that were true, he wouldn't have fallen for Zoe, the human embodiment of fun, in the first place. "But I cleared my day and brought you to…" He squinted at the one-story fleabag across from the Shell station. "A place with a motel called the Fourway."

"Bet it's named after the intersection," Evan mused.

"One would hope."

Evan laughed, but he sounded uncertain enough to assure Oliver that his son wasn't quite *that* precocious.

"Want to have even more fun, Dad?"

"If I can handle it."

"Let's go in that place called the Super Min and get Slurpees. I'm parched."

Oliver smiled at the word so few eight-year-olds would ever use. "All right. Let's live dangerously and see some local color."

Evan bounded out of the Porsche the second they parked in front of the store, full of energy and enough excitement over the modest adventure that Oliver had a pang of guilt. He'd worked a lot, and missed a lot, and now he'd moved away and ended his marriage. Evan might act smart and tough, but none of Oliver's decisions had been easy on the child.

And who knew better than Oliver what a lasting impact a parent's actions can have on a kid his age? He vowed to remember that this summer. No, he wasn't going to spoil Evan, but indulging him a little couldn't hurt, either.

With that promise in his heart, he watched the boy yank open the door and stopped to appreciate the old-fashioned bell that announced their arrival. Inside, they met the sharp-eyed gaze of a sixty-something proprietor propped on a stool behind the counter.

"Don't tell me," she said. "You're going to Casa Blanca."

Oliver and Evan shared a look. "How'd you know?" Evan asked.

"The car's a dead giveaway." She narrowed her eyes at him, giving Oliver a once-over. "And the designer threads. What's your name?"

Oliver bristled a little at the question, but had to consider where he was. In a town this size, everyone knows everything. "Dr. Bradbury," he said, approaching the counter. "Oliver Bradbury."

She straightened, giving him another, slow once-over, an awkward moment considering she was well north of sixty. Then she pointed to Evan. "Your son?"

"Yes." But Evan was already down the aisle, choosing a cup and a Slurpee flavor, avoiding local scrutiny.

"Where's his mother?"

Oliver, on the other hand, had obviously landed square on the radar. "On her way to Europe."

She made a face and wiggled her shoulders. "Well, la-di-da."

The Ritz was looking better and better. "How much for a Slurpee?"

She tapped a neon orange nail on the counter, studying him. "Married or divorced?"

"Are you serious?" He laughed softly.

"Dead." She stuck out her hand. "I'm Charity Grambling and, honey, I didn't get to be the eyes, ears, and source of all information on this island by not asking questions."

He'd have to remember that.

"Married or divorced to Ms. Euro Travel?"

He had no choice but to shake the busybody's hand. "Divorced."

Both painted-on eyebrows shot up well over the reading glasses perched on the end of her nose. "Really."

"I suppose you'd like to know the terms, too."

"Obviously you got custody."

"For the summer. How much is the drink?" he asked as the machine in the back made a loud sucking noise.

"Dollar fifty unless…" She leaned over the counter, lifting off a little stool she'd been perched on. "You want to work out a deal for a date."

He chuckled again. "I'm going to pass on that, though you're quite a, uh, compelling shopkeep, Ms. Grambling."

"Oh, I don't want you." She waved the fierce-looking fingertips at him. "I'm thinking of my extremely attractive niece, Gloria."

"Gloria." He smiled. "I'm sure she's lovely but—"

"Take my niece on a date and you can have free Slurpees all summer long."

"Free Slurpees?" Evan came up behind them holding a cup that was a little bigger than his head. "These twenty-two-ouncers?" he asked.

"Thanks, but we'll be happy to pay," Oliver said, taking a few dollar bills out of his wallet. "I'm sure Gloria is a wonderful girl—"

"Oh, she's no girl, trust me. But she has some very, oh I don't know how to say it without being blunt, but her taste in men is questionable." She shook her head. "That lame excuse for a deputy sheriff being one of them."

"You want me to go out with a woman who's seeing the sheriff?"

"Not that he has the you-know-whats to use his gun."

He glanced at Evan, who probably knew exactly what

the you-know-whats were, but he was busy sipping his drink and eyeing the candy offerings. "I'll pass."

"Why? She works at the beauty salon there at Casa Blanca. Except they call it a spa so they can charge three times as much, but…" She peered over his shoulder at the car. "You could probably afford a forty-dollar trim."

"I'm actually very busy. Thank you." He nudged Evan toward the door.

"You won't find anyone prettier on the whole island," she called out.

Oliver kept going, but Evan looked over his shoulder, then up at Oliver as the door closed. "Oh no?" he asked. "Bet she never saw Zoe, then."

Oliver almost tripped off the curb. One conversation with Zoe and poor Evan was smitten.

But then that was Zoe's gift. He had to remember that, too.

A few minutes later, he pulled the Porsche into the same spot he'd used the other night, surprised at an unexpected sense of anticipation gripping him. Just because he might see Zoe? *Might.* He had no guarantee she'd be around. And yet, when he'd called to talk to the owner and father of the newborn, he'd jumped on Clay Walker's casual invitation to drop by and see the baby.

Zoe wouldn't stick around long, no matter what her aunt's situation. And before she left, Oliver had to tell her what had happened in Chicago. Now that she'd met Evan, she deserved an explanation. If she hadn't already put two and two together and come up with…not quite reality.

Yeah, he had to set her straight. So he'd make some subtle inquiries and find her today.

A man came out of the entrance of Casa Blanca's main building, pushing the doors with assurance. Instantly Oliver recognized the long fair hair and muscular build. He hadn't talked much to Clay the other night; Oliver had been busy with the baby and Clay had been a typical overwhelmed new father.

This morning the man looked much more relaxed as he reached out a hand, then added an impulsive pat on Oliver's shoulder.

"Dr. Bradbury, it's great to see you here again. And this is your son?"

"Yes, this is Evan." Oliver gave Evan a little nudge to get him to shake Clay's hand. "This is the owner of this resort, Mr. Walker."

"Not technically the owner," Clay corrected as they shook hands. "I'm married to her. I am the architect, however."

"Then even more congratulations are in order," Oliver said, gesturing to the cream-colored building unlike any of the typical stucco Spanish-style buildings that marred the coast of Florida like carrot-topped behemoths. "This place is stunning. Great job."

"Thanks. We're really happy with how it turned out." He brushed his long hair off his face, revealing a tiny gold hoop in his ear. "We're not officially open, though we're taking a few early guests while we work out the kinks and get all the services up and running."

"All with a new baby," Oliver mused.

Clay laughed. "What can I say? My wife and I like challenges. It's really nice of you to come and see Elijah," Clay said to Evan.

"And Zoe," Evan said. "Is she here?"

And so much for subtle inquiries. Clay reacted with a slight frown, his hand clasped on a chin that hadn't seen a razor for quite a few days. "That's right, you two said hello the other night. I forgot you know her."

"You were distracted," Oliver said. "And how is the little guy? I feel invested now that I've brought him into the world."

Clay beamed, easily taken off track by the subject of his new baby. "You should. He might not be here if not for you."

"No, he'd be here. Your wife seems very strong."

"You have no idea." Clay gestured for them to climb into a waiting golf cart. "You want to drive up to our house, Evan?"

His eyes nearly popped out of his head. "I can't drive."

"Sure you can." Clay glanced at Oliver, who nodded easily. Better to keep his mind on a new adventure than drop any more hints about Zoe. He was rewarded with the biggest smile he'd seen from Evan in years.

After a moment and some quick instructions, Evan had the golf cart rumbling—slowly—under a canopy of exotic trees and palm fronds. They followed a path that cut through the resort and was built up enough to offer a stunning view of the Gulf of Mexico on the left.

"That inlet is Barefoot Bay, which is what the whole north hook of Mimosa Key is known as," Clay explained. "It's not very populated up here. Most of the residences on the island are on the south end, all the way down to Pleasure Point."

Oliver took in the tropical paradise, elegant but so much less ostentatious than the Ritz.

"We own the property along the water," Clay continued.

"From here up to our house and the acres of gardens to the east. We'd like to grow, eventually, but, you know, one step at a time."

"Looks like you've taken a pretty ambitious first step."

"It's been a fun ride," Clay said easily.

"Look, Dad. That's the house we saw in that flyer." Evan pointed to a waterfront villa they'd seen in the brochure, a truly gorgeous structure that matched the North African architecture with curved windows, multiple archways, and rich wood accents.

"Do you live there?" Evan asked.

"No, that's one of our six villas we rent out to guests."

Evan turned to Clay. "We could live there."

"Evan, eyes on the road," Oliver warned.

"You certainly could," Clay agreed. "That's Bay Laurel, our largest villa, and it happens to be vacant and ready for renting. You interested?"

"Yes!" Evan chirped. "We live at the Ritz-Carlton and I hate it there."

Clay gave an unsure look. "Am I walking into a land mine?"

Oliver shook his head. "Not really. I recently relocated here from Chicago, started a practice, and work with a clinic in Naples. I haven't had time to focus on buying a house, and Evan is not a fan of our hotel."

"Well, we could probably work out a better deal than you're paying at the Ritz, and you'd have a three-thousand-square-foot house with a pool and yard."

Evan slammed on the brakes and they all shot forward in their seats. "A yard for a dog?"

"Whoa, Evan." Oliver put his hand on his son's shoulder. "Easy on the brakes and the dog."

Clay shrugged. "We don't have a problem with animals in the villas. We actually welcome them."

"Well, then, that's something to think about," Oliver said vaguely. "Right now you should be concentrating on driving, son."

"I'll take you to look at Bay Laurel later, if you like," Clay said, obviously sensing that Oliver's enthusiasm was a little downgraded from his son's.

Of course it was. Zoe was living on this property. One more thing to remember.

They reached the end of the resort's road, pulling into the circular drive of another beautiful home, this one feeling lived in and loved and different enough from the rental villas that it was obviously not part of Casa Blanca.

Evan brought the golf cart to a not-quite-smooth stop, then turned to look at his dad. "I want to live here, Dad. For the whole summer." His voice almost cracked with the fervent plea. "I want to live here."

Right then, one of the double front doors opened and Zoe stepped out into the sunshine, a tiny baby in her arms and a blinding smile on her face. The sunlight spilled over her hair and straight through the white gauzy thing that barely covered her body.

"Can we live here this summer, Dad?"

Oliver's mouth went bone dry, his pulse doubled, and his brain went blank, forgetting everything he'd sworn to remember. "Yes."

"Woo-hoo!" Evan shrieked so loud the baby in Zoe's arms startled and opened his mouth to cry. In the time it took for him to gather his next breath, Tessa was on one side and Jocelyn on the other, ready to seize the coveted Elijah.

But then they both zeroed in on the arrivals and forgot the baby.

"Whoa," Jocelyn said in a low whistle. "I guess in all that chaos at the grand opening, I didn't notice how gorgeous our doctor in shining armor really was."

"Um, you were busy getting *engaged*," Zoe reminded her.

"He reminds me of George Clooney in the old ER episodes," Tessa agreed.

"More like McDreamy," Jocelyn said.

"And Doctor Hottie sure can't take his eyes off Zoe." Tessa whispered with the subtlety of a bad ventriloquist.

Oh, *brother*. "Don't you think this is too much sun for the baby?"

"Actually, vitamin D is great for him."

"Shut up, Tessa, and take him inside." Zoe did the hand-off quickly, especially because she was already quivering a little.

Oliver is here.

Surely he wouldn't have come to Casa Blanca just to see the baby, right? He had to be here because he'd rethought his response and wanted to help her. *Right?*

There was only one way to find out. She headed toward the golf cart, corralling every ounce of swagger she had.

"Hi, Zoe! Remember me?" Evan scrambled out of the golf cart and ran to her.

"Mr. Potty Mouth?" she teased, ruffling his hair. "Of course I remember you."

"We're moving here!"

She froze midstep. "What?"

"Dad said we can move out of the hotel and rent one of

these houses on the beach. Isn't that cool?" He came closer and lowered his voice. "No more Shitz-Carlton."

She stole a glance at Oliver, who approached slowly, as if he wasn't sure what to make of her...or the news.

He looked even sexier in casual clothes, if that was possible. A polo shirt fit snug on his broad shoulders, hanging over loose linen pants. He didn't smile, but studied her with the same intensity she was probably using on him.

"That was easy," he said, so softly only she could hear him.

"What was?"

"Finding you."

Heat that had nothing to do with the tropics rolled over her.

"Evan, why don't you follow Mr. Walker inside and go meet the baby I delivered last night?" Oliver suggested. "I need to talk to Zoe."

After a minute of negotiating Evan did as he was told, leaving the two of them frying under the blistering sun and staring at each other.

"You left too soon," he finally said.

"Story of our relationship, isn't it?"

He took a step closer, giving her a chance to see that a few beads of sweat had formed on his upper lip. They would taste...salty. And sweet. "But this time when I came after you, I found you."

She could have given up the fight right then and there. She could reach out, pull herself into him, raise her face, and let him kiss the holy hell out of her. Because that was all she wanted.

But not what she *needed*.

Braced by that thought, she lifted her face to him, but

not for a kiss. "I hope you came to talk about my aunt and what you can do for her."

"I came to talk about Evan, and how and when he was conceived."

Seriously? "I'm going to assume he was conceived the usual way and as far as when? I can add. Whatever, Oliver. It's hist—"

"And I found out in the balloon that day."

It actually took a few seconds for the words to process in her head. She opened her mouth to say something, but nothing came out. But the world slipped away, as if she'd caught a dangerous cross breeze.

"That's why I left so quickly," he said. "That's why I didn't really talk about your situation. I was too stuck on my own."

Still, no words. *In the balloon that day?*

"And of course, I had no way of finding you to tell you that I decided to—"

"Dr. Bradbury!" From the front door, Lacey called out, making them both turn instantly.

Her curls sprang in a wild strawberry-blonde halo and she looked like she was about to launch herself down the steps and across the driveway despite her post-delivery attire, which included bare feet, sleep pants, and a maternity T-shirt.

Aw, Lace. *Now?*

But Oliver instantly went to her, leaving Zoe hanging on a cliff.

Then Lacey was hugging him, thanking him, and dragging him inside. All he could do was shoot an apologetic glance over his shoulder.

Zoe let out a sigh of frustration. Lacey didn't know,

of course. She probably didn't remember she'd seen
Oliver before—in the lobby store of the Ritz almost
two years ago. Zoe had brushed off that chance meeting
back then, and she doubted that Lacey—especially in
her sleep-deprived, new-mom brain fog—would ever remember.

She waited outside for a few minutes, letting Oliver's
news sink in.

He found out in the balloon that day.

In the time since she'd met Evan and counted months,
that possibility had never occurred to her. Hell, in the
nine years that had transpired since that day, she'd never
even thought about those phone messages he'd received
up there, long before texting became part of everyday life.
She'd always assumed it was about a patient.

No, she really hadn't assumed anything because she'd
never thought much past his reaction to her announcement,
and his subsequent demands that she "do the right thing"
and talk to a lawyer or the police.

What would have happened if she'd waited? Would he
still have married Adele? Would he have forced her to try
to "resolve" things with the law and Pasha? Or would he
have deemed her unacceptable—too much of a risk, too far
off the grid, too flighty for a grounded guy with a potential
blockbuster career?

She wasn't sure she wanted to know the answer to that
question. And even if he told her, could she believe him?
It didn't matter. All she really wanted was for him to *fix*
Pasha. That's who was broken, not Zoe.

She walked toward the house, opening the door to find
Clay, Lacey, and Oliver talking in the entryway.

Oliver held the tiny baby in his arms and, shit, if *that*

wasn't the goddamned sexiest thing she'd ever seen, she didn't know what was.

Clay was laughing, putting a friendly hand on Oliver's arm. "We might have to put your little boy in charge of the sales staff. Why don't we take a look at Bay Laurel right now, then? You can move in this week."

Oh, Lord.

"Maybe Zoe should take Oliver," Lacey said quickly.

"That's all right," Clay said. "I'll take him down there."

Lacey shook her head and shot her husband a secret look that Oliver probably missed, but Zoe didn't. Maybe Lacey *did* remember the run-in at the hotel shop. And, of course, her friend would want to help. And by help she meant stick her little copper curls where they didn't belong.

"You'll just talk about rebar and I-beams," Lacey insisted. "Zoe can give the ten-dollar tour. Walk down the beach and really get the feel of the place."

"That'd be great," Oliver said, already putting a possessive hand on Zoe's shoulder. "You don't mind?"

Clay handed Zoe a card key before she could reply. "This'll get you into any villa on the property. We can entertain Evan for you, Oliver. That way you can make a decision without pressure."

"Good idea," Lacey added. "Can he go swimming with my daughter? She's an excellent babysitter."

"I'm sure he'd love that."

Lacey gave a warm smile to Zoe, her amber eyes dancing. "Then take your time and really let him fall in love...with the villa."

Holy crap, could she be any more obvious?

"Let me tell Evan," Oliver said, handing the baby to Lacey before he disappeared into the family room.

Instantly, Lacey's eyes widened. "You don't mind do you, Zoe?" she asked, nestling Elijah into her chest. "He obviously likes you."

"I think it's true that babies lower your IQ."

"Zoe, come on. He's totally hot."

Clay smiled, sliding an arm around his wife's shoulder. "She wants all of you guys married and mothering like her."

"Yeah, I've heard misery loves company."

Lacey shrugged, undaunted. "Take your time and close the deal."

It was futile to argue. And, honestly, Zoe wanted that time with him anyway. For Pasha, of course. Not for any reason other than Pasha.

Chapter Five

⌒

As they walked down the driveway and toward the beach, Oliver stopped at an overloaded hibiscus tree and plucked a red bloom.

"Peace offering," he said, holding it out to Zoe.

She gave him that look, that teasing mix of sarcasm and sweetness, and took the flower, sticking it in her hair. "I'll have to tell Lacey how effective her marketing brochures are."

"It wasn't the brochure that got me here."

She didn't react, just kicked off her plastic flip-flops as they reached the edge of the sand. "You won't want shoes."

He toed off his Docksides and impulsively yanked off his shirt, too, tossing it on the ground and getting a sideways look from her. "You don't play fair, doc."

"It's a thousand degrees."

She fought a smile. "So are you."

"Then I take it you're not mad at me anymore?"

"Never was mad."

"Oh, that's right. Sometimes you just disappear in the middle of things for no real reason."

"Define real, Oliver." She nudged him with her shoulder, forcing them both closer to the water. "Let's see, I discovered you have a son conceived before we ever dated, you're divorced and living a few miles from my closest friends, you're planning to live on the property where I'm currently staying, and you failed to tell me that you received life-changing news the moment I was revealing my biggest secret to you." She let out a sigh. "Anything I've missed?"

He stopped walking to roll up his pants and let the warm, foamy water splash around his ankles.

"My son wants you to be his nanny."

She let out a little grunt of disbelief.

"You asked if there's anything I missed, so I thought I'd better get that out there."

"Good call." She gave him another shoulder push, but not hard enough to get him in the water. More like she just wanted the body contact. And so did he. "Did you tell him I'd make the world's worst nanny?"

"I can't tell him anything," he said, fighting the urge to put his arm around her. "He's crazy about you."

She smiled. "I like him, too."

"I don't suppose you're looking for a summer job?" Son of a bitch, had those words just come out of his mouth? How did she get him to do and say things like he had no control?

"It depends."

Why did those words give him hope? Was he nuts? "On what?"

"Um…" She gave him another saucy smile. "The pay."

"What's your fee?"

All the tease disappeared from her eyes. "Quid pro quo. You take care of Pasha and I'll take care of Evan."

He closed his eyes on a sigh. "It's not that simple, Zoe."

"Too ironic for you? I mean, they are the two individuals who are responsible for taking us apart."

He stopped walking and turned to the water, staring out at the horizon. "I don't blame Evan for his timing. Maybe I did before he was born, but then, no."

"I'm glad," she said. "That would be an awful thing to put on his shoulders. Do you blame Pasha for her decision to leave?"

"I haven't," he said. "All these years I figured the guilty party was…"

"Me," she supplied.

"Pretty much."

She didn't answer. As she stood looking out at the water, the breeze lifted her see-through skirt and the sun poured over her like liquid gold. "I love it here."

"Enough to stay?" The question was out before he could even think about not asking it.

She shrugged, utterly carefree and so very Zoe. "Who knows? Want to see the villa now? It's right up here."

Without waiting for his response, she darted up the beach, leaving him alone and wet and staring at the most irrepressible, impossible, desirable woman he'd ever met. Of course, she was running away. And, of course, he followed.

He caught up to her at the path and they walked to the villa together.

"I'm not sure if I should sell this place to you or point out all the shortcomings," she said as she slipped the key into the lock.

"Why? You don't want me here?"

"It complicates things."

"You love complicated things, as I recall."

She pushed open the door to a large, inviting living area with more of the same Moroccan warmth. Dark wood gleamed and a wrought-iron rail curved up a staircase. Beyond the living room, sunshine bounced off the teal water of a screened-in kidney-shaped pool surrounded by a few chaises and a table.

Evan would love it here. And so would Oliver.

"Nice," he said, then gave her a quick look. "Unless it isn't."

She laughed. "On the positive side, it's gorgeous, brand new, all hand-crafted wood. You met Will the other night. He's the carpenter and Jocelyn's fiance." She led him through a small dining area.

"On the negative side?" he asked.

She pointed to the kitchen. "There's no room service yet, since Lacey didn't get a chance to interview chefs before the baby came and she hasn't officially opened the kitchen. So you'll have to cook." She squinched her face. "Unless Evan's nanny is expected to cook, in which case, we better hope someone can supply take-out menus."

He laughed, feeling himself so drawn to her he had to fight physically not to pull her into his arms and drag her to the nearest bedroom. He wasn't going to win that war for very long. "No, but the nanny might have to stay late."

"Because you work long hours?"

That wasn't what he meant, but he nodded. "Some days."

"We could arrange it," she said, gesturing for him to go down a hall. "Come see the rest."

She pointed out features as they went along, but all he noticed was the bright-green bikini under her dress. And she went on and on about the woodwork, but his attention was on her buttery skin, tanned and smooth. By the time they reached the doors to the master suite, he'd have bought the place if it meant he could have her...on that bed.

"All the trimmings of luxury: Jacuzzi, marble, a bed big enough to sleep three or four or nine." She grinned. "Whatever turns you on."

She turned him on. "Not three or nine," he said. Just one. The one he was looking at.

"Upstairs, there are two bedrooms and two baths. Also a game room furnished with a big TV, which I bet Evan would like. You want to see them or this lovely view?" She slipped by him and pushed open another set of french doors to the patio. "So you can roll right out of bed and go swimming every morning."

"With the nanny."

She tossed a look over her shoulder. "That's in the job description?"

Hell, yes. "It's on the negotiating table." He gave a rueful smile, joining her so they both stood in the doorway. He was close enough to her that he could see each individual eyelash tipped in gold as she narrowed her eyes at him.

"What do you think of the villa, Dr. Bradbury?"

"I like the tour guide." He leaned an inch closer, backing her against the wood frame of the door.

They did it against a door once.

He kicked the thought away, stuffing his hands into his pockets again, which seemed to be the only way to avoid temptation with her.

A kiss. That was all he wanted. One kiss. One long, wet, hot kiss to ease the ache that had already started low in his gut. Way low. Everything in him wanted to touch her, to remember the silky feel of her skin, the pressure of her mouth, the warmth of her tongue.

That very tongue darted to wet her lips, her eyes locked on his, the message in them so, so clear.

Kiss me, Oliver.

His reply was silent, too. Just a whisper of warm breath into her mouth that almost instantly became more. A warm, tentative, spark of a kiss that tightened every muscle in his body and did the opposite to his common sense.

She didn't move, didn't even breathe, as only their lips touched.

Slowly, he deepened the kiss, opening his mouth, darting his tongue over her teeth. Their mouths melded as one, and against every will he dragged his hands out of his pockets to cup her jaw and hold her pretty face in his palms.

"Do you interview all the sitters like this?" she murmured into the kiss.

"Just the mouthy ones. Do you give all the renters tongue?"

"Just the hot ones."

He pressed his body against hers, his cock growing against her belly, eliciting a tiny whimper that caught in her throat.

"Oliver."

He kissed her cheek, her ear. "Mmm?"

"You know where this is headed, don't you?"

"We're in the master bedroom, so I hope not far."

Breaking away from the kiss, she slipped from his

touch, out to the patio, pulling him with her. Sunshine through palm fronds dappled her in splashes of light, her eyes dancing with a tease. "As if I'd be such a cliché and fall into bed with you, Oliver."

"It was worth a shot."

"There's a *pool*." In a flash of snow-white gauze and lime-green silk and golden-brown skin, she yanked the dress over her head, tossed it in the air, and vaulted into the pool, splashing water all over him.

Once, about eight years ago, Pasha saw a moonbow.

Funny, she could remember the glimmer in the Colorado night sky even right now, bathed in the midday sunshine instead of nighttime shadows. The moonbow had been so rare and wondrous, with a hint of red and orange fading into a strip that looked so yellow it was white, then deep azure blues.

But it was more than a stunning vision in the mountains that stayed imprinted on Pasha's heart. The moonbow had been a clear message from Mother Nature: True love—the kind that happens once if you're lucky—would return.

But not, she knew that night, to Pasha. Her true love would never be back. So that moonbow was a sign not for her, but for Zoe.

That knowledge had always weighed heavy on her heart, but today it actually hurt her chest. Zoe's true love had returned...like the moonbow had predicted.

She'd always known that Oliver Bradbury would some-day return to Zoe. At least that was how she'd rationalized the decision to let Zoe leave Chicago when Pasha knew it was time to pack and run. That had been the time they should have ended their run together. Pasha had offered!

Maybe she hadn't *insisted*, but she'd have survived. Pasha had told Zoe she could stay in Chicago with Oliver.

But Zoe had chosen to go with Pasha.

And then Pasha saw the moonbow and knew that someday, somehow, Oliver would return to Zoe. Or maybe she hoped that he would, in order to assuage some of her guilt.

Oh, she hadn't told her darling Zoe, of course, who would scoff and say he was not her true love, something she claimed not to believe in anyway. But it wasn't that Zoe didn't believe in love. She'd just never experienced it, not even from the sidelines, like most children.

Pasha always hoped and prayed to every power in the universe that when Oliver returned, Zoe and Pasha would no longer be in hiding. That Pasha would no longer be running from the long hand that cast a shadow over her life.

But that wasn't the case, was it? That hand still held the power, and Pasha still spent her life paralyzed by fear.

The last thought made her eyes sting a little and put more pressure on her chest than the evil thing that was growing in there. No one knew what caused this sickness. Maybe it was all the fear and knowledge and guilt and remorse and indecision of her pathetic life rolled into a black ball that grew into *cancer*.

She closed her eyes and let her head fall back on the rocker headrest. Fact was, the longer she lived, the less chance at happiness Zoe had.

Pasha *owed* her that chance.

Pasha had only two choices: die or disappear. One she couldn't control and the other she wasn't sure she could pull off anymore. Pushing herself to her feet, she walked to the kitchen door, already overcome by the heat. And the truth.

Death was so permanent. Who knew that better than Pasha?

An old ache burned in her belly. That pain never disappeared. No matter what she did to replace it—run, hide, fill her heart with a child who wasn't even hers—the hole inside was always there, always black, always empty.

Exhausted, she walked into the tiny bedroom that had become her home for the time being, drawing the shades against the blazing sun. Zoe wouldn't be happy if she came home right now and found Pasha traipsing around instead of taking her afternoon nap.

But what if Zoe came home and Pasha was gone? Gone, one way or another?

Sliding out of her shoes, she dropped onto the bed, her gnarled fingers playing with a thread of the silky comforter. Did she have it in her? Could she do that? The thought of leaving Zoe was unbearable. But the thought of Zoe not having her chance at true love was unbearable, too.

And there was the most unbearable thought of all, the threat she'd run from all these years.

Her chest throbbed, and not like her heart was dancing with hope or fear. More like something was growing.

Because something was growing—and not only that hated tumor.

Hope was growing, too. Hope that nature would do her job and destroy this body so Zoe could have a proper life and a real home. She wished that there could be another way, less painful to both of them, but this was what the universe dictated.

Or she could run away until she died. Really, that was the only smart thing to do. She just had to figure out the perfect time, and then she could solve all their problems.

Chapter Six

⌒

Zoe stayed under water long enough to ice down her burning skin and corral her crazy thoughts and…

Come on, be honest.

Long enough to give Oliver a chance to strip and swim.

For the love of everything that was hot or holy, Zoe was starved for this. Craving more kisses, more touching, more Oliver. She had to have him. *Had to.*

When her lungs nearly burst, she popped up to see him sitting on the side of the pool, pants rolled to the knee, feet in the water.

She had to laugh at her dumb fantasies and his blasted self-control. "That's it? That's as reckless as you get, doc?"

He leaned back on his hands, watching her. "This is what you do."

Everything, every single thing, about that statement pissed her off, cooling her more than the water. "What the hell does that mean?"

"It means you do this." He gestured toward the pool.

"Swim?"

"As soon as things get messy, you do something impetuous and wild. You can't be trusted."

Damn him. She dunked herself, coming up to spit water in a perfect arc. "Since when is making out in a doorway *messy*?"

"Since you realized how much you wanted to make out in that doorway. Why jump in the water? Why not stand still and—"

"I can't stand still. Don't try and make me." She punctuated the admission with another dive, sliding down to touch the bottom. She blew some air and kicked back to the surface.

"Why can't you stand still, Zoe?"

She shrugged. "You know my history. Constant movement has been ingrained in me."

"You call it constant movement. I call it trying to catch liquid mercury with your bare hands."

"You're not trying to catch anything or you'd be in here." She slipped under the water, ready to count to thirty before she shot up again.

At fourteen, a splash rocked the whole pool, kicking her heart into high gear. He grabbed her from behind, the power of his arms so shocking that she sucked in water.

Instantly he pulled her up to the surface.

"It took you fourteen seconds to get your pants off," she sputtered.

"I had to use twelve of them to think about it."

She blinked water out of her eyes, vaguely aware that he still wore a pair of very wet boxer briefs. She snapped the elastic band. "Just think what you'd have done with two more seconds of thought."

"You're wearing something."

"For the moment. What did you think about for twelve seconds?"

"This." He pulled her into him and she automatically slid her legs around him while he got his footing in shoulder-deep water. "Oliver Bradbury, man in command of every situation, you got your underwear wet."

His mouth kicked up in a half smile. "I live here now. I can toss them in the dryer or go commando."

She took a deep breath, unable to keep from sighing it out as the image of him *commando* settled on her brain. "Would that be comfortable? You're a pretty well endowed man, if memory serves me."

"It serves you." As if to prove it, he grew a little harder and bigger against her stomach. She couldn't help it; she pushed against his erection, letting her bikini bottom swipe against its thickness, letting out an unintentional whimper of pleasure.

"You always loved riding me like that," he said, caressing her bare back, dragging his hand to the rise of her backside, and slipping one finger in the very top of her bikini bottom.

"What's not to love? It's sexy as sin."

He slid her up and down him again. "So are you."

She closed her eyes and leaned her head back as though she were offering her throat, but the truth was she didn't want to see the look on his face when she told him what she *had* to tell him.

He took the invitation and pressed his lips onto her skin, kicking up the pulse right under his mouth.

"I have to tell you something, Oliver."

He lifted his head. "Let me guess. You can't swim? That's a problem because I generally look for that in a nanny."

"Are we still interviewing?"

Once more, he dragged her up and down the ridge of his hard-on. "You're hired. Anything else you need to tell me?"

" I haven't had sex in four years." She squeezed her eyes shut so she didn't have to see the look on his face. After a beat, she peeked through her lashes. No shock, no laughter, just the quirk of an eyebrow.

"That's a long time."

"I'm really good friends with my vibrator, though."

He choked softly. "What a waste."

"Nah, it's top of the line and works like a charm."

He rocked the full length of his erection against her, making her suck in a little breath. "A charm like that?"

"Not quite that charming." His hair was smooth and slick as she slid her fingers into the locks, holding his head right in front of her so their mouths were as lined up as the rest of them.

He pressed again, their gazes locked. "Anything your vibrator can do, Zoe Tamarin, I can do better."

"You always were competitive. Top of the class, chief resident and all that." She rocked against him steadily now, heat searing her whole body. "But, I paid ninety dollars for him."

"Him?"

"Billy."

He choked softly. "He has a name?"

"Wild Bill Hickcock." She grinned. "But he's not that wild."

Laughing, he closed in for a kiss, lifting her into him and capturing her next breath in his mouth. Hot and wet and thorough, he kissed like he did everything—perfectly. A perfect annihilation of her lips sweetened by hands that slipped and dipped into private places, and the utter thrill of holding on to his strong, broad shoulders and riding his mighty hard-on.

Of course, she wanted more.

Just remembering the feeling of Oliver entering her made Zoe moan with deep, achy need.

"Better than Bill?" he murmured into the kiss.

"Bill who?"

He worked his hand up to the knot in her halter top. "Can Bill take your top off?"

"Depends on how tight the knot is."

"Not tight enough." He slipped the material through the knot and she felt the pressure on her neck disappear.

He peeled down the halter top to reveal her breasts, inching back to admire the view. "Too bad he can't see this."

"Too bad," she agreed, bowing her back enough to offer him access, blood pounding in her head, conveniently drowning out that stupid voice that might be saying things like *Stop*. Or *Run*. Or *Wow, this probably isn't completely made of smart.*

Right now there was nothing but the sound of their mutually strangled breaths, the splash of water, and the occasional groan of pure pleasure from both of them.

He eased her higher in his arms so he could suck one nipple, at the same time adding pressure between her legs, pounding a steady, maddening beat.

He lifted his head and looked at her, his face wet, his

eyes almost black, his jaw clenched as he ground into her again. "Bet your fucking Bill can't do *that*."

"No." Her throat caught as she fought for the next breath. "He doesn't have that setting."

He relaxed into a smile. "Then what the hell *can* he do?"

"He gets me off."

He pulled her so close no water could get between them, and pushed his hard-on against her, igniting a fire between her legs.

"Come on, Zoe, get off…right here." He picked up the speed, never taking his eyes from hers. His gaze held a challenge, the arrogant, arresting look of a man who had power and knew exactly how to use it.

She surrendered to the first twitch that squeezed into a spasm of pleasure, heavenly sensations radiating from her core, up her stomach, down her thighs, then deep, deep inside until she lost all control, and slammed helplessly against him, spiraling into her orgasm with shamefully little effort.

"Holy hell," she murmured, collapsing against his shoulder, her heart hammering so hard she felt the pulse in her toes.

He kissed her ear. "And no pesky batteries."

"I can't believe we just did that."

Drawing back, he gave her a strange look. "You started it."

"You finished it."

He thrust his hard-on against her. "Not yet."

"I…feel so easy."

"You haven't had sex for four years. You're not easy. You're…"

She put her hand over his mouth. "Don't say desperate."

"I wouldn't dream of it. Let's call it undernourished."

"I've had opportunities."

He ran his hands over her waist and tucked them under her backside. "I have no doubt. Every man who sees you wants this."

The words shot a hole in her heart. "Not every man." She slid underwater and pulled her top back up, hastily tying the straps behind her neck before emerging. "You gave me up."

"What? Sorry, but you went underwater and came up with changed history, Zoe."

"You would have," she insisted. "You'd have done the right thing. You'd have married Adele. And where would that have left me?"

His jaw opened, incredulous. "Wherever the hell you fled to, Zoe. I still don't know where you went when you vanished into thin air."

"Very thin," she said softly. "The Colorado mountains were my solace that year."

"Your solace?" His voice rose enough to know she'd hit a hot button. "I didn't have any solace, just empty promises that you'd wait and you'd talk and you'd stay."

She almost folded in half. "Did you try to find me?"

He let out a dry, wry laugh. "You might say that."

"What did you do?" And why did it matter so much? She didn't know, but it mattered. A lot.

He pushed a wet lock of hair off her face, his eyes on the strand, not her. "First? I talked to the landlord, and went to the post office, but your P.O. box had been closed with no forwarding address."

Of course it was. That was always Pasha's last errand on the way out of town.

"I left a letter in that box anyway."

"You did?" A longing so physical it ached like someone was in her gut twisting all of her insides. "You wrote me a letter?"

He shrugged. "I gave the prick fifty bucks, but I saw him toss the letter in the trash when I left. I wanted to tell you…" His voice faded out.

"About the baby on the way?" She waited, seeing the agony in his eyes and hating herself for putting it there. "Is that what was in the letter?"

"What was in the letter is moot now."

To him, maybe. "What else did you do?"

"Searched every place I knew you liked, every store, every bar, every park, every hot air balloon company in a two-hundred-mile radius."

Oh. "I'd always wondered. Then I saw that you had married and I assumed you went back to her right away because of…who I am. What I am."

He took her face in one hand, forcing her to look at him. "What you are is the woman I loved. I fully planned to support Adele and our child, but not marry her. I wanted to marry you."

"You did?" The bitter taste of regret filled her mouth, forcing a little mew of misery. Why had she gone with Pasha that day? She'd had the chance to stay and start over, without Pasha and with Oliver. Pasha had offered her the choice, but Zoe knew that would be the end of them. She'd never see Pasha again. And the way he'd acted in the balloon, she was so sure she'd lost him and couldn't imagine life without either of them.

So she did what she'd done most of her life because, deep inside, she didn't believe in the kind of love Oliver had tempted her with. It was meant for other people, but not for Bridget Lessington.

He stepped back, dropping his hands in the water with a small splash. "I went to your house that night, but you were gone."

The words hit like arrows to her heart.

Twelve hours. If she'd only stayed in Chicago for twelve more hours.

"Why didn't you tell me what Adele's message was?" she asked. Maybe that would have changed her decision...or maybe it would have made her run faster. There really was no way to know now.

"I couldn't tell you until I talked to Adele," he said. "I wasn't even sure she was telling the truth." He closed his eyes as if just remembering still hurt. "But she was and you were gone and, yes, I married her. And I stayed on a career course that was well guided by her father, and pretended that what you and I had was a crazy, brief fling instead of something real."

Twelve hours.

"If I had stayed," Zoe said softly, "how would you have gotten around the problem of my fake identity? Could you have gotten past the fact that I lived 'on the run' for all those years and might have to again?"

"I didn't see it as the problem you did. I absolutely believed we could have negotiated with someone for help and gotten her cleared or pardoned. I still believe that. We could have fixed that." He lifted a shoulder. "We still can."

"She won't even consider it. And now so much time has gone by it seems kind of...I don't know." She bounced a little on her toes; the conversation making her jumpy.

"She's too old to face that. By the time we have it sorted out, she could be…" *Dead.*

"Zoe." He reached for her shoulders, holding her still. "Why don't we fix both things at the same time?"

She stared at him. There were so many things to fix: their broken hearts, her dumb mistakes, Pasha's legal problems, and, the biggest thing of all, cancer. "How?" she asked, overwhelmed by her mental list.

"While I start treatment, you consult a lawyer. Let's attack the problems simultaneously." He was never overwhelmed, though. Methodically, he'd power through and repair the hell out of everything.

No matter what the consequences. "She'd feel so betrayed."

"Betrayed? If she's healthy and free?" he countered. "Maybe she'd feel relieved."

No. She'd be furious, hurt, and speechless at Zoe's treachery. "We have an unspoken pact."

"Maybe it's unspoken because it was so wrong."

"It wasn't wrong. She helped me, she saved me. And she's afraid."

"Of what?"

She let out a dry laugh. "Prison?"

"She's not going to prison."

"You don't know that. And we've always had this lifelong agreement."

He shook his head a little, sliding his hand under her hair to hold her head. "Is that the only lifelong agreement you want, Zoe?"

The words stunned her, like shock therapy to her whole body. "What are you saying?"

For a long moment he didn't answer, just traced her

lower lip with his finger, sending white-hot sparks through her. "I'm saying I don't want to be your replacement vibrator. I want a shot at something real with you, Zoe."

A wholly different kind of electrical shock sparked in her. "You do?"

He held her gaze. "Don't you?"

More than anything. But did she want it enough to hurt the one person who had stood by her through everything? The woman who'd saved her life and made sure she was educated and loved her wholly and fully—whether it was right or wrong?

"You're thinking awfully hard about this" He moved away so suddenly she bobbed in the water. "Forget I asked."

"As if that would be humanly possible."

He walked toward the steps, water dripping off his body. The wet boxer briefs clung to his stunning male physique. "You're asking me to pick you or Pasha."

As he climbed out, he turned to her. "And you made that choice already, didn't you?"

Yes, she had. And she hadn't really been deeply happy since then.

"Get dressed, Zoe. We should get back so I can sign the paperwork and you can tell Evan the good news."

"About moving in here?"

He picked up his pants from the patio. "About you being his sitter."

They'd confirmed that? "And will you see Aunt Pasha as a patient?"

"Yes, of course." He said it as though he'd planned to all along, which kind of pissed her off, but she was smart enough not to say a word. She'd gotten what she wanted.

And an orgasm.

* * *

Zoe was relieved to find Pasha asleep when she stopped by the bungalow after saying good-bye to Oliver. She wasn't quite ready for the inevitable discussion, which, if Pasha wasn't sick, could—and probably would—easily end with a pack-and-run.

But Pasha *was* sick, and this time everything was different.

And what Oliver was asking her to do? Turn Pasha in? The idea was still unthinkable to her. So she thought about other things.

I want a shot at something real with you, Zoe.

Yeah, she could think about that for hours. But Tessa texted that she and Jocelyn were still at Lacey's house, drawing Zoe like a magnet to her three best friends. As always, she'd have to hold some truths back from them, but even still, she could count on their friendship to make her feel better.

Plus, she wanted to hold that baby again. God, she was as bad as Tessa with the babies now.

Did "something real" include a baby? A life together? A home? She didn't know. The only thing she did know was that it would include a betrayal she wasn't sure she could make.

She took the back route along the gardens and ended up on Lacey's pool patio, where she found Jocelyn and Tessa nursing wine and Lacey nursing something a little bit cuter.

"And then there were five," she teased as she pulled open the screen door to join them poolside.

"Excuse me, this is my second child," Lacey said. "So that makes six."

"Yeah, but Ashley doesn't drink with us. Yet." At the

outdoor bar, Zoe grabbed a plastic stemmed glass and poured a liberal amount of Chardonnay. "Where is my god-daughter? Is she getting enough attention with the new baby?"

"I hope so. She went with Clay and Will to get us Mexican from the SOB," Tessa said. "Where have you been all day?"

"Selling real estate." She dropped onto an empty chaise and raised her glass to Lacey, who was curled up on her own chaise, her breast and babe covered by a pale blue blanket. "You're welcome, Mrs. Walker. Casa Blanca has its first long-term tenant in Bay Laurel."

Lacey smiled in gratitude. "We're over the moon about this rental, Zoe. This is huge for us."

"And how do *you* feel about it?" Tessa asked, sneaking a look at Jocelyn that practically screamed that they'd all been talking about her.

"Like I should get a commission." Zoe took a deep sip. "And the courtesy of not being gossiped about by my closest friends."

"We're not gossiping," Jocelyn assured her. "We're discussing your relationship with the newest guest."

"Who happens to be quite nice looking," Lacey said, cringing as she adjusted the infant. "I remember this being easier with Ashley."

"You were twenty-two," Zoe said. "Everything's easier then. Did you all lay bets on whether or not we kissed?"

"Five to one you kissed," Tessa shot back.

"Ten to one your bathing suit came off," Jocelyn added.

"I went all in for the whole enchilada." Lacey grinned. "And I don't mean the one I ordered from South of the Border."

Zoe rolled her eyes but didn't quench their pathetic curiosity.

"Zoe," Tessa said, her voice weary with frustration. "You know we hate secrets."

"You hate them, Tessa. The rest of us deal with them as part of life. Right?" She looked at the other two women, but Lacey peeked under the blanket and Jocelyn was suddenly interested in her wineglass. "Okay, let's get this over with, then. Start the inquisition."

Tessa dove right in, of course. "You *know* Dr. Oliver Bradbury."

"Define know."

"In the biblical sense," Tessa added.

Zoe almost spewed her wine. "You didn't really just say that."

"C'mon, Zoe, talk to us," Jocelyn said. "We know he's the guy that freaked you out that day at the Ritz."

Lacey leaned forward, her jaw opened. "The one who came in when you and I were buying me condoms."

"That you clearly forgot to use." Zoe pointed at the baby, then lifted her glass. "He was a stupid flash in my past, okay. I knew him years ago in Chicago for a couple of weeks. He's not a secret as much as a mistake, which you've all made." She took a sip, looking over the glass at three disbelieving faces.

"Oh, you haven't?" she demanded. "Jocelyn, the Alabama game, that's all I'm going to say." She put her finger in her mouth and fake-puked. "Lacey, I believe his name was David Fox and you have a lovely sixteen year-old daughter to remember him by."

Lacey shrugged. "Best mistake I ever made."

"And Tessa…" She dug into her memory for some misdemeanor, but Tessa hadn't committed a lot of them. "Surely you ate a burger and mainlined Splenda in a moment of unorganic weakness."

"Never." Tessa smiled. "Okay, once during finals. Stop trying to deflect with humor, Zoe. Spill the doctor dirt."

"There's nothing to spill." At Tessa's furious and unforgiving look, Zoe sighed. "It all happened a long time and a lot of men ago, okay? He doesn't matter except he's a paying guest of Casa Blanca and that's a good thing. Right, Lace?"

She looked up from the blanket. "Jocelyn said he was with his wife at the grand opening. Did you know he's married?"

"Not anymore, he's not."

"Was he married when you 'knew' him?" Lacey asked, the tiniest bit of accusation in her voice. Tiny, but as sharp as glass and straight to the heart.

"No." Zoe closed her eyes and swallowed hard. "But thanks for the vote of confidence, my friend."

Lacey looked suitably miserable for asking. "Sorry. Baby hormones."

"We're just trying to figure out what happened," Tessa added.

"Why?" Zoe spun on her, all the forgiveness she was ready to shower on Lacey gone. "Why doesn't 'we dated, had mind-blowing sex, and broke up' cut it for you, Tessa? Why do you have to know every soul-crushing, heartbreaking, dream-dying detail?"

Lacey pushed herself up slowly. "I'm taking Elijah inside."

"Oh, Lace, I'm sorry," Zoe said, putting her glass on the table to stand. "I didn't mean to lose my temper in front of the baby. Or any of you."

"Only me," Tessa said softly.

"Yeah, you." Zoe gave her a smile she had to fight to find. "We live to antagonize one another, remember?"

Still holding the baby in one arm, Lacey laid her free hand on Zoe's cheek. "Honey, we don't antagonize. We don't argue. And we don't want to pry. We want to help you."

Zoe closed her eyes, a whirlwind of emotion fluttering through her chest. Love, longing, friendship, and, damn it, the burning need to hang out without worrying about revealing everything. But mostly she wanted to respect Lacey, her home, and her newborn.

She nodded and stayed quiet while Lacey went inside, then plopped down again, directing her attention to Jocelyn. "You had a secret," she reminded her. "We didn't pry it out of you."

"I felt better after I shared," she said.

"Closer to us and happy to be honest," Tessa added, getting up from her chair to join Zoe on the chaise. "Don't hate me for wanting to help you."

Zoe fought the instinct to shake off Tessa's arm. "What happened that makes you think I need help? I saw an ex. He has a sweet son and now he's going to be a guest at the resort. What's the big deal?"

"Your face," Tessa said. "The way you look at him and the way he looks at you. And Pasha acted kind of weird, too."

Lacey returned, babyless this time, buttoning her top while looking at Zoe. "He came to see you, you know. His son let it slip to Clay."

"He came to see Elijah." But she knew that wasn't true.

"But you weren't surprised to see him," Tessa said.

Zoe speared her with a look. "You really should have been a lawyer."

Tessa didn't take the bait but rubbed Zoe's arm with love and patience. "He's more than just an ex, isn't he? He was important in your life."

How could she fight Tessa the Tsunami? "More than you know," Zoe finally whispered. The ache to say more twisted inside her, the need to know the bliss of pure, open honesty as powerful as any of the needs she'd been battling for a few days.

But she had never been allowed that privilege in her life.

While they were all quiet, Zoe took a sip of wine, considering how much she could tell them. Certainly it wouldn't hurt to share the news about Pasha being sick. That wouldn't break any promises, would it?

"The fact is, I went to see him first, the morning after the baby was born." She rubbed some condensation off the glass, not looking up. "He's an oncologist."

The word took a moment to sink in, then she got a chorus of two gasps and one "Oh my God."

"Not me," she said quickly. "No, I'm fine. It's Pasha."

"Oh, no." Tessa's chest sank like she'd been sucker-punched. "I've noticed how weak she seems. I thought it was old age."

Zoe dragged her curls off her face, the sense of relief palpable in her chest. Was it always this good to share secrets? "She's really sick. We got a quasi-diagnosis in Arizona and I talked to Oliver, who more or less thinks she might have esophageal cancer."

"More or less?" Jocelyn asked. "What does that mean?"

"I don't know. We're going to find out. He's going to see her," she said. "If she'll let him."

"Why wouldn't she?" Lacey and Tessa asked the question at the same time.

"Because..." She lifted the glass to her lips to buy time, but then realized that the wine would only make her more talkative, so she put it down. She was walking a very fine line with what she could reveal. "He broke my heart, as you've all probably figured out by now, so he's on her shit list."

And that was true enough.

"If he won't work, we'll find another oncologist," Lacey said. "In fact, I can make some calls now. I know some people in town who've been through chemo."

"No, no." Shit, now it was going to get tricky. "She... doesn't have insurance." Again, not a lie.

Jocelyn waved her hand. "We'll pool funds, Zoe. Did she have a doctor to refer her—"

"She doesn't want to see a doctor."

"If she has *cancer*?" Tessa was incredulous.

"Tessa, she will not see a doctor." At least not one who will make her fill out paperwork and have a legit Social Security card. "She's...terrified of them."

"What if she got a sign that she had to see a doctor?" Tessa asked. "You know how she responds to messages from the universe and nature."

"Like that pain in her chest and the doctor in Sedona using the C word isn't enough of a sign?" Still, Zoe appreciated the idea.

"We have to come up with a solution," Jocelyn said.

"This is not an insurmountable problem," Lacey agreed.

"As long as you're being completely open with us." Tessa gave Zoe's arm a slight poke. "And you are, aren't you?"

For several heartbeats Zoe stayed silent, a dozen different smart-ass quips threatening but not actually coming forth. It would be so easy to joke. To straight-arm her friends, who only wanted to help. To make sure that wall she'd started building at ten years old stayed nice and high and impenetrable.

She smiled at Tessa, only because, damn, the woman had tried for years to take that wall down. Really tried. And Zoe just shot sarcasm arrows at her year after year.

Her heart wobbled a little when she realized that Tessa loved her so completely that she took those arrows every time.

"Tess," she said softly, her voice cracking and her pulse ridiculously high. "If I told you that the truth could do more damage to Pasha than cancer, ending her life faster than any illness, would you let this one secret go?"

Tessa swallowed hard, obviously surprised by Zoe's response. "Okay, Zoe, you win."

When Tessa leaned over to hug, Zoe put her face in Tessa's shoulder and bit back completely unexpected tears. She might share a little and show a touch of vulnerability, but, damn it, she wasn't going to cry.

"*Hola!*" Ashley's voice called out from the kitchen. "SOB delivery is here." Carrying a large plastic bag, Lacey's daughter came out onto the patio, her fresh face and huge smile a balm to Zoe's heart. "Aunt Zoe! We thought you'd be out on a date with the hot doc."

Zoe shook her head, laughing. "*Et tu*, Brutus?"

Ashley squished her pretty face. "Does not compute."

Tessa pushed up from her chair to snag the bag. "It means we've been too rough on Aunt Zoe. And you better have remembered the whole-wheat tortilla and not let the beef touch anything I eat."

Zoe and Ashley shared an eye-roll, but Zoe appreciated Tessa's defense.

Will and Clay joined them on the patio, each of them drawn to the women they loved, pairing up naturally while they greeted Zoe. Tessa disappeared with Ashley into the kitchen.

Clay nudged onto the chaise with Lacey, whispering something about the baby, then smiling at her as they shared secret communication. And Will pulled Jocelyn from her chair, sat in it, and tugged her back onto his lap, giving her a not-so-secret kiss.

For one suspended second, Zoe felt utterly alone.

I want a shot at something real with you.

During that one moment of loneliness, the price she'd have to pay to have that shot—which might cost her Pasha—almost seemed reasonable. Almost.

If only there could be another way.

Chapter Seven

⌒

A soft ding pulled Zoe out of a dream about flying. She was up in a hot air balloon, way over the ocean, looking down at two people dancing on the sand. They were singing and laughing—

No, that wasn't laughter. That was the phone.

Damn it, only Tessa would text this early. Zoe stuck her hand out from under the sheet and patted the nightstand for her phone. Who else would text at the crack of dawn, probably looking for composting assistance or something equally riveting on a Saturday morning?

She managed to open one eye, blinded by streaming mid-morning sun. Okay, maybe not the *actual* crack of dawn. More like the gap of ten-thirty.

From the kitchen, a dish clattered and water ran, reminding her that she had to tell Pasha today. Pasha had been drowsy and disinterested last night when Zoe came home from Lacey's, but there could be no more procrastination. Maybe Zoe should hide the panic bag beforehand so Pasha couldn't convince her to run away.

Touching the phone screen, she squinted at the sender's name.

Oliver Bradbury.

An unnatural zing woke up every sleepy cell.

Her finger lingered over the screen, not quite ready to read what he'd texted.

Their good-bye had been quiet, like neither one wanted to talk about what could happen next. But she had to find out. Would he see Pasha soon? Did he really expect Zoe to go hunting down a lawyer to lay history to rest?

If Zoe even did that—the idea was still filed firmly under "unimaginable" in her head—it would be the ugliest betrayal she could imagine. But if she *didn't*, would Zoe ever have a chance for a relatively normal life?

Normal life now being a euphemism for "life with Oliver."

But he'd put a stipulation on it. He'd made it conditional. Conditional love—well, that was an oxymoron. Zoe wanted *unconditional*, balls-to-the-wall, no strings, no demands, no compromises, no betraying loved ones who'd given up everything for her.

Not that she believed for one second such an animal even existed, at least not one she knew how to hunt and bag.

"Are you awake, Zoe?" Pasha called from the hall.

"Out in a sec, Aunt P." She tapped the screen to read his text.

Moving in today. Meet us at the villa around noon?

With Pasha? Without? Did she have to show proof of a lawyer's bill before he'd help her? Or did he want her to come over and watch Evan while he got them settled in?

Throwing the covers back, she climbed out of bed, wishing she had a plan.

You hate plans, Zoe.

Yes, she did. Because it was so much easier to live in the moment and go with the flow and roll with the punches and dig for meaningless clichés that described her inability to make a commitment.

You wouldn't know how to handle a commitment if it bit you.

"Oh, shut up, will you?"

Pasha tapped lightly on her door. "Are you alone, honey?"

She blew out a breath and turned it into a laugh. "Only me and these male strippers I picked up at the Toasted Pelican. Come on, you guys, scram. Out the window." She opened the door. "Of course I'm al—" She didn't even finish, frowning at the ratty housecoat, flat hair, and washed-out face. "What's wrong?"

"Nothing."

Nothing? It didn't matter the day or time; Pasha Tamarin always drew in eyebrows, lined her lids with some kohl, and gelled her two-inch silver locks into a gravity-defying spike style. The woman didn't leave her room without a couple of pounds of silver and turquoise jewelry, and a blindingly bright muumuu draped over her narrow frame.

Not today.

Zoe frowned at her. "Why are you..." She gestured to the robe.

"Just feeling a little punk."

Oh, God. Zoe stepped into the hall, putting a hand on Pasha's shoulder to lead her toward the kitchen. It was time.

But she needed coffee to drop this bomb, and Pasha brewed it for Zoe every morning. Judging by the smell, today was no different.

Only it would be different in a few minutes because Zoe was about to break the news.

We got a doctor. And we're getting a lawyer.

Her heart tumbled down to the bottom of her stomach, landing with a thud. But this wasn't about how Zoe felt, and she had to remember that.

"Is it your chest ?" Zoe asked. "Or your throat?"

Pasha waved a hand as if to say it was nothing, but her pained expression screamed that it was most definitely not nothing.

"You're getting worse, aren't you?"

"I'm getting old," Pasha replied, letting herself be guided to a ladder-back chair at the little table, where the daily newspaper was still open, an empty teacup next to it. "And worse," she admitted softly.

Zoe turned to get a cup and pour some coffee, rooting around for the right words, the right way to start the conversation.

So, Oliver Bradbury, what a coincidence, huh? He's an oncologist, you know. Guess what, Pasha, he's agreed to see you and—

"Did you have sex with him?"

The cup slipped out of her hand, clunking onto the tile countertop. "Gee, Pasha, were you in on the bets my friends were placing? Apparently the odds are in my favor for getting laid."

She didn't laugh. "I know it's been a long time since you've been with a man, Zoe, and that one always had a way of, you know, getting you going."

There were some downsides to being this close to another person. "He doesn't 'get me going' anymore."

See, Zoe, you can lie to your Aunt Pasha after all.

Pasha snorted as if she could hear that inner voice of Zoe's loud and clear. She often could.

"Pasha, I *didn't* have sex with him." Not…technically.

"But you did kiss him."

Zoe carefully poured the coffee and scooped up an overload of sugar. "First of all, I fail to see what difference that would make in the scheme of things and I really fail to see how you could jump to that conclusion from the fact that he dropped by with his son to see Lacey and Clay."

"I think it was a little more than that."

On her way to the fridge for milk, Zoe leaned over the empty cup in front of Pasha. "Tea leaves talking this morning, Pasha?"

"No, Tessa was. She stopped over while you were still sleeping."

Zoe yanked the fridge door open with way more force than it called for. "So you *were* in on the gambling."

"She mentioned to me that you two disappeared for a couple of hours."

Was it that long? Felt like ten minutes. "I showed him Bay Laurel because he's—"

"Moving in there." Pasha flipped the page of the paper as if she were reading it.

Zoe laughed because, really, what else could she do? "I don't know why you'd bother with the *Mimosa Gazette* when you have the *Tessa Times*." She stirred the coffee until it frothed a little, tapped the spoon on the cup, the dinging sound announcing the next round.

"But here's something you don't know, Pasha, and you're going to be so happy to hear that—"

"He still loves you."

She practically sank into the other chair. "And Tessa knows this how?"

"Oh, Tessa doesn't have a clue." Pasha gave her a shaky smile, wide enough to show that she not only hadn't bothered with makeup or hair, she also hadn't put her bridge in that morning, leaving little gaping holes in her back teeth. "That I *did* get from the tea. But she mentioned he's divorced."

Zoe sighed, another laugh escaping. "And he has a son."

"I heard."

Of course she had. "Did Tessa tell you how uptight and serious he is? That he never met a rule he wouldn't follow, dots every *i* and crosses every *t*, and then takes anyone to task if they may have missed a detail?"

"Zoe, those were all character traits he had before and you *adored* him." She dragged out the word as though it were so…precious.

"What's not to adore?" she asked, lifting the cup to sip.

"He's a fine piece of ass, if I recall."

She almost spewed her coffee. "I created a monster with you."

Pasha gave a careless shrug and lifted her invisible brows. "He's good for you."

"You think I should get back together with him?" *He was the one who wanted to turn you in. And he still does.*

Pasha looked down at the newspaper, tapping a finger. "I thought you'd be interested in this advertisement for Sylver Sky." She inched the paper closer.

Zoe didn't look. "Answer me, Pasha."

"That's the name of a hot air balloon company in Fort Myers."

Zoe gave the black-and-white ad a cursory glance. "Nice."

"Maybe they're hiring." Pasha's eyes twinkled, maybe not as bright as they'd been for the past twenty years, but Zoe could still read that message.

"You'd live here?"

Pasha leaned back, crossing her arms. "I'd die here."

The words hit like a fast, unexpected slap. "You're not going to die."

"Darling girl, if I did, you'd be free."

"You're not going to die, Pasha!" Vaulting to her feet, she almost knocked the chair back. "And don't you even think that's some kind of ticket to my…my…"

"Happiness."

"Pasha!" She fell to her knees in front of the older woman, dropping her head on the bony lap she loved so much, wrapping her arms around Pasha's narrow middle. "Don't even say that. Ever, ever, ever." A lump formed in her throat just thinking that Pasha would even think her dying would make Zoe happy.

"I always thought there was a kind of magic in the air when you two were together." She threaded her fingers into Zoe's hair, looking down with a smile that only accentuated the deep, deep crevices of her paper-thin skin.

Was it possible she didn't remember that Oliver knew their secret? No, she knew. But maybe she thought if she were so sick that she—

"And Tessa told me that that magic is still there," Pasha continued.

"What didn't Tessa tell you?" Like did she mention that Oliver was an oncologist?

Slowly, Zoe inched away, returning to her feet, steadying herself for the conversation she couldn't delay any longer.

"She told me that Oliver's little boy is cute and your hair was soaked when you came back. Did you go swimming with him?"

Zoe smiled and took a seat at the kitchen table. "Yes. And we kissed. And we—"

Pasha placed her fingertips over her ears and sang, "I can't hear you."

But Zoe reached across and gently took Pasha's hands down and held them. "You have to hear this."

At her tone, Pasha looked at Zoe.

"We talked about you."

Pasha's eyes shuttered. "I'm sure you did."

"Not…that," Zoe said quickly. "We talked about how he can treat your condition and never report your name to any agency or insurance company or anyone." Just the lawyer he wanted Zoe to see. But she hadn't actually agreed to that, and with the way blood was visibly draining from Pasha's face, she wasn't going to mention a lawyer now.

"Do you understand what I'm saying, Aunt Pasha?"

She didn't even blink.

"He's an oncologist and that's a doctor that—"

"I know what an oncologist is," she said sharply, drawing her hands free of Zoe's. "And he's not treating me."

"Pasha, he's a very good doctor, in high demand, with a clinic that specializes in advanced, experimental treatment. He can figure out what's wrong with you and fix you." Zoe's voice cracked with the sheer will of trying to get Pasha to see the wisdom of this. "He's the answer to our prayers."

"He is," she agreed. "But I wasn't praying for a doctor, I was praying for your happiness."

"You being healthy would make me happy."

"Not as happy as love."

Zoe grunted softly. "Pasha! This is your *life* we're talking about. We need to know what's wrong and how to—"

"I *know* what's wrong with me. I have cancer."

She'd never said the word before. After the one time in Sedona when the doctor suggested the diagnosis, Pasha had refused to say the word *cancer*. And now it rolled off her tongue like her middle name.

"Then he's the perfect doctor for you since that's his specialty."

"I don't want to see a doctor."

"Did you not just admit that you have cancer?" It felt strange to say that out loud, because she'd been following Pasha's lead and letting the C-word be the silent elephant in their living room. Now Dumbo was lifting his trunk and spraying them.

"I did. I do." She angled her head and smiled, looking frightfully old without her makeup or jewelry or full set of teeth. "That's what Mother Nature gave me, and that's how Mother Nature's taking me. Unless I, you know, help her along a little."

"Pasha! Over my dead body!"

"No, child, over mine." She inched the newspaper closer. "Maybe you should talk to these folks at the balloon company. Get a job here in town." She gave the most unsubtle nod. "*Settle down.*"

Zoe bristled. "I don't settle down."

"And we both know why."

What was she saying? "You think my life is going to get better if you die, Pasha?"

Pasha leaned forward. "You gave him up once before for me."

"I gave him up for the wrong reasons," she said. "I thought he couldn't handle how we'd lived, but what he couldn't handle was the news on his phone."

Pasha didn't even hear her; she shook her head, waiting for a chance to speak. "I will not come between you two again. Your life will be so much better when I'm gone."

"Well, you're wrong." Zoe stood so fast her coffee splashed onto the newspaper, soaking the balloon company ad. "My life would *not* get better if you die. In fact, my life would suck if you die!"

"Zoe, you know as well as I do that my very existence is what's holding you back from being with Oliver."

"Are you crazy?" She grabbed the cup and walked to the sink, an acrid mix of coffee and anger and fear on her tongue. "There are so many things wrong with that statement I don't even know where to start. Your very existence is why I'm alive, Pasha. I'd have killed myself by thirteen if you hadn't saved me."

"You'd have survived."

She spun around, fire in her belly. "I'd have been raped sixteen ways from Sunday!"

Pasha flinched.

"And you are not holding me back from being with Oliver," Zoe said. "I'm doing that all by myself, thank you very much."

"Doesn't sound like you held back too much in the pool yesterday."

"Actually, I held…a little. You know what stopped me?"

"I hope it was your strong moral compass."

Zoe snorted. "Nothing so admirable."

"You didn't have a condom?"

"Pasha." She laughed softly. "How can you even think of dying? I need you to crack me up. And, no, that wasn't the problem, although I didn't even think about it."

"Well, you better. What stopped you?"

Zoe finished rinsing the cup and set it on the drainer, wondering how honest she should be. Normally, she'd tell Pasha everything. They had no secrets.

"Fear."

"Of what? Falling in love? You need to fall in love, Zoe. It's time. You're in your thirties. You need a home, a child or six, and a husband."

"I'm afraid." She looked out the window over the sink, her gaze focused on the very bright green of a queen palm frond swaying in the Gulf breeze. "I'm afraid I don't know how to stay."

"Another thing you can blame on me."

"I'm not blaming anything on you." She turned and walked to Pasha, her heart swelling with affection. "You sacrificed everything for me. Everything."

"And that's why you left him and went to Colorado with me."

"That's why I've done everything for the last twenty-five years. Do you think I will ever forget that you threw your life in a suitcase and ran into the night when I told you what happened? All you did to keep me safe? To educate me and love me and put me before everything else?"

The words seemed to pain Pasha and she hissed in a noisy breath, her lips puckering as she did so, her hand automatically rising to her chest—where the cancer was.

Tell her what he wants you to do.

Normally, Zoe fought to ignore that voice in her head. But right now something clicked and the instructions made sense. "Pasha," Zoe whispered. "If we could settle here and never run again, then I would be happy. Together, with you healthy. That's how I could be happy."

"That's…impossible."

Zoe crouched again, taking Pasha's withered hands. "Not if we clear your name."

Pasha whipped out of Zoe's grip with lightning speed. "No!" Pasha pushed her chair back, looking from side to side like a trapped animal, desperate for escape. "Don't ever suggest that again."

Zoe stood, reaching for Pasha as she tried to pass. "It's been almost twenty-five years, and—"

Pasha's dark eyes narrowed. "You know the law."

"We can get around that—"

"No." Pasha wrestled away from Zoe and marched toward the hall.

"Pasha, please." Zoe followed, easily catching up in two steps. "You aren't being reasonable. With a good lawyer, we could—"

"Stop it!" Pasha spun, her eyes filled and her color high despite her lack of makeup. "The answer is no. No. *No!*"

Frustration seized Zoe, wrapping around her throat. "Pasha, why can't we even try?"

"You can't try something like that, Zoe. The police, the newspapers…" She shook her head and put her hand over her chest. "I don't think I could take it."

Of course she couldn't. Zoe almost melted with self-loathing. How could she do this to Pasha? So she could have "something real" with Oliver? She would not hurt this woman who had saved her, raised her, and loved her.

Pasha was the only person who ever had loved Zoe *unconditionally*. Even Oliver's offer had come with stipulations, hadn't it?

"Okay." Zoe stepped back, holding her hands up in surrender. "I'm sorry I brought it up."

"Me, too." Pasha headed into her bedroom just as Zoe realized she hadn't done the one thing she had to do this morning: convince Pasha to see Oliver.

She swore under her breath as her phone buzzed with another text. Oliver, no doubt. What should she tell him? Was she going over to the villa today?

Of course she was. Because she was going to save Pasha's life—and not so she could spend the rest of it in jail. "Pasha?"

She didn't look up from an open drawer, where she was deeply involved in choosing her underwear for the day. "Hmm?"

"Can you go out with me today?"

She sighed. "I don't know. Where do you want to go?"

How could she convince her? She'd never say yes, not in this mood. Not when she was determined to die instead of getting legal help. Pasha Tamarin was a five-foot-tall, ninety-five-pound brick wall when she wanted to be.

But Zoe could climb that wall. "I thought we might go check out that hot air balloon operation. Maybe, you know, put an application in."

Pasha smiled. "I'd like that."

"All right. But I have to make one quick stop first on the way."

"That's fine, honey."

No, it wouldn't be. But she'd climb over that wall, too.

Chapter Eight

⌒

Oliver heard the Jeep from the kitchen, the low growl of the engine starting a matching rumble of anticipation in his gut. Already. It had taken two days to get stupid over Zoe.

And not only the hormones, adrenaline, and pheromones kind of stupid. That other kind—the illogical kind that made him agree to things that made no sense, like living on the same property, having her help him with Evan, taking care of her aunt, and getting close to naked the first time they were alone together.

But that wasn't stupid. That was inevitable.

And so was pain, heartache, and a few holes punched in the wall. This was, after all, Zoe Tamarin.

Evan's rapid footsteps pounded overhead. "Dad!" He tore down the stairs so fast he couldn't possibly have been holding on to the banister. "Dad!"

"Be careful on those—"

"She's here!" He swung into the kitchen, one hand on

the doorjamb, his dark eyes lit from the inside, his little face flushed.

So Zoe had that same inexplicable, stupid effect on him.

"I heard her car," Oliver said.

"It's actually a Jeep Rubicon," Evan told him, clearly proud of that knowledge. "Topless."

"Convertible." Topless was something else altogether. Although, with Zoe…

"There's an old lady in the car with her."

"That's her great-aunt." So she'd managed to get her here. The few texts they'd exchanged that morning had warned him that Pasha was lukewarm on the idea of seeing him. He wasn't sure if it was because Oliver knew her history, or because she wasn't keen on seeing a doctor in general.

Either way, he'd promised Zoe he'd let the visit be casual. Hell, he'd have promised her the moon to get her over here again. And not just because he needed to use her over-sized vehicle to get some stuff from storage, although he was looking forward to taking a drive with her.

"Let's go greet our guests," he said, folding a towel and placing it on the counter before gesturing for Evan to lead the way.

But his son didn't move, which seemed odd considering how overjoyed he was to see her.

"Move it," Oliver said, prodding Evan's shoulder. "She's liable to change her mind."

Evan didn't take the nudge, looking hard at Oliver instead.

"What's the matter, son?"

"Do you, like, like her, Dad?"

Ah, the downside of a genius IQ. It was impossible to get anything by this kid. "Of course I like *like* her. I think she's going to make a great sitter for you when I'm at work and—"

Evan scowled, reminding Oliver that his son was not as easily pacified as most eight-year-olds. "You know what I mean."

"Yes, I know what you mean." He searched his son's face, not exactly sure where to go with this—which seemed to be the story of their relationship. "Is that a problem for you?"

He lifted one shoulder. "Well, since Mom's gone to France with…" He rolled his eyes. "Mark *Ass*lowe."

"It's Bass…" He laughed softly. "I'm going to pretend I didn't hear that."

Adele had kept her relationship with the pharmaceutical CEO under wraps until the divorce was officially final, so Oliver had no idea how much his son knew about the man his mother was dating. Obviously enough to give Mark Basslowe an accurate nickname.

"So, is Zoe *your* new girlfriend?"

He opened his mouth to say no, but the denial didn't roll out. "She's a…friend."

Evan nodded, skepticism all over his little face. "I like her."

"Well, sorry, she can't be your girlfriend."

That got him a toothy grin. "I know. I mean, I guess you and Mom…"

Oliver felt his shoulders drop with the weight of the conversation. "We're not going to be together, Evan, but we both still love—"

"I've heard the speech, Dad." He worked to swallow, and Oliver was filled with sympathy. Evan had been a trouper through this whole thing, better than any parent could expect. "I, you know, don't want to get my hopes up and…"

"Lose someone again," Oliver supplied.

Evan glanced toward the ground, his cheeks pink.

"Trust me, son, I know how you feel." And he took the silent admission to heart. Zoe could leave two broken hearts behind when she left next time. "We better go." He gave Evan's shoulder another nudge. "I'm not kidding when I say she could change her mind."

The Jeep was still in the driveway when he opened the door, but the two women in it were making no effort to get out. They were deep in conversation, a dark expression on Zoe's face visible over Pasha's narrow shoulder.

Zoe looked up, a plea for help directed at him.

"Wait here for a second," he whispered to Evan, easing the boy back into the entryway. "I think this conversation requires privacy."

Evan agreed silently, and Oliver stepped out into the sunshine, approaching the passenger side. "Hello," he called out.

Very slowly, Pasha's gray-haired head turned to him. "Hello, Oliver."

Close to a decade had passed since he'd last seen the spry little woman who claimed to be a gypsy and told the future in the craziest ways. A decade that had changed her far more than it had changed Zoe or Oliver.

"Pasha, it's good to see you." He reached to give her a hand out of the high-stepped Rubicon, but she quickly shook her head.

"I'm not staying."

"Aunt Pasha," Zoe said, frustration in her voice. "Please come in and talk."

She closed her eyes. "I'm really not feeling up to it."

Actually, he believed that. Her hair, once lustrous and nearly blue-black, was only about two inches long in length, silver white, and facing straight into the air. She still wore too much silver jewelry, but instead of looking festive and wild, the chains and earrings seemed to weigh her down, which wouldn't be difficult on a woman who couldn't hit a hundred soaking wet.

But the doctor in him saw more than the obvious.

He recognized the sallow skin, the dim eyes, the full-body wasteness that consumed cancer patients.

"It's pretty hot to be driving around without air-conditioning," he said.

"She normally loves the top down," Zoe told him.

But Pasha held up her hand to stop them both. "I—I…" She turned to him again, this time looking at him as hard as he'd looked at her. "This is awkward," she finally said.

"It doesn't have to be," he replied quickly. "Come inside, have something cold to drink, and—"

"Can I come out now?" Evan asked, already halfway across the driveway.

Oliver seized the opportunity. "Meet my son," Oliver said with a smile. "Who has a hard time doing exactly what I say."

Pasha leaned around his shoulder as Evan came running out to the car. "Hi, Zoe!" he called.

"Hey, kid. How do you like your new house?"

"I love it! Come and see."

Zoe hesitated a moment, checking out her aunt. But Pasha's eyes were riveted on Evan, her mouth opened in a little circle of shock. "That's your son?" Her voice rose with an odd crack.

"C'mere, Evan." He gestured for him to come closer. "This is Ms. Tamarin, Zoe's great-aunt."

"Hi." He gave her a little wave.

"How old are—wait, wait, don't tell me. Eight."

"Exactly."

Had Zoe already told her? Or was he going to get flattened by disgust when Pasha realized that this boy had already been conceived during the month Oliver had been a fixture at their little rental in Chicago, dating Zoe?

"I knew it," Pasha said, staring and then surprising them by sliding her legs around to get out of the Jeep. "Going into third grade?"

He lifted a shoulder. "The dean wants me to skip third, but I'm not really sure if I should do that."

"He's advanced," Oliver explained, putting a proud hand on his son's shoulder. "We're trying to decide if moving him ahead a year is the right thing to do socially."

"He looks fine socially," Pasha announced, climbing down with no assistance whatsoever, still focused on Evan. "Give me your hand, little one."

Evan frowned for a moment, then reached out to shake Pasha's hand. "It's nice to meet you."

She flipped his hand, palm up. "Of course it is," she said. "Now let me see what you've got here."

Zoe came around the front of the Jeep, smiling at the exchange and then at Oliver, like they had shared a secret victory. She wore an ankle-length sunshine-yellow strapless dress as bright and sexy as her tanned face and summer-blonde curls.

Evan tugged his hand away. "What are you doing?"

"Pasha only offers to read your palm if she likes you,

Evan," Zoe assured him, with a gentle hand on his shoulder. "No need to worry."

Oliver took in the scene for a moment: Zoe so sweetly protective of his son, and the old woman doing her palmreading game, sun pouring over all of them with warmth and light.

And there went all those *stupid* things again. Braindead, gutsqueezed, hearthurt. Symptoms of something he really shouldn't be thinking about with Zoe.

She'd looked at him like he had three heads when he even suggested something more serious than pool sex. She'd never change. She'd never fit. She'd never *stay*. Why would he even ask?

"Oh, look at that," Pasha said, easing the boy closer.

"What?" Evan asked, unsure. "Is it bad?"

"No, it's all good," Pasha promised him, running her hand over his palm but mostly looking at his face with a little bit of wonder and a lot of joy. That's what it was; she'd absolutely brightened since she'd seen Evan. "What I see is someone whose fate line joins his life line at a critical juncture. That means he's a big thinker who knows exactly what he wants to be."

"A meteorologist," Evan and Zoe said at exactly the same time.

He did? How was it that Oliver didn't know that? And Zoe did? A little guilt smashed with envy in his chest as Pasha continued.

"Oh, my!" Pasha said with an exaggerated gasp.

"What?" Evan looked concerned. "Am I going to die?"

"Heavens no. Your life line is endless, and goes right past the edge of your palm, which means once you know someone, you'll give them your whole heart."

That must be hereditary, Oliver thought with another glance at sunny Zoe.

"Someone…like a dog?" Evan asked, getting a laugh from all of them.

Pasha laughed the hardest, and it caught in her throat, making her cough so hard it turned hoarse and gruff.

"Are you okay?" Zoe asked, instantly transferring her touch from Evan to Pasha, shooting a quick look at Oliver, making sure he'd heard.

He had, and that cough didn't sound good at all.

"Fine," she rasped, but it was a good fifteen seconds until the spell subsided.

"Why don't we get you inside?" Oliver suggested, half expecting her to freeze and return to the Jeep.

But Pasha smiled and kept holding Evan's hand. "Of course," she said. "I want to finish this reading because I do see something very interesting."

They walked toward the door, Evan leading the older woman in, his eyes wide with fascination. "What is it?"

"The center X."

"What's that mean?"

"You're very good at games."

"I'm a chess master."

"Oh, I was thinking about something a little less taxing for my old brain…"

They disappeared inside and Oliver stayed back next to Zoe.

"Well, that worked like magic," she said, watching them disappear into the house. "He's like the Pied Piper of little old ladies."

"She likes him, that's for sure," Oliver agreed, unable to keep himself from putting a hand on her bare shoulder. Her skin was so warm and smooth he had to fight the urge to bend over and put his lips right there and taste the sun on her.

"I really thought she was going to refuse to come in," she said.

"She was, but I guess she likes kids."

Zoe shook her head. "News to me. And, believe me, it wasn't easy getting her here. She thinks we're stopping for two minutes on our way somewhere else."

He nodded. "I can see she's very sick."

"Oh, is it that obvious?"

"I'm afraid so, but that doesn't mean she has cancer." Although he'd put his money on it.

"You have to work fast, then, Oliver." She looked up at him, squinting in the sunshine, her eyes moist. "She wants to die."

"What?"

"She thinks I'd be better off without her. I could have a...life." Zoe shrugged. "I think it's her solution to your more legalistic approach."

"Did you tell her you're going to talk to a lawyer?"

She shook her head. "It's not happening. She went batshit crazy. I can't do that to her. My God, Oliver, she's practically hoping the cancer will take her."

"Talk about batshit crazy."

"I'm serious. If she knows I'm considering that, I'm afraid she'll take her own life thinking it's best for me."

For a second he stared at her, an old but sickeningly familiar sensation washing over him. Numbness. Pain. Disbelief. Anger.

So much anger.

The feelings erased any of the much nicer emotions he'd

been nursing all morning. "We can't let that happen," he said simply, leading her inside. "We can't let that happen," he repeated, getting a strange look from Zoe. Of course she didn't know. In their brief month together, he'd held back a few things about his past, too.

"What can you do, Oliver?" she asked, obviously sensing he'd changed his tune a bit.

At the doorway, he hesitated. "I haven't told you much about my approach, Zoe. You have to understand something now. Our treatments are not typical, they're not proven, and they're not blessed by the FDA. Like I said, my clinic specializes in experimental treatment. And that has risks."

She looked dubious. "Is it legal?"

"Absolutely. We work with the National Institutes of Health, researchers, and some of the top cancer institutions in the country. Like I said, we're the last stop for the hopeless."

"And what kind of results do these hopeless patients get?"

He smiled a little, unable to hide his pride. "We have some miraculous stories, and I have the living, breathing, golf-swinging patients to prove it."

Hope brightened her eyes. "Would you take a living, breathing, palm-reading patient?" She put her hand on his arm. "Even if I don't talk to a lawyer?"

He nodded slowly. "Let me talk to her, and get her comfortable, then we'll see what's next. I'll want to consult with my partner."

She wrapped her arms around him, pulling her body right into his. "Thank you."

"Don't thank me yet. Let's take step one." With his

arm around her, they walked inside. The living room was empty, but the sound of Evan's laughter came from the patio. The two of them were already outside, at a table, with Pasha shuffling a deck of cards.

"Zoe, she's going to teach me the Egyptian game!"

Zoe put her hand to her heart, feigning pain. "Ugh, I've been replaced."

"No!" Evan almost jumped out of his chair. "You can play, too."

"It's more fun with two people," Zoe said. "But we'll watch. Your dad knows how to play." She shot him a playful look, memories of cards and tequila and disappearing clothes arcing between them like a thousand-volt defibrillator to his chest.

"*Dad plays cards?*" Evan almost choked with disbelief.

"I'm actually really good at that game."

He could feel Zoe's look.

"Sometimes," he added, nudging her playfully.

"You better pay attention," Pasha said, snapping the deck in front of Evan's face. "You need brainpower and speed to play this."

"I have a hundred-and-sixty-two IQ."

Oliver cringed. "You're not supposed to tell people that, Ev."

Pasha flipped the cards. "I don't care if you have a four-hundred-and-sixty-two IQ, this game takes skills."

"Nobody has an IQ that high," he said, ever the literal little guy.

"And nobody has ever beat me at this game on the first try."

"Oh yeah?" He shimmied closer to the table, and they were off. Oliver watched her teach him, a little in awe at how quickly his son learned, but also taking in as much as he could of the older woman.

Not a medical examination, by any stretch, but her cough was not in the lungs. And she unconsciously touched her throat more than her chest. With a gun to his head he'd say esophageal. But he had to talk to Raj before they did anything else. And so did Zoe.

He took her into the kitchen to talk privately. "I want us to meet with my partner. Today. He's at our clinic and you can talk to him about Pasha."

"Shouldn't we bring her?"

"I need you to know exactly how we work and what IDEA is."

She frowned at the acronym.

"Integrated Diagnostics through Experimental Analysis," he said. "Like I said, we have a team of top-notch medical researchers working tirelessly on advanced, untested treatments. But it's not unusual for our patients to be the guinea pigs of cancer treatments, even to be the case histories for the government organizations to study when they approve a new treatment. It's cutting-edge stuff."

"You know you're singing my song, doc." She glanced out to the patio. "But I don't want to leave them here alone. Let me call Lacey's daughter, Ashley, for some backup and we can go."

"I'll go tell them we're off to run some errands." He returned to the patio in time to see Evan snatching a card back with lightning-quick hands.

"Ha ha!" He pointed at Pasha. "Got it!"

She beamed back. "You are absolutely the...the... sweetest little boy I've seen in years."

Oliver interrupted the game long enough to tell them the plans.

"Just bring lunch when you get back," Pasha replied. "We're going to work up an appetite, right, Ma..." She hesitated as if she couldn't remember his name, then grabbed it. "Evan?"

"Right!"

She gave him a grin that put her whole heart on the line. Certainly not like a woman who was contemplating the unthinkable act of suicide. But then, she wouldn't be the first sweet lady to fool a little guy like that, would she?

Chapter Nine

You're great with Evan," Oliver said as they climbed into the Jeep. He adjusted the seat to his six-foot-one frame, sunglasses hiding his eyes but making him look cool. And hot.

"Not as good as Pasha. Good heavens, I've never seen her make such fast friends with anyone." Truth was, she made friends with so few people. "But he's a great kid, Oliver, as I'm sure you know."

"I know he's great. He's also tough."

She glanced at him as she pulled on her seat belt, not quite sure what he meant. "He seems pretty easy to me."

"That's what I mean. You make it look so easy."

"Maybe Evan and I are on the same maturity level," she teased. "Which is not meant to be self-deprecating. That kid is smart."

"Maybe too smart for his own good." As they drove off the property and into town, Zoe could tell he wanted to talk more about Evan, but she was itching to know about his clinic and the possibilities.

"I think you're trying too hard," she suggested. "You know, with the divorce and all, and him being in your care all summer. Relax and have fun with him."

He threw her a smile. "Fun is your specialty."

"You just need to be yourself with him." She put a hand on his leg, loving the muscle that tensed under her touch. "You don't need pointers, Oliver, honestly."

"I'll try." He turned the Jeep onto the causeway to the mainland, nodding like he was mentally filing the advice away.

"Tell me about your clinic and your partner."

"Sure. I met Raj Mahesh at that oncology conference at the Ritz a few years ago. When I saw you in the lobby."

"And in the parking lot."

He frowned. "I don't remember that."

She blew out a breath, embarrassed but not willing to lie. She'd freaked that day, seeing him and his wife, and had dived to the floor of a Rubicon very much like this one, the kind she rented every time she came to Mimosa Key and wanted a muscular convertible for the beach. "I was with Jocelyn and Tessa having lunch there, and you and your wife got out of a car at the valet parking."

He sort of shook his head, the moment probably not as crystal clear in his memory as it was in hers. "I remember meeting Mike Genovese, one of our investors, but I can't believe I wouldn't recall seeing you."

"You didn't exactly see me," she admitted. "I hid on the floor of the car."

"What? Why?"

"Why do you think?" She let out a dry choke. "I didn't want to see you or explain you or…" She waved her hand. "You were with your wife."

"What do you mean, 'explain' me?"

"To my friends."

"They don't know you have ex-boyfriends?"

"Of course they do, and they would want to know why we broke up and why I was…" *A basket case for the next two hours.* "So how exactly did you get involved with this clinic?"

She saw him react to the change of subject, but he let it go. "Well, Raj is pretty persuasive, as you will no doubt see," he said with a laugh. "And he happens to be one of the smartest physicians I ever met. He started IDEA himself because he was so sick of the bureaucracy of hospitals and administration and all the red tape and medical crap that gets in the way of saving lives."

His voice was deep with emotion as he shifted into another gear.

"So you left Mount Mercy to work with him."

"I couldn't resist. I'd been drawn to everything the clinic was doing and knew if I didn't move when I had the opportunity, it might never come along again. Gene therapy is so exciting, Zoe. It's a complete game changer in cancer research."

"What exactly is it?"

"It's the injection of vectors full of viruses into cancer cells to fire up immune systems and angiogenesis that can…" He slid her a look. "I'm losing you, huh?"

"Not at all."

"You're staring at me."

How could she not? Impassioned Doctor Oliver was even sexier than regular hot-as-sin Oliver. "No, I'm just impressed and happy for you. Everyone should find what turns them on so much."

He gave her a grateful smile. "But not everyone in my life was thrilled with the decision," he said. "Starting with my ex-wife, continuing to her father, and ending with my son. I gave up a lot for my passion, but it was worth it."

She considered that, looking out the window at the deep-blue water of the Intracoastal and curling her fingers around his hand to feel his strength.

His father-in-law was the CEO of Mount Mercy Hospital and, although Zoe didn't know it for a fact, she'd bet her last dollar he had been in line for that job. "So the decision to take this new position broke up your marriage?"

"Not exactly. It was the proverbial straw that whacked an already crippled camel." He let go of her hand to downshift and instantly scooped it up again, as if he couldn't stand a second without touching her. Zoe tried really hard not to let that little gesture worm its way into her heart. Tried, and failed.

"To be honest, nothing happened overnight," he continued. "I pushed at the hospital for change and a budget for advanced research, trying to use my position in administration but hitting the brick wall that happened to be Adele's father. All the while, she and I grew farther apart."

She swallowed, hating that she had to ask the next question. But she had to. "Were you ever…close?" *In other words, did you love the woman you married five weeks after I left you?*

The question hung in the wind, getting heavier as each second he didn't answer ticked by. "We tried," he finally admitted. "We got married because it seemed like the right thing to do and I was…"

On the rebound? She didn't have the nerve or heart to ask.

"Anyway, I tried. She tried. It didn't ever…" He puffed out a breath. "I never got over you."

"Oh." It was all she could manage under the suffocating weight of that confession.

"She knew it. She knew I was seeing you when she told me she was pregnant, and she thought that I gave you up to marry her."

But he hadn't. Zoe had taken off before they had any chance. "You didn't tell her I left town and we…lost touch?" Speaking of bad euphemisms.

"No, I didn't tell her that," he said. "I didn't want her to have horrible doubts about me. It was bad enough we *had* to get married. I didn't want her to be completely miserable." He pulled into a small parking lot behind a glass-and-metal three-story building, sliding the gear into Park but making no effort to get out.

She mulled the confession over. He hadn't been totally honest with his wife, but that reminded her that under all that authority and confidence and sex appeal was a guy who deeply cared about people.

"If she thought I married her because I couldn't find you, then I knew that she'd never believe in our marriage." The statement made sense, and a surprising wave of sympathy for Adele Townshend rolled over Zoe. No woman should have to marry a man who was in love with someone else, no matter how rich and bitchy she was.

"But we didn't really have a chance," he continued. "I never really loved her, I mean, not the way I…"

Loved you.

She swallowed and nodded, understanding why he couldn't even say it.

"Anyway, we faked a life for the sake of Evan," he said,

the words so softly she barely heard them over the hum of the engine he had yet to turn off. "At least we did until neither one of us could fake it anymore. And at the same time, I was so far removed from the reason I got into medicine in general and oncology in particular. This opportunity came up"—he gestured toward the building and the small sign that said IDEA near the door—"and I grabbed it. A chance to start over in a new city, a chance to do hands-on medicine again, a chance to break ground. And, of course, a chance to save lives."

"And she wouldn't relocate?"

He shrugged. "We were pretty far gone by then. Separate bedrooms, separate lives. Evan was the only thing even remotely keeping us together, so we worked out a custody arrangement when I left about eight months ago. Christmas, spring break, two weeks in the summer."

"Ugh. That's not enough time. So much for a chance to relax and have fun."

He gave her a tight smile and quick nod. "Don't I know it. But she surprised me with a trip to Europe this summer, and so I have this chance to be with him." His smile relaxed into a genuine grin. "And learn from the Mistress of Fun."

She winked. "I've been called worse, big guy."

He switched off the ignition and, as he unlatched his seat belt, she reached over to touch his hand, the words bubbling up. She owed him an apology. Not just for leaving without an explanation, but for longer-lasting effects.

"I'm sorry if I wrecked your marriage."

He smiled, but his eyes were dark and sad. "You didn't, Zoe. But you broke my fucking heart."

* * *

After a tour of the facility—which was surprisingly large, with multiple labs, in-house patient-care suites, a twenty-four-hour nursing staff, and a state-of-the-art surgery center—Oliver took Zoe into a conference room to meet with his partner.

Wiry, energized, and one of those keenly intelligent people who instantly make you feel at ease and yet in awe, Raj Mahesh was the perfect complement to Oliver's rationale approach to everything. Raj was the dreamer; Oliver made things happen.

And they were both very good doctors.

As Oliver brought his partner up to speed on the case, the other man's interest ratcheted from mild to wild. His clipped British-and-Indian accent couldn't hide the fact that the case electrified him and was exactly the opportunity they'd been looking for.

In a way that revealed none of the complex history of Pasha's life, Oliver let Raj know this was a patient who'd received absolutely no treatment by choice, leaving her free and clear of all other medical input.

"I'm deeply sorry for your aunt," Raj said to Zoe. "Please forgive me if I sound enthusiastic, because, of course, this is painful for you."'

Zoe nodded, seeing the honesty in his jet-black eyes. "I'm willing to do anything to help her."

"Gene therapy isn't anything," Raj said. "It's everything."

"How many times have you done the kind you're proposing for my aunt?"

"We're not proposing it yet," Oliver replied quickly. "Just thinking that she might be an excellent candidate. She doesn't strike me as a patient who could handle the standard treatments."

Zoe closed her eyes, a mix of relief and terror. "That's exactly what I think."

"And the other options are a ridiculously expensive trip to Switzerland for basically the same treatment, or peptide receptor radionuclide therapy," Raj said.

Zoe gave him a blank look, and he waved away the obvious question of what that was. "It wouldn't be right for someone her age. But to answer your question, I've done the procedure in Europe, but not here. However, we've done so much preliminary work for this, growing the vectors and planning for the possibility of finding the right candidate for the treatment."

He looked at Oliver, and Zoe easily interpreted the silent communication. Pasha could very well be that patient. A *test* patient.

"What exactly will you do?" she asked.

Raj answered. "We'd essentially be taking a disabled form of a very nasty virus, probably HIV, and using it to carry cancer-fighting genes to Pasha's T-cells. We'd be trying to train her own immune system to kill the cancer."

She glanced at Oliver. "I want to protect her," she said softly. "If this works, she can't be the poster child for new treatment or forced to meet with FDA representatives."

"Everything is private here, Zoe," Oliver assured her. "As far as the government, the identities of our patients are kept confidential. They, too, are only interested in results, not the personal lives of the patients."

And that was the perfect, ideal solution to Pasha's situation. Hope curled through her. "I'll try anything," she said. "Assuming it isn't going to kill her."

Oliver looked at her, silent.

"Shit," she murmured.

He leaned closer. "Obviously, without the standard tests, I don't know how sick she is right now, but I think she's in very bad shape. And we will send all of her initial tests to independent oncologists for a second and third opinion, I assure you."

Dropping her chin into her palms, she sighed. "Tell me the risks."

Oliver took over, referring to some rudimentary sketches he'd done when they'd first started talking. "The biggest risk is that these engineered T-cells could somehow attack healthy tissue," he said.

"But the odds are low," Raj insisted. "Not zero, but low. We'll know that within hours of the procedure, if she runs a fever or experiences swelling or low blood pressure."

She looked at Oliver. "Is this the only thing you'd recommend?"

"For a cure? Yes. To buy time? Of course there's chemo, radiation, surgery, and a standard sequence of treatments that can take months."

"And how much time do the standard treatments buy?" How could Zoe even think about life without her? She couldn't.

"Predicting time is impossible to say without measuring the tumor and getting a sense of how sick she is," Oliver said. "But certain treatments can buy you months, maybe more."

Months? Oh, Lord. Pasha could be gone in months? If she survived the treatment.

She leaned back, letting that sink in. But it barely did. "This isn't some nameless patient. This is…my only…" She closed her eyes and whispered, "Family."

"I know, Zoe." Oliver put his hand over hers, giving it a squeeze.

"What would you do if it were your aunt?" she asked both men. "What would you do?"

"There's not even a debate for me," Raj said. "Chemo and radiation can prolong her life. This could save it."

Oliver nodded. "That is the benefit that could outweigh the risk. Plus, if she fights the cancer and goes completely into remission, this treatment will be one step closer to approval for use in the United States, saving many, many lives."

Would Pasha be thrilled to have that role, or terrified of any sort of notoriety? It was hard to say. How much did she want to live?

That morning, very little.

"I'll be right back," Raj said, pushing out his chair. "I'm going to get some results from the international patients that I'm certain will erase any lingering doubts."

When Raj left the room, Oliver and Zoe sat in silence for a moment. She reached for one of the charts, the statistics and symbols meaningless without Oliver's simplified explanations. But she understood enough. This could save Pasha's life, but there were risks. Or they could go traditional, which probably wouldn't save her life and might even wreck any quality she had left.

Wordlessly, Oliver covered her hand with his, and Zoe's gaze shifted to his long, strong, capable fingers. A healer's hands. A lover's hands. Very slowly, she lifted her gaze to meet his.

"You really think I should do this, don't you?"

"After seeing her today, and this conversation, I'm inclined to say yes. There are some tests to run and we can start them tomorrow, but once she passes those, I think this is not only your best option, it's a brilliant one."

She smiled. "So humble."

"Trust me, I'm only the lead oncologist. You'll have a team of some of the finest, most talented professionals in the world."

The words settled over her like a cooling salve on an open wound. This was the best imaginable solution, better than anything she could have dreamed of. Except...

"What about your stipulations?"

He frowned and shook his head. "Did I have any?"

"About insisting I see a lawyer."

"That is entirely separate from this. I said I'll fix her medically and help you fix her legally. That wasn't a condition of anything, Zoe."

It wasn't? "But you made it sound like if I didn't—"

"If you don't, then we may end up with a healthy woman who's still running. That doesn't help her, and that doesn't help...us." He added a little pressure on her hand, kicking up her pulse. "Did you think about what I asked you yesterday?"

I'd like a shot at something real.

She shrugged. "I have a lot on my mind."

He gave her a half smile. "Then let's get it off your mind. The first thing you need to do is trust me."

"I trust you," she said. "It's me who usually lets me down."

He lifted her hand and brought it to his lips for a kiss so soft it was nothing but air and promise. "One more thing I'd like to fix."

"You can't fix everything, Oliver."

He grinned and kissed her knuckle again. "I can sure as hell try."

Chapter Ten

⌒

Pasha had gotten sleepy shortly after Ashley arrived, worn out by the game and sun and the little boy who had unknowingly dragged her down memory lane. She settled on a lounge chair in the shade, closing her eyes to listen to his childish voice, letting forty-seven years disappear. Time evaporated, along with the pain and heartache of running and hiding. And, of course, all the fear.

If Zoe ever found out...if Zoe ever knew what they were really running from. She blew out a sad, slow breath, and that forced her to press a hand on the pain in her chest.

That was the real reason for this tumor to take her, and fast. Although those dark thoughts of death had certainly lightened in the face of a little boy who reminded her of her own. A little boy who suggested by his smile and wit that maybe, just maybe, life was worth living a little longer, despite the risks.

That was probably because during those lovely mo-

ments of card playing and joke sharing, the little boy at
the table became Matthew Hobarth, seven-and-a-half years
old, a dark-haired dreamer who saw animals in the clouds
and had given his one and only four-leaf clover to Pasha
for her birthday.

This means good luck, Mama.

How do you know, little one?

*Because there are messages in the grass and promises
in the air. All you have to do is find them and figure out
what they are.*

"Dude, I'm so sorry I brought this puzzle. I thought you
were eight." Ashley's teenage voice pulled Pasha from her
reverie, making her startle.

"I am eight."

"A normal eight."

"He *is* normal," Pasha said. "Just very bright and excep-
tional." She grinned at him. How could she not? He was
the same size, about the same age, and had the same sweet
voice that hadn't yet developed a baritone—and he looked
so much like Matthew. The same inquisitive brown eyes,
the same upturned and freckled nose. Even his mop of hair
was the same shade of dark chocolate with hints of auburn
in the tips.

"Oh, Aunt Pasha, I'm sorry," Ashley said. "I didn't
mean to wake you."

"I wasn't sleeping," she assured them both. "I was day-
dreaming. Don't you ever do that?"

Evan shook his head. "I read or go on the computer. I
live on my computer."

Ashley smiled as if that amused her, but Pasha studied
his earnest expression.

Well, that wasn't the same as Matthew. There were no

computers in 1966, and her little boy was smart, but not quite this serious.

"You obviously do a lot of puzzles, too," Ashley said, selecting another piece. "I know this is My Little Pony, which probably isn't your favorite, but it is for seven-to-nine-year-olds and you're finishing it like a beast."

"I'm good at puzzles," he said, snapping a piece in place. "I do five hundred pieces in a day."

"Wow!" Ashley's eyes popped as she looked at Pasha. "Can you believe that?"

"I'm not lying," Evan said, his tone rising in self-defense.

"I know you're not," Ashley said. "I'm so amazed at that. I don't think I even owned a five-hundred-piece puzzle when I was your age, or even older. I might have, but if I did, it's somewhere in Barefoot Bay now."

Evan easily fit the new piece in place and looked up. "You threw it in the ocean? I mean, the Gulf. It's not the ocean, I know."

Pasha noticed very quickly that this boy couldn't stand to have his facts wrong. One more trait that didn't remind her of Matthew, but it didn't matter. She was already smitten.

"I lost everything I owned in a hurricane almost two years ago," Ashley told him.

"Oh, that was you! Zoe told me. I thought she said it was her friend."

"She meant my mom. I was fourteen and we lived about half a mile from here, down where the main building of the resort is now. During the storm, my mom and I spent the night in a bathtub with a mattress over our heads."

Evan looked suitably impressed. "That is so cool."

"No," Ashley said with a sarcastic roll of her eyes. "It was totally *not* cool. We lost everything, which is why the only puzzle I have left from when I was a little kid is this one. It was at my grandma's house."

Evan sat up, tucking his feet under his little body. "Was it a real hurricane, like a category five?"

"Four and, yes, trust me, it was so real."

"Was it loud? What did it feel like? Did you get hurt? Was there lightning? Were there tornadoes? Did you see them with your own eyes?"

Ashley laughed, and Pasha did, too. "Um, yes, it was as loud as a train. I don't remember any lightning or the tornadoes and, as a matter of fact, I was certain we were going to die. Why are you so obsessed with this?"

"Because I love weather," Evan said, shifting his attention back to the puzzle.

"He's going to be a meteorologist," Pasha told Ashley, getting rewarded with a gorgeous smile from the young boy. "What is it you like about weather so much, little one?" she asked.

"Everything, but I'm not that little."

"Of course not. Force of habit." She rose from the chaise and ambled over to the glass-topped patio table, taking a seat and resting her chin on her hands to watch him and *remember*.

She and Matthew used to do puzzles and play games like Hi Ho Cherry-O and Barrel of Monkeys. They'd play cards and take long walks to the lake for picnics. And, of course, they'd read the messages from Mother Nature, making up all kinds of funny things together. Every time she made a "prediction" now, it was really a secret whisper to heaven.

Could Matthew hear her—forty-seven years after that horrible night?

"The thing about weather," Evan said. "It always changes."

"It does indeed," Pasha agreed.

"And there's a reason why I like it." Evan hesitated with a puzzle piece, but not because he didn't know where to place it. There were only about six pieces left, and she had no doubt he knew where every one of them fit.

"Weather is the neatest thing in the world." He looked up, his eyes very much like his father's, keen and earnest, fringed with black lashes and bright with the emotion of talking about something he loved.

"It's certainly one of the most powerful," she agreed.

"Right!" He dropped the piece of the puzzle on the table. "Like nobody in the whole world can do anything about it," he said. "Weather just does what weather wants to do. And it does some really neat things. Did you know that if a butterfly flaps its wings in Hong Kong, it can change the weather in California?"

"That's not true!" Ashley said, earning a dire look from him.

"Oh, yes it is. You can look it up on weather.com or any of the really good weather Web sites."

Ashley gave another eye roll. "Like that's my idea of a fun time."

"Well, it's obviously his," Pasha said gently. "So you should respect that, Ashley. And, Evan, that might be the most interesting thing I ever heard."

"Oh, I know all kinds of things like that," he told her. "Like, do you know that if you weighed all the rain that falls on the earth in one year, it's like five thousand million million tons? That's *two* millions."

"That's a lot of rain," Pasha said.

They'd lost Ashley, who started putting in the last pieces of the puzzle, but Evan was on fire with excitement. "And you know what else?" he asked.

"Tell me," Pasha said, fighting the urge to reach out for his little cheeks and squeeze them. "What else?"

"Did you know the temperature of a lightning bolt is hotter than the surface of the sun?" He pushed himself up so he was practically kneeling.

"I did not know that," Pasha said. "Did you know that, Ashley?"

"That's super hot," she said, utterly bored. "You want to do the last piece, Evan?"

"No." He was locked on Pasha now, the two of them connected. "Did you know there's such a thing as a moonbow?"

Every cell in her body—the sick ones, the healthy ones, the old ones, the near-dead ones—froze for a moment.

"A *moonbow*?" Her voice shuddered a little.

"It's like a rainbow, but at night from the moon. Isn't that cool?"

She tried to swallow, but her damn wretched throat made it impossible.

"As a matter of fact…" Heavens above, maybe Mother Nature really did talk to her! "I saw a moonbow once." The announcement came out hoarse, and she had to work not to go into a coughing fit. She didn't want to ruin this blissful moment.

"Really?"

"Do you know what a moonbow means?" she asked.

"It means it rained and the moon's light is reflected through the water, creating a prism."

She shook her head, smiling. "It means that your one true love will return."

He squished up his face. "Ewww."

Ashley giggled. "You don't have a true love back at school in Chicago? A little third-grader you have your eye on?"

He curled his lip. "Hell no."

Ashley gasped. "Watch your mouth."

He ignored the warning and turned to Pasha. "That's not what a moonbow means."

"Yes it is."

"Aunt Pasha knows," Ashley said. "She can predict the future by looking at the clouds or dirt or even the foam at the beach."

Evan looked from one to the other, clearly not buying it. "I don't know anything about that. I only know what's real and scientific, not that kind of woo-woo stuff."

"Finally, something you don't know," Ashley said, pulling out her phone to tap on the screen. "Oh, Aunt Zoe texted. They'll be here in ten minutes."

"Good, 'cause I want to go on my computer and look up moonbows."

"You won't find what I told you on the Internet," Pasha told him.

"Then it's not true," he shot back. "'Cause everything in the world that's true is on the Internet."

Ashley snorted. "Not hardly."

"It's true," Pasha assured him. "I know things like that."

He looked uncertain, but then he smiled, revealing his too-large teeth and a gleam in his eyes. "'Kay," he conceded. "I like to learn things."

"Then we'll be a great team."

His smile was so real, so heartfelt, and so much like Matthew that for the first time in months and months,

Pasha almost wanted that black pressure in her chest to go away. She almost wanted to live.

"Hello, we're home!" Zoe came breezing onto the patio, her green eyes sparking like she had a secret, her hair wild from the wind.

Home? She thought of this as home already? Of course, with Zoe's life, she could think of a motel room on a rural highway as home. That was the sad, sad legacy that Pasha had given her.

Zoe came to the table, leaning over to give Pasha a kiss, her cheek warm from the summer air. Or was it that Oliver Bradbury gave her a flush of love?

The moonbow promised the return of true love. But whose love? A little boy like the one Pasha had lost, or a man like the one Zoe had lost?

The one Zoe had lost *because of Pasha.* "How was your ride, honey?" she asked Zoe.

"Amazing."

Pasha couldn't help but grin. "I like the sound of that."

Zoe slipped into one of the empty chairs, and Pasha got a good look at her face. Her sweet cheeks high with color, her ever-present smile as wide as ever. "I have so much to tell you."

"Is my dad here?" Evan asked.

"He's bringing some things out of the car," she said. "We stopped by his storage unit and picked up stuff for this house."

Evan's eyes grew wide. "I hope he remembered my Xbox. I had to use the system in the Shitz-Carl—" He gave Pasha a guilty look. "I mean the Ritz-Carlton. Be right back."

Pasha watched him tear back into the house and Ashley got up to follow. "I better keep an eye on that kid," Ashley said. "He's a cussing computer trapped in the body of an eight-year-old boy."

Zoe laughed, but Pasha sighed with contentment.

"He's wonderful," she said.

"You really like him, don't you?" Zoe asked, absently turning the puzzle spread out over the table.

"I do. He reminds me…" Oh, dear. *Careful, Pasha.* "He's a very endearing and intelligent young man."

"So's his dad," Zoe whispered, leaning close.

"Ahh, I thought you looked like a woman all smitten."

"Pasha, I've been to his clinic."

And that was what had her glowing? "Why did you go there?"

"Why do you think? Oh my God, I'm so excited. They can cure you."

"Zoe, I doubt—"

"Don't doubt!" Zoe squeezed Pasha's hand. "Do you want to talk to Oliver about it now? We've been with his partner, another doctor, and they can do gene therapy, Pasha. They can do amazing things that no regular hospital can do. It's this new—"

"No, no." Blood rushed in Pasha's head, thrumming and pounding.

"I know what you're worried about, Pasha," Zoe rushed on, undaunted by Pasha's protests. "This will be completely confidential and no one will have to know anything, not your name or identification. It's perfect!"

No, it wasn't perfect. "I'm sure it's dangerous and risky, though."

"Not as risky as dying!"

Pasha inched back at the outburst. "I don't think you should fight nature, dear."

Emerald eyes popped wide in response. "What are you saying? You won't treat this illness, even if it doesn't mean…exposure?"

Pasha turned toward the pool. The day had been nice. Warm sunshine and memories. But she'd made up her mind, and as long as she was alive and the threat existed, she was blocking Zoe from happiness.

"I'm tired and I want to go home." She put her hand on Zoe's arm. "Real home."

"Back to Arizona?"

"No, no, to the bungalow. Our temporary home."

Zoe's shoulders slumped. "They're all temporary, Pasha."

"Precisely." But if she were gone, Zoe could find permanence. "Please take me back so I can rest."

"He only wants to ask you some questions." She leaned closer. "Pasha, he's not a typical oncologist. I know what you're worried about, but there's no chemo, no radiation. He's working with this brilliant doctor and this really extraordinary research facility and they're doing all these exciting things like, oh, God, I can't even pronounce the words but it's a whole experimental way to treat canc—"

Pasha slammed her hand on Zoe's mouth. "Don't."

Zoe jerked away, the fire blazing in her eyes for a whole different reason now. "What is wrong with you?" she demanded. "I've found a solution!"

But Pasha had a better one.

She shook her head and conjured up some fake gypsy tears. "Please take me home, little one. I promise I'll come back tomorrow. Oh, no, tomorrow's Sunday. So maybe Monday, then. One day won't make a difference. And I will come back, Zoe. I enjoy that little boy very much."

Zoe dropped back into her chair with a sigh, shaking her head. "You can't outrun cancer, Pasha."

Pasha swallowed—mercy, that hurt—and cast her gaze over Zoe's shoulder.

"Hey." Zoe took Pasha's chin and angled her face so they had to look at each other. "We're a team, remember. I'll be with you every step of the way on this."

But the fact was, she wouldn't be. Not every step. Not this time. "'Kay." She gave a quick smile and prayed that Zoe couldn't tell she was lying.

Pasha was sound asleep by ten, leaving Zoe restless and bored and on the hunt for company. After a quick check on her aunt, Zoe slipped out into the moonlight, grateful to see a light on in the bungalow next door. But Tessa didn't answer Zoe's soft tap at the front door. She must have fallen asleep, and Zoe didn't have the heart to wake her so she headed back, considering a walk to Lacey's house. Surely *she* was up, with a newborn.

As she crossed the grassy area that separated each cottage, a soft sound from the gardens rustled through the air.

An animal? They were out here. Opossum, giant crane birds, and don't try to tell her a gator couldn't come from the canals on the east side of the island looking for a midnight snack.

With a quick shiver Zoe took a few quick steps, abandoning the idea of a walk through the gardens, however tempting a late-night girl talk might be. She took a few more steps, then heard the sound again.

That wasn't an animal. It was a person. A person...
sniffing.

Zoe headed into the shadows of the garden, her gut telling her exactly who was out here.

She found Tessa in between two rows of leafy greens, her arms wrapped around her legs, her face buried in her knees, her shoulders heaving with silent sobs.

"Hey," Zoe said softly, not so loud that it scared the crap out of Tessa, but loud enough to beat out the sobs. "And here I thought *I* needed a little girl talk."

Tessa lifted her head, the moon bright enough to reveal her red-rimmed eyes. "I don't want to talk," she said, the lie so pathetic Zoe almost laughed.

"Oh, I see you're out here weeding." She dropped into the soft dirt, praying that no nocturnal critters were out and about.

Tessa sniffed and wiped her eyes. "I said I don't need to talk."

"You said you don't want to talk. Needing and wanting are two different things." She lifted a leaf and examined the exposed vegetable. "Surely I'm better company than the..." She knew this; Tessa had told her. "Flying Chinese peas."

That got a smile. "Asian winged beans."

"Close enough. They look like caterpillars run over by a steamroller." She dropped the plant and eyed her friend. "Looks like something flattened you, too."

"Billy," she said softly. "That's the steamroller who flattened me."

"Oh, the fuckwad ex-husband. Don't tell me, baby number two was born and Billy the Bonehead just had to text you from the delivery room."

"How did you know?" Tessa croaked in disbelief.

"Oh, Tess. Really? Why would he do that?"

She nodded and swiped her nose. "The baby was five weeks early, and in his defense—not that there is one—he knows how I feel about everything not being out in the open. So he thought I should know right away and not hear it from one of our mutual friends."

"He's too thoughtful," Zoe said wryly. "I hate him."

"Zoe, you said you loved Billy when I married him."

"*Hello?* Wedding champagne. Anyway, have we not established that my taste in men is not the most reliable yardstick, hon?"

"Oliver's nice," Tessa said.

"Let's not talk about Oliver. I'd rather crucify Billy for a while. Did he marry that baby machine yet?"

"No, they're living together still, up to the eyeballs in diapers."

"Which means they're up to their eyeballs in diapers full of…oh my God that green stuff that Elijah makes. Have you *seen* that goop?"

Tessa sighed. "I wouldn't mind."

"Of course not. It looks like organic creamed spinach to you." But Tessa didn't laugh, so Zoe leaned closer. "Why don't you adopt?"

Tessa leaned back on a sigh. "We looked into adoption years ago and it's not as easy as you'd think unless you have a super-stable life. I'm a single woman who spent most of the last ten years moving from country to country, farming. By the time I got through the legal wrangling and qualified, I could be forty."

"So?"

"I want a baby now, that's all." She plucked a leaf. "There are other options for me to be a real mother."

"A *real* mother?" Zoe couldn't keep the disgust out of

her voice. "What the hell does that mean, anyway? You think Pasha wasn't a real mother to me?"

"No, Zoe, that's not what I'm saying at all, and I'm sorry, that was a poor choice of words. But she's your great-aunt, so there's blood there."

Zoe didn't answer, as a swell of guilt and discomfort rolled over her.

He knows how I feel about everything not being out in the open.

Lord, even Tessa's horrible ex was more forthcoming, out of respect for what was important to Tessa. Quiet, Zoe stuck her fingers in the soft soil and sifted it. She really should tell her best friends, but now she'd lied to them for so long she wouldn't know where to start.

"Do you even remember your mother, Zoe?" Tessa asked quietly.

Start right there.

No, she couldn't. The lies were so ingrained, so imprinted on her heart, that after a few dozen times of reciting them, they became truths.

My parents died in a car accident when I was ten. Aunt Pasha was my only relative. She raised me. We move a lot because there's gypsy blood in the Tamarin line.

"Barely," Zoe said, instead of lying by rote. "Pasha's my mother, for all intents and purposes. And you could be that person to another child who doesn't have parents. What you need is to get a kid that's been housebroken."

"Like a foster child?" Tessa asked. "I don't know if I could stand to give it away."

Zoe couldn't even respond to that. She turned away, certain that even in the moonlight Tessa could read her expression.

Could the door be open any wider?

The truth would feel *so* good. To sit here in the moonlight and share histories and secrets. Just to let the pressure of a lifetime of lies lift from her heart would be so liberating. Sure, Tessa would be mad as hell, but they'd be closer and more trusting, wouldn't they? It would be a breakthrough moment, and they'd tell Jocelyn and Lacey, and surely they'd all rally round Zoe. They'd finally understand what made her tick, forgiving her deceptions, and be all *Fearsome Foursome, go team go*. Right?

Or would they hate her for hiding the truth for all these years?

And if she told the truth, even whispered it right here in the moonlit garden to a woman whose perspective could change if she knew Zoe's history, would Zoe be breaking a promise to someone who'd been so much more than a friend?

What a bitch of a dilemma.

"Anyway, I'm not sure I'm equipped to handle a foster child," Tessa continued. "Some of them have been abused and neglected and God knows what."

Yeah, God knew what and didn't do a damn thing about it. But Pasha did.

"You could probably handle it, Tessa." Zoe's hands shook a little as she played with a row of strange bean pods, popping one off and snapping it to find three splotchy red lima beans inside.

"I want a baby to keep and raise, not a social services project I'm scared to get attached to," Tessa said.

Was *that* what she'd think Zoe was? Had Pasha? Of course not. Pasha had just scooped Zoe out of her life and saved her ass. Which is why Zoe owed her complete loyalty to Pasha, not Tessa, who was actually pissing her off even more than usual right that moment.

"A child like that needs love, like any other kid."

"But don't you have to give a foster child away at some point?"

"How would I know?" Zoe said, sounding irrationally defensive and not giving a shit right then. The misconceptions about foster kids made her crazy, and so did this conversation. "I don't think all of them are like delinquents or crack babies. You might get your maternal instincts appeased for a while."

"Well, that's not what I want."

"What about what they want?" she demanded. "Why is it always about you, Tessa? You and your uterus. Don't you ever think about those poor kids and how much one of them could be transformed by living here, learning from you, loving you, eating this tie-dyed bean?"

Tessa gave a weak smile. "That's a Christmas pole lima bean, Zoe. And, honestly, this isn't about my poor, empty uterus. It's about the one thing I wanted to be in my whole life. A mother forever. Isn't there anything you ever wanted to be or do, something that burns inside of you like a lifelong dream, the thing that would make you so happy and whole that you just know you have to have it someday?"

Oh, yes, there was. A permanent, stable, enduring address to a place that had history and happiness in every corner. But nothing could make Zoe say the ultimate four-letter word out loud.

Home.

"Isn't there?" Tessa demanded.

"No," Zoe lied. "I just want to be a hot air balloon pilot

who drifts from city to city without any chance of putting
down roots that could do nothing but strangle me."

Even she could hear the sarcasm in her tone and, damn
it, she wanted that line to come off as the truth.

"Roots are what I live for." Tessa leaned forward, her
eyes piercing. "Roots don't strangle if the plant is well
tended, my friend. Roots nourish. They provide stability.
They make sure the plant doesn't merely survive, but
thrives and grows and produces a fruit or vegetable."

"Enough with the gardening metaphors. You know what
I meant."

"No, I don't, Zoe. You don't really like this…this whimsical, immature life you're living, do you?"

She snorted. "Excuse me, but I am not the one sobbing
in the dirt."

"You just keep on pretending to be someone I know
you're not."

Zoe gasped a little, shocked at how the conversation had
turned on her. "I am? You know this how?"

"You're always pretending to be some sex-loving, hard-
drinking, joke-making party girl, when deep inside you're
really a sweet angel who would do anything for her old
aunt and gets tipsy on a glass of Chardonnay."

Oh, God, Zoe, just tell her.

"You know damn well it takes two glasses." The tease
tasted like vinegar on her tongue, but she said it anyway.
Because she couldn't face the truth. "And now that we have
me all figured out, why don't we talk about you and your
issues?"

"Nah." Tessa stood up, brushing dirt off her jeans. "I
feel much better. And I know what you should do, Zoe."

"Stop pretending?"

"Well, that, yeah, and you should move."

"Oh, I'm sure I will. That's my life."

She held out her hand to help Zoe up. "Here."

"Thanks."

"No, I mean *here* is where you should move. Right here, to Barefoot Bay on Mimosa Key. I think this is the one place you can have that thing you're longing for, that dream that will make you whole and happy."

"You sound like Pasha the Predictor now."

Tessa ignored the comment. "A home, Zoe. This can be your forever home. And isn't that what you want more than anything?"

So much for *secret* longings. How did Tessa know that?

"You're not going to deny it, are you?" Tessa asked.

"Home is overrated," Zoe said, looking up to the stars, suddenly imagining the utter peace and security of a night balloon flight wrapped in silence and sky. "I prefer to be untethered."

Tessa sighed. "I guess that's the difference between us, then. I'd kill for a few tethers I could diaper and love."

Zoe put her hand on Tessa's shoulder, handing her the lima bean. "Here. There were two little beans in this pod. Pasha would say that's a sign you could have twins."

"I wish Pasha's predictions were right."

Zoe angled her head, surprised. "They are."

Tessa looked a little hopeful when she took the bean and headed into her bungalow, seeming much more light-hearted and leaving Zoe feeling exactly the opposite.

What was stopping her from telling the truth? Habit? Fear? The anger and disappointment she'd see in one of her closest friend's eyes?

And yet she wanted to talk about it so much. She walked

toward the bungalows, aware of a pressure on her heart so heavy she almost couldn't breathe. What was that?

This can be your forever home. And isn't that what you want more than anything?

Considering how well her friends knew her, it was a miracle they hadn't figured out the truth by now.

She kicked the dirt and peered up at the moon, suddenly turning in the opposite direction, toward the other side of the resort, no longer concerned about night critters. Her heart ached with untold secrets. Her body tensed with the need to tear down that wall that surrounded the *hard-drinking, joke-making, sex-loving party girl who never lets her feelings show.*

Meandering through the back of Casa Blanca, she made her way to another wall—a wooden fence, actually. On the other side of it was…the thing she wanted most right then.

Chapter Eleven

⌒

The Glenlivet burned on the way down his throat, but Oliver didn't bother to chase the shot with water. Instead he drew in a slow, deep breath so the bittersweet flavors of the scotch worked their way up into his head, clearing it.

And still he stared at the silver-blue pool and imagined he could see Zoe, swimming naked like some kind of laughing, loving water nymph with flowing blonde hair and luscious wet skin.

Well, that beat the darker images that usually haunted him when he was alone in a house. So far the little villa on the beach hadn't triggered any old memories, but maybe that was because Evan was here. In Chicago the house had never been empty; even if Adele had been traveling and Evan had been sent to stay at his grandmother's, they'd had live-in staff.

He'd never had to come home to an empty house.

He pushed the glass to the side and returned his attention to the tablet computer on the table, forcing himself to finish the report to Raj and the team, bringing them all up to speed on their newest case and the schedule for tests and treatment.

Still, the words blurred in front of him and his mind wandered back to Zoe.

She wasn't going to try to fix Pasha's legal problems. Why did Zoe have to be so driven by loyalty and emotions and an invisible sense of duty when that could be steering her aunt all wrong?

He tapped into the Internet and opened a search bar, an attempt to pull up some facts based on the little information she'd ever given him.

Bridget. Corpus Christi. Foster Child. Missing.

He sipped while a few results flashed on the screen, mostly recent stories that couldn't possibly be connected to something that had happened about twenty-five years ago.

He took another drink and started to skim the links but a sound at the fence caught his attention. Looking past the pool screen, he peered into the darkness, expecting to see an animal.

Every light in the house was off, the fiber-optic pool lights were too dim to cast much glow, so he listened, definitely hearing something thud against the privacy fence.

And the soft intake of breath.

An intruder at the resort? Without making a sound, he unlatched the screen door and stepped onto the narrow strip of grass around the patio. He walked along the wall, cocking his ear.

Another thud, and this time two hands appeared at the top of the fence, along with a loud bump—someone hoisting themselves up on the other side, probably balancing on the crossbeam that ran along the back of the stockade-style wooden fence.

A ballsy intruder, then.

He hid behind a thick hibiscus bush, placing himself between the intruder and any entrance to the house. He didn't have a weapon, but he had his bare hands and he'd use them before anyone got near—

Blonde hair popped over the fence.

What the *hell* was she doing?

Zoe pushed herself up higher and one foot in a bright-yellow flip-flop came over the fence, a short black dress riding up to reveal her bare thigh. Turning her head from side to side, she peered into the darkness and then hoisted herself higher.

Jesus, she was fearless. And crazy. And gorgeous. And *here*.

He managed not to make a sound or move, watching as she maneuvered over the fence and angled herself to—she wouldn't jump, would she?

Of course she would. She'd do anything. That was why she made him hard and hot and flat-out insane with how much he wanted to capture her and hold her down and force her to *stay still* and *be his* and *not leave him*.

But if she did that, she wouldn't be Zoe. She wouldn't be the woman who climbed fences and…

Jumped. He sucked in a breath as she leaped into the air like a bird, arms out, hair flying, dress high enough for him to see that she was bare-ass naked underneath.

She landed with a soft thump, tumbling to her knees like she was born to be a cat burglar. But something told him she wasn't here to steal anything, except his sanity. And his breath. And his heart.

Or maybe she just wanted to get laid.

"Can I help you?" He stepped out from behind the bush and earned a loud gasp of shock.

"Oh my God, you scared me!"

He smiled, the irony too obvious to comment on. He reached down to give her a hand. "Let's see…you didn't want to knock and wake Evan?"

She let him pull her up. "I was strolling the grounds and ended up back there."

"By chance?"

"Luck." She grinned. "Did you think I was a heavily armed intruder?"

"Not when the dress flew up. Don't know where you'd hide a weapon." He gestured toward the screen door, letting her brush by him. She left a trail of something that smelled like honeysuckle and sin behind her.

And he followed like a fucking dog in heat.

Inside the patio, she went straight to the table and his heart stopped. If she looked at that tablet screen…

What difference did it make? Why not let her know exactly what he was doing? He was trying to help.

She lifted the glass and sniffed, made a face, then sipped. "Ewww. That tastes like lighter fluid filtered through swamp water. Why would anyone drink that?"

"It's manly."

Laughing, she dropped into his empty chair and draped her arms over the side. "Can I have something girly? Like, you know, beer or vodka?"

"Stay here."

He went into the kitchen and grabbed the bottle of Grey Goose he'd picked up when supply shopping, telling himself it wasn't because he knew she liked it, poured it over

ice, tore into a juice box, and added a splash. Before going back out, he slipped into the living room and broke the
bloom off a bright-pink flower from a bouquet to garnish
the drink.

He half expected her to be skimming his tablet and following his last Internet search when he came out, but she
was sitting at the edge of the shallow end, her feet dangling
in the water.

He joined her, sticking his feet in the pool as he presented the drink. "Girly enough for you?"

"Perfect." She raised her glass. "Let's drink to…"

"Whatever made you come over here."

"Dead batteries."

He laughed. "At least you're honest."

"Except when I'm not." She tapped his glass with hers,
casting her eyes downward. "It's hard to live life as a liar
when you're as open as I am."

"I imagine it is."

She lifted the flower and laid it down before sipping
her drink, closing her eyes and moaning appreciatively.
"Damn, that's good." She tasted again. "Cranberry
juice?"

"Apple Raspberry Juicy Juice."

She smiled. "The mixer of champions."

"So, Zoe, why don't you stop lying if it's so hard for
you?"

"It's become a way of life." The blunt candor actually
surprised him. "In fact, just moments ago, life handed me
the perfect opportunity to share all my secrets with one of
my very best friends and what do you think I did?"

He didn't answer because he was still trying to process
that her friends didn't know her past.

"That's right," she answered for him. "Nothing. Not exactly a lie, unless you count omission."

"You mean to tell me that Lacey and Tessa and Jocelyn don't know that Pasha's not really your great-aunt?"

"They know she's sick," she said, as if that were a huge bit of progress. "But the rest of my sad tale of woe?" She lifted her glass again. "Only you, doc. Only you."

He would have liked to hold on to the sideways compliment, but he was still too perplexed by her confession. "But they're your best friends, Zoe. They can give you advice and be sounding boards."

"And I might even be able to return the favor by helping them. At least I could set Tessa straight on the truth about foster kids." She splashed her feet in the water, creating ripples that danced across the teal water. "But there is a downside."

"Surely you don't think they'd turn Pahsa in."

"No. But they might hate me for not coming clean."

He let his knuckles brush her exposed thigh, trying not to think about what wasn't on under that thin dress. It would take one second to have her naked and in his arms. One second.

He lingered on the thought for a lot longer than that, watching her drink and think.

"I don't believe they'd hate you," he finally said. "You are judging yourself far more harshly than they would."

"Hate's a strong word," she agreed. "But how do you think they're going to feel when I tell them I'm not…" She closed her eyes and whispered, "I'm not a girl named Zoe Tamarin."

He put down his drink and reached for her, wrapping his hands around the slender column of her throat and holding her jaw with his thumbs. "No one cares what your name is, Zoe. You are *you*. An amazing, funny, beautiful woman. You owe your friends the truth."

She looked away, refusing to make eye contact.

"What's the worst that could happen?" he asked.

"I could lose them, like I…lost you."

He tightened his grip. "You didn't lose me. Surely you believe that by now."

Finally, she shifted her gaze to meet his. "I'm ashamed," she said softly.

"You were a kid."

"But I let this lifestyle go on and on for years," she said, inching free to make her point. "Every time I had a choice—including that day in Chicago when Pasha said I should stay—I took the chickenshit, lazy, easy, loser choice."

Yet she was none of those things. "You and Pasha simply got yourself painted into a corner, Zoe. She protected you and you protected her and neither one of you could get off—"

"Don't make my excuses for me." She took a lusty gulp and put the glass down so hard he thought it might crack on the stone pavers. In a second, she turned to him, her eyes bright.

"Then don't make your own," he said.

"Touché. So you noticed that I'm naked under this?" She fluttered the hem of the dress seductively.

Of course, she wanted to plow over the tough stuff with sex. And as much as he wanted to drive that plow, he refused.

"Why don't you tell me what happened?"

Her brows drew together. "When?"

"I know you say Pasha's at risk of being charged for kidnapping, but what actually happened?"

She tilted her head, a smile pulling. "You don't want to have sex with me?"

"I'm going to assume that's a rhetorical question. What I don't want to do is derail this conversation yet."

Without warning, her hand landed on his crotch, squeezing, a bolt of lightning shooting right into his balls. "What are you doing?"

"Making sure you're a guy."

He put his hand over hers and pressed, his erection growing with each passing heartbeat. "I'm not *a* guy. I'm *the* guy. I'm the one who knows you, Zoe." Very slowly, because it hurt like a motherfucker even to think about making the move, he lifted her hand and put it on her lap. "Now tell me the story. What happened when Pasha 'kidnapped' you? I take it she didn't throw you in a trunk and drive off." He frowned when she didn't reply. "Did she?"

"Of course not." She picked up her hand and looked at it like her very fingers had betrayed her. "I'm really losing my touch."

"Your touch is…" *Insane.* "Fine. And my kid's asleep upstairs," he added, more to assuage her humiliation than anything. "I've waited nine years, Zoe."

"For sex with me?"

"For this story."

Puffing out some air, she leaned back on her hands, breaking their contact but staying close enough that he could feel the silk of her calves against his and the splash of warm water between them. "She did drive off. But I was in the passenger seat, not the trunk."

"Ten years old?" The threads of her story had stayed in

his mind over the years, but no real tapestry had emerged. She'd been in trouble, run away, found safety with Pasha, and—that was all he knew. "How did it happen?"

She didn't answer for a while, drinking instead.

He gave her leg a nudge.

"Okay, okay. I'm getting fortified." One more luscious sip, this one with her eyes closed and head tilted back. It took everything in him not to dip his head and kiss her exposed throat. "I have never spoken this story out loud," she announced as she set the drink down next to her. "Not once, not even to myself. So bear with me."

"I have all night and an eight-pack of Juicy Juice. Talk to me."

She exhaled a soft whistle and looked out over the water, gathering her thoughts. "I was raised in foster homes. I think I mentioned that on our balloon ride."

He nodded his head, but she didn't even look at him. "Yes, you did. But when we were dating, you told me your parents died in a car accident, and that Pasha was your father's aunt and your only living relative and she was appointed as your legal guardian. But…" His voice trailed off as it hit him then—really hit him like a brick to the brain.

Zoe had lied to him from day one. She'd *never* told him the truth.

She glanced at him, no doubt reading his expression. "And I only knew you a month. Can you imagine how my lifelong friends are going to feel?"

Yes, actually, he could. They'd feel betrayed and hurt and cheated. Those emotions strangled enough that he couldn't talk.

"Sometimes," Zoe said, "you tell a lie for so long it becomes the truth."

"No," he managed to reply. "It never becomes the truth."

"I'm sorry, Oliver." She angled her head toward him. "I wasn't happy about lying to you. That's why I took you on that balloon ride. I wanted to tel! you the real truth up there. I did, I tried, anyway."

"Tell me now, down here."

"Okay. I might have to go back to, you know, the beginning." She took another drink, then continued. "I have no idea who my father is. I doubt my mother did, either, but she overdosed when I was four, I think. I really don't know. I was truly an orphan—she was a runaway, too, and…" Her voice cracked.

"Shhh. Zoe, don't cry." He put his hand on her shoulder, but she wiggled out of his touch.

"I'm not crying. My voice always cracks when I'm nervous."

"Why are you nervous? This is me."

She looked at him and, for a woman who said she wasn't crying, her eyes were pretty bright. "I'm nervous because it's *you*. And you matter."

Which might have been the nicest thing she'd said since she'd shown up in his office. "Zoe, it's not your fault who or what your mother was."

"It's my legacy. A long line of runaways. Not exactly the bloodline you married into."

"Adele isn't here, and she won't ever be. You are. Please." He managed to settle his hand on her bare thigh. "I'm not judging you."

"All right." She reached for the drink, then shook her head and put it down. "Anyway, they put me in foster care and from there the State of Texas pretty much forgot I existed until whatever family had me got sick of me."

"How could anyone get sick of you?"

She gave a dry laugh. "I was mouthy, sarcastic, irreverent, impolite, and never met a rule I couldn't break."

"All the things I love about you."

She startled a little, making him realize what he'd said. He opened his mouth to correct himself, but closed it again.

For a long, heavy moment, neither said a word, but when he looked down at the water, her toes were curled into tight little balls.

"Anyway," she continued, "I was in Corpus Christi last, with a family who had three foster kids. I really don't know why they took fosters, probably for the subsidy money and free labor. And free…" She shook off the thought. "Anyway, about two doors away, this incredibly sweet lady moved in. Her name was Patricia Hobarth."

"Pasha?"

She nodded. "She lived alone and we became friends that summer. I'd visit her almost every day. She taught me how to play cards and do crafts and"—she laughed softly—"read tea leaves. She was…sad. Lonely and lost, like I was, and we formed an unlikely friendship."

She was quiet for a moment, maybe holding on to an old memory, but he let her go, waiting for her to finish.

"So I spent a lot of time there because…the father at the house where I lived…" She fought for a breath and his heart fell down somewhere into his gut.

"God, tell me he didn't hurt you." White-hot rage blasted through him, and she hadn't even told him anything yet.

She swallowed hard and shook her head. "Not me. At least, well, no. He had sex with one of the other girls. She was fourteen."

"Fuck."

She closed her eyes and stayed quiet a really long time. "Every night. In the next bed."

"Oh, shit, Zoe. How do you handle something like that?"

"Run, Zoe, run." The words were no more than the breath of a sad sigh, hardly discernable.

"Excuse me?"

"That's when the voice started." At his look, she gave a dry laugh. "No, I don't hear voices. Well, one. And it's mine, but it's…loud. Usually telling me to do something that goes against common sense. But it started in that room, on those nights, when I'd stick my head under the pillow and try to drown it all out. The voice…helped."

He reached for her, putting his arm around her back, pulling her closer, trying to warm the chill that probably started deep inside her. "This voice told you to run."

"Fast and far. I wanted to get…away."

"So it's not your life on the lam with Aunt Pasha that makes you so impossible to hold."

"I have to have an escape route," she admitted. "In fact, I kind of freak out if I don't have a way out of…anything."

Anything like a relationship, a permanent hometown, even her friendships. Very slowly, threads of that tapestry that was Zoe started to form a picture.

"Life with Pasha just magnified that trait," she said. "First, Pasha *was* my escape hatch, then that lifestyle felt normal. I know anyone hearing this, even close friends, will have a hard time understanding that, but it's true."

He tried to imagine that life but couldn't. Not that he couldn't imagine how she had lived that way, but why?

"Why not try to change the situation? Why run? Why not fix it?"

"I'm not the fixer you are, Oliver. I'm the runner, remember?"

"But why didn't you report the guy to the social service people who checked on you?"

She shook her head as if the question was crazy. "You don't understand. The other girl threatened me."

"*She* threatened you?"

She lost the battle not to drink, picking up the glass and gulping. "It wasn't rape. She wanted to have sex with him, and in return she got stuff: clothes, money, drugs. She was his favorite, and it worked for her. I had to shut up and cover my ears, always, always under that pillow."

He tried to imagine the suffocating feel of the bedding, the sounds, the horror for a little girl, and it turned his stomach.

"But I listened to that voice," she said quickly, as if she were more concerned about how he felt right then than the memories. "The voice would soothe me. The voice told me what it would be like when I ran, when I was safe, when I could roll around beautiful green hills or even *fly*." She smiled wistfully. "I wanted to fly so much. And not a plane, although I had to take those flying lessons, too, but I wanted to float." She closed her eyes and sighed the word. "Just go up and away and hear silence. That was my greatest fantasy. A quiet, far away balloon has always been my happy place."

"So Pasha helped you?" he asked.

"That summer, foster asshole guy lost his job and he was home all the time with that girl." She closed her eyes.

"They…did stuff all the time. So during the day I spent every possible moment with Pasha."

"Did you tell her what was going on at your house?"

"No, I was too scared. But she knew something was wrong, because she read my palm."

"And figured it out?" He couldn't keep the incredulity out of his voice.

"She saw the fingernail gouges from me digging into my own hands." She gave a wry smile. "Say what you will about her fortune-telling skills, the woman is intuitive as hell, and she recognized a kid who was getting progressively more fucked up as the days went by."

"Is that why she took you?"

Zoe shook her head, kicking her feet in the water to make waves again. "That girl, the fostertute, as I liked to call her, got taken away. There was some trouble or something. The state services person was on the take, I think. I don't know. I was too young to understand it, but when she was gone, I knew I'd be next."

More unholy heat blasted through him. "What happened?"

She turned, her eyes dark with pain. "He managed to corner me and…try. Got his hand down my pants and his tongue down my throat."

He buckled a little like he'd been shot. "You were *ten*?"

"He liked 'em young, doc."

Bile rose in his throat. "What did you do?"

She almost smiled. "What do you think?"

"Ran?"

"After I bit his fucking tongue until it bled and slammed my knee in his nuts, yeah. I ran like hell to Pash—Mrs. Hobarth's." She nearly drained her glass before finishing.

"And Pasha, it turned out, has a superpower. That woman can pack and disappear in less time than it takes most people to take a shower. She knew it was no use reporting that guy, and it was only a matter of time until I was his next…" She shook her head. "The voice screamed 'Run, Zoe, run,' and, this time, I did. With her."

"She saved you, Zoe."

She turned to him, her eyes wide. "Duh. Why do you think I'm so determined to do the same for her?"

"You're covering for her by running and hiding," he shot back. "That's not saving her."

She didn't answer, turning away.

"You could argue that to any judge," he insisted. "Or police or FBI or sheriff—"

"Stop. I would never talk to those people."

"Or a lawyer," he continued, undeterred. "She doesn't have to live with this sword hanging over her head anymore. Hell, you could find that foster father and—"

"He's dead. I've kept tabs on him and he died in a house fire. I hope he's still burning." She shuddered a little. "You have to know what Pasha did is illegal, by any stretch. She broke every law there is by using fake IDs and dead people's Social Security numbers. She had this whole underground network of people who are all up to their asses in criminal shit."

He thought about Pasha for a moment, about how little he knew about a woman whose life he wanted so much to save. "How'd she do it? Didn't anyone check up on you? How did you get into schools or rent apartments or make money?"

"Pasha has money, thousands in cash, she keeps stashed in places like the freezer or—God, this is so cliché but true—under the mattress."

"Where does it come from?"

"I really don't know, but we never were destitute. She always found odd jobs, and then I did. Waitress, sales clerk, cleaning lady, seamstress. Whatever, until people started asking questions and then, sometimes for no reason I could figure, we'd blow out of town and move to the next place."

"How did you get into college?" he asked.

"Miracles. Strings pulled. Pasha's relentless determination that I get a degree. She homeschooled me and made sure I passed every test. She managed to find people who make fake IDs and create real people out of thin air. I even have a birth certificate and I do have a Social Security card. I got into the University of Florida, for crying out loud. She made that happen—it was so, so important to her that I go to college."

She kicked her legs a few more times, the soft splash punctuating the pride in her voice. "But that's just the story of what happened, Oliver. That's not the *story*."

He gave her a questioning look, not following.

"What I mean is, that's not who or what my Aunt Pasha is made of. She saved me, yes, and maybe what she did was illegal and wrong in the eyes of the law, but she sacrificed her entire life for me, too. She's my friend, my confidante, my mother, my sister, my soul mate. She would die for…" She dropped her head into her hands. "But I don't want her to."

He settled her against him the way her pain settled on his heart. "We'll do everything possible and more," he promised.

"Can you save her life?"

He inched her around to look at him. "Zoe, I will do everything in my power and in the power of my team to save this woman who saved you. You have my word."

She inched back. "There's a 'but' coming."

"There is," he acknowledged. "I'll save her if I can, but what will you do with that life if we save her?"

She didn't answer.

"Zoe, I can see the agony in your eyes and practically hear that voice in your head."

"Yeah? What's it saying?"

"Take the easy way. Run, hide, and avoid the trouble. Protect yourself and Pasha and don't take any chances."

She gave him a slow smile. "You can hear that voice in my head?"

"Loud and clear."

"Then why don't you do what it's screaming at you to do?"

He leaned closer, wrapping both arms around her. "This?"

"You must be stone deaf." She put her hands on his face and brought his mouth to hers. "*Kiss me, kiss me, kiss me. Hear that now?*"

He did, and it was music to his ears.

Chapter Twelve

Heat like she'd never felt before rose up from deep, deep inside her, burning a hole in her chest and making her want to scream with the need to relieve it. And yet Pasha's whole body was chilled.

She had a fever.

The kind that made her eyeballs ache and her arms numb.

She turned again to place the cool cotton pillowcase against her inflamed cheek, but almost instantly the material was as warm as she was.

At least Pasha hadn't lied to Zoe. Not tonight, anyway. She really did feel so punk that she'd had to rest all afternoon and into the evening. She really had felt the urge to nod off every time Zoe tried to have a conversation with her—as if she hadn't known where *that* was going—and she really had been too tired to sit at the table and eat dinner.

And as the evening wore on, Pasha felt worse, trying harder to hide it with each of Zoe's efforts to make things better. She'd come in and brought Pasha food, even put a little vase of flowers on the tray, but Pasha couldn't eat.

Zoe had sat on the edge of the bed and tried again to explain about an experimental treatment that involved putting viruses in her body, making it sound like that was a good thing, but Pasha had nodded off.

And, even when Zoe had attempted small talk and asked Pasha questions about the little boy and how sweet he was, it had been nearly impossible to stay in that conversation. But Pasha had told Zoe how much she loved her. And that was the truth; the only thing that burned hotter in her cancer-filled chest than pain was her love for Zoe Tamarin.

Little Bridget, the desperate, terrified, talkative child who'd come into Pasha's life when they were both at rock bottom, had given Pasha a reason to go on. Now that little girl was all grown up, and she deserved more than this. She deserved better than a life with Pasha.

She deserved *him*.

With each hour the fever got a little more intense, like it was burning the common sense right out of her. Because an idea had planted itself and it wouldn't let go. If only she could have a sign so she could know if that idea was right or not.

She needed a sign.

She'd been waiting for one since Zoe had left, around ten o'clock. Maybe she'd gone to Lacey's house, but Pasha would put her money on Zoe choosing a different soft place to fall tonight. Pasha knew exactly where that girl had gone. Right to his arms. Right to where she belonged.

It was quite possible she'd be gone all night.

Very slowly she pushed back the covers, sending a cascade of goose bumps over her exposed skin.

Time to get into action, Tricia.

It had been a while since she'd thought of herself as Tricia. Maybe *that* was the sign that it was time to go.

In her closet, she pulled out a small duffel bag that had never been unpacked. The essentials were always there: cash, toiletries, clothes. Lifting it was a challenge, despite how light it was, but she got it to the bed and looked around for what she should take with her.

She always left room in her panic bag for the most important things. A picture of Zoe. Her favorite earrings. Hair gel. Some aspirin and Tums. She stood in front of the bureau deciding what else to take, her gaze landing on the vase Zoe had brought in with Pasha's dinner. The pink flower was unusual, more like a ball of fuschia-colored needles.

The mimosa flower, Zoe had said, the official flower of Mimosa Key.

She reached to touch the silky needles that stuck straight out like Pasha's hair when she managed to get it perfect. As she brushed the bloom, her finger started to shake. With a sudden spasm, she toppled the vase, the water spilling, the flower fluttering to the ground.

She let out a cry, but that made her cough, then choke, igniting more fire in her windpipe and making her lungs feel like someone was pressing a steam iron on them.

The flower lay on the floor in a little mess, water dripping down the side of the bureau like tears. What was nature's message in that mess? She dug through everything she knew, every possible interpretation.

Pink. Pink. Pink always represented innocence, youthfulness, the indefatigable spirit of a child.

Who had that more than Zoe? And a river of water, always leading toward something better. Eternity for Pasha, but for Zoe—happiness. Maybe that was a stretch, but her head was throbbing and her body felt like it burned at a thousand degrees.

That sign would have to do. She turned to the bag and mentally went through her list of things she couldn't live without. She had it all, didn't she?

Zoe would be heartbroken.

The reality of that hit her harder than the fever. Like so many things she'd done in her life, this was selfish, the act of a coward. How could she let Zoe know that? How could she be certain that Zoe wouldn't mourn her?

And then she knew the answer.

She crouched down to dig into her bottom drawer, feeling around for the edge of the envelope, the paper soft and familiar and worn. Without even looking at it, she placed the envelope on the edge of the dresser.

That would do the trick. When Zoe read that, she'd understand why she deserved someone better than Pasha.

Prickles of heat stung at Pasha's neck, the inside kind, like the hot flashes she used to get in her fifties. But this wasn't a hot flash; this was the sickness inside her screaming to get out. Somehow she found the strength to slip into loose pants, a long-sleeved T-shirt, and sneakers. Running clothes, Zoe would call them.

Running-away clothes.

Please understand, Zoe darling. Please. This is for you. So you can have the life—and love—that you deserve.

The house was quiet as she walked through, letting herself out the front door into the moonlight.

She started walking, following the path out of Casa Blanca, finding her way to the beach road. It had rained earlier, before Zoe had gone out, one of the flash showers that came through Florida and washed everything for ten minutes, then disappeared.

Was this the right thing to do? Had she gotten the right signs? She lifted her gaze from the ground, where she had been watching her every step, then looked up at the night sky.

"Oh my word," she whispered, bringing herself to a complete stop. "A moonbow!"

A hint of red and orange fading into a band of soft yellow, then deep azure blues, all curved around a three-quarter moon.

The sign that true love would return.

Pasha shivered, the fever pounding at her head, the pain screaming in her chest, the pressure of every decision hammering her into a quivering mess. It didn't matter. She had to go. She had to run. Just like she had ever since the day she'd heard that word: *mistrial*.

She'd been on the run for forty-seven years. What was a few more weeks until she died?

The scotch tasted a hell of a lot better on Oliver's tongue than it would have in the glass. Smoky and fierce, a fiery flavor that was exactly as he described it: manly. So were his hands, strong and secure, holding her exactly where he wanted her for this kiss.

Drunk on the release of pent-up emotions and ancient history, and maybe a wee buzzed from the vodka, Zoe sank into Oliver, lifting her legs from the water to hang them over his lap and curl deeper into the warm, familiar pleasure of his kiss.

The voice in her head was blessedly quiet, and all she

could hear was his soft breathing, the rustle of clothes, the gentle moan in his throat as he intensified their kiss.

He knew everything now. And still he kissed her with something that felt so tender and precious…and sexy. The thought was as potent as a whole bottle of vodka, heating her blood, squeezing her lungs, and fluttering a ribbon of white-hot lust right through the middle of her body.

"Now this," she whispered into his mouth, "is why I came over here."

He broke the kiss, frowning. "Really?"

"Booty call, totally," she told him. "I told you I'm naked under this dress."

"I did notice a distinct lack of undergarments when you, uh, flew in."

"What do you think?"

"Who can think when *Zoe*, *naked*, and *booty call* are all in the same sentence?"

She ran her hand along his thigh. "You've proven your-self a worthy opponent to my vibrator."

"So, you want sex?"

She inched back, not quite sure how to take that. "Don't you?"

He didn't answer right away, and her heart dropped.

"Don't you?" she prodded, a soft flush of embarrass-ment rising.

"*You* don't want sex," he said.

"My damp thighs beg to differ."

His eyes flickered with interest at the thought. "That's a physiological response."

She choked softly. "Seriously, doc?"

"Zoe." He stroked her cheek, way too gentle for the kind

of stroking she had in mind. "You came here for an es-cape."

"Maybe I did," she replied, tamping down an irritation that didn't mix well with arousal. "Sex can be a great es-cape. And it beats the hell out of disappearing. *Again.* Don't you think?"

He finished the last of his scotch, his throat moving with the gulp.

"Oliver. You mean you're saying no?"

"I'm…not…" He stood suddenly, leaving her cold and alone. "Not sure," he finished. "I'll be right back. You want a refill?"

"Water, please." She stayed right where she was while the sound of his footsteps disappeared into the house.

Well, *hell*. This wasn't turning out as planned. First he'd dragged out a confession that made her ache in a way that—well, in a way that she hadn't ached in a long time. And then he made her ache in a whole different way and didn't seem inclined to satisfy it. What the *hell*?

Maybe he'd gone for a condom. Maybe he'd gone to be certain Evan was asleep. That gave her hope, because she needed this. So what if it was an escape? It would be an amazing, wonderful, delicious escape.

In one easy move, she slipped the cover-up over her head and slid into the water. It had worked very well with a bathing suit on, and now it would—

"What are you doing?"

Maybe not work so well. Shit. "Skinny-dipping. That against the law?"

"In some states." He had two bottles of water, which he set on the stones as he sat back down on the edge of the pool. "I'll watch."

Watch? "Suit yourself." She dove down to the bottom, staying as long as she could, letting the water cool her. Would he jump in and join her? She kicked to the surface, each stroke taut with anticipation.

He hadn't moved, but sat there chugging a bottle of water.

She stayed immersed up to her shoulders. "So, what's your game?" she asked. "Hard to get?"

He shook his head and finished the last of the water.

"Make me beg?"

Another shake.

"Fear of failure?"

He laughed. "Never a problem for me."

She put her hands on her hips and stood straight so that her whole upper body was exposed. He stared and she didn't move, knowing full well he never could resist her breasts. "Then why won't you fuck me?"

The response was almost imperceptible, but she caught the little flinch. "I don't want to fuck you. I want to make love to you." He lifted the other bottle and held it toward her. "When you're ready."

For making love or the bottle? "Color me baffled, doc."

"A water color," he fired back. "Looks great on you."

"Then join me."

"No."

She slapped the water with the same force that the word hit her. "No?"

"No."

"At the risk of sounding a little overly cocky, why the hell not?"

He angled his head a little, like he was considering

the question. Or just wanted to stare some more. "Damn, you're hot."

Her jaw loosened a little. "Then why don't you dive in here and get burned?"

"Because…" He took another sip of water. "That's not what I want."

What did he want? A commitment? A romance? A flipping ring on his finger? Or maybe he didn't want her now.

"Was it everything I told you?"

He actually laughed softly, as if she'd said something absurd. "Zoe, I'm going to hold out for something better than pool sex with you."

"The bedroom's right there."

She saw the longing. It flashed in his eyes, passing quickly, but not so fast that she didn't get it and know—absolutely know beyond any shadow of a doubt—that he wanted her in that bedroom. But something was stopping him.

"Is it because Pasha's your patient now?"

He laughed again. "You don't get it, do you?"

"Evidently not."

"There's more to it…than sex." The words were soft, almost a whisper, and as loving and tender as anything she'd ever heard.

"More to what?" Her heart thudded softly as water sluiced down her bare breasts and his gaze followed each droplet.

"More to everything." He gestured toward her discarded dress. "Your clothes are vibrating."

"My cell." She strode forward, water sluicing down her naked body. "Can you pull it out of the pocket and read the ID? I want to be sure it's not Pasha."

He didn't take his eyes off her as he found the phone. He looked at the screen and drew back.

"Who is it?" She forgot her nakedness and need. "Pasha?"

"The sheriff."

"Very fun—" She blinked at him. He wasn't joking. Shaking water off her hand, she reached for the phone and tapped the screen, a dark feeling of dread building inside her. "Hello?"

"Ma'am, this is Deputy Slade Garrison of the Lee County Sheriff's Department."

Holy, holy crap. They'd been caught. This was the call she'd dreaded her whole life. "Yes?"

"I'm with a woman by the name of Pasha Tamarin. Do you know her?"

She almost sank right into the water. "Is she okay?"

"No, ma'am, she's not. She's not okay at all."

Chapter Thirteen

⌇

Doctor Bradbury was a godsend in a crisis. During the blur that was the next hour—two?—Oliver handled everything. Everything. With calm, unquestioned authority, not the least bit ruffled by a life-and-death situation.

He took the phone and talked to the sheriff, helped Zoe dress, called Tessa to come and stay with Evan, talked to a doctor in the ER at North Naples Hospital, and, through it all, he stayed completely calm as he drove them over the causeway.

Zoe, on the other hand, was a wreck, with two words echoing through her head the whole time Oliver dealt with one thing after another: She left. She left. *She left.*

Pasha had packed the fucking panic bag and *left,* only to collapse in the parking lot of the Super Min and be found by the night clerk, Gloria Vail, who happened to work during the day at the Casa Blanca salon and also happened to be dating Deputy Garrison.

Gloria recognized Pasha and called Tessa and got Zoe's cell number.

Otherwise, Zoe might never have learned where Pasha was until she got home and discovered her missing and then called every hospital and law-enforcement agency in the county.

She had to remember to thank Gloria for calling the sheriff.

Now if that wasn't irony, what was? Thanking someone for doing what Pasha and Zoe had been actively avoiding for twenty-five years.

At the hospital they wouldn't let Zoe see Pasha. When the desk clerk had asked for insurance, identification, and other *normal* information that *abnormal* Zoe didn't have, Oliver had swooped in once again, promising to handle it—how?—and demanding that Zoe sit in a waiting room to *wait*.

And there she stayed, in a blue leather chair that stuck to her bare legs, staring at a TV with no sound and vaguely aware that people walked by while her world crumbled into a million pieces.

"Hey."

Zoe jumped at the greeting, yanked from her miserable meditation to see Tessa and Jocelyn hustling down the hall toward her. Even in T-shirt and jeans, Jocelyn looked completely collected, her dark hair pulled back in a smooth ponytail. Tessa didn't look quite so together, but they *had* gotten her up from a sound sleep to stay with Oliver's son.

"Where's Evan?" Zoe asked, standing up to meet them.

"He woke up and I took him to Lacey and Clay's house. She was up anyway with the baby, and we wanted to come and be with you." Tessa handed her a plastic supermarket bag. "I happened to notice you were next to naked and thought you might want something to wear."

Zoe nodded thanks and gave them both quick hugs.

"You okay?" Jocelyn asked, a gentle hand on Zoe's face. "'Cause you look like hell on a stick."

"I am hell on a stick. She ran away!" The words tumbled out on a sob.

"Why would she do that? Was she trying to find you?" Tessa asked.

"My father has run away," Jocelyn said.

"But he has dementia," Tessa replied. "Pasha has…"

All three of them were quiet, almost refusing to say the word.

"Cancer," Jocelyn finally said. "She has cancer and now she's going to get help. She can't fight you on it, no matter what her reasons."

Tessa looked hard at Zoe, the silent question all over her face. *What are her reasons?* "Why do you think she ran away, Zoe?" she asked instead.

Zoe fell back into her chair, the leather still warm. The girls bookended her in the chairs on either side, both instantly grabbing Zoe's hands.

Zoe gave them both a death grip. "I don't…" She swallowed the standard response—also known as a *lie*. "She ran away because she doesn't want…" No, that was another lie. She hadn't run from doctors and the opportunity to be cured; she'd run from reality. She ran away… "So I can have a normal life."

They both stared at her.

Zoe closed her eyes, the lids burning with exhaustion and stress and fear. And probably some tears.

Her friends were going to be so hurt. So mad. So insulted that they hadn't been close enough to be trusted. Especially secret-averse Tessa.

"What are you talking about, Zoe?" Tessa asked.

"I haven't told you…everything." Zoe couldn't take her gaze from Tessa's, hoping the depth and sincerity of her apology was coming through. But, judging from the look of abject misery on Tessa's face, Zoe was failing.

"Zoe," Jocelyn said again, adding a squeeze.

Zoe ignored her, still looking at Tessa. It wasn't Jocelyn who worried her, frankly. She'd hid enough of her own past from them that she'd be the most understanding of the friends. But Tessa, oh, *Tessa*. She'd only asked for honesty and Zoe had withheld it for all these years.

It was time.

"Zoe, look." Jocelyn yanked her hand, and finally Zoe turned, her gaze snagged by a man in forest green walking toward them. With a big bad mother-effer of a gun on his hip and a Lee County sheriff's badge on a sizable chest. "I think Deputy Garrison wants to see you."

Zoe instantly recognized the buff build and sandy hair of the young deputy sheriff who was such a presence around Mimosa Key.

"Ms. Tamarin." He nodded.

Slowly Zoe stood, her heart walloping her ribs. So this was it—the moment she'd dreaded for as long as she could remember.

"Deputy Garrison." She reached out her hand to shake his. "Thank you very much for taking care of my…of Pasha."

"I'm wondering if you could help me with some paperwork, ma'am. She didn't have any identification and

I have to fill out some forms. Did you bring her license?"

"She doesn't drive." Or have a shred of legitimate identification.

"Can you give me her social and permanent address?"

"Actually, I don't know them." Because they don't exist.

"How about a birthday and place of birth so we can plug that into our system?"

And find nothing? Zoe shook her head. "I'm afraid I can't, Deputy."

He frowned a little. "Then we do have a problem because—"

"What exactly is the problem, Sheriff?"

Zoe whipped around at the velvety, powerful sound of Oliver's voice, her heart vaulting to her throat at the sight of him in scrubs. Had he operated on Pasha? Treated her?

"How is she?" Zoe asked, the sheriff momentarily forgotten.

He nodded, reaching out a hand to her. "I'll tell you in a minute. I'm Dr. Oliver Bradbury," he said to the sheriff. "Pasha Tamarin is a patient of my private practice. I'm on staff at this hospital. We'll get the paperwork to you tomorrow, Sheriff. Ms. Tamarin needs to see her aunt now."

Slade nodded. "I understand that, but I need to get something into the system as far as identification. Can you tell me her full, legal name?"

For a long moment no one said a word. Zoe was aware of Jocelyn and Tessa just a few feet away, frozen in uncertainty. And Oliver, clearly waiting for her to…stop running.

"Her name is…" Zoe swallowed and looked at Oliver,

seeing the silent plea in his eyes but hearing another in her head.

Don't do it, Zoe. Run. Lie. Keep that pillow over your head and imagine. Float away from this moment.

Not this time.

"Her name is Patricia Hobarth," she said softly. "And as soon as I know she's going to survive this, I'll tell you everything else you need to know."

Slade looked satisfied with that, stepping aside to let her get to Oliver, who reached out and pulled her into his chest with a full-body embrace. "That's my girl."

Was she his girl? Well, they were certainly a step closer to that, weren't they? "How is Pasha?"

"Come on. I'll take you to her."

Zoe stood in the doorway of Pasha's room for a few minutes, holding on to Oliver's arm as she watched a nurse change an IV bag. Pasha looked as tiny as a child, pale and frighteningly close to death.

"What exactly happened?" she asked Oliver.

"Extremely high fever, severe fatigue, and indigestion. We've got those symptoms under control, but now we have to treat the cause."

"Cancer?"

"Tests will confirm what I already know but, yes. Esophageal cancer, advanced." He put his hand on her back, strong and sure. "We should do the gene therapy, and fast, Zoe."

Hope. She dug deep into her heart and grabbed it with two hands. But it felt so damn slippery. "Okay."

The nurse finished and gave Zoe a nod. "She's awake," she said, "but there's some antianxiety and a sedative in that

IV so she'll crash soon. She might not be completely lucid or remember this conversation, but you can talk to her."

"Thanks." Zoe headed to Pasha's bedside, aching to reach out and hold her. "Hey, Auntie," she whispered, putting a hand on her narrow shoulder. "You in there, sweetie?"

Her wrinkly eyelids fluttered.

"It's me, your little one," Zoe said, using the age-old nickname.

Pasha smiled just enough to give Zoe's heart a joyride. "How *is* my little one?" Pasha asked.

"I'm fine."

Her eyes opened, foggy and distant, but open. "No, my little boy. Matthew."

"Evan," she corrected. "He's fine, too." Zoe leaned closer, trying not to reprimand and scold the old woman for running. "You're going to be fine, too, Aunt Pasha."

Brown eyes slid to capture Zoe's gaze. "I was arrested," she whispered.

"No, you weren't. You collapsed in a convenience-store parking lot, which, by the way, you shouldn't have been in"—she couldn't resist a little reprimand—"and the sheriff got you to the hospital."

"I told him I was innocent."

"Don't worry about it now, Pasha. Oliver's here and he's going to take care of you. As soon as you're stronger, we'll move you to his clinic and start the treatment to get you on the road to recovery."

"Zoe…" She struggled for a breath. "Don't believe what they say."

What *who* say? "I don't believe anything," she said, placating her. "Just get better, okay?"

"I mean it." Her eyes cleared for a moment, like the fog had lifted, then it descended again. "They're going to tell you things and, I swear, Zoe, I swear to you, I didn't do anything to hurt anyone."

"Of course you didn't." Pasha really was foggy, and since she was sedated and wouldn't remember the conversation, Zoe added, "And I started the process of making sure you can live the rest of your life in the open and free."

Pasha's dark eyes flashed. "What?"

"Don't worry." The words sounded hollow, but she did her best to infuse them with hope. Oliver was right. This was the right thing to do. "I promise you, Pasha. No judge or jury is going to put you behind bars for saving a little girl and getting her away from a dangerous situation. I'll fight to the end for you." She squeezed Pasha's shoulder, trying to transmit the fire in her own veins to Pasha's.

"They might try, though," Pasha said. "They did before."

"No, no." She was confused. "No one did before."

"The mistrial was right, Zoe," she rasped.

The what? "Miss who?"

She closed her eyes. "I'm innocent, little one. I'm innocent."

"I know you are, Aunt Pasha. You did what you thought was right and it was right. You saved me. Please. Now isn't the time—"

"If only I could prove that."

"I can prove it," Zoe said. "I remember what happened and what he did."

"So does he."

"Pasha, that man is dead."

But Pasha shook her head and then let out a long, slow breath. Her eyes closed as if they weighed too much for her to battle any longer.

Zoe sensed Oliver approaching. "I think she's asleep now," she whispered.

"I'm not asleep."

Zoe startled, turning back to Pasha. "You should be," she said. "You need sleep."

Pasha's eyes opened and her gaze shifted to Oliver. "I always liked you," she said softly.

He smiled. "I like you, too, Pasha."

"Because you loved Zoe. I could tell."

He nodded.

"She's really not lucid," Zoe said quickly.

"If I weren't here…" Pasha tried to lift her shoulder.

"Shhh." Zoe hushed her by moving closer. "You *are* here and you are going to be here for a long time. Oliver's going to see to that."

"I will," he promised.

Pasha made a small groan. "I tried to leave."

"You failed, thank God," Zoe said.

"No, I mean I tried to leave back in Corpus Christi."

"You succeeded in that." Zoe leaned over and kissed her cheek. "And I'm eternally grateful. Go to sleep."

Pasha closed her eyes and they waited a moment, and then stepped away from the bed. As they reached the door, Pasha called out, "Zoe?"

"I'm going to go out in the hall now, Aunt Pasha. You go to sleep."

"You believe I'm innocent, don't you? No matter what they say?"

She gave a look to Oliver, who mouthed, "Strong sedative."

Zoe nodded. "I believe you, sweetie. Go to sleep."

"Because it was a mis…"

Zoe waited for her to finish, but the drugs hit home, and Pasha fell asleep.

Chapter Fourteen

Is there anything as sexy as a woman nursing?"

Lacey rolled her eyes and shifted on her pillow, shooting her husband a look. "Yeah, a woman sleeping."

"Seriously, Lace, I always thought those amazing breasts of yours were for form, not function."

She smiled and brushed his hair affectionately, sliding a long strand behind his ears. "You're such an architect, Clay."

"And I'm a father." Pride rolled through every word, and even in the darkened bedroom, Lacey could see the moisture in his eyes.

"A darn good one," she said.

"That remains to be seen."

She gently elbowed him and he let himself fall to the pillow. "You're a great stepfather to Ashley."

"I try, but…"

"Hey, she's a sixteen-year-old girl who's never been

easy to raise. She totally loves and trusts you. And…" She leaned over to kiss his cheek. "So do I."

He looked up, a sly smile on his face as he twirled a lock of her hair. "I miss you, Strawberry."

"It's going to be a few more weeks."

"Oh, hell, I'm not complaining." He scooched closer to the baby. "Elijah's worth every sacrifice, personal, physical, financial, professional."

"That's why God makes them so cute, so you'll give up everything else for them."

"He sure made this one cute."

"And asleep," Lacey whispered. "Can you get him into the cradle without waking him?"

"Of course I can. Unplug the little monster and I'll toss him in."

She smiled as she eased the baby's mouth away from her breast and exhaled with relief and exhaustion as Clay took over. Expertly he lifted Elijah, patting his tiny back until he let out a belch.

"That's my boy." Clay slid out of bed to lay the child in the cradle a foot away.

Leaving her pajama top open to let her sore, cracked nipples dry, Lacey fought the first wave of sleep that threatened. She wanted five more minutes to talk to Clay. Just five more minutes to kiss and exchange—

Clay stood straight up from the cradle. "What was that?"

"Shhh. That's the sound of silence. Enjoy it."

He shook his head, his whole body on alert as he made his way to the closed door.

"Someone's walking around."

Lacey sat up. "Do you think Evan woke up?"

A light knock on the door answered that question. "Mrs. Walker? I can't sleep."

"Oh, boy," Clay said.

"Two of them, in fact," Lacey replied. "Get one asleep, and another wakes up. Let him in, Clay." Lacey quickly pulled her top closed and adjusted herself, any possibility of sleep nothing but a sweet dream now.

"Hey, bud." Clay opened the door, crouching down to Evan's height, giving Lacey's heart a little tug of appreciation and love. He really was going to be an amazing dad. "You need water? Trip to the boys' room? Midnight snack?"

"I'm worried about Aunt Pasha."

Lacey sat up completely. "We all are, honey, but she's in really good hands. She's in your dad's hands, so what could be better?"

"I really want to go home."

"Home to…" Chicago? The Ritz? Where was home for him?

"That house we moved into. I want to see my dad. And Zoe."

The fact that he was already attached to Zoe ignited a little flame of hope in Lacey that maybe something could actually work out for her and the single father.

Clay stood. "If you're dad's back, I'll take you down there, bud. Not a problem. But if he's still at the hospital, you need to stay here, okay?"

"Let me call and see if I can reach Zoe," Lacey said quickly, scooting out of bed and reaching for her cell phone. "You guys stay here and if you wake that baby, prepare to die."

Clay gave Evan a fake scared look, which made him

laugh, and again Lacey's heart swelled with love. "Thanks," she whispered on her way out, tiptoeing down the hall to shoot a text to Zoe. A few seconds later her phone vibrated a response.

Zoe Tamarin: We'll come & get him in 10 min...need to talk to you. Tonight. Impt.

Tessa had texted from the hospital that Pasha was better but spending the night there. What was so important that... Lacey sighed. Sleep was nothing but a memory.

In the bedroom, she found Clay at the window with Evan, getting a brief astronomy lesson.

"Actually, that star moves every twenty-five thousand years or so," Evan said, "but not enough that we can see it."

Clay looked down at him, shaking his head. "You're ready for college, you know that?"

"My mom already has me signed up for some special classes at the University of Chicago," he said, more resignation than pride in his voice.

"You don't want to go?" Clay asked.

He shrugged. "I just want to be normal."

"Who doesn't?" Lacey teased.

He turned around. "You sounded like Zoe when you said that. I like her," he added wistfully.

"Then I have good news," Lacey interjected softly. "Your dad and Zoe are on the way. Pasha's being kept overnight for the doctors to watch her, but she's doing much better."

He nodded, then frowned, thinking. "My dad and Zoe really like each other."

"Well, they've known each other a long time."

"Two or three days."

"More like ten years, I think."

"Ten years?" Evan's voice rose in shock.

"Shhh." Lacey put her fingers to her lips, but it was too late. Elijah stirred and Lacey's heart dropped. Still, she was a little relieved for the distraction. She'd clearly gone into not-yet-covered ground for this kid. "Let's go wait for them by the front door, okay? Clay will stay with the baby."

A few minutes later, the growl of a sports-car engine and the harsh glare of halogen lights cut through the darkness of Barefoot Bay as Oliver's Porsche rolled into the driveway. Zoe was out before the engine was off, instinctively reaching for Evan.

"Hey, kid."

He didn't run forward but stiffened a little, waiting until his father got out and walked around the car. "Keeping pretty bad hours, Ev."

He shrugged and walked by Zoe, stiffly enough that she inched back in surprise. "You okay?"

"I'm tired," he said, whining enough to prove that no matter what their IQ, eight-year-olds can get cranky.

Zoe turned to Oliver. "Take him home and I'll stay here."

His disappointment was palpable. "Are you sure? Don't go to your bungalow alone."

"You can stay here, Zoe," Lacey said quickly, stepping forward, getting a grateful look from her and a quick glance from Oliver. "Whatever you want."

Zoe put her hand on Oliver's chest. "This has been hard on Evan, too. Take him back and we'll talk tomorrow."

His gaze flickered over her face, intense enough that Lacey felt like she should back away, as if the moment was private.

Oliver reached out to brush Zoe's cheek, making the exchange even more intimate. "I'll call you tomorrow. Get some sleep."

She nodded, and as he walked away they held each other's gaze. "Thank you," Zoe mouthed.

Lacey caught his final look, saying nothing until his car pulled out. Then she stepped next to Zoe. "A person's hair could fry from all the electricity out here," she whispered.

Zoe, her gaze on the disappearing lights of the sports car, barely smiled. Lacey waited for the smart-ass quip, the sex joke or bit of sarcasm.

But Zoe turned to her, an expression of pain and fear changing her normally bright and happy features to something Lacey barely recognized. Behind her, lights bathed the driveway again, and Lacey and Zoe turned to see Tessa and Jocelyn jump out of a car the second it stopped.

"I got your text," Tessa said to Zoe when they came inside. "And I thought you were going home with Oliver."

"I changed my mind," Zoe said, looking from one to the other. "I think what I really want to do is…" She took a slow, deep breath, the only other sound the splash of the Gulf waves in the distance and a chorus of cicadas. "Something I should have done a long, long time ago. I want to tell you guys a story about a girl named Bridget Lessington."

"Who the hell is that?" Tessa asked.

Zoe turned to her, eyes brimming with tears as she tried to smile, but her lips quivered. "You're looking at her."

Evan was dead silent on the way home and trudged upstairs without much of a good night. Oliver chalked it up to sleep deprivation, which was taking its toll on him as well.

Collapsing on his bed, he wished like hell Zoe had

stayed and was next to him. Under him. Wrapped around him.

Except he'd had his chance with Zoe—naked and swimming and begging for company.

What the hell was wrong with him? He certainly wanted her body, wanted her...

That's what was wrong with him. He wanted her. More than anything.

He didn't want to be her human vibrator. He didn't want to be her escape or distraction or *fuck du jour*.

She hadn't been with anyone in four years?

Well, he'd done nothing but go through the motions of sex with a woman he barely liked, let alone loved, for the past nine years. There'd been no one else, not one single indiscretion, since the day he'd left Zoe's house and driven to Adele's, his decision made.

Thank you, but he'd had enough meaningless sex to last him a lifetime. If he needed to get his rocks off, he'd do what he had to do. He was old enough, smart enough, and lonely enough to know what he wanted.

"Dad?"

He reached up and turned on the light, blinking into the brightness. "What's the matter, son?" His heart thudded when he saw that Evan had been crying. "Shit," Oliver mumbled.

"Exactly."

He almost smiled. "Come on." He patted the bed. "Sleep down here for what's left of the night."

Without a moment's hesitation, Evan scrambled onto the oversize California king, slipping right under the covers. "I miss Mom," he admitted, his voice sounding very small.

Evan might be a genius, but he was still a little boy who had been thrown into a situation he didn't understand, and his mother was an ocean away. And if Oliver, of all people, didn't get that, then he didn't deserve to have even part-time custody.

"That's perfectly understandable, Ev. It's going to be daytime in Europe soon. Do you want to call her?"

He thought about that for a minute, squirming a little, as if the need for sleep was wreaking havoc on his little body. "I thought about it, just to ask her…"

"Ask her what?"

He screwed up his features, clearly building nerve, but Oliver had no idea what for.

"Was Zoe the girl Mom used to talk about?"

Son of a bitch. Why had Adele told Evan about this history? How could a child understand? "What girl?" he asked, even though he knew.

"She said you had a girlfriend before her and you still liked her even though you married Mom."

How the hell did he answer this? He wouldn't lie, but he didn't want to paint Zoe as some kind of home-wrecker. The whole thing was too much for Evan, no matter what his brainpower.

"Well." Oliver dragged the word out a good two seconds. "If you mean did I know Zoe before your mom and I got married, yes."

"And did you like her more than Mom?"

Like. Now there was an understatement. "I liked her…differently. But I had to make a choice."

"Because of Grandpa?"

Oliver frowned. "What does your grandfather have to do with it?"

"Mom said that you married her because Grandpa Walter made you."

Actually, Adele's father wasn't exactly thrilled that his daughter walked down the aisle with a baby on the way. But he'd always liked Oliver enough to forgive him the mistake, and he'd paid for a country-club wedding with all the trimmings despite the fact that it was rushed to accommodate Adele's growing belly.

At the reception, Walter had taken Oliver to the side and offered him a career-changing position at the hospital, focusing on administration and grooming him as the next CEO of Mount Mercy.

Oliver had accepted the position, because, with a baby on the way, it was the right thing to do.

"Grandpa Walter didn't make me do anything."

"But she told me. She said Grandpa tried to kill you."

He choked back a laugh. "No, Evan, he never tried to kill me."

"Then why did she say he had a shotgun at your wedding?"

He did? Oh, of course. Realization dawned, and he knew why Evan thought that. "Did she use the expression 'a shotgun wedding,' by any chance?"

He nodded. "I figured it was because Grandpa would kill you if you didn't marry her."

"That's more or less what that means, but it's just an expression. It doesn't mean he literally had a shotgun there."

"I didn't think Grandpa Walter owned a gun."

He smiled. "I doubt it, too." He patted Evan's shoulder. "It's all history and it doesn't matter anymore. Your mom and I both love you and that's all that really—"

"So what does it mean, a shotgun wedding?"

Oliver stared at him. He could lie. He could make something up, like you would with any normal eight-year-old, but this was Evan. He'd Google the expression in the morning anyway. "It means that…"

Hadn't he ever done the math? Or did his young mind not work that way yet, despite its advanced capabilities?

"Your mom was already pregnant with you, Evan. And that's an old expression that means the mom was going to have a baby before the couple actually got married."

He waited for the reaction, which, with Evan, could range from innocent shock to a lecture on the gestation period of the mammal.

Evan didn't react at all, though. He turned away and looked up at the ceiling, saying nothing.

"So, you can stop worrying about Grandpa Walter shooting me."

"Okay."

Oliver gave his arm a pat. "This is serious stuff for the middle of the night, son. I don't think we've ever talked about anything more serious than the weather."

Evan gave him a sly smile. "Which is serious stuff."

A rush of love almost choked him. His son had a sense of humor, a heart of gold, and a hunger to know everything. Zoe was right. All he had to do was relax and parenting came naturally.

Turning, Evan wrapped his arms around the pillow, a sleepy smile working on his mouth. "Pasha's right. You and Zoe should get married."

Just when he thought he had things under control. "Pasha said that to you?"

"When we were playing Rat Screws," he said. "You

guys were gone a long time and she said something like that. I don't think she knew I heard her, but I did."

Oliver blew out a breath and stole a look at the clock. "Hey, it's almost three-thirty. Can we table this until I get some sleep? I have to be a doctor tomorrow."

"If you tell me a story."

Oliver could have cried. "You're kidding, right?"

Evan looked at him. "A good one. Like when you were my age."

"When I was your age, I…" Had a perfectly normal life in Wilmington, Delaware, with a dad who went to work every day as an engineer at DuPont and a mother who laughed a lot and played a lot and had a crazy streak that made her do impulsive things. "I liked to ride my bike a lot."

"Where'd you ride?"

"You know, the usual. School, the baseball park, library."

He lifted his head, shocked. "You were allowed to ride your bike to school when you were eight? I'm not."

"Different world. Is this a story or an inquisition?"

Evan smiled. "Story. Tell me the best thing that ever happened to you."

"You," he said without hesitation.

"Okay, the worst."

He knew that without hesitation, too. But he wouldn't tell his son. That wasn't exactly a bedtime story. He reached for the light, switching it off and bathing them in darkness.

"I broke my arm jumping off a cliff near a graveyard."

The sheets rustled as Evan sat up again. "Nuh-uh! You? You never do anything that fun."

"Damn it, Evan, I'm going to rid you of that notion if it kills me. I *love* fun."

A soft giggle was the only response.

"I'm going to prove it, too," he added. "I just haven't figured out how yet." He thought for a moment. "Anyway, the cliff. I was sailing along at about twenty miles an hour on my bike and there was this kid who dared me to jump a cliff and, man, if that isn't a lesson not to pay attention to idiots, I don't know what is. So guess what happened?"

Silence.

He leaned over and heard the steady breathing of an exhausted child.

Lying back on his own pillow, Oliver stared up into the darkness, a maelstrom of emotions zipping through him.

Why was it so hard to do this most of the time? Was it because Adele had been around and he didn't think Evan needed him? Was it because he didn't really understand this complex child with an adult's brain and a kid's soul?

Or was it because Evan reminded Oliver of himself?

The truth thudded in his chest.

And next year, when Evan turned nine, he'd be the same age Oliver was when his perfectly normal life crumbled and everything he believed to be true turned out to be a lie.

The day Oliver had come home to an empty house and climbed up the stairs, then up to the attic…then felt the whole world fall away.

Zoe's voice echoed. *I have to have an escape route…In fact, I'm terrified if I don't have one.*

There wasn't anything that scared Oliver more than a woman desperate to escape.

Chapter Fifteen

~⌒~

The soft vibration of her phone pulled Zoe from a surprisingly deep sleep, followed by a split second of confusion. Where was she?

Then she remembered last night. The disbelieving stares, the dropped jaws, the confused questions, and, finally, the silent click of the door when Tessa walked out into the gray whispers of dawn. Zoe had crawled into the guest room to sleep.

From somewhere in the house a baby cried and high-pitched women's voices replied—Jocelyn and Lacey cooing over Elijah.

The phone vibrated again and she reached for it, longing for news about Pasha and, almost as much, a call from Tessa. Oliver's deep voice greeted her with a simple, "Hey," and that was enough to send off a flock of wild hummingbirds in her stomach.

"Hey back. Any news?"

"I just talked to the hospital, and Pasha's doing very well."

She looked skyward, silently thanking whatever power ran this universe. "Should I go and get her now?"

"They're going to release her this morning and I'd like to take her straight to our clinic. We have round-the-clock care and she'll be in good hands. We have a battery of tests to do before we can actually perform the gene-therapy treatment. I want to start today."

His competence and confidence covered her like the puffy down comforter she curled under.

"What about Evan?" she asked. Funny how he already figured into her logistics.

"I'll have to figure something out."

"I'm still at Lacey's. Why don't you bring him here? Ashley can watch him."

"Perfect. We'll be over in a few minutes. You need anything?"

"Just you." The words were out before any sleepy brain cells could engage and stop her.

He didn't answer right away, sending a little wave of heat and nerves through her chest as she waited.

"I can fix that, Zoe," he finally whispered.

She closed her eyes, falling on the pillow with a dreamy smile. "Ah, the man who can fix anything."

"We'll see, won't we?"

The guest bedroom doorknob twisted and, very slowly, the door inched open, not revealing who was behind it. *Please be Tessa. Please be—*

A hand holding a coffee cup jutted through the door. "I come in peace."

Tessa. She almost melted with relief.

"Hey, I gotta go, doc." When she clicked off, she put

down the phone and took a deep breath before asking, "Two sugars and extra cream and no arsenic?"

"The garden is fresh out of arsenic," Tessa replied from behind the door.

"Then you may enter."

Tessa stepped in, her doe-brown eyes much softer than last night. "We are growing a bumper crop of humble pie and I'm planning to eat some for breakfast. Join me?"

"Oh, Tess." Zoe sighed the exclamation. "You don't owe me an apology. I owe—"

"No." Tessa waved the hand not holding the coffee, coming closer. "I lost count of how many times you said you're sorry last night. It hit triple digits, though."

Zoe took the mug and patted the bed next to her. "I feel one more bubbling up."

"Drink instead."

She did, letting the warm liquid comfort her throat and send much-needed life into her veins. "Where are Joss and Lacey?"

"Where do you think?"

She thought about that for a minute, frowning. "Listening outside the door?"

They appeared almost instantly, making Zoe laugh so hard she almost spilled the coffee. Baby Elijah stirred in Lacey's arms.

"You guys," Zoe said, shaking her head and carefully setting down the mug. "I love how predictable you are." She reached out. "Let me smell the mini-guy."

Lacey obliged, propping herself on the edge of the bed to hand the baby to Zoe. Jocelyn came around the other side, and then all four of them were on the bed, surrounding Zoe and the baby.

"Look at us, all gathered on one bed on a Sunday morning for a rehash of Saturday night," Jocelyn said. "This reminds me of dorm days."

"Only I'm not hungover," Zoe said, cuddling the tiny bundle of boy into her arms. "And there were no itty-bitty sweet wittle babies."

"Trust me, he wasn't so sweet at one, three, four-thirty and six-eighteen," Lacey said.

Zoe looked up. "Don't let the kid take all the credit for annihilating your sleep. I own that wreckage."

Elijah made a soft shuddering sigh, and they all used the excuse to stare at him and not say a word. Last night's conversation was obviously not over yet.

"We've been talking about you, Zoe," Jocelyn finally said.

"I'm sure you have," she replied. "I have provided gossip fodder for years to come."

Lacey looked indignant. "We don't gossip about each other."

Zoe lifted a brow. "You whisper about me behind my back. What's the difference?"

"The difference," Jocelyn said, "is that you gossip about strangers or people you don't care about or someone who isn't…"

"Family." Tessa supplied the word, and put her hand on Zoe's. "Because, like it or not, we are yours."

Shit. Now she was going to cry. She finally met Tessa's gaze, her brain rummaging through a lifetime of smart-ass answers for the right one. Nothing came. "Thank you," she managed, her voice cracking. "And I'm so—"

"Don't." Tessa squeezed her hand. "We know you're sorry."

"And I know you're hurt by all the years of lying. I hope that, over time, you can forgive and forget."

"Zoe, we love you," Lacey assured her. "You know that, don't you?"

She nodded, her throat tightening.

"Do you know what that means?" Jocelyn asked.

Sometimes she wondered. But not now. Not right this minute, wrapped in a lifetime of friendship. "It means I'm forgiven?"

"Before you even woke up," Lacey said.

Zoe tried to smile, but her lips quivered. "You guys always were very productive while I slept."

"You have no idea," Jocelyn told her. "I've already made a list of all the things you need to do to address this issue, personally, professionally, and emotionally."

Zoe smiled. "Ever the life coach, Joss."

"And I've gotten the phone numbers for three attorneys," Lacey added. "Right in Naples, so you can meet with them soon."

"Oh, thanks." *I think.*

"And I picked a whole sachet of herbs," Tessa said, reaching into her pocket. "I have a mix of tumeric and meadowsweet in a compress to get those swollen eyes back to normal, if you promise me no more tears today."

But she was already breaking that promise, over-whelmed by the three women who loved her more than any family could. "You guys…" Moisture blurred her vision and she attempted a laugh. "I'm sorry." She blinked, and one tear rolled right onto Elijah's cheek.

"Oh, boy," Jocelyn said, wiping it away. "Pasha would probably say that means it's going to rain on his wedding day or something."

"Speaking of Pasha," Tessa said. "Latest?"

The doorbell rang before Zoe answered. "She's good and that's Oliver. He's bringing Evan here and we're moving Pasha to the IDEA clinic to start the whole process of preparing for the gene therapy."

"I'll go let him in," Lacey said, reaching for the baby. "You better get dressed."

"I'll get you my list," Jocelyn added, following Lacey out the door.

"Thanks." Zoe didn't move for a minute, looking at Tessa and waiting for her to chime in. But Tessa didn't say a word, even though something was clearly troubling her.

"What is it, Tess? I know it's going to take you a while—"

"No." She shook her head. "That's not it. I want to…I'm sorry, Zoe."

"You have nothing to apologize for."

"I do." She took Zoe's hand and lifted it. "I'm sorry for what I said about foster children."

"Oh, that." Yeah, Tess probably did owe her an apology for those comments. "You didn't know."

"I should have been more sensitive."

"I should have been honest, so we're even."

From the living room they heard the baritone of Oliver's laugh, and Zoe's eyes widened in response. Zoe threw back the covers and leaped out of bed.

"Like him, do you?" Tessa asked.

She shrugged, but Tessa snagged Zoe's T-shirt and kept her in place. "Hey. No more secrets, Zoe Tamarin."

Zoe turned slowly, a typical retort brewing, but she tamped it down. "I more than like him, Tess, and that's what scares the holy shit out of me."

"Why? He's great, Zoe. He's smart and gorgeous and charming and obviously makes terrific babies."

Zoe laughed. "Yes, from a sociological and reproductive standpoint, he's a ten."

"Then what's the problem?"

Zoe shook her head, tugging her T-shirt free. "I can't, Tess."

"Can't what? Tell me? Take a risk? Stop moving long enough to make a commitment? We're going to work on all that for you, Zoe, and you'll be able to—"

"I can't do a whole…long-term, permanent, happily-ever-after thing."

"Also known as marriage."

Zoe waved off the word with a shrug. "Whatever you want to call it."

Tessa snorted. "That's generally what it's called."

"Whatever name you give it, Tess, I don't know how it's done."

"*What*?"

"I don't…I've never…I don't have a flipping clue what the rules are," she finally managed.

"It's not a card game, Zoe. There aren't rules and winners and losers."

Really? "I beg to differ. Lacey's a winner."

"Then I'm a loser."

Zoe closed her eyes, cursing herself for causing the hurt in Tessa's voice. "Look," she said. "This is hard for most people to understand, but I never had *parents*, Tessa. I lived in shitty foster homes and then spent the rest of my life with a crazy old lady who was ready to move every time a librarian asked for ID when we tried to take out a book."

"And that's what's stopping you?" Tessa sounded dumbfounded, and Zoe didn't blame her.

"Nothing's stopping me. Trust me, I'm doing my level best to get the man in bed."

"Just in bed?"

"Well, I tried the pool but, you know, he's a traditionalist."

"*Zoe.*" Tessa smashed a decade and a half of exasperation into both syllables of Zoe's name. "You know there's no future, and yet you want to have sex with him?"

She held out her wrist. "Pulse, beating." She touched her lower abdomen. "Body parts, female." Then her forehead. "Pituitary gland, operational. Yes, I want to have sex with him."

Tessa just stared.

"What? You've never fucked for fun, Tessa? It's *always* for a baby?" She heard her voice turn thickly defensive, and mean. God, why did she and Tessa always fight? "Sex is normal. It's natural, it's—"

"A cop-out."

Zoe closed her eyes and turned away, walking to the bathroom as fast as she could, but only because she couldn't get up enough speed to *run.*

At the end of a long day that had put Pasha through a battery of tests and examinations, Oliver and his team had almost everything they needed for an accurate diagnosis, second and third opinions, and then a final decision on the treatment.

Driving over the bridge back to Mimosa Key, they'd left the top of Zoe's Jeep down, and the wind whipped so loudly there was no chance for conversation. Oliver had given Evan permission to stay at Lacey's for dinner and then go to a late movie with Ashley and Clay, so he and Zoe drove in a comfortable quiet.

The clunk of the tires on the metal bridge, along with a sense of peace that there was truly hope for Pasha, nearly put Zoe to sleep, but Oliver's hand on her leg woke her up when they reached Mimosa Key.

"How about dinner," he suggested.

She moaned softly. "I don't want to go into a restaurant. Let's pick up."

"Choices?"

She thought about them. "There's bad burgers at the Toasted Pelican, gooey enchiladas at the SOB, or some of those lovely might-not-really-be-meat hot dogs that Charity overcharges for at the Super Min."

"The Super Min is the convenience store?" He slowed at the corner. "How about I grab a frozen pizza and beer?"

"Heavenly. Can I wait here?"

"Sure. Be right back."

Before she answered, he climbed out of the car. Almost instantly Zoe closed her eyes, drifting off to a peaceful place, too tired to think about anything but the need for—

"Ms. Tamarin?"

She jumped, blinking into the fading light and seeing a vaguely familiar face, then bolted upright when she realized who it was. "Deputy Garrison."

He nodded, coming closer. "I'd hoped to hear from you today."

Oh, yeah. She owed him a call and information. "It's Sunday," she said quickly. "I thought you'd be off today."

"So I did a little research on your aunt."

Oh, this can't be good.

"How is she feeling today? I understand they released her from the hospital."

Crap. Crap. *Crap.* He was totally on to them. Every old instinct rose up and dusted itself off; Zoe began wondering where the hell they'd put the panic bag.

Run, Zoe—

No. Not anymore. Not tonight, anyway. And she surely didn't have to give any more information to a law-enforcement officer until she talked to one of those attorneys that Lacey'd lined up.

"She's in a clinic in Naples getting a special treatment for esophageal cancer," Zoe explained. "So it'll be a week or more before you can talk to her."

"I had a hard time pinning her down on any database."

Zoe pushed up in the seat, completely awake now. How could she answer that? And she *had* given him Pasha's real name, so it was only a matter of time until he found out—

"I found seven U.S. citizens named Patricia Hobarth who met her general description and age. They're all in old-age homes, incapacitated, or dead."

She'd be the dead one.

Raking her hands through her hair, Zoe didn't say a word. She wasn't ready to do this yet. Not now, in this parking lot. Not this tired, not this…not yet.

"The dead one was wanted by the law before she passed, actually."

Fuck! "You don't say."

"Seems she was involved with a missing child."

She slid a look to the door of the convenience store, willing Oliver to come out and save her. But if he did, he'd probably spill the beans to the sheriff because it was *the right thing to do.*

Maybe it was, but she couldn't do it yet. She would, when Pasha was strong and healthy and cured and Zoe had the comfort of a lawyer on her side. Right now, she sat silent.

"But she was cleared of that murder," he added.

What? Murder? "That's not my aunt," she said.

"Oh, obviously," he replied, a little color rising. "'Fraid I have a weakness for those interesting cold cases and I got wrapped up in the reading. Anyway, be sure to call me when she gets settled so I can finish that paperwork, right?"

"I will." Relief poured through her as he stepped away. Then she felt a sudden burst of goodwill. "Oh, and— Deputy." When he turned, she gave him a genuine smile. "Please tell Gloria thanks again for helping out when Pasha collapsed. It was so sweet of her."

His shoulders slumped a little. "I would, but…" He blew out a breath and looked toward the store. "We're not together right now."

"Oh, sorry to hear that."

He came right back to the car and she silently cursed herself for not letting him leave before Oliver came out and made a full confession. "Yeah, speaking of aunts," he said with a thumb over her shoulder. "If there were an Olympic event for meddling, Charity'd take the gold."

Zoe offered a sympathetic nod. "I've heard she's got…opinions."

He laughed. "You can say that again. So you'll have to thank Gloria yourself, if you see her around Casa Blanca."

"I will. I hope things work out for you." She gave him a little wave. "I'll give you a call."

He nodded good-bye and walked to the sheriff's car parked across the lot. As he crossed in front of the store, Oliver walked out, nearly bumping into him.

Zoe held her breath as the two men greeted each other. Her fingers squeezed the leather seat until her nails dug in. *Please, Oliver, don't push this.* Don't do the right thing, not now.

After a quick second Oliver walked away, and Zoe collapsed against her seat with relief. When he got in and turned to put the bags in the back, she grabbed his face and pulled him into her for a kiss.

"What was that for?" he asked.

"Because…" Oh, she was too tired to explain. "Just because."

He smiled. "You thought I was going to tell him, didn't you?"

"Yeah."

He leaned forward and kissed her. "I've got, what? Three or four hours alone with you? You really think I want to spend it being interrogated by the local sheriff?"

"How do you want to spend it?"

He tunneled his hand under her hair and angled her face for one more kiss. "Like this."

Chapter Sixteen

ᶜ~

In a perfect world, Zoe would step out of the shower and into the guest room, where Oliver would be naked in bed, waiting for her.

Sadly, despite the promising kiss in the Super Min parking lot, this was not a perfect world. But it was close. Lacey had left the villa bathroom stocked with honeysuckle-sweet body butter, which Zoe applied liberally. And Oliver had thoughtfully laid out a pair of comfy-looking scrub pants and an ancient, well-washed Chicagoland 5K T-shirt for her to change into.

Although she'd have happily waltzed back downstairs wearing just a towel and a smile. Because…that had to be what he meant by that kiss, right?

The wait was over, the fight finished? Easy, breezy, slightly crazy sex was on the horizon?

Because if he freaking wanted to talk, she was out. She didn't want to talk or think or analyze the situation. She didn't want to review the medical issues or weigh the chances of success. She didn't want to rehash the past or fantasize about a future.

Lord, she *really* didn't want to do to that.

She just wanted the sweetest, fastest, loveliest escape she could find…in Oliver's arms. In Oliver's bed.

Pulling the shirt over her head, she let her hair soak the shoulders, not bothering to do more than quickly towel-dry it. Then she stepped into the scrubs, pulled the drawstring as far as it would go—the pants still hung low on her hips—and tossed a quick look in the mirror. Fine. Let's…

She looked again.

Okay, maybe not completely fine. She brushed a finger along the slightly violet circle under her eye, a color that should really be called sleep-deprived indigo. The compress had made her bags go away, but her cheeks were pale, the whites of her eyes a lovely shade of road-map red.

Maybe she *should* go down in a towel and distract him. Because, really, who wanted to take the walking wounded to bed?

Oliver Bradbury, that's who.

For once, the voice was dead-on. That kiss had said sex and she was answering the siren call.

She padded downstairs, spying Oliver in deep thought on the patio, shirtless in a pair of cargo shorts, a beer bottle in his hand, his eyes focused on the silver sky as dusk fell hard once the sun was down.

She stepped outside, but he didn't move.

"Hey."

He turned at the sound of her voice, his expression dead serious. "Hey."

"Are you all right? Is everything okay?"

He nodded, then dropped his gaze over her. "Damn, you kill a pair of scrubs."

"You like?" She lifted up the T-shirt to show her belly, fully exposed as the pants skimmed her pelvic bone. He stared right there and heat coiled through her.

Thank God she wasn't going to get turned down again.

"I'll have some, thank you." She walked to him and took the beer out of his hand, "Pizza in already?"

"Yep."

"I love when you cook." She took a long, deep draw on the beer bottle, the biting brew cold on her dry throat. When she finished, she held up the half-empty bottle with a sly smile, shaking the liquid and peering into the bottle. "Now I suppose you want me to read the foam like Pasha."

"If only that were possible."

She pulled out a chair, sat down, and propped her feet on his lap. "You don't believe Pasha can see things?"

"Not for a minute." He instantly wrapped his hands around her feet. "She's intuitive and understands people, like you said." Long, strong fingers took ownership of her size-sixes, rubbing a thumb over an arch, sending chills over her body and tingles up her spine.

"So you think she's a charlatan in addition to being a kidnapper? Well, thank God she's not a murderer, like that stupid sheriff tried to imply."

He was staring at the logo on the T-shirt, the entire top half wet enough that it stuck to her skin. "What?"

She almost laughed, the feeling of victory so close. Under her foot, she felt his cock stir and grow, and another wave of heat and satisfaction rolled over her. Finally.

"Foot rub, please."

But his hands were still. "What did the sheriff say?"

"Nothing." *Please touch, not talk.*

"She was wanted for murder?"

"God, no." Thankfully, he started massaging again, his knuckles pressing under her foot and hitting some sweet spot in her brain. Perfect.

"What did he say?" Oliver asked.

"He was searching databases for Patricia Hobarth and found one who was involved with a murder, but she's…oh, please don't stop that. In fact…" She closed her eyes and dropped her head back. "Put your fingers between my toes, Oliver."

"I love it when you talk dirty."

"And suck them."

He lifted her foot to his mouth and she laughed softly but didn't even open her eyes. When nothing happened, she wiggled. "They're clean."

Cupping her heel, he stroked the skin again, running a finger over her baby toenail. "Who paints their toes aquamarine?"

"Girls." She wiggled again. "Are you going to suck them or not?"

"Then what?"

"Then work your way north, big boy." She tugged at the scrub pants, revealing a turquoise ankle bracelet.

Very slowly, he lowered her foot, silent.

Aw, really, Oliver? She lifted her head and looked at him from under her lashes. "Is toe sucking against the no-sex rules?"

"I don't have…" He let his voice drift off. "Yeah, it is."

Blowing out a disgusted breath, she yanked her feet away and stood suddenly. "I'm starving." She grabbed the beer bottle and walked into the kitchen, her head already buzzing with options. Through the front door, out the garage. There were plenty of ways to escape.

But she paused in the middle of the kitchen, waiting for his footstep, waiting for him to come in and grab her and kiss her and tell her he was kidding and drag her off to...

Silence.

She turned to see that he hadn't moved. He still stared at the sky, his back perfectly straight, a man clearly at war with himself.

Well, she did not want to be this battle's casualty. She hissed in a breath, her own private war raging. She didn't want to run, damn it. She didn't *want* to leave him.

He didn't want her. No one did. The only person who ever really wanted her was lying in a clinic, sedated, and dying.

She looked again.

He still hadn't moved, but sat like a freaking statue...staring. What was he thinking about? What was he feeling?

He doesn't want you. Could he make it any clearer?

With a soft grunt Zoe set the bottle on the counter and felt something old and familiar and hot in her belly, a pressure that felt like it could explode or at least come out in the form of a primal scream.

Holding it back, she walked out of the kitchen, through the living room, and stood at the front door, her hand on the knob.

Couldn't she stay? Couldn't she tell him about all this pain that bubbled up and threatened to suffocate her? Or, better yet, couldn't she just lose herself in sex and sleep and forget everything?

No.

She turned the knob, opened the door, and his hand landed on her shoulder like a vise grip.

"Where the hell do you think you're going?"

"Home."

"You don't have one."

She closed her eyes under the impact of the words. "Ooh, below the belt, brother."

"Why?"

She shook her head. "You don't know me at all, do you?"

"What does that mean?"

"It means you don't even know what matters to me, and I don't mean sex." She stared ahead at the door as she spoke. "Do you have any idea how much I want a home? A place to put down roots and stay and grow and live and die?"

"Then why don't you get that?"

She choked softly. "I'm leaving."

"You're not running away, Zoe."

Oh, yes, she was. She had jerked away from his touch and made one step onto the front porch before he snagged the T-shirt and pulled her right back into the house, whirling her around. She was stunned when she looked at him.

His eyes were as red as hers, and, good God... "Are you crying?"

He blinked, and, sure enough, there were tears. "You're not running away, Zoe," he repeated, the words more mantra than demand.

"What's wrong with you?"

He pushed the door closed with one hand, still holding her with the other. "You're not running—"

She put her hand over his mouth. "I get it. What is wrong with you, Oliver? Why are you crying?"

"I'm not," he lied, swallowing what had to be a basketball in his throat. "I'm just so fucking sick of you leaving me." With both hands on her shoulders he pushed her against the door. The carved mahogany pressed into her bones.

"Well, I'm so fucking sick of you turning me down."

He drew in another breath, frustration and fury coming off him in waves so thick she could practically taste his anguish. "Zoe, I…" He put his head on her forehead, his grip growing tighter on the wet fabric of the T-shirt. "Don't leave me."

"I feel like I'm throwing myself at a man who doesn't want me."

"I want you." Pressing his whole body against her, he answered that question with a firm and mighty erection. "See?"

Her hips, the little traitors, rocked right into him. "You don't want me with the right head, Oliver. I can feel you're a human male and I'm in a wet T-shirt. That doesn't mean you want *me*."

"What do you want me to say?" He pulled her a little higher, making her crotch slide against the length of him, burying his face in her neck.

"I want you to say…" She lost the fight and closed her fingers over his arms, sliding up to his shoulders, riding that hard-on one more time just for the sheer thrill it sent through her body. "Yes."

He grunted and dragged one hand over her breast, cupping and caressing.

"Say it, Oliver."

He slid his hand under the T-shirt, palming her flesh, tweaking her nipple.

"Say it." Just say *yes*.

He half laughed, half moaned, his other hand over her hips, tugging at the pants, taking them right over her backside.

"Say it, damn it."

Pulling back, he used both hands to push down the drawstring pants, and they fluttered to her ankles. His eyes were still damp, but they were also dark with arousal, his jaw set, his nostrils flaring as he unsnapped his shorts and pushed them down. His erection sprang forward, pulling her gaze as it pulsed and glistened with a drop of semen.

That said yes, but still he didn't.

"Oliver." She mouthed his name, unable to find her voice or possibly stand for one more second. "Please say it."

He lowered his face to hers, closing his eyes as he put his mouth against her lips, making her dizzy with need and curiosity.

"Say it," she murmured into his kiss.

"I love you."

Chapter Seventeen

~⁓

With three dangerous and dizzying words, Oliver lost the fight. Emotion won. Desire won. Risk won. Need won. *Zoe won.*

Common sense, self-preservation, and any hope of not getting hurt folded like a paper house in gale-force winds. Everything collapsed with one confession, three words that hadn't stopped being true for nine long years.

He loved her.

The admission rocked him, but Oliver couldn't deny the truth as he laid Zoe down on the bed and kneeled over her. The T-shirt had ridden up, exposing her torso, her hips and the sweet, sweet slender strip of dark blonde hair between her legs, the scent of flowers and lemon and woman actually making his mouth water.

Good God, he couldn't stop looking; his fingers aching to touch her everywhere.

"You've seen me before, Oliver."

"So I have."

"Then why are you staring?"

"Trying to decide where to start. Top or bottom."

She propped up on her elbows, sandy-colored curls cascading over the still-damp shoulder of his shirt. "Middle."

His cock throbbed between them, too hard and sensitive for much foreplay. Way, way too anxious to get back to where he loved to be most…inside Zoe. As far as he could go, bearing down with everything he had, not letting her run away.

"Middle it is." He lowered his head to her navel, curling his tongue into the precious indentation. Instantly, her fingers tunneled into his hair and her hips rose, inviting him lower.

He trailed kisses over her abdomen, flicking his tongue over that tuft of hair, showering kisses on her thighs. He kissed his way back up to her breasts, shoving the T-shirt up to fully expose every inch of her, sucking one, caressing the other.

"You skipped my toes again."

"I don't want your toes," he said gruffly, licking her nipple until it budded under his tongue. "I want you."

She moaned softly, reaching down to stroke his hard-on, coaxing him between her legs. Her fingers were hot and strong, sure and fast, easily working him the way she always did.

"Condom," she murmured.

"Nightstand," he answered, reaching over to pull the drawer open.

"Lacey thinks of everything."

"I thought of it." He raised himself off her to get the foil packet.

"When?"

"Move-in day." He tore with his teeth. "After the pool. Well, after the second cold shower after the pool."

She took the package from him. "I'll do that," she said. "I want to stroke you."

"Be a nice change from doing it myself."

She closed her hands over him, looking up. "You take care of business a lot, do you ? Thought you were married for all those years."

He snorted.

"It's hot," she said, pumping him once, hard and fast, making him suck in a breath.

"What is?"

"Thinking about you jacking off."

"You have your vibrator, I have my fist."

She stroked again, slowly, staring at his dick, her mouth slack, which might be the sexiest damn thing he'd ever seen.

"Shower or bed?" she asked.

"Yes. You?"

She smiled. "I like the bathtub. But once in a while on a long drive alone in the car."

He almost lost it in her hand. "You make yourself come when you're driving?"

Her eyes widened. "I know, right? What crime *won't* I commit?"

He wanted to laugh, but she punctuated the question with another squeeze, while she cupped his balls with her other hand. Fiery sparks flashed up his body and a few gallons of blood rushed to put out the flames. He grew bigger in her hand, dying to get inside her but unwilling to stop this…this intimacy.

"What do you think about, Zoe?" His voice was barely

a whisper, since talking took way too much of the energy he needed not to shoot right into her hand.

"I think…" She leaned up again, easing him closer to her mouth. "About that time…" She flicked her tongue over the wet tip. "We did it on the stairs up to your apartment."

He grunted when she put her mouth on him, the memory of driving into her on the hardwood steps at three in the morning still one of the sexiest five minutes of crazy in his whole life.

"Me, too," he admitted.

She lifted her head, looking up at him. "We were good together, Oliver."

"We *are* good together," he said, reaching for the foil packet she'd set on the bed. "Let me show you."

She didn't argue, thank God, but pulled out the condom and placed it on his head, then slid it so maddeningly slowly he thought he might cry. Lying back, she spread her legs and gave him a silent look of invitation.

He braced himself, feasting on every move and muscle of her body as she let him in, her soft, soft sigh of contentment as he filled her up. Their eyes met as he started to move faster, and hers shuttered closed as the sensations took over.

Everything was new to him. The angle of her face when she turned her head, the shape of her breasts as they moved with her body, and the intense, tight, squeeze of her body around him. All new, all brand new.

She stopped moving suddenly, reaching up to touch his face. "I just lied to you."

He slowed a little, causing a small insurrection in his balls. "What?"

"I don't think about the time on the steps."

Forcing himself to focus and stop moving, he looked at her. "What do you think about?"

"I don't. If I think about you too much, I start to cry." A single tear escaped from the side of her eyes. "So I don't think. I…escape. I go away in my mind."

He lowered himself, wrapping her narrow frame in his arms. "Don't go away now, Zoe. Stay here, right here. With me. Don't go anywhere."

She nodded, biting her lip, as he started pumping into her again. He plunged deeper and faster, finally letting go of his last shred of control to hold her as close and tight as he could and spill everything into her.

A second later she shook with her own loss of control, murmuring his name, biting her lip, and then giving into an orgasm that pulsed around him. Immediately, she pulled him closer, wrapped her arms around his neck, and clung to him as if she would never let go.

They stayed that way until he slipped out of her and the sheen of sweat on their skin cooled under the air-conditioning. For what seemed like the most perfect ten minutes of his life, Zoe didn't voluntarily move a single muscle. She breathed quietly, and her heart slowed to a steady, normal beat. But everything else was…still.

Until the high-pitched beep from the oven reminded them of dinner.

Only then, when he'd slowly eased himself to the side, did she move, and that was to trap him with her leg.

"Let it burn," she said. "I can't get up."

"This is the longest time you've ever been still," he whispered.

He could feel her cheek smile against his. "A magic orgasm."

"Better than anything at sixty on the highway?"

"Eighty."

"Please tell me you're lying about that."

She laughed softly and he inched away, dealing with the condom and then pulling up the light blanket from the foot of the bed to cover her. "Stay here. We deliver."

"No kidding." She rolled around like a contented cat while he stopped in the bathroom, washed up, and grabbed boxers. In the kitchen, he assembled a tray of pizza and beer. When he came back, he half expected an empty bed, but she hadn't moved, except to take off the T-shirt and toss it on the floor.

He put the tray on the bed, gave her a fresh bottle of beer, and sat cross-legged as she pulled herself up. The blanket fell away, revealing the sweet slope of her breasts as she lifted her bottle for a toast. "To masturbation."

He choked softly. "The end of it, you mean."

"For now."

With a soft grunt, he lowered his bottle. "Already looking for an exit strategy, Zoe?"

"Just covering my bases."

"Well, cover your headlights instead so I can stop staring and start eating."

She grinned and, of course, did exactly the opposite, squaring her shoulders to jut out her breasts, still pink from handling and so round and sweet and soft.

"Think of them as visual aids for when you're alone again."

He dragged his gaze to her face. "Why should I be alone again?"

She didn't answer. Instead she took a slice of pizza and held it poised to her lips. "Do you have to turn our post-sex pizza party into a commitment conversation?"

Hell, yes, he did. "What do you have against commitments?"

She took a bite, chewed, and shrugged. "What do you have against masturbation?"

"It's lonely, depressing, and leaves you worse off than before."

"Then you're doing it wrong."

"Zoe." He slammed his beer onto the nightstand. "Why are you doing this?"

"Why are you?" she asked, far more calmly than he had. When he didn't answer, she plucked a piece of cheese from the topping, stretched it, then opened her mouth like a bird to feed it to herself.

"Because we just made—"

She held out her hand, a strand of cheese on her lip and fire in her eyes. "No, we didn't."

"Then what the fuck do you call it?"

"I call it…that." She raised an eyebrow. "Fucking."

He let both hands fall with a disgusted sigh. "Why do you have to do this?"

"Oliv—"

"Why do you have to get all tough and funny and hard-ass and put that goddamn brick wall around you?" He ground out the words, fighting the fury that rose.

She looked at him, almost imperceptibly nodding.

"What?" he demanded.

"She's right."

"Who is?"

"Pasha. She's right about you and all that anger you carry around. Who are you mad at? Me? I just spread my legs for you and gave you my *all*, Oliver Bradbury. You took down the wall and got *inside me*." She kneeled a little, narrowing her eyes. "That's all I wanted. Take it or *leave it*."

Each word pushed him farther away. Each word reminded him that whenever he trusted a woman, she proved not to be worthy of that trust. Zoe was no exception.

"Just tell me why," he demanded.

"I don't know any other way." Her tone was flippant and pissed him off more than what she'd said.

"What? When we were together we were just 'fucking'? Is that right, Zoe? You don't call that a commitment."

She angled her head. "Now we're fighting."

"Can you see this from my point of view?"

"Can you just be a normal guy who wants sex without being tied down?"

He pushed his paper plate away and practically leaped off the bed. "I can't do it," he said roughly. "I can't just…do it. And I don't know why or how you can." He froze and stared at her. "Do you not trust me? Is that it?"

"I trust you," she said softly, looking down at the food as if she couldn't handle the intensity of his gaze. "It's me I don't trust."

Air came out of him in a whoosh. Well, that made two of them who didn't trust her.

"I'm not hungry anymore." He went into the bathroom, closed the door, and turned on the shower.

Maybe she'd come in and they'd wash away all this…mess. Hey, an idiot could hope, right?

He stayed in the shower until he depleted the supply of hot water in the tank and the spray turned ice cold. And, of course, she didn't come in.

Still he let the water sting against his back, then his face.

He closed his eyes and tried to picture Zoe…Zoe on the stairs of his apartment.

But when he imagined those stairs, they became another set of wooden stairs. Up higher and higher, the house quiet and empty…but for the sounds of a child's footfall on each step.

All the way to the third-floor attic.

With a push that nearly broke the shower door, he knocked the glass open, stepping out without bothering to turn off the spray. He had to tell her. She had to know.

"Zoe!" He threw open the door and blinked into the light. She'd left the room immaculate. The bed made. The pizza and beer gone.

All that remained were his scrub pants, fallen on the floor with the legs curved in the shape of a heart.

Had she done that on purpose?

He stood and listened for a moment for any sound, but, of course, she was gone.

He'd lost the battle…and her.

Chapter Eighteen

～

Pasha reached for Matthew, but just as her fingers closed over his narrow shoulder, he disappeared into the ground. Then he reappeared, but he was different this time. Instead of Matthew, it was Evan.

Behind him, a moonbow flickered in the sky.

True love will return.

The true love of a mother for her son?

"Miss Pasha, time to wake up, dear."

She startled at the voice, then stayed very still on the bed, the room dim but for a small green light on something electronic in the distance. A machine hummed somewhere, a soft, lulling sound.

"I know it's early and you're probably foggy from the sedatives."

The nurse's voice pulled Pasha out of her reverie, but Wanda was so sweet and soft-spoken that she didn't mind. Her strong hand landed on Pasha's shoulder, comforting and sure.

"We need to do a bone scan now, love."

"Mmm." Pasha drifted away. What time was it? Morning? Evening? She had no idea anymore. It was all sleep and dreams. Dreams about Matthew.

And Evan. That sweet little boy who made her want to live again.

"The drugs make you groggy, don't they?"

"Not really. I'm just…" What was this feeling? So unusual and unfamiliar. She was… "Happy."

That was it. She was happy. How strange was that? She still didn't open her eyes, for fear that the happiness would float away like a soap bubble.

"Drugs can do that, too," Wanda said with a chuckle, making Pasha picture the nurse's beautiful chocolate-colored face breaking into a glorious smile. She had lovely teeth and such a warm, natural smile. It made Pasha feel good. Everything made Pasha feel good.

"Very happy." That had to be Evan's influence. There was no other explanation.

"Well, that's nice, Miss Pasha. Not too many people in this situation are happy."

"Not too many get what I got." A second chance…with Evan.

"The T-cell gene therapy? You can say that again. There are hundreds of patients trying to see Dr. Bradbury and Dr. Mahesh. Getting on the list for this procedure is like being handed a miracle."

No, Evan was like being handed a miracle. An eight-year-old miracle and another opportunity to love a little boy.

She barely opened her eyes as she was taken down the hall to another room and put on a new table. Still that didn't change how happy she felt.

"Don't move, Pasha," the nurse said, ever so slightly tightening her grip. "I need to have you right in the perfect place before I start the scan."

Pasha tried to keep every muscle in her body completely motionless, but one of them refused to cooperate. "Is it okay if I smile, Wanda?"

Another soft chuckle. "I can't say anyone's ever asked me that going in for a scan. I think it's fine if you smile."

So she did.

"You know, Miss Pasha, you are such an inspiration to me."

"I am?"

"Absolutely. A positive attitude is the most powerful thing you can bring to this party." The nurse situated Pasha on the bed and patted her arm. "Is it all the gypsy hoo-hah stuff you were telling me about before? When you looked at the ice in your water and said those two cubes meant two people who were supposed to be together had found each other?"

Pasha nodded. "That's right, Wanda. You have a good memory."

"Not like I'd forget something like that. So that's why you're smiling? Here—I'm going to lift your head ever so slightly, dear."

As Wanda's strong hands slid under Pasha's neck, a warm, trusting feeling rolled over her. She liked Wanda. She liked everyone right now; she really hadn't been this happy in years.

And not because she was finally going to die and free her darling Zoe. But because—

"You'll be having a full blood transfusion in the next few days and I hope you'll be smiling through that, too."

"Oh, you never know. I might be smiling." Heck, she might be laughing by then. Laughing and loving and so happy to be alive. "I'm not afraid of anything anymore."

The nurse tilted her head, and said, "Let me guess. You love Jesus?"

"Well…" She'd never been particularly religious, so no. Of course, she could lie. It certainly wouldn't be the first time in her life. "He's okay."

"Because the people who are thinking about God are usually the ones who are calm during this part of the whole thing."

"It's not Jesus who's making me happy," Pasha replied.

"Family?"

"Not exactly. I mean my family, most of it, is gone."

Wanda nodded knowingly. "So, you think the worst that could happen is Dr. Bradbury fails and you get to see someone you love again, don't you, dear? Who's up there? Your husband?"

She looked right into Wanda's trusting eyes, the trance still carrying her on a cloud, the blood in her veins not boiling in fear for the first time in so, so long. Instead, she felt at peace and certain of everything. So calm and detached and, yet, so happy.

"My son," she rasped. "My son, Matthew Hobarth, is up there."

Wanda closed her eyes and sighed. "Oh, my dear. Your son. The hardest thing in the world to lose a child, I say. God knows, I've seen some mighty miserable parents in here."

"It hurts," she agreed.

"I'm going to slide your shoulder a little to the left now. How old was your son when you lost him, Miss Pasha?"

"Seven and a half."

Wanda gasped softly. "Oh, Lord. So young. I'm very, very sorry to hear that." She patted Pasha's shoulder gently. "Was it cancer?"

Pasha took a slow, deep breath, not answering.

"I hope you have lovely memories of him," Wanda said quietly.

"I do. I think of him laughing, climbing a tree on our last day together, getting a chocolate-milk mustache as a reward, cheering a card game win, finishing a puzzle. No, no that's not Matthew." She felt her brows draw into a frown, but, honestly, that effort was more than she had in her right now. "That was Evan," she finished.

"Evan? You mean Dr. Bradbury's little boy? He's something, isn't he?"

"Oh, yes. He's wonderful. He reminds me of Matthew."

"That's nice. Evan's smart like his daddy and…" Wanda laughed softly. "Not really anything like his mother. Which is a good thing."

Pasha might be in a little bit of a fog, but not so much that she couldn't recognize an opportunity when it was presented to her. "So why did he marry her?"

Wanda looked surprised by the question. "I surely don't know Dr. Bradbury's business," she said. "But his former wife's father is a bigwig in the medical community. Now you didn't hear that from me, Miss Pasha."

Pasha smiled. "And you didn't hear about my son from me," she whispered. "I have secrets, you know."

"I bet you do," she replied with a soft laugh. "Now, I need you to hold very still, sweetheart, because this long metal arm is going to pass over your whole body and scan your bones. If you move, we have to do it all again."

"Okay."

"Anything you want to get out before we start?" Wanda asked. "You know, another smile, a quick prayer, more secrets?"

"One more secret," she said, even groggier than when she'd first awakened. "One more," she mumbled.

"Go right ahead. Your secret is safe with me, darling."

The trance was starting again, the lulled-to-sleep feeling where there was no pain, no worry, no trouble, no secrets. No secrets. "My name's not really Pasha," she whispered.

"Oh?" Wanda had a little smile in her voice, as if she liked this secret. "What is it?"

"Patricia."

That strong hand patted her again. "Pasha suits you much better. It's a great nickname."

"Not a nickname," she said. Then something sort of broke off in her head, like a branch snapping from a dead tree, needing to be pruned. "And my little boy didn't die of cancer."

On her shoulder, Wanda's hand stilled. "Oh, really." She sounded like she might be searching for the right thing to say. But what can anyone say? "What happened to him?"

"He was killed." She wanted that dried old branch gone, forever.

"That's a—"

"Murdered."

Wanda's hand lifted as she let out a slight gasp. "Oh my God, Pasha. That's awful. I'm so sorry for you."

"It was awful." But she had Evan now, and he was every bit as dear and precious as her son.

"Don't think about that," Wanda said. "Think about that little boy climbing trees and drinking chocolate milk. And hold still for me, dear. Here comes the arm."

Pasha drifted off, vaguely aware of that humming again, in her head and in her heart.

When Zoe arrived at the clinic she was braced to see Oliver, but a much younger version greeted her when she walked into Pasha's room.

"Hello, Evan," she said when he looked up. "Didn't expect you to be here."

"My dad didn't want to ask you to babysit since he figured you'd want to spend time here today."

A little bit of guilt zinged. She had offered to watch him and then done her disappearing act. Although Oliver hadn't called her all morning, either. So they were both on eggshells.

"Do you know where Pasha is?"

"The nurse said she's getting tests, then coming back here." He reached into his back pocket and pulled out a deck of cards. "Wanna play Rat Screws while we wait?"

It was, actually, the last thing she wanted to do. "Sure. Where's your dad?"

"Meetings, I think."

She sat down opposite him at the tiny round table by the window, studying the face that was so much like the one that had haunted Zoe's dreams all night. "Is he going to be here today?"

Evan nodded and started to shuffle, eyeing her as he did.

"What?" she asked after an uncomfortable moment.

"So you and my dad knew each other a long time ago, huh?"

Whoa. She hadn't seen that one coming. "Very long time ago."

"Before Mom."

Actually, after. "More or less." She gestured toward the cards. "You gonna split that deck, cowboy?"

"I'm counting the cards."

"With your thumbs?"

He nodded, then split the deck and handed her half. "I can remember what order they come out in, too, so I know if you've been through your deck once what the next card will be."

Her jaw unhinged. "You would be quite valuable in Vegas, you know."

"That's what your aunt Pasha said."

Zoe snorted. "She would."

"I like her. 'Cept when she calls me Matthew."

"She does?" Zoe shook her head. "She likes to make up names for people. You can go first."

He put a card down and Zoe responded with a king, then he slapped down three more cards and the last one was a jack, so Zoe had to put one down. A seven.

"Oh." She made like she'd been shot. "You get the jack."

"That's how you win this game," Evan announced as he scooped up the pile.

"Sure is."

"Can I ask you a question, Zoe?" He looked up with eyes so big and deep her heart nearly folded.

What did he want to know? About his father? About their past? She took a deep breath, prepared at least to color the truth if not lie outright to protect this child. "Sure, what do you need to know?"

"It's kind of, I don't know, out of line for me to ask."

"Out of line is my specialty. Fire away."

He leaned forward. "Would you talk my dad into getting me a dog?"

"Is that Evan I hear?" Pasha's voice came from the hall, sparing Zoe the answer.

"Hi, Pasha." Evan popped up from the table, his face bright. When the nurse wheeled her in, Pasha's expression matched.

An entirely unbidden thought popped into Zoe's head: What if they really *could* work this thing out? If Pasha could live and be free, maybe Zoe really could stop running and Evan could stay with them and all four of them could live in a big house together. Forever. Maybe they could have another child, and that dog Evan wanted.

Inside her chest, a pain as palpable as the one Pasha complained of gripped Zoe so hard she couldn't breathe. She had no right to have fantasies like that, like some kind of fairy—

"Zoe, are you all right, honey?" From her wheelchair, Pasha scowled. "You look worse than I feel."

"Oh, I'm fine." She stood quickly to give Pasha a kiss hello. "I'm just…" *Dreaming like a fool.* "So happy to see you looking bright and chipper."

"I don't know how bright I am, but they said all the tests are done for today and now I can rest." She turned to Evan, putting a hand on his face. "How wonderful to see you, little one."

He gave a shy smile. "Hi, Pasha."

"Oh, I know, you're not little," she teased. "And I see you brought the cards for us."

The nurse came around the front of the chair. "I don't think you're going to be playing cards, Miss Pasha. Dr.

Bradbury has strict rest orders today since the treatment begins tomorrow and you need to sleep."

Pasha's shoulders slumped like a disappointed child. "Right away?"

"Well, let's get you into bed and we'll see."

The nurse, Wanda, easily got Pasha into the bed and smoothed the covers. The two of them obviously shared a nice rapport. For the second time in a few minutes, Zoe let contentment and hope roll over her.

"Thank you," Zoe said to the nurse when she'd finished. "I promise we won't keep her up too long."

Wanda cocked her head toward the hall and gave Zoe a look to come out and talk to her. Evan settled into the chair next to the bed, so Zoe gave her aunt another pat on the shoulder.

"One game," she said sternly. "And no swearing. Either of you."

They both gave her fake smiles, neither one willing to make a promise they knew they wouldn't keep. She rolled her eyes and followed Wanda into the hall.

"She really does need to sleep," the nurse said. "Tomorrow's a full transfusion and that's going to really exhaust her."

"I promise we'll cut out in a few minutes." She glanced down the hall, unsure what she should do about Evan. "Is Dr. Bradbury here?"

"He's looking at the bone-scan results," she said. "And I can tell you that test gave us some excellent news."

"Really?"

She nodded, her dark eyes dancing. "This is unofficial, but I can tell you that scan showed no cancer in the bone."

"Was there a chance of that?"

"There's always a chance of that. The reason it's good in this case is because they can focus on the soft tissues. I know you have other oncologists giving outside opinions on the test results, but assuming they agree, there's going to be a T-cell transfusion here tomorrow." She reached for Zoe's arm. "That's historic and exciting for all of us. Thank you for giving us this chance."

Zoe took the nurse's hand. "Thank you for being so kind to her and making her comfortable. It's made everything so much easier."

"Oh, I haven't done much," Wanda said. "She really has a good attitude."

Some laughter came from the room, reminding Zoe that Evan had a lot to do with Pasha's change in attitude.

"You can't underestimate how important that is," the nurse continued. "Especially after what she's been through, it's understandable."

Had Pasha told this nurse what she'd been through? Impossible. "You mean collapsing and going to the ER the other night?"

"She told me everything."

"Everything?"

Wanda waved her hand. "Don't be shocked. People tell me stuff all the time. I think it's the combination of the dark test room and the lorazepam. That stuff's like truth serum. No surprise she'd mention her son."

"Her *son*?" Zoe had to be sure she'd heard that right.

"Well, I guess he'd be your uncle, if she's your great-aunt."

But she's not my great-aunt. "My…uncle?"

"She said he died when he was seven, so obviously you never knew him but, oh, what a tragedy. It's no wonder sometimes she wants to end it all and be with him, but to-day she seemed quite happy about being alive."

Zoe had no idea what the nurse was talking about. "He died when he was seven?" she asked.

Wanda gave her big eyes. "And how awful that he was murdered."

Murdered? For a second it felt like the world slipped away and left Zoe behind. All she could hear was the sher-iff's words.

But she was cleared of that murder.

He'd been talking about another Patricia Hobarth. *Hadn't he?* Cold trickled through her veins.

"Don't look so stricken, honey. The drugs bring out all the skeletons." Wanda patted her arm. "Really, don't worry. Secrets are safe with me. I won't even remind her that she told me her real name is Patricia."

All the happiness and hope started to seep out of the bal-loon that she'd dared let fill her chest.

"Zoe, there you are."

She turned to see Oliver's masculine silhouette moving down the hall, backlit by the window streaming morning light. Another wave of dizziness threatened, but this one was more primal and feminine, caused by the width of his shoulders, the certainty in his stride.

"Hey." It was all she could manage in the face of the on-slaught.

He reached her and gave a slight, secret smile. Had he forgiven her for disappearing last night? Hell, had she for-given herself for the little temper tantrum? She'd certainly suffered for it overnight.

From the looks of his face, he hadn't suffered at all.

"I bet Wanda told you the good news."

Wanda laughed as she walked away. "I'm lousy with a secret."

Then would she be spreading the news about…*Pasha's son*?

"We'll progress with the transfusion as soon as the oncologist reports are in." Oliver reached to touch her shoulder. "You okay?"

"I am," she finally said, forcing a smile. "I'm…I'm really sorry," she said suddenly. "I shouldn't have left."

He angled his head, a rare look of uncertainty on his face—rare at least in these surroundings, where he never looked less than sure of everything.

"I freaked out," she admitted before he could answer. "It was really intense and I—"

Evan stepped into the hallway, interrupting the conversation. "She's asleep!" He announced, devastated.

"That's what we want, son," Oliver told him. "I've given her something to keep her resting today. Tomorrow's going to be the biggest day of her life." He turned to Zoe, a spark of warmth in his eyes. "First day of the rest of it, I hope."

"What should I do, Dad?"

Zoe knew what *she* wanted to do. Internet searches for…the truth.

"Well, I guess you could hang around here or…" Oliver gave a beseeching look to Zoe.

She pulled herself together and looked down at the little boy. The one Pasha called *Matthew*. She *had* to know more about what that nurse had told her.

"You know what?" Oliver said suddenly. "I've put everything aside for Pasha today and we're ready to roll tomorrow." He put an arm around Zoe and reached for Evan's hand. "Let's do something together."

Oh, the fantasy balloon was inflating again, damn it.

"Like what, Dad?"

"Anything you want," Oliver replied.

Evan looked up at Zoe with a longing so clear she could practically hear him barking his plea to her: *Tell him I want a dog!*

Zoe inched back, shaking her head. "You two go off and have a father-and-son day. I've got...stuff to do."

Disappointment flickered in Oliver's eyes. Of course he thought she was running away, bailing before things got too stable and steady.

But that wasn't true. Still, she couldn't tell him. Not until she knew more.

"You go." She eased away, toward the door. "I'm going to whisper good-bye to Pasha." She escaped before either one could argue, slipping into the room where Pasha slept.

She hesitated for a second, then walked to the bed, taking in the peaceful countenance of a woman she thought she knew.

Pasha wasn't capable of murder; Zoe would bet her life on that.

But then, hadn't Zoe bet her life on everything Pasha said and did? Hadn't she let this woman make every call and dictate every move and insist on a lifetime of lying?

Had Pasha given up everything for Zoe, or had Zoe given up everything for her? *Everything*.

The fairy tale. The family. The love of a good man. *Everything*.

What was she *doing*? Oliver was offering it to her again. And her answer? To run, of course. Maybe she thought she was running to smooth out this new wrinkle—whatever it was, however it affected them—but she was running none-theless.

Damn it. When would she stop? When would she run *to* something wonderful instead of *away*?

With one last glance at Pasha, Zoe spun around and darted to the door, looking down the hall to catch that same silhouette and a much smaller one right next to it.

"Oliver! Evan!"

They both turned.

"Wait for me!"

Chapter Nineteen

~

Oliver actually heard his own breath hiss through his teeth when he turned and saw Zoe running down the clinic hall, her eyes shiny and sparkling.

"Dog," she said, a little breathless.

"What?"

"Yes! We're getting a dog!" Evan jumped noisily.

Oliver opened his mouth to protest, but when Zoe slipped her slender fingers into his hand and tugged him, any chance of saying no to anyone about anything disappeared.

"We're getting a dog?" He echoed Evan's statement, only less enthusiastically.

Zoe didn't answer, but fished her keys out of her pocket. "We'll take my Jeep so there's room to get a crate and all the stuff and…" She looked at Evan. "A nice big pooch."

He jumped again and Oliver finally found his common sense. "Whoa, just one second." He shook his head, hard. "Not so fast."

"Dad!"

She looked from one to the other, settling on Oliver. "Okay, what exactly are your issues with a dog?"

"Taking care of it."

"I will!" Evan said.

Oliver rolled his eyes. "What about when you go back to Chicago in the fall?"

"I'll bring it with me."

Oh, that would go over big with Adele. "Uh, your mother is not a fan of dogs."

"She'll *love* my dog."

"Not its pee on her white carpets."

Evan giggled. "We'll house-train it before I go back."

"You think we can have a dog at the villa?" Oliver asked.

"Yes, Miss Lacey already told me I could." Evan looked downright smug.

"Dogs are a responsibility, Evan. This isn't a stuffed animal. It's a living, breathing creature who needs attention and love and devotion…" His gaze shifted to Zoe, his chest suddenly tight. "That's an awfully big commitment that some people can't imagine making."

She barely flinched at the not-so-subtle dig.

"I can do it, Dad." Evan squeezed his other hand. "I promise I'll take care of it, I'll walk it, I'll feed it, I'll do everything, I'll love it. And it can sleep in my room. I promise. Dad, please? Please?"

Zoe smiled. "How can you say no to that face?"

Knowing he had what he wanted, Evan slathered it on, grinning his most adorable smile.

Shit. "You can't change your mind, Ev," he said. "You

can't take it back if it turns out to be more than you can handle."

He held up his right hand, the image of solemnity. "I swear, Dad. I swear to you."

Oliver let out a sigh and dug around for anything at all that could counter that. Nothing showed up.

"All right, then," Zoe said, scrolling through her phone. "Let's find the local rescue shelters."

This time Evan froze. "I want a puppy."

"Well, they have puppies. Sometimes."

He frowned, seeking support from Dad. "Don't you want a puppy?"

"I think I've made my feelings clear on the subject. And if it's your dog, you can get whatever you want."

"Oliver!" Zoe's eyes were wide. "There are rescue dogs who need homes."

But Evan stepped forward to make his own argument. "Zoe, I want a puppy. There's a pet store in the mall about ten minutes from here. I already Googled it."

"Of course you did," she said. "And you're right. It's your dog. Let's go see what they've got."

Half an hour later the three of them stood in front of a glass partition, looking at about fifteen puppies of various shapes and breeds, sleeping, eating, and generally looking adorable in their little cages.

Zoe leaned against the glass, watching as Evan walked back and forth, eyeing each critically, completely involved in the selection process. Oliver let his son go and stood next to her.

"So what changed your mind?" he asked.

She shrugged. "Pasha was sleeping and I had nothing else to do."

"I meant last night, when you disappeared."

"You know…things got dicey."

He took her chin and tilted her face up to him, lost for a moment in inviting green eyes. "Things get dicey in life, Zoe. You can't always—"

"I can't decide!" Evan popped in front of them. "I love the Yorkie, but that's not a very big dog."

"Little is good," Oliver said.

"But there's that fluffy white thing."

"American Eskimo." Zoe nodded. "Pretty dog, too."

Evan sighed. "I also like him." He pointed to a black-and-white rat terrier, sound asleep and looking far more peaceful than he probably was when awake.

"Rat terrier? Sounds like he might bring home some unwanted friends," Oliver mused. "But you pick the dog who speaks to you."

Still pondering, Evan walked back down the glass, leaving them alone again.

"You were saying?" Zoe asked.

"I was saying you shouldn't have left."

"It was time."

On whose clock? "I want you to spend the night."

She gestured toward the dogs. "Gonna get crowded in that house."

"I want to sleep with you next to me, Zoe."

She inched away as if the very idea gave her claustrophobia. "Not tonight. You have a big day tomorrow."

"We're all ready, and so is Pasha."

At the first mention of her aunt's name, a shadow crossed over Zoe's face. Instantly she walked away to join Evan. "Did you see that little dachshund?"

"Yeah, he's cute, too." He put his hands on the glass and shook his head. "I can't pick."

Oliver stood behind them, the urge to put a protective hand on both of their shoulders surprisingly strong. But Zoe would just duck and run.

"Listen, Evan, the man who owns the store has a lot of information about each dog, including how big they'll be and what their temperaments are. Why don't we get a copy of that and take it to lunch and you can make a more informed decision?"

Zoe turned and smiled. "Such an Oliver-like idea."

"Logical and sound," he agreed. "What do you say, Evan?"

He hesitated, his attention darting from dog to dog; he was clearly overwhelmed with the weight of the doggie decision. "'Kay. I'm hungry."

The inability to pick a breed lingered over lunch at the mall deli, distracting Evan enough that he barely ate his burger. Side by side in a booth with Zoe, Evan pored over the list from the pet store, troubled.

Zoe asked him questions and helped the boy hone in on what was important, while Oliver relished the connection between them, enjoying her quips and the sight of his son next to the woman he...

No. It didn't matter how he felt. He could love Zoe from now until he took his last breath—and, damn it, he might—but would that ever be enough to hold on to a woman like her? No matter what her circumstances? How many times would he come out of the bathroom to find an empty bed? Home from work to find an empty house?

Zoe pushed the paper away from Evan. "Stop thinking so hard, kid. Eat your food and think about something else and the right answer will come to you. You, too, Dad." She winked at Oliver, obviously aware he wasn't listening to this conversation.

"Is that what you do? Think about something else when you have a problem?" Evan asked.

No, she runs off.

Zoe shrugged. "No, but you're not me. You're way smarter and you have too much information now, and you're no longer going on your gut. Plus, it doesn't matter." She picked up an onion ring and used it to point at him. "You're going to love this dog no matter what you get."

"Do you have a dog?" he asked.

She shook her head and dipped the ring in ketchup. "I move around too much."

Like, constantly. Oliver swallowed the retort along with some iced tea.

"Did you have one when you were a kid?" Evan asked.

She shook her head, then stopped as if reconsidering that. "Actually, one place had a beagle. ..." Zoe's voice trailed off as she caught herself. She shared a look with Oliver.

She'd told him earlier that she'd finally come clean with her friends. Would that honesty extend to others now, too? To Evan? Oliver sat perfectly still as he waited to find out.

"One place? You mean you don't remember?" Evan asked.

Zoe put down the onion ring without eating it, brushing her fingers so some crumbs fell on her plate. "I..." She took a slow breath, her eyes cast down. "I lived in a lot of places."

"Did your parents move a lot?" he asked.

Oliver held his sandwich poised in the air, watching and

waiting and wondering what was going on in Zoe's head. She still didn't meet his gaze.

"My parents..." She swallowed. "I didn't really have parents."

Evan looked up, ready to argue, but then his expression softened. "Aunt Pasha raised you, right?"

There, she had her usual out. Oliver waited for her to take it, to quip about life with her gypsy aunt, to mention that her parents died in a car crash when she was ten.

Basically, he waited for her to lie to his son.

"She did raise me," Zoe said. "But before that I lived in foster homes."

Something in Oliver's chest slipped.

"Like, you were an orphan?" Evan asked.

Zoe nodded. "Yep. Little Orphan Zoe." But the humor didn't ring true. And he could feel discomfort rolling off her in waves. Oliver wanted to step in, help her out, change the subject, anything to take the agony out of her eyes, but something told him not to.

This was Zoe's confession to make and all he could do was love her for making it.

"What was that like?" Evan asked, a little tentative, as if he knew it wasn't polite to ask questions about being an orphan.

Zoe tried for a casual shrug, but her shoulder stayed up and her expression dissolved from a woman about to make a joke to...a face he saw so rarely. Her eyes, which normally glittered with her easy smile, looked wide and sad.

"It sucked," she said quietly. "Hope I can use that word in front of your son."

"He's said worse."

"Much," Evan agreed, but his attention was riveted on Zoe. "How come nobody adopted you?"

Finally that shoulder dropped in a slow slump. "I got too old and most people want babies."

"But you're so much fun."

She gave him an elbow nudge. "Just like the dogs in the shelter that you don't want to consider."

Evan's expression changed as that hit home. "How many houses did you live in?" he asked.

Oliver stepped in to save her. "Hey, it's personal business, Ev, so—"

"It's okay." She waved him off as if she were trying to convince herself as much as them. "Really, I'm ready…it's okay." She leaned back and took a second to compose herself, then said, "I lost count after fifteen families. Sometimes I was only at one for a few weeks, sometimes longer. I never knew when the call would come that I had to move on. And so I wasn't really nice to those people because I figured if I got too…" She closed her eyes.

"Zoe, you don't have to—"

She caught the hand that Oliver held out. "I want to. I want to tell him this." She added a smile. "But thanks."

"Zoe doesn't tell a lot of people this, Evan," he said softly.

"But I'm telling him, now." She let go of Oliver's hand and turned to Evan. "The hardest part was that I didn't want to get too comfortable. If I felt like something was mine—like my closet or my drawer or my bed or my family—then, sure enough, some old bag would show up at the door and tell me I had to leave."

Evan was silent, mesmerized. And Oliver simply

wanted to punch a wall. How had he never considered this aspect of her life?

She'd said she always wanted to get away from that last horrific home, and he'd accepted that as her reason for running. But it was even deeper than that. Staying—staying *anywhere*—meant getting hurt.

"So, as you can imagine," she said, fighting for that light tone of hers and losing the battle, "it's always been easier for me"—she shifted her gaze to Oliver, slicing him in two with the sincerity of it—"to not get attached. That way, when I left the closet or the drawer or the bed I liked so much, I didn't miss it too badly."

Of course. It made perfect sense. Now all he had to do was figure out how to convince her that wouldn't happen. And trust her to love and not leave.

Was that even possible with a woman as damaged as Zoe?

"But then you got with Aunt Pasha," Evan said, like a child determined to find the happy ending. "And it was like somebody took you home, huh?"

Zoe shook her head. "Not exactly, but it was better." She reached across the table to touch Oliver's hand, as if she understood that her message had finally sunk into Oliver's skull.

Evan pulled out his phone.

"What are you doing?" Oliver asked.

"Googling."

"Foster homes?" Zoe smiled. "You want to know everything about everything, don't you, little Einstein?"

He tapped a few buttons and scrolled on the screen. "I want to find the closest animal rescue shelter." His finger paused and he looked up at her. "I bet we could find a dog that needs a real home."

"I bet we could." Zoe beamed at Oliver, her eyes brimming with tears. "Mission accomplished."

Zoe ended what had felt like a nearly perfect day by pouring a heavy-on-the-vodka-with-a-molecule-of-tonic and settling onto her bed with an open laptop. Oliver had practically begged her to stay after dinner and she'd been so tempted, but the siren call of the Internet was too strong.

She had to know more.

Her fingers touched the keys, ready to type. *Patricia Hobarth...Corpus Christi...Matthew Hobarth.*

Matthew Hobarth? Was that even his name? How would Zoe know? Because the one person she loved and trusted and depended on for everything had *failed to tell her.*

How? How could Pasha have had a son and never even told Zoe about it?

A white-hot spurt of betrayal shot through her, and not for the first time that day. She'd managed to run from the heartache and escape to something better with Oliver and Evan, even with her honest admissions over lunch.

She was tired of hiding the truth about her life. But, evidently, Pasha was not.

Had Pasha lied to Zoe all these years? Whether out of omission, fear, or just plain guilt—God, no, please. Not that.

She had to know.

Still, she couldn't type the words. Instead she took a deep, long drink, the vodka harsh on her tongue. A second gulp was a little better, but she still didn't feel numb enough to face this search.

Whatever had happened, *if* it had happened, had taken place over thirty years ago. There might not be anything on the Internet.

That gave her the strength to begin clicking. She closed her eyes as the links popped up, praying that this was misinformation, a coincidence that the sheriff and nurse had used the same word: *murder*.

She finally opened her eyes and read the first link, dated just a few months earlier.

Police reopen 1965 murder of Matthew Hobarth.

Shit. *Shit!*

She sipped some more, put the glass on the table with a thud, and stared at the words. She jumped when a knock at the bungalow door pulled her out of the sixties and back to the moment.

She popped off the bed, gathered her wits, and listened for the next knock.

What if it was the sheriff?

An old, familiar fear crawled up her back. *Grab a bag, get out the back door, hide until it was clear and they could run.*

But Zoe didn't have to run. She picked up the glass to down the last sip but didn't drink, carrying it to the door.

"Zoe, are you home?"

Tessa. Relief hit as hard as the vodka as Zoe blew out a breath. Tessa was better than the sheriff. Better than anyone, right now.

She flung the door open. "Tess."

"Where have you been all day?"

"With Oliver and Evan. We went dog shopping. Got a lovely mutt who has a heart of gold and paws the size of basketballs."

"Really? And you're not over there doing an assist on the house-training?"

She managed a smile. "They can't bring him home for forty-eight hours. Shelter rules."

Tessa inspected Zoe's face. "You okay?"

No, she was not okay. Zoe grabbed Tessa's arm and pulled her in. "I need your help."

Inside, Tessa took the drink from Zoe's hand and sipped. "Whoa. Ever hear of a mixer?"

"Overrated. Come back here. I need you to read something for me."

"Too drunk to read?"

"I'm not drunk," Zoe fired back, her voice cracking. "I'm..." What was she, other than shocked, devastated, and dismayed? *Hurt.* She was hurt down to the bone. "It's Pasha."

Tessa reached for her. "What happened?" The question was loaded with fear and a hint of dread. "Is she okay?"

"I don't know," Zoe said glumly.

"Did she have a setback? Is the treatment still scheduled for tomorrow? What's the matter?"

"Everything. Nothing. I don't know, except that I can't stand to do this alone."

"Do what alone?"

"Find out the truth."

Tessa practically folded Zoe into her arms, patting her back with as much love and understanding as Zoe had ever felt. "Hey." She gave her a hug. "We're good, you know that. Whatever it is, tell me the truth. No judging, I swear."

The words were like a balm, and incredibly empowering. "I'm not sure what the truth is. That's the problem."

"Then let's figure it out together, can we?"

"Maybe." She handed Tessa the glass. "Mix me up

another vodka-and-vodka and get a little something for yourself. You're going to need it. Meet me in my room."

An hour later, neither one of them had finished their drinks. But Tessa had read aloud every single word they could find, which wasn't much, but it was enough to leave them both in stunned silence.

Seven-year-old Matthew Hobarth had been stabbed to death in the backyard of his Pennsylvania home.

That alone was enough to make Zoe nearly throw up.

The child's father, Harry Hobarth, the owner of a string of very successful car dealerships all over the state, had been at a car show in Philadelphia when Matthew was killed. His mother, Patricia, a housewife, was the only real suspect. After scouring for clues around the body, which had been found at the far end of the property, investigators honed in on scratches on the mother's arms. She'd claimed they'd been climbing a tree together that day; the child had similar scratches. And she'd failed a lie-detector test but the evidence wasn't admitted into court.

The trial had ended with a hung jury, and the judge had declared a mistrial.

With each new fact that Tessa read, Zoe curled more tightly into a ball, wrapping her arms around her pillow, closing her eyes, trying to accept this unacceptable news.

In a story written about five years earlier in the *Pittsburgh Post-Gazette* about unsolved crimes in the area, a reporter had discovered that Harry Hobarth had divorced his wife and remarried, and Patricia Hobarth had moved away from the area. A search of obituaries listed her as dying of natural causes in Lubbock, Texas, in 1988—the year

Zoe and Pasha had started their twenty-five-year run from the law.

But the case was now open due to new evidence.

"You okay?" Tessa asked, stroking Zoe's arm.

She nodded but kept her stinging eyes shut tight.

"What do you want to do?"

"Scream in her face. Demand to know why she never told me." Was it because she was guilty? Was that even possible? "She doesn't have a violent bone in her body."

"Zoe, you don't think she did this, do you?"

Did she? "No, I don't, but why didn't she tell me? Why has she been running and hiding and pretending to be dead all these years?"

Tessa angled her head, frowning. "You know why. Because she basically kidnapped you and would have to face the charges for that, even now. She was protecting you."

"Was she?" Zoe pushed herself up. "Or was she protecting herself?"

"It was a mistrial."

"Hung jury. That's not a clear verdict of not guilty." Every word hurt to say. The very idea that Pasha could harm a child went beyond unthinkable. "But why be so secretive about it?"

Tessa gave her a rich look. "Says the queen of subterfuge."

"For a reason."

"She has her reasons, Zoe, and, frankly, I'm kind of shocked that you'd even consider that she's capable of something like this. She's probably terrified of being falsely accused again."

Guilt tweaked. No, it did more than tweak—it stomped all over Zoe's heart. "I know she didn't do this," Zoe said, the truth of that so powerful it rocked her. "I absolutely know she's not guilty. I'm angry at her. I'm hurt and disappointed and miserable and…I feel cheated." The last one took hold and she nodded, letting the emotion ricochet through her. "She cheated me out of a chance with Oliver."

"She thought she was doing the right thing for you, didn't she?"

Zoe looked at the screen, where the last story was still visible, but she couldn't bring herself to lean closer and read every damn word. "What does it say about the open case again?"

Tessa skimmed the words. "They have the killer's DNA now, something they didn't have the technology to get back then. But they haven't matched it to anyone in any database."

"And of course," Zoe said softly, "the number-one suspect, Patricia Hobarth, is dead."

"Except she's not."

"And I'd stake my life on the fact that she's innocent."

"You certainly have buckets of DNA if you wanted to…"

Turn her in. "Whoa." Zoe blew out a breath, falling on the pillow to stare at the ceiling. "Talk about a betrayal."

"If she's innocent you'd be helping her. And maybe you could negotiate for the kidnapping charges because she came forward."

"Except she wouldn't have come forward. I'm busting her." Zoe's whole body tightened like a coiled spring, the first prickles of a cold sweat breaking out on her neck and scalp.

Could she do that? Could she even think about it?

"Why don't you talk to Oliver?" Tessa said. "You trust him."

Zoe slid her a look. "I slept with him last night."

"That's what you wanted, right?" When Zoe didn't answer, Tessa leaned forward. "How'd it go?"

"I can't believe you didn't feel the earthquake."

"When you shared thundering simultaneous orgasms?"

Zoe smiled, but her eyes were already brimming. "When I ran out the minute he wasn't looking."

"Oh, Zoe." Tessa reached for her with another of her mother-bear hugs. "Baby, you're a mess."

She gave in to the tears and the hug and the delicious overdose of nurturing, letting Tessa stroke her hair. Lovely as that was, it wasn't what she needed. It wasn't who she needed.

For the second time that day, Zoe wanted to run. But not away. She wanted to run *to* someone.

"What are you going to do?" Tessa asked.

Zoe turned a little to look up at her friend. "I'm going to talk to Oliver."

"Talk?" Tessa looked dubious.

"Talk after."

"After another simultaneous orgasm?"

"That or maybe after tomorrow," Zoe said. "We got the other oncologists' opinions today and everything's a go for the transfusion and gene therapy in the morning. I think I should wait and do some more research. Maybe…talk to the sheriff."

Tessa gave her another hug. "If you need me to go with you, I will."

"What I need is…"

"Tell me, Zoe."

"Oliver." She mouthed his name.

"See? That wasn't so hard." Tessa gave her a peck on the cheek. "Have fun and stay with him."

Zoe's eyes popped. "Forever?"

Tessa laughed. "I meant tonight, but hey, who knows?"

Chapter Twenty

~

Oliver's front door opened before Zoe even knocked, leaving her to wonder what was sexier: the sight of him bare-chested in soft blue doctor's scrubs or the utter lack of surprise on his face when he saw her.

"You were expecting me, weren't you?"

"A guy can hope," he said softly.

"So you're standing sentry at the door?"

He smiled. "I was upstairs checking on Evan and I saw you walking down the path. Usually when you come over you take shortcuts and climb fences."

She smiled. "I had a cocktail with Tessa, so I didn't trust myself to climb." She glanced behind him. "Evan asleep?"

He nodded, reaching for her, touching her face with his gentle but capable fingers. "You okay?"

"Yeah," she said vaguely, the need to tell him everything she'd just learned plaguing her. Of course he'd demand info, want to see the stories, and—worst of all—maybe he'd believe Pasha was guilty.

How would that affect the delicate gene-therapy procedure he was supervising the next day to save the woman's life?

He drew her closer. "You coming in?"

She hesitated, looking at him, inhaling the mix of salty humid air and the soapy smell of a man who'd just showered. "I guess," she said.

"You guess?" he laughed softly, sliding his hands to her wrist.

"I didn't just come over for sex," she said, not sure why it was important that he know that.

Still smiling, he eased her into the villa. "That's fine. We're a full-service operation. What will it be? Food, drink, pool, shower, or a cuddle on the couch where you can unload whatever it is that has your pulse so erratic?"

She rolled her eyes. "Come to a doctor for comfort and you get diagnosed."

His face softened as he closed the door and walked her to the overstuffed sofa. "Is it comfort you want, Zoe?"

An unexpected lump formed in her throat. "Yeah," she admitted. "That's what I want. No-questions-asked consolation and tenderness." She looked up at him with a hopeful smile. "Can I buy some of that here?"

"Better yet, we give that away at no charge." He eased her down on the sofa cushions and laid her back on the armrest. He sat at the other end, lifting her feet to his lap, sliding off her flip-flops and letting them drop to the floor. "Somehow I keep getting sent back to your feet."

She smiled, closing her eyes as he gave her a gentle foot rub, lost in the power of his hands.

"Are you worried about tomorrow?" he asked. "Is Pasha on your mind?"

She most certainly was. "Of course. I can hardly think about anything else."

He gave her foot a squeeze. "She's in great hands. Our team is amazing and prepared. I'm now one-hundred-percent convinced this is the right way to go."

His confidence was as reassuring as his touch. "How long until we know if it worked?"

"In hours we'll know if it didn't work—that's actually a better way to look at it. If there is toxicity or inflammation from the bad cells we're injecting, we will know within hours. Certain symptoms will alert us."

"What will you do?"

"Stop and reverse the therapy, but…" He stilled his fingers and waited until she opened her eyes to finish. "That might be too late."

"I'm aware of that risk, and so is Pasha."

"Good. But remember, this process could save her life and many more." His voice grew tight and his grip even tighter.

"That's why it's so important, huh?" she asked.

"No, Zoe. It's important because your aunt, whom you love, has trusted us with her life."

She swallowed some guilt. Yes, she loved Pasha. Nothing could ever change that. But should Oliver know what Zoe knew now? Would it matter? Would it be right or wrong to tell him on the eve of this important event? The indecision squeezed at her chest.

"But," he continued, "I won't lie and tell you this isn't major, potentially career-changing, and without a doubt the very reason I walked away from my position at Mount Mercy and opened a practice in Naples to work with Raj."

The passion in his words hung in the room, as attractive

and powerful as any language of love. She studied him from under her lashes, her heart swelling so much that the observant doctor could probably feel the physiological responses just by holding her feet.

"You love what you do," she said, unable to keep the raw admiration—and maybe a little envy—out of her voice.

"I do," he agreed. "Saving lives, hands-on medicine, especially the kind that has potential for huge and important change, is the reason I became a doctor and definitely the reason I went into oncology."

A story about his grandmother drifted up from her memory banks. "I thought you chose oncology because of losing your grandmother to breast cancer when you were in college."

He nodded slowly, his expression a little distant. "I did."

She inched up a little. "It sounds like there's more."

"There's...always more." He inhaled deeply, and, on the exhale, he let go of her feet and climbed up the sofa, covering her body with his as he lay down next to her.

"Done with the comforting foot rub?"

"I want to do a comforting full-body rub." He tucked her into his chest, wrapping a leg around hers to hold her securely on the sofa.

"Shouldn't we do this behind closed doors? You've got an eight-year-old upstairs."

"We will." He brushed her hair back and angled her face so they were looking right at each other. "I want to tell you something. It's serious and important and I don't want to get sidelined by...by what happens when we get near a bed."

She tensed a little, waiting for him to finish.

"Zoe, I don't want to have any secrets or anything that could change how you feel—or not—about me."

Guilt churned her stomach—she was the one holding in a secret on this sofa—and that pain mixed with a burn of curiosity. "Something about your marriage?" she guessed.

He shook his head. "Long before."

"Before that, there was…me."

"Before that."

She tried to sit up, but he held her right where he wanted her, heart to heart, face to face. "I want to tell you about the very first woman who hurt me."

She blinked at him. They'd talked about former lovers when they'd dated; she knew all about Adele Townshend and even a few girls from college. "Your first love?" She had deluded herself in thinking *she'd* been his first love.

"Every boy's first love, I guess."

"Your mother?"

He nodded and she dug back into those memory banks for information. All she knew was that his mother had died young, his father and grandmother had raised him, and…that was it.

"Did she die of cancer, too, Oliver?" Maybe that was the death that really put him on the track to this life, a boy who wanted to save lives because he'd lost the one that mattered most.

But why wouldn't he have told her that?

And why did his face register nothing but agony right now?

He stroked her cheek, brushing an imaginary hair, his gaze beyond her as he visibly gathered his thoughts. "When I was a little older than Evan and nowhere near as smart, I might add, my mother died."

Sympathy swelled. "That must have been so hard. What happened?"

"She…" He closed his eyes. "I came home from school and the house was so quiet."

It was his turn for his heart to race and his body to tighten. She caressed his bare arm the same way Tessa had stroked her earlier. Calming, soothing, and comforting.

"It was never quiet," he said. "My mother didn't work outside the home. She was a housewife supporting my dad's engineering career. When I came home from school, there was always music. Early-eighties rock and roll, mostly, but really anything. She would be dancing around in some kind of crazy outfit, putting together a play for the neighborhood kids, or organizing a garage sale, or planning a party. She was the original good-time girl."

"I like her already," Zoe said with a sly smile.

His eyes narrowed. "You would have…" He shook his head. "You're very much like her, Zoe."

Something told her that wasn't a compliment.

"She was the center of attention, always making jokes, never taking anything seriously, filling her life and our house with…"

"Joy?"

He shifted his gaze to focus on her. "Fake joy."

For a moment she couldn't speak. Then she asked, "What is that?"

"That's when…" He curled a strand of her hair around his finger, winding it like a spring. "You convince the world you are so happy and always laughing and joking and singing but inside you are very, very…damaged."

The word was like a quick stab to the heart. Damaged sounded familiar.

"What happened to her, Oliver? Just tell me."

"I went upstairs." He paused, getting composure. "She wasn't in her room or anywhere else. Then I went up to the third floor. We lived in an old Georgian-style house outside of Wilmington. It needed a lot of work and, in fact, that was what my mother was supposed to be doing—hiring contractors or carpenters because my dad was working fifty, sixty, even more hours at DuPont." He took a moment for a breath, and Zoe realized their hearts were beating in unison—way too fast.

"She wasn't on the third floor, either, so I had to go up to the cupola. The very top of this old house, which I'm sure could have been restored to greatness, but my mother was too…distracted."

"What happened, Oliver?" She could barely whisper the words, like a child listening to a scary story and knowing the very bad thing was right around the corner.

"I found her." He closed his eyes and bit his lip. "She'd hung herself."

Zoe sucked in a deep breath, the shock of that hitting her brain. A happy, joyful, music-loving, easily distracted, party girl had killed herself.

And her nine-year-old son had found her.

"Why?"

He shrugged. "We never knew. No note, no issues, no hidden secrets, no journal, no safe deposit box, no friends came forward, no history of instability, nothing. But it was suicide and she was clearly a troubled, depressed woman who hid behind a façade of happiness. There had to be a reason, but it defied logic. *She* defied logic."

Zoe stared at him, chugging all that in, and, man, it tasted bleak.

"Wow, I'm sorry. I can't imagine how hard that must have been for you," she said, placing her hand on his face and forcing him to look at her.

"It was horrible," he agreed. "It changed me, forever."

"How?"

"I guess I've studied enough psychology to know it's why I have a need to fix broken things." He gave a quick smile. "I spent the next five or more years wondering if I could have fixed my mother."

"Not if you didn't know anything was wrong with her," she said. "Not if no one knew the way she was feeling."

He didn't answer, still playing with one of her curls, his eyes unfocused as he no doubt relived the memory and its aftershocks.

"You think I'm like her, don't you?" she asked in a soft whisper.

Now his eyes focused, and he looked right into her eyes. "In some ways, yes. In others, no."

Some ways. "You think my tendency to run is just another way of escaping life when it gets tough."

He didn't answer. He didn't have to.

Oliver's chest felt lighter than it had in years. Even though they'd rolled to a more comfortable position on the couch and Zoe was more or less draped over him, squeezing the breath from him, he felt nothing but buoyant inside.

It was as if the confession had freed him.

But not Zoe. She had a million questions, which he did his best to answer, reserving judgment on his mother's decision, convincing her that with no note and no indication that she'd been unhappy at all, the family had learned to live with a scar they'd never understood.

"But you're not living with it," Zoe said. "It's still haunting you. I bet that's the reason you're scared of heights."

"That might be a stretch, but okay," he agreed. "I know it's why I hate to come home to an empty house. None of that means I'm letting the incident define me."

"You said it had a lasting impact."

"But not one that defines me. I won't let it." He pulled her into him, as close as he could get her, but there was nothing sexual about the move. He wanted her to understand how important his next words were. "I'm not letting it define us."

She shuddered out a breath. "There is no us, Oliver."

"There could be. You know how I feel. I love—"

She inched up, warning flashing dark green in her eyes. "Don't say it, Oliver."

"Why not?"

"I can't say it back."

"You never could," he said on a dry laugh. "Remember, even when I tried to teach you." He sat up next to her and held her face in his hands. "I…" He nibbled on her lower lip. "Love…" He sucked that lip into his mouth, wanting to rush and get the last word out, but really wanting to taste her. "You."

Amazingly, she didn't stop him or jerk away. Instead, she kissed him, her mouth open, her tongue sweet and slippery, her hands closing around his neck.

"Zoe?" he asked when they finally broke the kiss.

"I can't, Oliver."

She never could. She never had. And now he knew why. She was afraid of having the rug pulled out from under her the minute she took a chance standing on it. She needed time. "Will you spend the night with me?"

She didn't answer right away, and he could practically feel her rooting around for excuses.

"We'll do nothing but sleep, I swear."

"I don't have any clothes for tomorrow and I need to shower and…"

He stood, pulling her up with him. "Listen, go into my room, take a hot shower, and climb into bed. I'm going to run over to your bungalow, get you clean clothes and whatever you need. We'll wake up early, before Evan's even up, and he'll think you arrived in the morning."

She searched his face, then nodded with one last sigh of resignation. "You win."

"It's not a battle, honey." He stroked her cheek. "I'm going to hold you all night and when you wake up and look at me, you're going to say the first words that pop into your brain and those will be the unvarnished truth."

She smiled. "You sound like Pasha and her signs and wonders."

"Go." He nudged her toward the master bedroom. "Give me your key and tell me what you need."

"Key's under the front mat. Something clean that looks like I'd wear it. Don't forget underwear. And my toothbrush."

He kissed her on the forehead. "Be right back."

She eased back, unsure. "Aren't you worried that you'll come back and I'll be gone?"

"Not in the least."

She gave him a playful punch. "Well, look at that. Big breakthrough for Doctor B."

"Now it's your turn. Go and shower and *stay* here. All night. Can you do that, Zoe? For me?"

"I can." She leaned forward to kiss his cheek. "I can do that for you, doc. Trust me."

He watched her walk to the bedroom door and, as she opened it, she turned, a heartbreaking smile tipping her lips. "I kind of...do. You know? I do. I always have."

Now that right there was a breakthrough. Zoe style. He smiled right back. "I know."

He waited until she disappeared into his bedroom and then he left, jogging down the Casa Blanca beach path, cutting through the gardens to make his way to the little cul-de-sac of bungalows where Zoe was staying. He rounded her Jeep parked in front, found the key with little problem, and let himself into the darkened living area. Turning on a lamp, he glanced around while his eyes adjusted and headed toward the hall, turning that light on, too.

There were doors on either side, both leading to tiny bedrooms. The one on the right was smaller, with a single bed and a nearly empty dresser. That would be Pasha's room. As he was turning to the other room, something on the dresser caught his eye. White, square, familiar black lettering.

His whole being froze as an icy splash of disbelief shot through his veins.

Very slowly, he turned, the blood pounding in his head so hard he could literally hear his heart rate rise with each passing second. As if he couldn't bear to put his eyes on it, he looked downward, at a fallen vase with a few dead flowers, any water long evaporated.

But he knew what he'd seen. He knew it.

He lifted his gaze up the side of the dresser and let it finally land on a time-yellowed envelope with familiar black writing.

"*Fuck.*" He stared at it so hard he damn near willed it to be a figment of his imagination.

But it was real. Three-dimensional, nine years old, and

chock full of so much love and so many promises that, in the right hands, it might have changed everyone's lives.

If it had ever gotten *into* those hands.

He picked up the envelope, vaguely remembering the postal worker who'd shaken his head and told Oliver no, that box was closed, no forwarding address. Turning it over, he could see the envelope had never been opened.

Small consolation to know that no one had ever read it. It wasn't like Pasha had read his outpouring to Zoe, but still, she had kept it. Hadn't she?

He looked around the room, imagining her last few moments before she had run off and hoped to die. She must have left the letter as an explanation or apology. Or because she knew they'd reunited and everything he'd said in this letter would get said again, in person.

Hell, he was ready to say half of it tonight.

Zoe mustn't have gone into Pasha's room, so she'd never even seen it. How would she feel when she did? Furious? Frustrated? Worried that he wouldn't do his job right tomorrow in vengeance against a woman who, unwittingly or not, had controlled their future?

Because he believed in his deepest heart that if Zoe had read this letter, she would have come back to him before he ever married Adele.

Had Pasha known that?

He examined the seal again, admittedly no expert in steaming and resealing; maybe she *had* read the letter.

He stuffed the letter into the side pocket of his old scrubs and turned to Zoe's room to get what he'd come for. His hands shook a little in anger as he pulled open a drawer and found a mess of pastel silk, plucking out a polka-dot thong and a purple bra.

His hands better not shake tomorrow, he thought ruefully. Not when he'd be working to save the life of the woman who had ruined his.

Pushing the thought away, he yanked open the next drawer, grabbed a navy tank top, and tossed it all on the bed next to an open laptop. Turning to the closet, he examined a row of long skirts, imagining which Zoe would want.

Behind him, the laptop hummed to life, probably bumped by the clothes. He should turn that off and not let it go to sleep, he thought, plucking the white skirt he remembered her wearing to his office. It was wrinkly and soft and a little bit see-through.

The letter still burned in his pocket as he gathered up the clothes. What would he say to her? Would he give it to her tonight? Tomorrow morning? Wait until she told him she loved him? She was so close.

Maybe after the treatment, when Pasha was healed.

When was the best time to break the news to Zoe that her beloved aunt—

The computer lit up, the black letters of a large headline filling the screen. Where was the power button? He searched the keyboard, reaching for the shut-off key with his pinky since his hand was full of skirt and underwear.

Just as he hit the button, he glanced at the screen.

Police Reopen the Cold Case of Murdered Seven-Year-Old.

Frowning, he read the smaller print below that.

New DNA Evidence Uncovered but Prime Suspect, Patricia Hobarth, Released after Mistrial, Now Dead.

A whole new wave of emotions hit him so hard he dropped down on the bed. The screen flickered, then turned blue.

No, no. He had to know. He stabbed at buttons, his

hands still so damn shaky, desperate to call the story back up, but the computer went silent and dark.

For a long moment he sat there and stared at it.

He could have turned on the machine, found the Internet browser, and followed the electronic trail to read to the end of the story, but did he have to? Didn't he know enough?

The reason why Pasha lived on the run. The reason why she'd sacrificed Zoe's happiness for her own safety. The reason why she'd never given this love letter to her niece.

Not her niece—some stray she'd picked up and decided to use, probably to help change her identity when she got herself declared dead.

All the facts rolled from his logical brain and landed in his stomach with a thud.

The letter made him mad. The news made him sick. But the fact that Zoe had known this when she'd shown up at his door looking for comfort but didn't trust him enough to share…that hurt like hell.

Finally, he pushed himself off the bed and grabbed the clothes.

Did she think he wouldn't do his level best to save Pasha if he knew this? If so, she really didn't know him at all. And he didn't know her.

I kind of…do. I always have.

That might have been the closest thing to the "I love you" he wanted that he'd ever had. And as meaningless as the sex they were about to share.

And anything she said or did with him tonight was meaningless, too. She ran and she hid—everything. How the hell could he ever love a woman like that?

On his way out, he threw the letter back on the dresser where he'd found it.

Chapter Twenty-one

⌒

Zoe climbed naked in between the sheets, making a mental note to compliment Lacey on the fine Egyptian cotton she'd chosen. She sighed and rolled onto Oliver's pillow, taking a whiff of his spicy scent, which still lingered from the night before. She was anxious to smell the real thing when he got back.

And say the real thing. Not just *allude* to it.

While she was at it, she needed to come clean with everything. She'd tell him what she'd discovered and how firmly she believed Pasha was innocent. While he was administering the treatment that would save Pasha's life, Zoe would be meeting with the sheriff, talking over the facts, and asking for help and arranging for Pasha to submit DNA evidence.

It would be a long, grueling legal process, compounded by the crimes Pasha *had* committed along the way. But if she were alive and healthy, she and Zoe could fight this. Lives could be saved and then changed.

Oliver would do the first and she would do the second, without running away, not once. He'd like that. They'd be fixing things together.

She heard the front door open and close and she tensed in anticipation, ready, willing, and right where he wanted her to be when he got home. No doubt he expected her to pull a Zoe and—

"Dad?"

Dang it. Evan was up.

"Hey, son. What're you doing down here?"

They were right outside the room, close enough that Zoe could hear the exchange perfectly.

"I can't sleep."

Okay, no sex tonight. But that was fine. She stayed still and soundless, waiting for Evan to go back upstairs.

"Go on," Oliver said. "I'll be right up to tuck you in again."

"Can I just go in your room again, Dad? I'll be really quiet."

Whoa.

"No, that's not a good idea, son."

"Dad, please. I'm so excited about the dog that I can't sleep and I'm starting to get really nervous."

"You'll be fine."

Zoe could hear tension in Oliver's voice and didn't want him to be in this bind. She rolled out of the bed, tiptoeing toward the bathroom.

"Dad, I'm scared I can't take care of him or something will happen or Mom will hate him or…" The litany of Evan's fears quieted when she stepped into the bathroom and closed the door silently, grabbing the clothes she'd worn over here.

Now what? She could hardly get out without being seen.

She opened the door a crack and listened. Evan's voice had risen to a soft whine and she could hear him sniffing back tears.

"Just a second, son. Wait here." Oliver came into the bedroom and Zoe inched the bathroom door a little wider.

"Pssst."

He looked over and saw her, pointing over his shoulder toward the living room and giving her a "What can I do?" shrug.

"Should I leave?" she whispered.

For a moment he looked at her, and even in the dim light she could see something unreadable and confusing in his expression. He looked sad, not amused at the slightly comedic situation. No, he looked like a man disappointed by far more than his child's nighttime problems putting a crimp in the plans.

"Yes," he said simply, the one word like a block of ice. "You should leave."

Zoe blinked at him, not quite believing what she heard. Just because Evan was awake? "Oh, okay." She stepped out of the bathroom dressed in the shorts and T-shirt she'd been in all day, the bottom strands of her hair still damp from the shower dribbling cold water down her arms.

He didn't move, but stared at her, that look so…harsh.

"Dad, please, can I come in?"

"I'll go out the patio and climb the fence," she said.

He shook his head. "I'll take him upstairs and you can leave."

Something about his face, his words. Something was wrong. "What's the matter?"

He didn't say, just stared.

"Oliver, what's the matter?"

He shook his head, almost as if he couldn't speak.

She frowned, stepping closer, hoping with her whole being that he'd pull her into a kiss, whisper that she should wait so they could have that long night of holding each other they both wanted and needed so badly.

But his expression was raw and icy.

"Dad!"

"What's wrong?" she asked.

"Daddy!"

"I'm coming, Evan." He took a step back, his face pale and angry and hurt. That was what he was—truly, truly hurt. "You'd better leave, Zoe."

He backed out of the room, leaving her paralyzed with disbelief. She didn't move until she heard his footsteps on the stairs and his voice fading as he walked his son back to bed.

She stared at the door, stunned. Did Oliver really want her to leave? After all this time he'd been trying to get her to *stay*?

She listened for the voice and the usual mental instructions, but her head was as silent as a balloon midflight. She didn't want to run tonight. She *wanted* to stay and tell him everything, no matter what he had to do tomorrow. She wanted to...

You'd better leave.

At the echo of his command, she quietly walked through the villa, opening and closing the front door without making a sound except for her soft gulp as she swallowed back a lump of tears.

It was warm and clear, and the last thing Zoe wanted to do was go back to that bungalow and feel utterly and com-

pletely alone. Instead of rounding the path and picking her
way through the gardens, she walked down to the water,
drawn to the moon-drenched Gulf of Mexico and the cool
sands of Barefoot Bay.

She kicked off her flip-flops and made her way across
the beach, inhaling the salty air and counting the stars that
seemed to multiply the longer she looked at the heavens.

The moon was just about cut in half, bright enough to
cast shadows and highlight the beachside tables and chairs
on the pool patio of Casa Blanca's main building. Those
were new, she thought, since the restaurant hadn't opened
yet and Elijah's arrival had put a delay in Lacey's poolside
decorating efforts.

Maybe she could sit up there and lick her wounds.

About twenty feet from the tables, Zoe heard a voice.

Was someone out here? Up by the tables?

Her heart rate increased, and she suddenly realized how
vulnerable she was, despite the safety of Barefoot Bay and
the security of the resort. But someone was definitely out
there.

From the unfinished patio restaurant, she heard the low
tenor of a man, the softer high pitch of a woman.

"You can't do that!" The woman's voice got lifted by
the Gulf breeze, the cry serious enough for Zoe to pick up
her pace and begin walking toward the patio, cocking her
head to hear more. If the discussion seemed benign, she'd
slip away without being seen. But if someone was hurt...

Stepping into the shadows near a side entrance, Zoe
slowed her step when she heard the woman sob.

"What will I do if you leave? I don't want to live without you."

Oh, a lovers' quarrel. *Join the club, lady.*

"You have to decide what matters to you, Glo."

Glo…that would be Gloria Vail, an employee in the spa, so the man must be—holy shit. The sheriff, Slade Garrison.

Zoe stayed still now, hidden by a low wall near the side entrance but able to hear the voices from the patio.

"My family matters and you matter," Gloria replied. "But…"

"But what?" Slade's voice rose with frustration, pulling more empathy from Zoe. Was there a bad moon rising over Barefoot Bay tonight?

She glanced around, looking for an escape route. Just then, one of the chairs scraped over the pavers, and Slade got up and walked to the railing to look out at the water, making it impossible for Zoe to escape unnoticed. She had to stay perfectly still in the shadows.

"I know what's going on in your head, Gloria. You think Charity is right."

"I don't," she replied. "Not…really."

Eeesh, yes she did. Whatever they were fighting about, Glo agreed with Charity; anyone could tell from that response.

Slade certainly could, because he turned and even in the dim light Zoe could see the hurt look he gave Gloria. "Well, I have news for you, Glo. That's about to change."

"What is?"

"My career."

Now Gloria stood, making it even more difficult for Zoe to move. She really didn't want to get busted eavesdropping on this conversation. Couldn't they go inside or walk the beach?

"What's going on?" Gloria asked, coming up next to him. Zoe could see their silhouette against the moonlight.

They stood face to face, leaning toward each other like they couldn't resist the pull. Why did people who loved each other fight it so much, she wondered, lost for a moment in the image of the handsome young deputy and the hairdresser who loved him.

"I'm going to be a good catch. You'll see."

He *was* a great catch, Zoe wanted to call out. Good looking, well respected, and he carried a big gun. What did Gloria want? Or what did that old bat Charity want?

"It isn't going to be speeding tickets and expired car tags anymore," he said.

"Don't take that transfer," Gloria pleaded. "Working in Orlando is going to be dangerous. And so far."

"Well, hell, I want the job in Naples, but I don't have the record they're looking for. Although…"

"Although what?"

He didn't answer right away, then, "Look, I can't give you the details because it's big, but I really think I'm on to a case that could change my career."

"Oh my God, what is it?"

"I can't tell you until after I have a meeting with… someone," Slade said.

"Slade, you have to tell me!"

Yeah, you do, Zoe thought, invested in the conversation now.

"It's a cold case. A murder."

A bad, bad feeling slithered up Zoe's spine. There was that word again. Murder.

Gloria gasped. "A murder on Mimosa Key?"

"Not here. It was in Pennsylvania, years ago."

Oh, God. Oh, *God.* Zoe swayed a little, holding the wall for support.

"What does that have to do with you and your jurisdiction?"

Zoe took a careful step closer, praying for a different answer than the one she already knew she'd hear.

"I can't tell you who, what, or how, Glo, so don't ask. But I can tell you that someone who's been living for years under a fake name, moving from place to place, is involved and living right here on Mimosa Key."

Zoe bit her lip to silence any noise. She leaned against the wall to keep from running forward and demanding to know more. Or running away altogether.

But if he saw her, he'd be the one demanding to know *more*.

"Don't you dare say a word to anyone, Glo. Especially Charity."

"Oh, Slade, how is this going to change anything?" Gloria's voice lifted up a few notes, and Zoe knew she was taking the conversation away from murder and back to love. *Not yet, Glo. I need more information before I go in and see him tomorrow.*

"It's going to change everything," he insisted. "If I can solve this murder, I can get the promotion in Naples. That's more money, better cases, and I'm still able to live here. Then we have to get married, Gloria." His voice cracked a little as he pulled her closer. "We have to."

Gloria wrapped her arms around his neck. "Lacey said we could be the first wedding at Casa Blanca and she'd use all the pictures in her new 'wedding destination' brochure. It would be free for us, too. Just expenses."

"Honey, trust me on this." He pulled her in for a kiss.

Oh, puhlease. There's a murder we need to discuss first. How much did he know? What was he going to do? Would they arrest Pasha or just question her? "If I can solve this case, and I really think I can, we're going to be Mr. and Mrs. Slade Garrison."

Gloria's sigh was audible, and so was the noisy kiss.

Zoe'd heard enough and she sure as hell didn't want to stick around and watch the make-out session. She bent over and picked up a seashell, raising her arm to pitch it to the other side of the patio.

At the sound, they broke apart and looked in the other direction.

"What was that?" Gloria asked.

Slade started walking across the patio, holding out a hand to keep Gloria back. So protective, and so loving.

In a moment, he waved her closer and they both disappeared from sight, off to make out or spend the night together or plan their future. All he needed was to...find a killer.

Who was right over in Naples in a clinic.

No. No! Shut up! She actually put her hands on her ears to silence the voice.

She couldn't let herself even think that for a moment. The minute she could talk to Pasha, she would.

Certain she was alone again, Zoe slid down the side of the wall and let her backside land on the sand, hating that she'd even think the unthinkable about Pasha.

Pasha had protected her. *Or had Pasha protected herself?*

No matter what it cost, Zoe would find out the truth.

Chapter Twenty-two

⌒

D̲id you bring Evan?" Pasha's first question—before even saying good morning, hello, or *holy hot dogs this is a big day*—made Zoe hesitate in the doorway of the dimly lit room.

"He's with Tessa. I came super early to see you before the transfusion."

"Oh, I wanted to say good-bye to him."

"Good-bye?" Zoe reached the side of the bed, taking in Pasha's pale complexion, somehow made even more dramatic by the tubes coming out of her nose to help her breathe without having a coughing fit. "Where are you going?"

"You know, just in case."

"In case what?" Zoe tempered the bite in her question. Now wasn't the time to do anything but wish her luck. There'd be hours, days, and, she hoped, years to find out the truth of her past. Minutes before a life-saving procedure wasn't the time. "You're going to be fine."

Pasha let her lids close, then open again, working to focus on Zoe.

"Did they give you more sedatives?" Zoe asked.

"Mmm. I guess. I feel pretty woozy." She attempted a smile. "Wild dreams, too."

"Oooh. You love those." Zoe tugged the light blanket higher over nearly childlike shoulders. "See any good signs?"

"Just Matthew."

Oh, Lord. Matthew. "Really? Who's that?" Her pulse jackhammered as she waited for the answer.

"My sweet little boy." Pasha turned her head from one side to the other as if she were looking for someone. "It was like he was here."

"But he wasn't." *What happened to him, Pasha?* The question danced on her tongue, but Zoe managed not to let it out. But it sure would be good to have something concrete to take to the sheriff.

"So did you dream about this little boy?" she asked.

"Yes, but then he changed into you. When you were about eleven or twelve and I bought you that green-and-white polka-dot ruffled top. Do you remember?"

Every thread. "I loved that top."

"You looked so pretty in it, Zoe. Your eyes looked as green as grass and the ruffles bounced a little when you walked. You always...trusted me."

"Yes, I did." Her voice was flat and Pasha opened her eyes, blinking until they momentarily cleared.

"In my dream, you were up onstage, singing in front of hundreds of people."

"That's not a dream, it's a nightmare. You know I can't sing."

"But you could in my dream. You know what that's a sign of?"

"Too many sedatives?"

"That your voice is about to ring out loud and clear."

Zoe opened her mouth to answer, then closed it. Yes, her voice *was* going to ring out—to the sheriff.

"And what you say is going to be the truth, Zoe, no matter what people tell you."

"Are you…" *Really innocent?* "Sure?"

A knotted hand crept out from under the blanket, shaking a little. God, Pasha was old. Eighty-four, she'd finally confessed during one of her medical tests, an age that was confirmed in some of the articles Zoe had read online last night.

"You don't believe in my signs, do you?" Pasha asked. "You're humoring me all the time when you talk about them, aren't you?"

Zoe played with a few different answers. "Yes, I am. I don't believe in signs." She added a smile. "Well, there you go. I did just ring out the truth, didn't I? So you always have a bit of something right in your predictions."

Pasha patted Zoe's hand. "Listen to me, child. In case I don't come back from wherever I'm going, listen to me."

Zoe stayed very still. "I'm listening," she whispered.

"I had a very good reason for everything I did."

Doubt and hope sucker-punched her gut. "Everything?"

"Everything."

Zoe's skin prickled with the need to know. "Everything?" she asked again.

"If you can find him, you'll know the truth."

Oh, Lord. What did that mean? "Find who, Pasha?"

"Matthew."

He's dead, Zoe wanted to scream. How could she find him? It was the drugs, of course. The sedatives making her confused. This was not the time for a serious conversation of any sort.

"You just be strong, Pash—"

"But don't let him know." Her hand shook hard now and she struggled for breath in spite of the oxygen tubes. "Ever. Promise?"

Zoe shook her head. "C'mon, you have to calm—"

"Good morning, Pasha." Oliver's voice startled them both, making Zoe twirl around to face him.

Whoa, game face *on*. Every feature was set in a stern, expressionless stare, and he didn't look nearly as sleep deprived as Zoe felt.

"Good morning," Zoe replied, absently patting Pasha's hand as if she could soothe them both off the cliff they were teetering on.

"We're ready to go." He nodded to Zoe. "You can leave now."

She blinked in surprise, biting back a comment about bedside manner. But it wasn't a time for jokes. A woman's life was at stake. Their issues had no place in this room right now.

Pasha reached for her, unaware of the dynamics. "Zoe, remember. Matthew."

Oliver's eyes flashed for a second, so fast anyone else would have missed it. But not Zoe. She knew every nuance of his face and…

Holy, holy shit. He *knew*.

"We're here, Dr. Bradbury." Two nurses hustled into the room. "Dr. Mahesh is ready in the treatment room."

Zoe could feel the blood drain from her head.

"Let's get her prepared," he said.

For a second Zoe couldn't move, everything in her body wanting to scream. He couldn't possibly know who Matthew was, could he?

But instead she leaned over Pasha's bed and put her lips on soft, familiar cheeks. She knew this woman, right? She did, and, no matter what, Zoe loved her.

"Go get 'em, tiger," she whispered into Pasha's ear. "I love you."

As she straightened she caught Oliver's quick, dark look, then he turned away and began talking to one nurse while the other put her hand on Zoe's arm. "No worries, dear. We'll take great care of her."

Zoe turned to Pasha, but Oliver blocked her view.

"Zoe!" Pasha called. "Find Matthew! Then you'll know, then you'll understand everything! Find Matthew and you'll be safe."

Oliver turned and looked at her over his shoulder, his face telling her everything.

He knew, and he believed that the woman whose life he was responsible for saving had taken the life of a child, a child very much like his own.

Would Oliver Bradbury, the man who always did the right thing, do the right thing now?

She had to trust him.

And she had to *find Matthew*.

The Lee County sheriff's satellite office in Mimosa Key was tucked away on Center Street between a florist with the unlikely name of Bud's Buds and a very small teahouse that had three outdoor tables under a spread of live oak trees. Zoe parked a half-block away and sat very still. The midmorning sun was already strong enough to warm the leather upholstery of the topless Jeep, making Zoe's legs feel like they were stuck to the driver's seat.

Or maybe that was raw terror keeping her trapped in her seat.

Because she *was* trapped. For as free a spirit as she fancied herself, Zoe Tamarin-*cum*-Bridget Lessington was really as tethered and shackled as a woman could be. The realization hurt her chest, as if a great big elephant sat on it, crushing her.

An elephant named Matthew Hobarth.

A little boy who'd died before Zoe was even born had somehow inexorably tied Zoe down and trapped her.

She dropped her head back and looked up at the Florida blue sky, a distinct cloudless Wedgwood color that was like a siren call to her spirit. When running wasn't enough, Zoe wanted to fly away. To get in that gondola, pitch the sandbags with a soft rebel cry, and lift off this earth to somewhere silent and safe.

She ached like an addict who'd kill for a fix. Every fiber of her being wanted to rise out of this situation and escape. But that would mean leaving Oliver. And Evan. And Lacey, Tessa, Jocelyn. And Pasha. Barefoot Bay and—

How had that happened? How had this little island become a different sort of sanctuary, with friends and happiness, with family and…love?

She closed her eyes and thought of Oliver, but instead of seeing his face when he smiled or laughed or looked at her with a touch of awe in his eyes, she could only conjure up his last expression.

The one that said he knew—and he was hurt she hadn't told him.

In the time since she'd driven from Naples back to Mimosa Key, she'd figured out what had happened. He'd seen her computer screen; he knew that there was more to what his patient was hiding than the "kidnapping" of a foster child. She'd come to him for "comfort" and listened to his own story, but never once said, *Uh, I have to tell you something*.

No wonder he'd kicked her out.

And this morning there'd been no time to explain or talk, obviously, not moments before he was about to start Pasha's transfusion and treatment. She tried to swallow, but her throat was bone dry. Maybe an iced tea at the outdoor tables, a quiet moment, a bit of...delay.

A delay like all afternoon and into tomorrow. Get out of here, Zoe, before you do something stupid.

"Shut up," she murmured to the anonymous, hated voice that screamed from her gut. That voice was never right! She pushed open the door and climbed out, her sandals hitting the pavement with a snap. Oh, Lord in heaven, she didn't want to do this. She didn't want to walk into that little office and sit down in front of a sheriff and betray a woman who'd been like a mother to her.

Find Matthew.

Now that voice wasn't anonymous; it was Pasha's. What had she meant by that? Was it some kind of obscure message?

No! It was the rambling of an old, sick lady who had cancer and some dark secrets growing inside of her.

Secrets...like murder.

No! Zoe put both hands on her temples like she could squeeze the voice out. Pasha hadn't killed a child; Zoe knew that like she knew her own name.

Except you barely remember your own name.

"Ugh," she grunted out loud, hesitating while a car passed, her gaze locked on the building down the street.

What if the sheriff wasn't there? He was out a lot. Half the time he was over at the Super Min sniffing around for Gloria Vail, who often worked a second shift for her Aunt Charity. She glanced at the convenience store and lost a mini-battle. She was dying for something cold to drink.

That wasn't such a bad delay tactic, was it? A cold soda on a blistering hot day?

Yes, the convenience store called to her.

She darted across the street, her thin cotton skirt swirling around her ankles as she practically pranced to this much, much more welcome destination. Inside a little bell rang, snagging the attention of the Super Min's owner, first class town snoop Charity Grambling.

It wasn't Zoe's first encounter with the woman, but mostly she stayed off Charity's radar.

"Oh, you're the doctor's little harpy," Charity announced in greeting.

Zoe froze, frowning at the older woman, who adjusted tortoiseshell glasses on her nose like she simply had to have a better look.

"Excuse me?"

"I've seen you with him," Charity said, giving Zoe a slow up-and-down. "He's very handsome."

"What the hell is a harpy, anyway?" Zoe asked. She was so not afraid of this woman who had tried to stop Casa Blanca from ever being built. "Other than fantastic, fresh, and fabulous, of course?"

Charity didn't smile, still busy eyeing Zoe. "He has a son, you know."

"Must be that wicked-high sperm count." She headed to the back, her eye on the coolers full of Coke. And not diet, damn it.

"I thought he might go out with my niece, Gloria."

She opened the fridge and looked at Charity through the frosted glass. "Isn't she dating the sheriff?" *The same sheriff I should be standing in front of right now, confessing.*

"Not anymore."

"They'll get back together." She grabbed the can and closed the fridge. "And you'll come around to like him."

The other woman made a harrumphing noise that would probably be engraved on her tombstone, placing her hand on the register. "He might not be so bad after all," Charity said.

We'll see how bad he is—will he arrest Pasha before or after she gets out of the clinic? Zoe smiled. "I bet you like him more than you're letting on. You just like to make trouble."

"Of course I do." She hit a key and grinned back. "Like trouble, that is. Anyway, he's about to get a break on some big case."

You have no idea, lady.

"He was just in here this morning, trying to kiss up to me and tell me stuff he surely shouldn't have been telling me."

"Which of course you'll repeat."

Charity bared aging teeth. "Of course."

Good to know the sheriff couldn't keep his mouth shut. No doubt Charity would know Zoe's deep, dark secret by nightfall. She slid a five across the counter and popped the top of the soda can, the crackling fizz tempting Zoe to drink before she even got her change.

But there was no change, because Charity lifted her

skinny butt off her stool, looked side to side as if the CIA were hiding behind the magazine rack, and whispered, "Things like this don't come along very often in Mimosa Key."

Zoe shrugged, taking a huge, icy gulp.

"The FBI is in town."

And spit Coke all over the counter.

Charity jumped back. "Oh my—"

"The FBI?" Those right there were the three scariest letters in the English language. She'd grown up in fear of them, imagining them as dark-suited, sharp-toothed, beady-eyed Kidnapper Hunters bent on tracking down every old lady who'd ever snagged a foster child, no matter why.

Charity's mouth turned down at the soda sprinkles on the counter. "You can buy some paper towels in aisle two."

She set the can down. "Keep the change. And the Coke." If she ran out of here she'd look guilty. Like she knew exactly where the murderer was hiding. Charity would be on the phone before Zoe left the parking lot. The FBI would be after her, lights flashing, bullhorn screaming, charges flying.

She was ready to deal with the town sheriff—well, sort of ready—since she knew his weaknesses. But the *FBI*? No. That was like walking into hell to face the devil.

Her heartbeat echoed so loud she couldn't hear Charity talk, although her lips were moving. She couldn't remember how to breathe or think or make a joke that could get her out of this.

All she could do was run. So she did.

Chapter Twenty-three

⌒

When the transfusion and gene-therapy treatment were complete at three o'clock, Oliver and Raj crashed in the conference room, both quiet as they came down from the process of injecting vector carriers into Pasha's cells and monitoring her response.

Raj paced the room, vibrating like an overstrung violin. "I think we did it, Oliver. She responded so well, even better toward the end than I'd thought."

Oliver nodded, still too preoccupied to talk.

"I think we have everything we need to take this one to the NIH," Raj added.

The process of getting this far in the testing protocol and working with the National Institutes of Health had been long and arduous. But every roadblock with the government organization would have been worth it if they saved Pasha's life—and many, many more—because of the job they'd done.

"Look, we have three major risk factors," Raj continued, as if he felt he had to convince Oliver they'd succeeded. "One is reproductive, so not a factor with an eighty-year-old woman. One is infection of healthy cells, and we'll know that in a matter of hours. And last is overexpression," he said, using a term that meant they'd caused inflammation. "That never happened once in the international cases or any other testing I've tracked."

Oliver nodded, taking a long draw on his water.

Raj stopped pacing, coming to a stop in front of his partner. "And then there is the risk that this could get too personal for you."

"Every patient is personal for me, Raj. That's my weakness."

"And your greatest strength. But when you know and care about the patient—"

"I care about every patient."

"She's practically family."

Oliver shook his head. "No, she's not."

"She's the aunt of the woman you love." At Oliver's look, Raj waved a hand. "Don't deny it. I'm practically suffocated when you two are in a room together."

"That makes two of us suffocated."

Raj dropped into a chair. "What the hell does that mean?"

It meant he couldn't breathe for how much he needed her, missed her, wanted her—and he was furious because she didn't trust him enough to tell him everything. "It means that love, if that's what you want to call it, can be suffocating."

"It can also be life changing."

"Says the committed bachelor."

Raj had the decency to grin. "Hey, I don't want my life to change. You, on the other hand—"

"I don't want my life to change, either."

"No?"

Yes. Of course he did. "The truth is," Oliver said on a sigh, "that woman can't stay in one place long enough for anything to change."

Raj frowned. "Where *is* Zoe? Shouldn't she be here celebrating?"

"See what I mean?" Oliver had called her four times since they'd finished, but each time he was sent to voice mail. He'd talked to Tessa, who they'd agreed would watch Evan today. Tessa had exchanged texts with Zoe but had no idea where she was.

Frustration pushed him up from the table and to the door. "Like I said, she has a tendency to disappear."

"Where are you going?"

"Check on the patient."

"Keep it impersonal, Oliver," Raj warned. "Stress is the enemy."

Oliver shot Raj a look as he walked out. Did he think Oliver didn't realize that?

The patient room was dim and Pasha's eyes were closed, but he knew better than to assume she was asleep. Still, he moved around quietly, checking the monitors but mostly watching her face.

Her expressionless, calm, and very much alive face.

God, he wanted to save this woman's life, despite the fact that he suspected she didn't have a lot of years left. Still, if she made it to eighty-five or eighty-eight or even ninety, he'd have given her a gift.

What would she do with it? Hopefully, explain why

she'd sat on that letter for nine years, then left it as some kind of explanation or act of goodwill.

Her lids fluttered and she opened her eyes slowly to focus on him.

"Hello there, Pasha," he said softly.

"Actually, my name is Patricia."

Either the drugs made her want to be honest, or the realization that she could be knocking on death's door had done the trick. Either way, he took a slow step closer to the bed. "I know that," he said simply.

"And Zoe's name is Bridget."

He nodded. "I know that, too."

"I know you do. I remember it all."

Was she lucid enough to remember why she'd hidden the letter he'd written that somehow did manage to get forwarded to her? Because he'd sure as hell like to know. And why she decided to share it now? And while she was remembering things, what had really happened with that boy of hers?

But not now. The doctor in him knew the timing of those questions could be fatal.

Instead, Oliver gently lifted her hand to touch her pulse. "You don't need to remember anything right now, Pasha. I want you to sleep. The more you sleep, the more your cells are going to reproduce and become healthy."

She gave him a dubious look. "If it's that easy, why isn't everyone who has cancer having this treatment?"

"Everyone might, someday, thanks to pioneers like you. Are you in any pain?" he asked.

"No. Yes. Heartache."

"Your chest hurts?"

"My heart. There's a difference. It's actually aching because I think it might be broken."

"No, no, Pasha," he reassured her. "Don't get emotional. Not now."

Her eyes flashed open. "Then when?"

"When you're healthy and this has been a rousing success, then you and Zoe can—"

"Where is Zoe?"

He wished to hell he knew. "She's not back yet."

"Are we alone, then?"

"We are, but Pasha, I don't want your blood pressure to go up and I don't want your heart rate to increase, so I'm going to give you a seda—"

"I don't want to sleep anymore."

"You have to. Sleep is nearly as important a part of this treatment as the gene therapy itself. I'll prepare an IV for—"

"I always knew you were the one for her."

Then why screw with their chances by hiding that letter? He tamped down the question and put his hand on her thin shoulder. "Not now, Pasha."

She looked up at him. "What if I die?"

"I don't think that's going to happen," he said with true confidence. "I think you're going to live, and live well."

"The only way for me to live well is to know you and Zoe are together."

He clamped his mouth shut and turned to a cabinet where IV bags were kept.

"You know I'm right," she said. "You should be together."

"It seems we always have obstacles that keep us apart." *Like you.*

"Has she found the letter yet?"

Damn it. He wasn't going to spend the day pushing the

boundaries of modern medicine only to see her fail because of anxiety that he could have avoided. He didn't answer, signing the forms as he entered the security code that kept the cabinet locked.

"Is she mad at me?"

I am. "We've been too focused on today. As you should be," he added with a stern look over his shoulder.

"Doctor…Oliver…I need to say something." Her dark eyes flashed with desperation. "There's so much more to the story than you understand. There's more to my life, my past.…"

The heart monitor started to beep. "Not now, Pasha. You need to say it when you're better." He attached the sedative to the existing IV bag, snapping the opening in place to connect to her port.

"What if I die?"

"If you die, Zoe will be heartbroken, so I recommend you sleep."

"But that…child…my child…"

The drip started, the IV open and successful. Nothing that was said now could upset her; she'd be asleep in a matter of two minutes.

In fact, in the next thirty seconds, thanks to the meds surging into her veins, every word she said would probably be the absolute, unvarnished truth. Might as well get it. There'd be no reaction to stress now, and she'd never remember what she'd told him.

"What about your child, Pasha?"

"You have to find Matthew."

He let out a slow breath. "I don't think that's possible anymore," he said as calmly as he could manage. "Matthew's dead, isn't he?"

Her eyes widened, more from fighting the need to close the lids than from alarm.

"Find him," she whispered.

"How can I do that?"

Her eyelids fluttered. "All these years, I had to run from him."

"From his memory or from what…happened to him?"

"From…the…killer. From Matthew."

Oliver startled at the words, but Pasha did exactly the opposite, slipping into a deep sleep, completely still and completely silent.

"Dr. Bradbury!" In the hall, Wanda's voice rose with an uncharacteristic note of panic. She stopped at the door, a little breathless.

"What's the matter?"

"I got rid of them, but…" She shook her head. "It wasn't easy."

"Them? Who? What are you talking about?"

"The sheriff was here, with an FBI agent. They wanted to take Ms. Tamarin."

"Take her?"

"She's wanted in connection to a murder, Doctor."

The murder of Matthew…but she'd just said he was the killer. Someone named Matthew had killed Matthew. Is that what she'd meant? And she'd been running from *him* all these years?

He glanced at the sleeping woman, his heart squeezing to put the puzzle pieces together with the same ease as his brilliant son assembled toy puzzles. Something was missing, someone named Matthew. Would Zoe know who Pasha was talking about? Would the sheriff and the FBI agent who'd just been sent away?

Someone knew, and Oliver meant to find out. Hustling out of the clinic, he realized that Raj was right. He cared about this patient. He cared about her, because Zoe did.

Now he had to fix her inside—and out.

"You are really, really good at this." The balloon pilot, a sixty-something charmer named Syl, had let Zoe take over the operation of the balloon about twenty minutes after they hit their cruising altitude.

Since they'd been out, almost two hours now, Zoe had waited for the happy, light, mind-numbing relief that ballooning always gave her. It never came.

Sure, she'd enjoyed the excursion, floating over the Intracoastal Waterway and up the coast, and now she could see the question-mark-shaped island of Mimosa Key, which gave her a little thrill. "Do we have time to fly over Mimosa?"

"If you can get us there." He gave her an easy, toothy smile. "Which I'm certain you can, since I'm gonna say you're the best damn pilot I've seen in a long time."

She laughed. "I'm pretty good at it, I'm not going to lie."

She twisted the parachute regulator, pulling the cord to let some air escape, which dropped the balloon a few feet so they could catch an easterly breeze.

"You read the wind," Syl said, his arms crossed as he leaned against an extra propane tank and watched her. "That's not something that's easy to teach."

"Better know how if you want to go anywhere but up or down."

"You do it on instinct," he said, his voice rich with admiration. "I've seen older pilots fight the wind like a battle to the death. And lose. Men, too."

She smiled, not fazed by his sexism or ageism, more concerned with the redline on the thermistor. But that was all good. "I lose other battles, but not with the wind. Oh, here we go." The breeze caught the balloon and it swayed left, then right, then left again, drifting closer to Mimosa Key. "The trick will be getting us back to the mainland."

"I can call my runners when we land," Syl said. "That's all part of my business."

"If I can land up in Barefoot Bay, I could walk home."

"You live on Mimosa Key?"

She pulled the chute again, catching a breeze like a windsurfer, the movement almost taking her breath away. But not her heavy heart.

"I live there temporarily," she said. And wasn't that the story of her life?

"Where you from?" he asked.

Good question, with no answer. "I live in Arizona. At the moment."

"Good ballooning in Arizona. You pilot there?"

She turned her face to the sun, the breeze taking away all the heat, leaving nothing but glorious warmth on her cheeks. This was usually the moment she felt free, unencumbered, and safe.

But she didn't really feel any of those things right now. She felt lonely and scared and so, so tired of running. "Yes," she replied. "I freelance pilot wherever I live."

"Why don't you move here and work for me?"

Zoe almost laughed at the irony of that—exactly what Pasha had suggested she do when she'd seen the ad in the paper. Which, Zoe had to admit, might have been why she'd driven toward Fort Myers when she'd run off, checking the skies until she had caught a few glimpses of a bright-red-and-white balloon. On instinct, she'd followed it until she'd reached an open airfield owned by Sylver Sky.

It had taken a few hours to get a balloon, but she'd gotten to know the owner, Sylvester McMann, and just being at an airfield made her feel a little better.

Before she'd taken off she'd checked with the clinic. Everything was going well. Then she'd texted Tessa, who had informed her that Evan was enjoying a day working in the greenhouse. Cleared of her immediate responsibilities and forced to turn off her phone, Zoe seized the chance to get as far away from the sheriff—and the FBI—as she could. For now.

Then she waited for that natural high that came only with a good escape. But with every foot they climbed, she felt lower.

"Look, there's the causeway," she said, peering out at the long bridge that connected Mimosa Key to Florida's mainland. From up here, the eight-mile-long and two-mile-wide curved island was even more beautiful, a forest-green sanctuary trimmed with white sand beaches, boat-studded harbors, and long docks reaching out like tentacles all around.

At the northern end, the west-facing inlet of Barefoot Bay glimmered like a necklace of emeralds and sapphires.

As they floated over the northeastern side of the island, Zoe got a look at the undeveloped side of Barefoot Bay, where there were no roads, homes, or people. Toward the coast, she spotted a clearing big enough to land.

"I could put us down there," she said.

Syl launched an eyebrow in the direction of the balloon's crown. "You could land us in the water, too. Don't you dare."

"The beach winds are kind of unpredictable, but I could do it."

"One wrong cross breeze and…" Syl leaned over the basket and then grinned at her, his hazel eyes dancing. "You could probably do it."

She puffed out a breath. "No *could* about it."

"Okay, young lady, if you drop this baby right on that clearing, I'd pay you twice what you're making in Arizona to work for me."

A funny lightness popped in her chest—was *that* the release she'd been seeking all day? "You would?"

"Hell yeah. I have a dozen customers a week asking to come over here to Mimosa or one of the other islands, and I've never had a pilot qualified to land it."

"Damn, Syl, I love a challenge."

"Go for it."

A ping of excitement shot through her, and for the next few minutes Zoe sparred with the Gulf breezes, depending on instinct and experience to guide her as she adjusted the valves and took the balloon up, down, and directly over the clearing.

"Woo-hoo!" she called out, exhilarated with her success as she curled her fingers confidently around the maneuvering vent.

Syl lifted his hand. "Don't get too cocky!"

Just as he said that, a gust pushed them off course, whipping the basket toward the west. She responded instantly, twisting the valve to shoot out more gas and take them above the breeze, high enough above the tree line that she could now see the buttercream rooftops of Casa Blanca tucked into the foliage and beach.

"My friend owns that resort," she said proudly. "Her husband is the architect."

"Really?" He leaned over the side of the basket while she gave full attention to the burners. "I figured it was some corporate conglomerate who owned it."

"Nope, just a mom-and-pop deal, but it's top notch."

"Think you could get your friend to send some of those rich clients my way?"

Zoe struggled with another gust. "Done and done. Okay, I'm going to try this again."

"Looks like they spotted you, though."

She turned to look, her gaze scanning the resort until it landed on the rooftop of Bay Laurel and the driveway in front of the villa. There, two men stood side by side, one of them pointing straight up at the balloon.

At the sight of Oliver, even a thousand feet below, her heart flipped. Or maybe that was a reaction to the man he was talking to. And the car parked in the driveway—a dark sedan that Pasha would say "screamed" FBI.

"Those tourists are ripe for the picking, don't you think?" Syl asked.

Someone was about to be picked. Someone up here.

She could only imagine what Oliver was saying. *There she is. There's the woman you're looking for.*

Had he already turned Pasha in, too?

She swallowed the metallic taste of betrayal and let out a long sigh. "I can't do it."

"What?"

She stepped away and gestured to Syl. "You do it. Take

us back to the mainland and call a runner to meet us. I can't get down on that island."

"I thought you were so sure."

"I'm not sure of anything or anyone," she admitted. "Let's get out of here."

"Come on, you can do it. I want to see you land this thing."

She shook her head. "I'm not feeling it today, Syl." Not feeling free or safe or untethered or any of the things she loved about flying.

Just numb.

"Hmm." Syl stepped to the valves to do the work. "I didn't really take you for a quitter, miss."

Inside her chest, something slipped and gripped and hurt. What was she so afraid of? Whatever the truth, whatever it cost, she had to face this. Until she did, she had no chance at love or a home or the real freedom she'd been searching for all these years. She *had* to do this.

"You know," she said to Syl, "I'm not a quitter. Let me at that valve."

Chapter Twenty-four

~

Before Oliver could find Zoe, Special Agent Nicholas Fitzgerald showed up at Casa Blanca looking for her. The woman at the front desk sent him to Bay Laurel, and as they greeted each other in the driveway, a brightly colored spot in the sky told Oliver exactly where Zoe was. The agent was alone and made no mention of the sheriff who had been with him when they'd been sent away from the IDEA offices. Maybe they'd decided to split the effort, sending the FBI here and the sheriff to get Zoe.

When the agent asked about her, Oliver pointed to the balloon. His gut told him exactly who was in it, if not flying it.

Oliver wasn't exactly sure what he was going to say to the agent, so he let the visit unfold to get a feel for the man. His impression wasn't entirely positive, based on Fitzgerald's cool demeanor during their conversation, which didn't change even after Oliver invited him inside.

"I really wanted to speak with Pasha Tamarin personally," the agent said. "But the staff at your clinic made that impossible."

Oliver made a mental note to give Wanda a raise.

Once they were seated in the living room, the other man leaned forward and looked earnestly at Oliver. "I'm not sure how much you know about the subtleties of DNA, Dr. Bradbury."

He managed not to smile. "I know a little."

"Your patient, whose real name is Patricia Hobarth, is allegedly enmeshed in multiple crimes, the worst of which is the murder of her son."

"She didn't do it."

Fitzgerald's crystal-blue eyes sparked. "Perhaps you know a little bit about DNA, Doctor, but determining innocence or guilt really isn't part of your job."

"Maybe it isn't, but her health is my number-one concern right now. Ms. Tama—er, Ms. Hobarth has undergone an extremely delicate and experimental procedure today. Stress could grossly undermine the treatment. So my job is to keep you away from her. When she's healthy, I'm sure she'll talk to you."

"You're sure?" Fitzgerald choked softly. "She's changed her name, used false identification, fraudulently reported her own death, abducted a child, and God knows what else to avoid being tried for this murder."

"She *was* tried for the murder and acquitted." He'd done a little research himself after Zoe had left last night.

"She was not acquitted," the agent corrected. "And she most certainly can be retried. She can no longer escape the power of technology and our ability to find fugitives. Obviously, she's living in fear of that."

"Maybe she's living in fear of something else," Oliver suggested. "Like the real killer."

Fitzgerald shook his head and sighed. "There's never been another serious suspect."

"There's never been any hard evidence."

"And you're basing that on what knowledge, Doctor?" Fitzgerald demanded. "Talking to her about it or reading ancient news accounts?"

The latter, but he was undeterred. "I won't let anyone near her for at least a week."

"We can end this very, very quickly, Dr. Bradbury," the other said. "We don't even have to talk to her. The FBI has DNA evidence and wants to compare it to Ms. Tamarin. We need access to her to get a clean sample."

"You want DNA? I have vials of her blood. It's yours. Moreover, I have mitochondrial DNA, which, if you do a little studying, you'll discover that you can match with zero doubt and quite quickly, too. In a matter of hours, not weeks."

The agent shook his head. "We need to verify that it's her blood, not a random vial from some local health clinic."

Ire whipped up Oliver's spine. "You may go to my clinic and examine the vials that were taken during a transfusion today. You may stand at the door and watch the nurse take any sample for DNA testing. But you may not talk to her."

"Why not?" he asked. "Why can't I at least question her?"

"She's eighty-four and battling for her life," Oliver told him. "And I might add that if she wins that battle, she may save hundreds, even thousands, of others. But not if she collapses under the stress of this investigation."

Fitzgerald sat back and crossed his arms, unrelenting. "I'll get a warrant."

"She's sound asleep. She can't tell you anything."

"But I can."

Both men turned at the sound of Zoe's voice as she stepped around the entryway wall into the living room. Her hair wind whipped, her cheeks chapped, her eyes bright from tears or fear, she walked into the room and managed to avoid eye contact with Oliver.

But he couldn't take his eyes off her.

"How'd you get down here so fast?" Oliver asked.

"I'm that good," she shot back, her attention on the FBI agent. "And the driver broke land speed records. I'm Zoe, er…" She reached out her hand as he stood. "Bridget Lessington."

"Special Agent Nick Fitzgerald." The man gave her enough of a once-over to really irk, but Oliver stood slowly, waiting for the introduction to be complete before he walked over to Zoe.

Finally, she looked at him, and the hurt in her eyes punched a lot harder than Fitzgerald's smart-ass attitude. "How is she?" Zoe whispered.

"She's good. She's sleeping, and I'd like to keep it that way." Oliver nodded to the other man. "Special Agent Fitzgerald has other ideas."

"I don't want to hurt your…friend, Ms. Lessington."

She closed her eyes for a quick second in reaction to the name. "Please call me Zoe. And she's my great-aunt, even if that's not what some piece of paper says. What do you want from her?"

"An interview," Fitzgerald said. "What do you know about the murder, miss?"

She brushed a hair off her face. "I didn't know she had a son until a few days ago. She's never mentioned him."

"All those years of living together and she never mentioned she had a son? Don't you find that odd?"

Zoe didn't answer, but worked to swallow.

"She never mentioned her trial?" he asked.

"No."

"She never mentioned her life in Pennsylvania?"

"Rarely."

"She never mentioned her marriage to Matthew Harold Hobarth?"

"Not once."

"She never—"

Oliver shot between them. "That's enough."

But Zoe's eyes were wide, along with her mouth. "What was his name?"

"Hobarth. Matthew Harold, but he goes by—"

She grabbed his arm. "Goes by? He's *alive*?"

"Barely, but yes."

"Have you talked to him?" Zoe and Oliver asked the question in perfect unison, each taking a small step closer to the other.

The FBI agent shook his head, shutting them down. "First of all, he can't talk. He suffered a stroke in an assisted-living facility outside of Columbus. I met with him before coming down in a failed effort to get more details about Patricia's relationship with her son and really get a better handle on her motive. To be honest, Harry isn't going to live out the month."

Zoe's eyes narrowed at the news, but Oliver moved in, putting a hand on her shoulder to ask the question burning in him. "Did you happen to get *his* DNA for testing while you were there?"

"No, Dr. Bradbury," Fitzgerald said, taking note of the protective stance and flicking an interested eyebrow. "Mr. Hobarth's alibi is ironclad and was never at issue during the trial, so don't even go there."

"I'll go wherever I want," Zoe shot back. "Including to Ohio to clear my aunt's name."

"Ms. Lessington, she is not your aunt." All warmth was gone from the man's eyes as he met Zoe's gaze. "And you are not an investigator. I suggest you cooperate as fully as possible, as our investigation shows you have long gone past 'victim' in this case."

Oliver stepped forward. "I think it's time you leave."

"Why?"

"She doesn't have a lawyer present." Oliver ushered him to the door. "I'll call my clinic and if you go there right now, they will arrange for you to get the DNA sample from Ms. Hobarth. You can verify it, take it, test it, and compare it to whatever you have."

"And then—"

"And then," Zoe said, cutting him off. "You can clear her."

He gave her a long look, then nodded. "We'll see about that."

Oliver walked him to the door, watched him drive away, and returned to the living room to find Zoe madly dialing a cell phone.

"Who are you calling?" he asked.

"Slade Garrison."

"The sheriff? How do you think he can help you?"

She smiled. "I think I can help him." She held up a

finger and talked into the phone. "Slade? Zoe Tamarin. Wanna get married?"

Oliver almost fell over.

Oliver nodded throughout Zoe's conversation with Slade, obviously not the least bit surprised as he listened to her arrange a meeting at the Naples sheriff's office so she could break the case wide open for the young deputy.

When she disconnected, they stared at each other for a beat and she waited for the inevitable litany of questions. *Why didn't you tell me about her son last night? What are you hiding? Is Pasha a murderer?*

"Her ex-husband killed the child," he said instead.

Relief rocked her. "How do you know that?"

"She told me."

She stood speechless.

"The same way she told you," he explained. "She told me to find Matthew. She didn't mean the son, she meant the father."

"They're both Matthew," she finished. "But the newspaper said M. Harold Hobarth, so I figured he went by his middle name."

"Whatever he went by, that's who she's been running from, Zoe, not the FBI or police."

She stabbed her fingers through her hair, every follicle tingling with frustration. "God, if I'd known this earlier, I wouldn't have wasted the day in a balloon, running away."

Oliver reached for her hand. "Stop running, Zoe."

"I should have that tattooed on my arm."

"You should have it tattooed on your heart." He pulled her closer, looking so deeply into her eyes the intensity rocked her. "I'll be happy to do the work."

"You forgive me for not telling you last night?"

"Yes, but why didn't you?"

"The treatment was today and I thought…" Her voice faded, the idiocy of that decision so clear in today's light.

"You thought I'd screw up somehow?" She could hear the hurt in his tone.

"I underestimated you," she said softly. "My bad."

"Yes, you are bad." He eased her closer to kiss her forehead. "Let's talk in the car. And you can tell me why this information is going to get Slade married. I'm assuming not to you."

She just smiled.

On the way to Naples, she shared the conversation between Slade and Gloria, and they discussed all they'd been able to glean about Matthew Harold Hobarth from the news accounts.

"He's crazy rich," Zoe said, remembering a detail about him being on a Greek yacht during the trial. "Could she have been blackmailing him all these years and that's how we've had cash? But what about his 'ironclad' alibi?"

"You answered that with your first statement. Crazy rich can buy alibis. I doubt she's a blackmailer, but think about what drives your aunt."

Zoe glanced out the window, following the sharp curve of white as a boat turned and changed its course and cut a new wake through the waters of the Intracoastal. Pasha would look at that and say something like *That's a sign that there's an unexpected turn coming in our path.* "She's driven by nature's clues."

Oliver shot her a look. "She's driven by fear."

A breath of realization whooshed out of Zoe's chest. He was right. "She ran, she hid, she changed her name, she stayed under the radar and out of the spotlight and off the grid."

"Shitty way to live, isn't it?" he asked.

"Point taken," she conceded. "Why is she afraid of an old guy who had a stroke?"

"He wasn't old years ago, and, as you well know, some very bad behaviors get so ingrained that they become the way you live."

"All right, all right." She fisted her chest. "You're hitting home." But then she relaxed her hand and reached over the console. "I'm so glad you're here with me," she admitted. "I wouldn't want to do this alone."

"You don't have to do anything alone, Zoe."

She closed her eyes and let the feelings wash over her, everything mixed together like a waterfall of gratitude and hope and contentment and…love. Wow. This was no half-assed admission that she couldn't quite form in her mouth.

She *loved* him. She loved this man.

"Here's the sheriff's office," he said, whipping his little sports car into the parking lot and yanking her from lovely realizations. She'd tell him later, she promised herself. The very first minute she could.

A half hour later, in a brightly lit conference room, Zoe and Oliver held hands under the table, a united front sitting across from Deputy Sheriff Slade Garrison.

"You were eavesdropping?" Slade asked for the third time, glancing around as if one of his cohorts might have heard.

"I was walking the beach," she said. "And I happened to hear you."

He narrowed his eyes at her. "What did you hear?"

"Enough to know you want to solve this case." She

pointed at the name and information on the table between them. "Go up to Ohio and snag some blood from this guy before he keels over and dies. I'm telling you this will get you the glory and Glor*ia* all in one swoop."

He almost smiled at her joke, but shook his head. "I'd need to involve another sheriff's office, and the FBI wouldn't like it."

"You want the FBI to solve this crime?" Zoe asked.

"Because that Fitzgerald guy will beat you to it," Oliver added.

"How do you know him?" Slade frowned, confused. "When did you meet him?'"

"He came to my rental villa," Oliver told him. "Without you. He wants the glory, too, I think, and I doubt he wants to share it with the local sheriff."

Under the table Zoe gave his hand a squeeze for the perfect assist.

"First we have to deal with Patricia Hobarth," Slade replied. "Once she's cleared, we can worry about other people who were tangentially involved and had watertight alibis."

"But what if you were to preempt the FBI?" Zoe asked. "You'd be a hero."

"You'd solve a cold case," Oliver added.

"Gloria would be so proud of you." Zoe narrowed her eyes to make her point. "Charity would talk about it from now until the end of time."

He smiled slowly. "You really know how to get a guy, don't you?"

Next to her, Oliver snorted softly. "You have no idea."

"You're right," Slade finally agreed. "I'll fly up there tomorrow."

"Tonight," Zoe said. "The guy is knocking on death's door. Don't miss this opportunity."

"I'll have to talk to my supervisor," he said, standing up.

When they left, Zoe still felt buoyant with hope as they walked to the car and drove through Naples. She was waiting for the perfect moment. In the car? Over dinner? Later on, in bed?

"Shit," Oliver murmured.

"What?" She followed his gaze, realizing they were on the street where his office was located, the wide boulevard where, not so long ago, Zoe had found him and begged him for help.

On the sidewalk outside of the charcoal glass doors of Oliver's practice two people stood in deep conversation, and Zoe instantly recognized the FBI agent who'd been in Oliver's living room and... "Is that Attila the Receptionist?"

"'Fraid so."

"Why is she talking to him?"

Before Oliver answered, the redhead handed a file to the agent, who nodded and walked away, getting into his dark FBI-mobile and driving off without seeing them.

"C'mon." Oliver pulled into a reserved spot next to the building, his jaw set in determination. He walked so fast that Zoe had to practically jog to keep up.

As he pulled open the doors, they found Johanna at the desk, fishing in her bag. She jerked up with a surprised look when Oliver walked in.

The offices were dark, clearly deserted for the evening.

"What did you give him?" Oliver asked.

She didn't reply but shifted her icy blue eyes to Zoe. "She's involved in a crime. I hope you know that."

"You're unemployed. I hope you know *that*." He held the door for her. "You can leave now, Johanna."

She didn't even flinch, but scooped up her bag and walked by them, giving Zoe a wide berth lest she pick up a criminal germ or two.

When the door closed behind her, Oliver snapped one lock and then another.

"Long overdue," he murmured.

"You know what else is long overdue?" Zoe pushed him against the glass and pressed her body up against him. "This." Up on her toes, she kissed him with everything she had, getting an equally passionate kiss back.

"You like that I fired her," he whispered into the kiss.

"I love it. And…" She inched back to look into his eyes. "I love…"

He lifted a brow, waiting.

But the words wouldn't come out.

"Aw, Zoe," he whispered. "You really need to see a doctor about this problem." He lowered his head and kissed her again, deep and slow.

Chapter Twenty-five

Oliver kissed Zoe right across the marble floor, tugging up her T-shirt with one hand as he opened the door to the offices with the other; the hallway was even darker than the waiting room.

"I can enter the sanctuary?" she asked. "I don't have an appointment."

Laughing, he eased her into the wall and pushed his whole body against hers. "This is an emergency. The doctor will definitely see you now."

She smiled into his kiss, flattening her hands on his chest and bunching his shirt, pulling it from his trousers. "I'd like to see him, too." She attacked his mouth with hers, like she was as starving for a taste as he was. "Every inch."

He led her down the hall and into his office, locking the door behind him with a crisp and meaningful click even though he was certain everyone was gone by now.

She glanced around with a questioning look. "Couch? Wall? Desk? Or from that pretty chandelier?"

"Yes."

Laughing, they came together, kissing while she unbuttoned his shirt and pushed back the sleeves and he made his way under her top to caress every bit of skin beneath. Planting his lips under her jaw, he sucked the salty sheen, then licked his way back to her mouth.

"You gotta pick your poison, doc," she whispered. "Fall to the floor?"

"Not for what I have in mind." He walked her across the office, knowing that what was on the other side would surprise her. "My favorite patients get special treatment."

He opened a door to the tiny studio apartment he'd had finished when he'd first moved to Naples. It was dimly lit by shuttered windows that let the last whispers of dusk reveal a king-sized bed.

"Well, well, well." Zoe checked it out as he ushered her straight to the bed. "Doc's got a secret crib."

"When I first moved here I lived in this room."

She sighed. "Lonely."

It was. And Zoe had no idea how many nights her memory had kept him company. "Convenient."

"It is now," she agreed. They stood together for a moment, suspended before the big fall, heat coiling between them.

"Here's my problem, doc," she whispered. "I can't say three little words."

"That's a symptom, not the real problem."

She closed her eyes in acknowledgment. "No wonder you're in such demand. You're so good at diagnosing."

"Damn right. We know the problem," he said. "Now we have to figure out…" He lowered his head and placed his lips on hers with an air-soft kiss, flicking his tongue over her lip. "Why."

He added enough pressure to force her mouth open, then he slipped his tongue inside and curled it around hers. "So we need a very careful…" He eased her onto the bed. "Examination."

As he stood over her, he rolled up his sleeves, like there was work to be done. Pulling him closer, she finished the last of his shirt buttons and slammed her hands onto his chest with an appreciative moan.

"When did this problem start?" He lifted her tank top, dragging it over her breasts and sliding it over her head.

"A long time ago."

He reached around, unsnapped her bra, and slipped her out of it. "Be specific."

"A *very* long time ago."

Laughing, he took a few seconds to enjoy the sight of her breasts, pink and round and tipped by perfect nipples, before dipping his head to suckle her sweet, salty skin.

"Have you ever told anyone you loved them?" he asked.

"I tried. I wanted to." She gripped his head and lifted it to look at him. "I almost did. …"

"But you couldn't."

She shook her head. "I don't know why."

Without answering, he kissed his way over her belly to her skirt, tonguing her belly button while he unsnapped, unzipped, and undressed her.

Once she was gloriously naked, he straddled her, his

shirt hanging open and his pants tented with an erection. She reached for his belt buckle, but he seized her wrists and gripped her, shaking his head.

"I'm still asking questions. Do you *think* these words you can't say?"

She nodded slowly.

"Do you whisper them to yourself?"

Biting her lip, she nodded again.

"When?"

She looked down at his trousers again, which made him harder. "When...I...when...you..."

"When you're with Wild Bill the vibrator?"

Fighting a smile, she looked up at him. "Yeah."

"So you can say you love me when I'm not there, but now you can't?"

"Pretty screwed up, isn't it?"

He grazed one pointed nipple, earning a shudder in response. "I can fix this."

"Of course you can," she said with a laugh, but quieted when he placed another hot kiss on her stomach and worked his way down, kissing her hipbones and stroking her skin with his tongue, suckling her enough to pull a groan of need from her chest.

He lifted his head and gave her a sly smile. "Part of the problem is down here."

"What seems to be the problem?"

"It's hot. And wet."

"And right now, it aches like hell."

"Definitely something I can fix." With one slow stroke of his tongue over her swollen flesh, her legs instinctively widened. He licked again and again, lost in the sweet and unexpected flavors of Zoe, feeling her body vibrate under his hand and mouth, on the very edge of an orgasm that damn near dragged him to one himself.

Seconds before she lost it, he kissed his way back up her body, lingering over every precious inch.

"Now let me work on this…" He returned to her breasts and placed his mouth right over her heart. "Up here."

He turned his head and pressed his ear to her chest. "This heart sounds perfect to me now."

"Beating fast enough," she agreed.

"Then our problem must be…" He crawled up her body and put his hands on her face again, tapping her temples with his index fingers. "Right here."

Which was what they both knew anyway.

Closing her eyes, she pumped her hips once. "Can't you just fix me with…" Another pump. "That."

Not good enough. He wanted to hear the words, wanted to watch her mouth as she admitted what he had long ago realized. "Just say the words to me, Zoe. Say the words you think in your head and whisper when you're alone. Tell me."

"Oliver, why do three overused words matter so much to you?"

Didn't she get it? "The words don't matter, Zoe. I don't want this to be…meaningless." That's what mattered to him. "For so long I've gone through the motions and felt nothing but a natural release. But with you, Zoe, I feel…everything. I want you to feel it, too."

"I do."

"Then…" He lifted both brows.

"I…love…" The word choked her. "I…love…" She shook her head, her eyes full of pain. "Oh, God, Oliver. I don't know what love is. I've never seen it, I've never known it, I've never lived it. How do I know for sure if what I feel for you is lust or love? How do I know?"

"You? The girl who gets in a basket, turns a knob, and trusts it to fly? You know it will work, like you know you love me. You've *always* loved me." He cupped her face, holding her still. "Zoe, you love like you breathe. You don't need to have seen it or lived it before. You love without trying."

"How do you know that?"

"Because I know you. And because, Zoe, I love you." He gave her a teasing smile before coming in for another kiss. "See how easy?"

It wasn't easy. It was hard. *Everything* was hard. Oliver's arms. His kiss. And, oh God…*that* was hard.

He intensified the kiss but somehow kept it so tender that it almost hurt for the sweetness. Easing himself over her, he held her close and let that kiss go on and on until the room spun a little and each breath became an effort. Until blood started to thrum fiery through every vein, and every carefully placed brick in the wall around her heart just tumbled and crashed and turned to dust.

"How does that feel?" he asked, whispering the words into her ear, flicking his tongue over her lobe.

Like her whole world was spinning into magic. "Really…" Amazing. "In need of help."

"Guess what?"

"You can fix that?"

"It's my specialty." He rolled over and grabbed a condom he must have had in his wallet, sheathing himself before positioning himself over her.

"You like fixing things," she said, watching every move. "That's what turns you on."

"*You* turn me on," he murmured. "And you're talking too much."

"You better fix that."

He did, kissing her mouth as he entered her body, stealing all her breath and doing a damn good job of shutting her up. And of making her forget how to speak, actually, because right then, all she could do was…feel.

And it scared her. Why?

She closed her eyes, tears stinging. All she could feel was pressure…on her head, over her ears. Darkness, heat, the smell of musty cotton and the muffled sound of…

Suffocation. "Oliver!"

He shot up from the kiss, blinking at her. "What?"

"Suffocation." She barely mouthed the word but it hit her in the gut like a cannonball. "That's what I'm scared of."

The trapped feeling of a pillow over her head and the desperate, burning, panic because she needed to escape. The dark nights in that foster home when there was no way out. When that voice started demanding and demanding the same thing. Three different words, so different than the three Oliver wanted and needed to hear.

Run, Zoe, run.

As long as she could run, she could survive. But if she didn't run this time, if she could stay right here with Oliver, no matter what, then she could beat the memories of that house and that man and even that voice.

"What are you scared of, Zoe?"

"Him. The foster father who Pasha saved me from. I can't breathe when I think about…him. About how much I needed to escape him." The sob trapped in her throat nearly strangled her. "I would put that pillow over my head and

try to suffocate myself. It was my only escape." Until Pasha
was her real escape.

Oliver held her, kissing her forehead, her eyes, her
mouth.

"He's gone, Zoe. Long, long gone. You're not going
to suffocate if you stay." He reached up and grabbed the
pillow, holding it in the air. "You're safe. With me, you
will always, always be safe. You don't have to escape. You
don't have to suffocate yourself just to hide."

He tossed the pillow on the floor, where it landed with a
soft thud.

For a long, quiet moment, she searched his face, memo-
rizing every line, every lash, every cell. This man who was
completely inside her head, heart, and body. This man who
had so much patience and tenderness and ability.

This man she absolutely, positively… "Oliver," she
whispered, touching his face.

"Yes?"

"I love you."

He smiled. "I know."

"Then why all the work to make me say it?"

"So *you* know." Very slowly, he began to move in and
out of her again, deeper with each thrust, farther and closer
and longer. They broke the kiss, their cheeks smashed together as the intensity sharpened every time he plunged
into her.

All the feelings of suffocation were gone. He'd done
that for her! Zoe could breathe. She could hold him and cry
out his name and say those three words and *breathe*.

Was this what it was like to love? To be free?

A shimmer of sparks showered low and deep inside
her, forcing her to rise up and meet each thrust and

cling to his arms like she might fall off the edge of the world.

"I have to…" She struggled with the words, her throat weirdly closed and tight. "I have to…"

He slowed his movements, then stopped, and her eyes popped open in disbelief. "I *have* to," she insisted.

Still, he didn't move, holding her shoulders and his position inside her.

"Aren't you going to fix that, doc? I *need* to come."

"You need to love."

She frowned, biting her lip, rocking into his immobile hips. "I…can't…"

"You can." He started to move again, taking her with him.

"I do, Oliver. I love you. I *do*." Every muscle spasmed at the same time, twisting and turning with exquisite pleasure, fluttering first, then thundering to a complete release.

Oliver lost it, too, closing his eyes and gritting his teeth as he gave in and pounded deeper and harder into her, finally lifting her shoulders off the bed with unexpected might and grinding into her as he came.

They fell on the bed, hearts hammering, neither one really able to get a deep breath.

She finally turned her head to look at him and enjoy the way that made her heart swell. "You think that's all it takes to fix me?"

"Absolutely not."

"No?"

"You need this prescription regularly. Maybe every day. Maybe forever."

"Forever?" She waited for the grip of terror, but none came.

"Don't leave me, Zoe. No matter what, please stay with me. Promise me, Zoe." He stroked her cheek. "Promise me."

"'Kay."

"'Kay? " He let out a dry laugh. "What kind of promise is that?"

"That's my kind of—"

On the floor the phone beeped, and not a soft ding of a call, but a high-pitched alarm that pierced her brain.

"Fuck." He shot off the bed and grabbed the phone, stabbing the screen and angling it to read. Even in the darkness she could see the blood drain from his face and she knew exactly what that meant.

"Pasha?" She sat up, gathering sheets frantically.

"She's had a heart attack." He was already in motion, getting clothes, making a call, barking orders, but Zoe sat stone still in shock.

She'd just learned to love. Would she have to learn how to lose?

Chapter Twenty-six

～

For once, Zoe sat very, very still. Not that she could actually bounce off the walls of the waiting room, since Jocelyn held one hand, Tessa had the other, and Lacey stood behind the three of them with her hands on Zoe's shoulders.

It was like they were, literally and symbolically, holding her in place. Was that what it took to keep Zoe still?

Or had Pasha's heart attack paralyzed Zoe with fear?

"She's going to be fine," Lacey whispered.

"She's too tough to die," Jocelyn added.

"She's in the best possible hands." Tessa gave Zoe a little nudge. "You know that."

A nod was the most she could muster. Closing her eyes, she imagined Oliver's hands—not how they'd just been all over her, but healing with that competence and authority. *Please, Oliver, heal her.*

He'd been stunned by the news of a heart attack. This wasn't a side effect of the treatment; there was no connection to her heart, and the pretreatment tests showed her heart to be strong and her arteries healthy.

Yet she'd suffered a massive myocardial infarction, with no warning or reason, and her life hung in the balance down the hall.

Across the room Evan stirred under a blanket a nurse had supplied.

"He can't be comfortable," Tessa said, eyeing the child. "Maybe I should see if they'd give us a pillow."

"Don't even think about it," Lacey warned. When all three of them turned to give her a look of disbelief, she didn't flinch. "Sorry, but you never move a sleeping child. That's a law of nature."

Zoe studied Evan's profile and felt a totally unfamiliar flutter in her chest. Was falling for this kid a law of nature, too? Because she was, and fast.

"What?" Jocelyn asked, concern in her voice.

"I didn't say anything," Zoe replied.

"You groaned."

"Of course she groaned," Tessa jumped in, squeezing her hand. "We're holding vigil in a hospital. She's terrified."

"A vigil?" Zoe choked on the word. "Isn't that when you wait for someone to die?"

"It's when you wait for someone, period," Tessa said.

"Exactly." Jocelyn added pressure to Zoe's other hand. "We're waiting for Oliver to walk through those doors with good news. We have to hold that positive thought."

Zoe opened her mouth to say something about Jocelyn's platitudes but closed it again. Sarcasm had no place in this waiting room, with these friends who had left a warm bed, a dear husband, a hot lover, or a newborn baby to sit with her.

The impact of that sacrifice exploded inside her. "God, I love you guys," she said, the admission coming out on something embarrassingly close to a sob.

Well, *that* was easy to say.

"We love you, too," Lacey assured her.

"And I kind of love him," Zoe added, her gaze still on Evan. It was like Oliver had unlocked the dams and love was pouring out *everywhere*. "He didn't even complain when I pulled him out of bed. All he cared about was Pasha." Affection twisted through her, wrapping around her throat and making it tight.

"He's a great kid," Tessa agreed. "So smart and sweet. He's insane about getting that dog—"

"The dog!" Zoe slapped a hand over her mouth and sat bolt upright. "If we don't get that dog today, he might be given away to someone else."

"I can take him to the pound," Tessa assured her, but then added, "'Cept I'll probably pick one up myself."

"You should," Jocelyn said. "It would be good for you to have a dog."

They were all quiet for a moment, the obvious, unspoken, and uncomfortable truth hanging over them: *A dog was no substitute for that baby Tessa wanted so much.*

"I'm getting coffee," Lacey said quickly. "There's no sleep in my near future."

Zoe dropped her head back and looked up at her friend. "And by near future, you mean the next seventeen years."

"At least." Lacey gave Tessa a tap. "Wanna come with me? I'm sure we can scare up some organic tea."

"Sure." She stood slowly. "What do you guys want?"

"Coffee for me," Jocelyn said.

"Hot chocolate," Zoe added.

Tessa screwed up her face. "Seriously?"

Zoe jutted her chin toward Evan. "For him. I don't want anything, but he's going to wake up soon."

Jocelyn and Tessa shared a look and Lacey sort of tilted her head and smiled.

"What?" Zoe said. "Why are you all looking at me like that?"

"You got it bad," Jocelyn said.

"The mommy bug bit," Tessa agreed.

"Mommy bug?" Zoe almost choked. "Because I feel bad that I yanked the kid out of bed and threw him on a hospital waiting room sofa and want to give him some hot chocolate? This is now a cry for motherhood?"

"Yeah," Tessa said.

Zoe pointed at her. "You're projecting. Isn't she projecting, Joss? You were the psych major."

Tessa shook her head and walked off with Lacey, no doubt to gossip about Zoe's detonating ovaries.

"Jeez," Zoe mumbled, crossing and uncrossing her ankles. "She can piss me off faster than anyone else."

"You're tired, Zoe," Jocelyn said.

"And scared. And miserable. And lonely. And..." She closed her eyes. "Doesn't matter. She can piss me off after a good night's sleep and multiple orgasms. Which..." She slid a look to Jocelyn. "I was about to have before Oliver got the call."

"That's the least of your problems."

"No kidding." Zoe sighed for what seemed like the three millionth time since they'd arrived at the hospital in North Naples. "How do you do this, Joss?" she asked, referring to the many trips she and Will had made to doctors for Jocelyn's father, who suffered from Alzheimer's.

"We haven't had an ER or ICU incident…yet."

"But…"

Jocelyn nodded. "We will, of course. There's no way to avoid the inevitable of his disease."

"How do you deal?" Zoe asked. "How do you keep from imagining life without him?"

Jocelyn snorted softly. "You may remember that not so long ago I *preferred* life without him. But now…"

"Now you don't, so it's got to hurt to worry about him."

"It does, but it helps to have Will." She gave an easy smile that lit her eyes. "It changes everything to have Will."

"Because he shares the worry?"

"Like everything else in life."

"Wow, that sounds good," Zoe admitted.

"Something you want?"

As much as her next breath. "I don't…yeah. Sure. Who doesn't? But that's not the question."

"What is?"

"I don't know if I can give that kind of unconditional love back," she admitted. "I don't know if I'm capable of it. I've spent my whole life avoiding it. But I think Oliver wants it. He wants everything from me—my heart and soul and trust."

"So what's stopping you?"

"I've been stopping me." Zoe turned away, the confession too raw and way too honest for this particular moment.

"How? Why?" Jocelyn turned, trying to force Zoe to look at her. "Have you made a list of all the possible reasons?"

"I would get stuck in the waiting room with a life coach."

"Answer the question."

Zoe plucked at a chip in the fake wood armrest, reliving the incredible breakthrough she'd had in Oliver's office. "Every time in my life that I ever got even close to an attachment, it blew up in my face. A family I liked or a new friend at school and, wham, I had to move. Then with Pasha, I'd get settled in a place and put down one little root and, bang, it was time to go to the next place. I fell in love and the same thing happened." She looked at Jocelyn through blurry eyes. "Why would it be any different this time?"

Jocelyn closed her hands over Zoe's shaking ones. "You've kept us through all these years."

"You guys work at that. If the three of you didn't hound me with phone calls and e-mails, I'd have probably lost touch."

"And you have had Pasha."

Yes, she had. And now…

"Zoe."

She blinked, the light blocked by a large figure coming through the doorway, in scrubs. "Oliver."

He crouched in front of her, his face a wasteland of misery

"Is she…" *Dead?* Zoe couldn't make the word form.

He shook his head. "She's stable, more or less."

"What does that mean?

"It means you can see her now."

Zoe practically leaped out of the chair. "Is she in pain?"

"No." He stabbed a hand through his hair, exhaling pure exhaustion and frustration. "It was a massive attack, though, and her heart is weak. The real irony is that she isn't rejecting the vectors. In fact, the very earliest indicators are that the gene therapy is working exactly as it should."

"Oliver, is she going to…" She couldn't bring herself to say it.

"I don't know."

They walked down a long hall in silence, so fast the rooms and nurses and soft hospital colors blurred in Zoe's vision. When they reached a room at the end of the ICU hallway, the nurse next to it looked up in greeting.

"Any change?" Oliver asked.

She gave her head a quick, negative shake.

He nodded thanks to the nurse and reached for the door. "Go ahead in, Zoe."

But she stood, frozen in place, collecting the thoughts and feelings that ricocheted around her head and heart, unable to capture any of them long enough to know what she wanted to say to Pasha if this was their last time together.

Could this be their last time together? Oh, Lord, not again. Not another…detachment. She couldn't lose Pasha!

"Zoe?"

She gave him a sad smile. "For a change, I can't move."

He didn't smile. Instead, his eyes darkened as though they reflected the pain in her heart. "I've done everything possible, Zoe. Everything."

She nodded.

"I don't know if it's enough." He worked hard to swallow. "You better go in now."

In other words, say your good-byes.

"Hey, Auntie."

From somewhere in the dark, quiet place where she slept, Pasha could hear Zoe's voice.

Zoe! Is that you, little love?

But nothing came from her mouth and no muscle in her body moved. Even her eyelids were still. It was like she was trapped, able to hear, smell, think, and feel, but her body would not cooperate. And that low, slow, deep burn had started in her chest again.

The touch on her shoulder was light and familiar, along with the scent of a girl who had, in so many ways, saved Pasha's life.

"Pasha?" Close enough that Pasha could feel Zoe's warm kiss on her skin, and the contact gave her just enough energy to open her eyes.

"Hi," Zoe said on a whisper, taking Pasha's hand.

Pasha blinked once because it was easier than talking. For a long time, she soaked up the sight of Zoe's sweet green eyes, which was always a little like walking barefoot in the grass. Cool and inviting and just plain fun.

"At the risk of asking the obvious," Zoe said with a smile, "how ya feelin'?"

"My heart…" *Hurts.*

"Yeah, apparently it's on the attack. But you're going to be fine."

Zoe didn't sound so sure, and she'd be even less so if she could feel the pain in Pasha's chest.

"But I'm right here with you, and Oliver and the doctors are taking care of you."

Oliver. Oh, *Oliver*. "The moonbow." She had to tell Zoe. "True love…returns."

Zoe kind of shook her head, not getting it. "Evan's outside, too."

No, not Evan. He wasn't the true love, though Pasha may have imagined that at first. It was—

"And the girls, too. All gathered round because you're a *great* great-aunt to all of us, Pasha." She was keeping her voice bright and chirpy, like she did in the car when they were beelining out of yet another town and Pasha was scared, looking at the rearview mirror and expecting…him.

He'd hunt her down and kill her, too.

"I'm sorry…" Pasha eked out the words, and they sounded empty and useless. As they should.

"Stop," Zoe said.

Pasha tried to take a breath to say more, but her chest felt like someone was stabbing her heart, using knives sharpened by guilt and self-loathing and fear, each strike worse than the one before.

What seemed like an eternity passed, but it probably was just the time it took for Zoe to stroke Pasha's arm and run her knuckles over Pasha's old fingers. The loving touch broke her heart even more.

"Pasha, I want you to listen to me." She got right next to Pasha's ear to whisper. "I know about Matthew."

Pasha closed her eyes. "I didn't—"

"I know." Zoe put a hand over Pasha's heart, the touch somehow soothing. "His father did it, didn't he?"

For a long time, Pasha didn't move, then she nodded her head, no more than a centimeter.

"I thought so," Zoe said. "We're going to prove that and you're going to be cleared. And I'm getting a lawyer to fight anyone who charges you with kidnapping me. So everything is going to be fine. Better, in fact."

"I never hurt him. …" She had to know the *truth*.

"God, I know, Pasha. I never imagined you did."

"No," she croaked. "I was so scared of him. Of Matthew…Senior."

"Why?" Zoe asked. "If you knew he…did that, why not tell the police what he did? Surely not because of me? There were years between your trial and finding me."

"I had no proof, just my gut." Her heart hammered and immediately one of the machines in the room started beeping.

"No, no," Zoe said with a touch of panic in her voice. "Please don't get worked up, Pasha. We'll talk about it later."

"Not later." There might not be a later. "Now."

Zoe didn't answer, and, in her eyes Pasha could see that there really *might* not be a later.

Digging for every ounce of strength, Pasha whispered, "I didn't see him do it, but he was in a rage. So angry at the boy for…nothing. They ran out and then…neither one came back. I waited and waited."

Old feelings welled up, making her rib cage feel like it would burst with the pain, but she had to get this story out. She'd tried to tell the police, but nobody believed her. Or they'd taken some of that mountain of Hobarth cash.

"He got away, drove to some convention, paid people to say they'd been with him. People would do anything for that man. Anything for money."

"Did you tell your lawyer this? The judge and jury during your trial?"

"Nobody believed me. He had an alibi and I was home with my son, had scratches on my arms. But a few of the people in that courtroom believed me. Enough."

"Enough for a hung jury," Zoe said.

Pasha forced a nod. "But he knew what I knew. First, for years, he gave me lots and lots of money and, God help me, I took it. I didn't have any other way to live and…"

"Shhh," Zoe whispered. "It's okay. You don't have to tell me this now, Pasha."

"But I do." She knew her body well enough by now. Time was running out and she couldn't die with Zoe thinking anything bad of her. "He stopped giving me money," she said. "When I was in Corpus Christi."

She remembered the call so well. His gruff voice, his dark threats. Times had changed since the murder. They had tests now, blood tests, and her ex-husband was scared. And scared people did terrible things.

One word, Patricia, and I will find you and cut you to ribbons.

"When you came to me that day, Zoe, I was already packing to leave. You were like...a sign." And added protection. She'd done the research and knew how to change her identity, and he'd never be looking for a woman with a ten-year-old child in tow. "So I kidnapped you."

Zoe nearly choked on her reply. "Like hell you did."

The machine chirped a little faster and Zoe patted her arm some more, glancing at the monitor with worry in her eyes. "None of this matters, Pasha. He's going to be caught, you're going to be free, and—"

"I'm going to die."

"No! The gene therapy is already working. This is a little setback." Zoe leaned so close some of her hair brushed against Pasha's cheek, the sweet smell of her lemony shampoo like a balm on Pasha's pain. "Do you need a sign?" Zoe asked. "I can tell you a very happy secret about Oliver and me."

A fist squeezed at her heart. She had to finish her confession. "Zoe."

"Shhh. No more."

"Yes. More." The letter. She'd been so shocked when it arrived a year after Oliver had mailed it. That was a sign—a very real one—that she wasn't doing a bang-up job of covering up their trail from town to town. "It was wrong to keep it, but I was scared you'd go back to him and we'd get caught."

Zoe sighed softly. "I don't know what you're talking about and I want you to stop talking."

The fingers on her heart clutched a little tighter. "You didn't find the letter?" She looked right into Zoe's eyes and tried to hold on against the pain, that incessant beeping getting louder and faster.

Zoe looked panicked by the sound, her worried gaze shifting to the flashing light. "Pasha, please, *please*. Don't talk anymore. Your heart."

"Is breaking." Cracking in two, bleeding out, exposed for the selfish choices it made. Was loving Zoe selfish? Was taking her selfish? Was keeping that letter selfish?

Yes, yes it was. Everything she'd done was selfish and motivated by fear.

Fire shot through her chest, worse than anything she'd ever felt and entirely different from the last time. This was sharper and deeper, somehow. Worse.

"Don't be afraid, Zoe."

But the look in her darling girl's eyes was pure fear.

"Don't…let…fear…stop…you."

"Pasha!" Zoe backed up, her voice barely audible over the alarm.

"I'm sorry." She could only form the words, with no sound. "I'm so, so sorry."

"Don't be sorry." Tears welled up in Zoe's eyes. "You saved me from a very bad man."

"But kept you…from a good one."

Agonizing white sparks exploded behind her eyes and everything, every part of her body, felt numb and black and…distant.

"Pasha!"

"Step away, ma'am."

"What is it? What's going on?" Zoe cried.

And then the loudest noise she'd ever heard screamed in her head, one long, deafening, endless screech that blocked out everything but Zoe's voice, rising in terror, calling her name, begging for help.

"Code Blue! Code Blue!"

Pasha didn't know what a Code Blue was, but something told her that was one very bad sign.

Zoe's voice was distant now, a wild, desperate, shrill squeal…no, that was the alarm. The heart alarm. The death alarm.

Her time had come.

"Pasha, please, I love you. Don't…"

"You need to leave, ma'am. *Now.*"

"No! Aunt Pasha!"

One last time Pasha forced her eyes open, searching wildly until they landed on the child she'd loved like her own. Zoe. *Zoe.*

"We'll call you Zoe," Pasha whispered. "It means 'new life.' "

But Zoe's face faded into a soft white light and disappeared from Pasha's sight.

Chapter Twenty-seven

⌒

Zoe ran as far and fast as she knew how, through a parking lot, down a street, into an alley, across a road, finally reaching a public beach somewhere in Naples.

There, she hurried down a set of weatherworn stairs, her feet pounding on the wood until they finally hit sand. She curled up against a post under the boardwalk and let go of the sobs she'd been holding in.

She cried until her eyes were dry and her breaths nothing but shuddering sighs. And still she didn't move, watching the occasional passerby, listening to the splash of the surf, the sound of steps overhead, the mournful squawk of a seagull.

Nice work, Zoe. You escaped. Now what?

Guilt pressed on her, kicking her stomach and heart until they were black and blue. She should have stayed. She'd tried to, waiting with the others, shaking and crying. And then, just as Jocelyn had predicted, Oliver had come back through those doors to deliver the news.

Only it wasn't the news Jocelyn had promised.

Anguish had mixed with anger, threatening to spew as Zoe tried to accept the unacceptable. She almost hurled words of blame—words Oliver didn't deserve but that her grieving heart wanted to throw anyway. So she did the only thing she could. She hit the road.

She couldn't face life without Pasha, couldn't *imagine* life without Pasha. They'd been a team for so long, the two of them against the world.

And now the world had taken her away. Once more, Zoe was left in the cold, alone, unattached, unsure of where she'd go next.

She kicked the sand so hard her flip-flop shot into the air, landing in the sunshine. No way was she moving to get that. No way was she coming out of this shadowy covering that protected her. No way was she—

Oliver.

She put her hand to her mouth as she stared at the man backlit by the sun, a silhouette she'd recognize anywhere. He still wore the same soft green scrubs he'd had on in the hospital. He held a phone to his ear as he strode down the beach, looking from one side to the other.

"No sign of her." His voice bounced over the sand and hit her right in the gut.

Oh, God, they were all probably looking for her. She couldn't hide here like…like she was trying to escape the pain. Because she *couldn't* escape the pain.

Clearing her throat, she pushed up and Oliver turned, dipping his head to squint into the shadows. She stepped out from under the boardwalk, the blast of the sun like fire on her skin.

"I've got her," he said into the phone, then he dropped it into his pocket and stared at her.

Her heart, even broken and bruised and battered as it was, still managed to thump against her ribs as he took a few steps closer. Yes, she loved that man. Loved him wholly and completely...which was why she couldn't bear the inevitable.

"You left," he said.

"Shocker, huh?" She inched back, the sun too hot, the shadows behind her too tempting. She forced herself to stop moving.

"Zoe, I'm..." He reached up, then let his hands fall to his sides. "You have no idea how sorry I am."

"Not as sorry as I am."

He flinched at the direct hit, but the bullet hole gave her no satisfaction.

"I swear to you that neither heart attack was related to the treatment, but even knowing that, I feel like a complete...failure." His voice cracked enough to make her want to go to him.

"I know." She did know that; it didn't help alleviate the ache, but she didn't want to add to the misery etched in his face by placing blame where it didn't belong.

"There was nothing we could do. We tried everything, but her heart simply wouldn't..." His voice faded out with the next crash of the sea behind him. He looked up, over her shoulder, beyond the boardwalk. "Your friends are here for you."

She turned to see Jocelyn and Lacey marching across the road like a little cavalry coming to the rescue.

Right behind them marched a man Zoe instantly recognized as the FBI agent. "And they bring company," she said.

"I already talked to him," Oliver said. "The preliminary

mitochondrial DNA test came back and she's cleared. I guess he wants to tell you in person."

Zoe almost stumbled backwards. "Pasha missed this by—what, hours?"

"She knew she wasn't guilty, Zoe. She died with a clear conscience."

"She did…say she was sorry." She squinted up at him, the sun so powerful it made her tear. Or something did. "She said she was sorry she kept me from a good man. She meant you."

His gaze flickered and he opened his mouth like he was going to say something, then stopped.

"What?" she asked.

He shook his head. "We can't get past this, can we?"

Her heart did a double dip. "I don't know." Would she ever forgive him for something that probably would have happened anyway? Could she hold his hand and not blame those healing fingers for not fixing what he'd promised to fix? Pasha…and her.

Neither one of them was better off. Pasha was gone and Zoe had run. No one was *fixed*. "And I can't seem to stick around and face reality, so we're both to blame."

A gull screeched nearby and some kids came running down the boardwalk steps, laughing and tossing a football.

Life went on for everyone else, Zoe thought bitterly. It would have to go on for her, too. Without Pasha. And without Oliver.

"Zoe." He was close enough that she could see the sheen of perspiration on his forehead and the abject misery in his eyes. "I don't want to…" He tunneled his fingers in his hair, dragging it back, letting out a soft grunt of resignation.

"Listen." She took a slow breath in, knowing she had to

tell him the truth. "I don't want to make any more promises I can't keep."

His brows furrowed. "What are you saying?"

"I can't," she admitted on a soft cry. "I can't…do…this."

The agony on his face fell to something different, raw disappointment and disbelief. "You don't trust me?"

She put her hands to her mouth as if she could hold back the words, but she couldn't. They had to be said. "I don't trust *me*. I don't trust my history, my life."

"Change history," he insisted. "Fix your life."

"It's so much easier for you to—"

"No, it's not, Zoe!" He closed the space between them, putting his hands on her shoulders as if he could cement her into the sand and force her to see it his way. "I've lost people, too. My mother, my marriage, and you. Twice, it seems," he said with a dry laugh. "Nothing is inevitable. You don't have to assume the worst will happen."

She closed her eyes and all she could see was Pasha's pale face, her fading eyes, her last words. *We'll call you Zoe. It means "new life."*

When the hell was she going to get one of those? "I thought you were going to fix me," she whispered.

"I thought I was, too." Very slowly, he opened his fingers and lifted his hands, his palms suspended over her shoulders, but not touching, as if he were letting go to see if she'd…run away. "Once, a long time ago, you took me up in a balloon. Do you remember?"

She gave him a look. "You know I do."

"Do you remember why you took me up there?"

To confess the truth. "I wanted to tell you about my life."

"You took me up there to face my fears. That's what you said."

The moment drifted back; they'd been in his car, with a blindfold. She nodded, remembering.

"I've faced mine, Zoe. And it's time for you to face your own."

She took a breath, ready to shoot one more arrow, but she had nothing left. He was right.

"If and when you do," he said quietly, taking one more step back as Lacey's voice floated toward them, calling Zoe's name, "I hope you remember that I love you."

"I know you do."

He reached out one hand and brushed his thumb along her jaw. "I wish that were enough."

She sighed. "So do I."

But, after one more touch of his thumb, he walked away, leaving Zoe ice cold in the burning sun.

Oliver woke later than usual the next morning with a dry mouth, an empty gut, and a sense that there was something he needed to do, but he couldn't remember what it was.

Oh, yeah, save a woman's life.

The hot sear of failure slipped through his veins. Fuck. *Fuck.*

Was that all? No, he had to get over the loss of the only woman he'd ever loved—for a second time.

A different pain gripped him, the thud of defeat. Zoe. All that laughter, all that love, all that Zoe.

Anything else? Yep. He had to meet with Raj and the team to try and figure out if they could have done anything differently.

What a complete mess. Nothing was right in his life. Nothing except *Evan.*

He blinked into the morning light, listening for sounds

of life in the little villa. But it was very quiet. Grabbing a pair of shorts, Oliver headed out of his room, checking out the first floor for signs that he'd been around already. But there were no telltale cereal crumbs on the table, no half glass of juice in the sink.

Oliver walked to the steps and was partway up before the complete silence made him freeze. No soft hum of a television, no digital melody of a video game, no sound.

An old fear pressed on him, almost strong enough to send him right back down the stairs. He gave the feeling exactly two heartbeats before he physically shook it off and bounded up the last three stairs in one giant step.

"Evan." He bolted through the doorway and froze at the sight of an empty, unmade bed.

The sound of a distant voice from the beach pulled his attention, a child's voice, a happy voice. Snapping the shutters open, he squinted toward the sand, letting out a soft grunt of relief at the sight of Evan running full speed down the beach, a very large dog hot on his heels.

What the hell?

He didn't hesitate; he was back downstairs and out the front door before he could process how Evan had even gotten out of the house without making enough noise to wake him.

"Dad! Come and meet our new dog!" Evan tore toward him, barely keeping up with a large dog that Oliver guessed was a retriever of some kind, definitely not the same dog they'd applied to receive the other day but never got because of Pasha's death.

"Evan, did you just leave without waking me?"

"Sorry, Dad, but this guy was barking outside of our door. Didn't you hear him?"

The dog came to a stop in front of Oliver, looking up with complete trust in his sweet brown eyes as he sat obediently, panting softly. "No, I didn't hear a thing."

"Can I keep him, Dad?"

"I'm sure he belongs to someone." Oliver looked up and down the deserted beach, spying a couple in the distance he recognized as a travel agent and her husband who were staying in one of the other villas, but no one else.

"He doesn't have a collar on," Evan said, as if that made him fair game. "I think Pasha sent him from heaven."

Oliver stood straight and looked at his son. "Don't start dreaming about keeping him, Evan. We'll get you a dog as soon as the shelter opens this morning. If the dog at the shelter is gone, then we'll be approved for another, I promise."

"She sent this one."

"Evan, please, don't be—"

"She told me she'd be sure that I got a dog if it was the last thing she did." He dug his little fingers in the thick blonde coat. "Maybe it was."

Oliver put his hand on Evan's shoulder and the dog barked, nuzzling into both of them. Oliver wasn't the only one feeling sorry for himself, and Zoe certainly wasn't the only one grieving Pasha's loss. He had to remember that.

"Son, that's a nice thought and it sounds a lot like something Pasha would do, but just in case this guy belongs to someone, I don't want you to get your heart set on keeping him."

"She said I'd know my dog when I found him because we'd have a special connection. Watch this, Dad. Sit, boy."

The dog stayed where it was.

"See?" He grinned. "Now watch this. Speak!"

The dog barked twice, getting an excited laugh from Evan.

"But, Ev—"

"Laugh!"

"Dogs can't—"

The dog leaped up on its hind legs, faced the sky, and made the most hideous howl Oliver ever heard.

Evan squealed with equally loud laughter. "Who else could find a dog who could do that but Aunt Pasha?"

Oliver couldn't help chuckling, too. The dog was ridiculously cute, and obviously well trained. He looked around again, certain he'd find the owner, but the only other person he saw was Clay Walker, heading toward them on an electric golf cart.

"He'll know whose dog it is," Oliver said as he waved for Clay to stop. When he did, Oliver jogged over to him. "Any idea who owns this fellow, Clay?"

Clay climbed out of the cart and came over, shaking Oliver's hand and checking out the dog. "None of our guests have dogs now, and no one on staff owns him." The dog went right to Clay and sat down again, practically begging to be petted. "Friendly, isn't he?"

"Can I keep him?" Evan asked.

The two men shared a look.

"Can you ask around the resort?" Oliver suggested. "And I can check in town to see if anyone is missing a dog."

"Then can we keep him?" Evan asked.

"We'll find his owner, son."

"Until we do, he's mine. Roll over, boy!"

The dog obliged, instantly on his back.

Clay chuckled softly. "Uh, I don't think that's a boy, buddy."

Evan's jaw dropped in surprise, then he shrugged. "Whatever. Maybe Pasha wanted me to have a girl. Run, girl!" Evan took off and the dog followed.

"He thinks Pasha somehow managed to send him a dog," Oliver explained. "I hate to see him get disappointed when we find the owner. I'll have to take Evan to the shelter as soon as we find out where this one belongs."

Clay nodded in understanding. "Hey, I'm really sorry about Pasha."

"Yeah, it was tough."

"She doesn't blame you, you know." At Oliver's surprised look, Clay added, "Zoe spent the night at our place."

Ah, so that was who had comforted her when he couldn't. He tamped down the knot that came with that thought, the one that had twisted in his gut all night long.

"Zoe knows the heart attack was unrelated to the treatment," Oliver agreed. "But it would be natural for her to place blame."

"Actually she's not. She's sad, of course, but so many things about her aunt's past have been cleared now. We're waiting for some word from Slade Garrison, who's up in Ohio now." Clay turned to watch Evan and the dog romp on the beach. "Listening to her reminisce about her aunt last night, I realized something I'd never known about her."

Oliver waited, wondering what of the many, many surprising things about Zoe had struck the other man. Her capacity to love? Her basically joyous nature? Her unshakable faith that somehow life would all work out?

Because those were just some of the many things about Zoe that Oliver...

No. He *had* to stop loving her. Except that would be like

asking the wind to stop blowing, the sun to stop shining, and Oliver to stop breathing.

"For a person who never really seems to settle down, she's remarkably grounded," Clay said.

"Yeah." Maybe that was why Oliver felt so unsteady without her in his life.

"In fact, she had some great ideas for the resort," Clay continued. "The four of them were up most of the night making plans."

Plans for where she'd live next, where she'd go, where her spirit would take her, no doubt. But then he did have doubt, and he had to ask. "What kind of plans?"

"The wedding package that Lacey wants to create for the resort. Zoe had some amazing ideas, and if we can swing some of them, we could turn Casa Blanca into one of the top destination-wedding resorts in the country. I didn't even know there was such a thing," he added with a laugh. "That's where I'm going now, as a matter of fact."

"A wedding?"

"A meeting. Apparently a whole parcel of land up on the east side of Barefoot Bay is going up for sale, and I want to see if we can get part of it for the resort. But we can't bite off the whole thing. I'm hoping someone will want a few acres and Lacey and I can buy the rest to expand. If her wedding-destination idea takes off, we're actually going to need more rooms to accommodate bigger parties and…" Clay waved an apology. "Hell, I'm sorry, doc. You got enough on your mind today. I'll let you know if we find out who owns the dog."

"Thanks, Clay. Good luck with the meeting."

Clay put a hand on Oliver's shoulder. "Good luck with Zoe."

He inched back. "I don't think luck's going to do it for us, man. There's too much…" *Wrong.* "Going on."

Clay nodded. "Hey, you never know. Stranger things have happened, and I'm living proof. Zoe is nothing if not unpredictable."

But could Oliver hold on to that hope again? Or should he just get on with his life? And his life was—

"Dad, I taught her to shake paws!"

His life was Evan. *Just like last time.*

"Don't get too attached," Oliver said, walking toward his son. "I don't want your heart broken when…she's gone."

But Evan laughed. "She's not going anywhere."

Oliver guessed Evan would have to learn the hard way, like he had.

Chapter Twenty-eight

⁓

The morning of Pasha's service, Zoe dressed in white. Because she felt lighter than she had in days, and it was a bajillion degrees outside.

Plus, Pasha would want white. No black, no tears, no agony, no regrets. Oh, there was a hole in Zoe's heart, no doubt about it. A couple of them, in fact. But she kept stuffing those holes with hope to stop any bleeding, and that seemed to do the trick for now.

Death was final and sad, but so utterly inevitable. No matter how hard Zoe had been trying to stave off the unavoidable consequences of cancer and old age, no matter how she'd begged, borrowed, and stolen extra hours and days, no matter how much she willed Oliver to play God with Pasha's life, nothing could change what was meant to be.

She was learning to accept that, and she'd gone a few hours without crying each day. Instead, she took solace in certain melodies of the wind, in the sight of a butterfly, and even in a random splatter of tea leaves. Pasha was everywhere, or at least her memory was, and Zoe would stay connected to her forever.

But she would have to go on with her life, different as it might be now.

Last night, Zoe had finally slept in her own bungalow again, trying to think of the little place as her "home." Could it be? Lacey had said she could live there permanently if Zoe really decided to move to Mimosa Key, work for Sylver Skies, and help build the destination-wedding business.

But, deep inside, Zoe hadn't decided anything yet. First, she had to gather with her friends on the beach and celebrate the life of a woman who'd left a mark on all of them. Then she'd make a decision about staying or not.

She'd never had the option to make that decision on her own before, and the feeling was more than a little heady. It made her dizzy.

She listened for that voice in her head to bark an order or two, but it had been unusually quiet this week.

Stepping back from the mirror, Zoe checked out her understated sundress and fluffed her hair. Maybe it was too understated. This was *Pasha's* funeral, after all. That called for outrageous silver earrings.

Automatically, she went to the door, almost ready to call out to Pasha and ask to borrow some hoops. A now-familiar pain twisted in her chest. That's what she'd miss: the everyday companionship of her very best friend. Tears threatened, but she blinked them away.

Zoe had other friends, and they wanted her to stay here permanently. For the first time in her life, Zoe was actually considering that, but there were complications.

Complications named Oliver.

He'd left her alone, of course, as she'd expected him to. *But now what?*

He'd made it clear the door was open, but did she have what it took to walk through? The pain of losing Pasha was still fresh enough that the idea of taking that chance, of connecting to one more person she might ultimately lose, was still enough to keep her from even thinking about Oliver.

First she had to hold this ceremony for Pasha. For that, Pasha would want her to look good, and that required those giant earrings Pasha loved so much.

Swallowing any trepidation, she walked across the hall into Pasha's room, entering it for the first time since she'd died. Actually, the first time since Pasha had run off and ended up in the hospital.

Well, she'd have to come in here sometime, right? She couldn't put it off forever.

The soft scent of talcum lingered in the air, along with an eerie quiet that seemed so unfamiliar. Zoe stood completely still next to the bed and waited for chills or heartache or even a whisper of air over her skin.

But there were no ghosts in this room. No spirits of fortune-tellers. No Pasha. Zoe started to close her eyes against a wave of grief, but just as she did she spotted an envelope.

Zoe frowned at the rectangular paper on the dresser, halfway under Pasha's jewelry box as if it had been tossed there. Had Pasha left a farewell note?

Now Zoe got chills *and* heartache.

The letter lay facedown, making Zoe scared to turn it over and see Pasha's right-leaning distinct handwriting. A letter would make her cry, for sure. A weepy missive from Pasha would wipe away all those solemn oaths about accepting death and being strong and looking forward. Something like that would surely gouge at those holes in her heart, and today, of all days, she wanted those holes firmly shut.

Then she noticed that the paper was yellowed with age, the corners softened like they'd been folded away forever.

Picking up the envelope, she turned it over and stared at the front, at a different handwriting than she'd been expecting, addressed to *Ms. Zoe Tamarin*.

Holy God, no.

In the upper left corner—oh, *no*.

Zoe's legs buckled, forcing her to back up and fall on the bed. She held the letter with trembling hands.

I left a letter in that box anyway. I saw the postman toss the letter in the trash when I left. I wanted to tell you...

This was Oliver's letter. How long had Pasha held on to this? The answer was in the postmark, of course. Nine years.

Why? *Why?*

That answer had died with Pasha. A new feeling welled up inside her, rough and raw. Anger. Zoe ran her finger over the back, certain the seal was the original. No one had ever read this letter.

Another wave of anger took hold, different than she'd been feeling as she went through what Jocelyn called her stages of grief. This was pure fury in all its glory.

"How dare you!" she screamed out, slapping the letter on the bed. "How could you not give me this?"

Then Zoe remembered Pasha's cryptic words as the alarms had been blaring in the hospital room during the chaotic last second of her life.

It was wrong to keep it, but I was scared you'd go back to him and we'd get caught.

Yes, Pasha, it *was* wrong.

Once again, fear had held Pasha back. And Pasha's fear had kept Zoe from knowing what Oliver had written in this letter. And fear was keeping Zoe from...everything she wanted.

Don't...let...fear...stop...you.

Zoe sat straight up at the sound of a voice. It was the first time she'd heard it in days.

Except that it wasn't an unknown voice; that was Pasha's voice. A soft, lilting, sweet voice that usually made Zoe feel better. This voice was telling her not to make the same mistakes Pasha had made. This voice was telling her to walk through the door Oliver had opened and not be afraid of whatever life held.

Don't let fear stop you.

Anger gave way to a soft appreciation. Pasha had done what Pasha thought she had to do. But Zoe did not have to live with those same shackles on her wrists.

Zoe took the letter and pressed it to her heart, then to her lips.

Standing up, she slipped the envelope into the pocket of her skirt, saving it for later.

Less than an hour later, a very small crowd of about a dozen people milled about the beachside patio of Casa Blanca, where Clay and Lacey had set up the chairs for the service. Zoe's friends were there, along with a few of the townspeople or staff who'd met Pasha while she'd lived in Barefoot Bay, the whole thing as intimate as a small family gathering.

Zoe stayed in the middle, greeting guests, accepting condolences, quietly listening to people share tidbits and vignettes about their interactions with Pasha.

"She read shampoo bubbles when I did her hair," Gloria Vail said as she stood flanked by her cousin, Grace, and her aunt, Charity, who looked around like she was determined to find someone doing something she could criticize. "Said I'd found true love."

"You have found true love," Zoe said. "I could see it all over Slade's face when I met with him the other day."

Goria beamed. "How can we thank you enough, Zoe? Closing that case by proving Matthew Hobarth Senior had murdered his son was the best thing that ever happened in his career."

"He's in Naples, meeting with his new boss." Gloria smiled, brushing back her dark hair in a nervous gesture. "He's so excited about the promotion to the Naples office."

"He should be," Zoe said. "Thanks to him, we not only got the DNA sample the FBI needed, we got a confession."

Next to Grace, Charity snorted. "It wasn't like Slade muscled it out of the guy using his state-of-the-art interrogation techniques."

Gloria closed her eyes, fighting for patience. "It doesn't matter how he got it, Aunt Charity. He got it."

"On the man's deathbed while he was getting last rites." Charity rolled her eyes. "Puhlease."

"I'm eternally grateful," Zoe said quickly, pulling Gloria to her with a kind hand. Not only had Slade gotten the DNA evidence to prove Pasha was innocent and her ex was guilty, he'd convinced the FBI to drop any and all charges against Zoe for aiding and abetting a kidnapper and using false identification. She had a clean slate now

At the thought, she added another hug to Gloria. "Your boyfriend is a hero."

"I know he is," Gloria said, shooting a look at her aunt. "I couldn't be more proud of him."

Tessa signaled Zoe from across the patio. "You ready?" she mouthed.

Zoe nodded and walked to the rail that faced the Gulf. Tessa pressed a button that worked the sound system, and the first strains of an old Romanian folk song played through the speakers. When everyone sat down, Zoe stayed standing and started her short speech.

"Pasha would tell you all that today's cloudless sky was a sign." She skimmed the faces of the few guests, lingering for a moment on Tessa, then Jocelyn and Will, who sat with Jocelyn's father between them. Last, she looked at Ashley, next to Lacey and Clay, who bounced baby Elijah in his arms.

She might be burying the only "family" she'd ever had today, but that didn't mean she didn't have family…and a home.

"She'd say it meant clear sailing straight to…" Just then, Oliver stepped onto the patio, with Evan next to him. "Heaven," she finished.

Everything stopped. Time, her heart, her very next breath. She couldn't help staring at him, inhaling the sight she'd missed so much the last few days.

He met her gaze, but his only movement was to put a comforting hand on his son's shoulder, reminding Zoe that Evan had cared for Pasha and he must be devastated, too.

"Today, we're going to sprinkle Pasha's ashes in the water of Barefoot Bay and while the tides will carry her from place to place in a way that would please any gypsy, I hope that a piece of her will stay here in our hearts forever."

She stole another look at Oliver, easily able to read the question in his eyes.

Pasha will stay forever, but will you?

Somehow, she pulled it together and made it through the rest of the service, stepping aside while her friends spoke about Pasha. Then, arm in arm in arm with her three best friends, Zoe walked down to the shore to bid Pasha good-bye. The ashes fluttered in the breeze, then landed on the water, spreading slowly to start Pasha's next journey.

After that, Zoe felt ready to face Oliver, but he was gone.

The sharp, unexpected pang of disappointment was as powerful as the heartache she'd felt when she'd flung the ashes.

"You okay?" Tessa asked.

"Ready to go in for lunch?" Lacey took her hand and tugged her toward the resort. "We're christening the new kitchen."

"I want to walk for a little bit," she said. "Can you go up with everyone and start? I need a few minutes alone."

With understanding hugs, they left, and Zoe turned to the private beach that curved for nearly a mile. The solitude beckoned, and she kicked off her shoes and let a brisk walk become a run. The Gulf breeze whipped over her face, drying her tears before they spilled.

Tears that weren't for Pasha, but for Oliver.

He'd left, of course. She'd made it clear that she didn't trust herself or her lousy track record, that she couldn't endure the pain of loss, that she'd never seen what true love looked like up close, so how could she even know how to live that kind of fairy-tale life?

She'd buried him with excuses and lost him, too.

She glanced over her shoulder. She was a good half mile from the resort now, and completely alone. Finally, she dropped down to the sand and reached into her pocket for the letter.

What would have happened if she'd gotten this letter when Oliver had intended her to? What could he have possibly said that would have changed her life? She slipped her finger into the old seal and started to tear.

"Dear Zoe."

She whipped around at the sound of Oliver's voice, a gasp on her lips.

"Those are the first two words."

Unable to speak, she watched him approach, silent until he sat down next to her.

"Want to hear the rest?"

"I thought I'd read it for myself."

"You can, or I can tell you what it says." He reached his hand out and waited.

She hesitated, then slipped the envelope between his fingers. "Read it to me."

"No need. I remember exactly what I wrote."

"You do? Every word?"

"Every word." He held it up to the sun, like he was trying to see through it, or offer it up as a sacrifice to the gods of star-crossed lovers.

"Dear Zoe," he said again.

She smiled. "I got that much."

He placed two fingers in the middle of the envelope

and took a breath. "Imagine my shock and sadness when I found you'd left."

For a moment, she wasn't sure if he was reciting the letter or talking. But before she could ask, he tore the envelope…right in half.

"What are you—"

"I cried like a stupid kid," he said, looking out to the horizon as he spoke. "Just sat in that living room where we'd once played Strip Egyptian Rat Screws and you cheated—"

"I did not!"

"So that I had to play for ten minutes in nothing but socks."

A half laugh caught in her throat. "It was a good ten minutes," she whispered. "I dominated that round."

He turned the two squares of paper sideways and ripped again. "You want to hear the rest?"

"If I'm hearing the real letter. Otherwise…" She looked at the torn pages. "I'm never going to know what it said."

"This is exactly what it said," he assured her, clearing his throat to recite again. "After I realized you weren't coming back, I started a search for you. A search I doubt will ever end."

The sound of tearing paper—and of breaking hearts—punctuated that sentence. Nope. She'd never know what was in that letter now.

"And?"

He took another breath, still looking at the water. "Zoe, I want you to know that unless you come back, I'm going to make a life-changing decision that you might not understand or agree with. But I know it's the right decision, at least I hope so."

"The decision to marry Adele and be a father to Evan?" she asked.

He nodded.

"It was the right decision," she whispered.

"I'm making this decision with full knowledge that I currently do and probably will always love you." He had the letter in very small pieces now, his fingers still. "And I believe that, even though you never told me, you love me, too."

"I did." *I do.*

"And no matter that everyone and everything is against us…" He turned his head to look at her. "We are meant to be together."

"We are." The words came out in a hoarse whisper, caught in a sob.

"Forever." Once last time, he tore what was left of the letter, the pieces no bigger than an inch by now. "So if you ever find it in your heart to come back to me, Zoe, I will change my life in whatever way is necessary to make you the biggest, best, and most wonderful part of it."

Was this Oliver's letter of yesterday or Oliver's heart of today speaking to her? She didn't ask because she was lost in his eyes.

"Many things will change in our lives," he continued, "but one thing will never ever change. I'll make mistakes that I can't fix and so will you, but through it all, Zoe Tamarin, I will love you. I love you now and forever. If there is any way you'll spend your life with me, I want you to know I am yours. Always."

"Always?"

"Love, Oliver."

He opened his hand and twenty tiny pieces of paper fluttered into the wind, like those ashes she'd just released. Zoe reached for one and snagged it, glancing at the white square and the three words it captured:

life-changing decision

And another, fluttering next to her foot, that said *come back to me*.

"So you didn't make that up? That's really what the letter said?"

"It is."

"Why wouldn't you let me read it?"

"Because I wanted to say it to you."

She watched one more piece picked up on a breeze float on the wind, like she loved to do. "Why couldn't I keep it?"

"It's history, honey." He touched her chin and turned her face toward his. "You can't be a prisoner of history when it's time to look forward and start a new life."

New life. "That's why Pasha gave me the name Zoe. It means new life."

He leaned forward to kiss her. "Zoe Bradbury. You know what that means?"

A little thrill danced from her scalp to her toes. "It means new life...with the man I love."

He kissed her so tenderly the tears threatened again.

"Was that all that was in the letter?" she asked.

"P.S." He cupped her jaw and held her face. "I bought some land in Barefoot Bay and I'm going to build a house. Would you marry me and make that our home forever?"

Our home forever.

Chills washed over her skin like certainty over her heart. She closed her eyes as his mouth touched hers. "Yes." When they broke the kiss, she searched his face for the truth. "Did the letter really say all that?"

He eased her back on the sand, blocking the sun with another kiss. "Every word except the P.S."

"That was the best letter I never read."

"And you're the best woman I never seem to be able to pin down."

"You're doing a pretty good job right now."

He smiled, satisfied, and kissed her again. "You want to go up and share the good news with all your friends?"

"You know what I want to do?" She caressed his cheek and brought him closer.

"Hmm?"

"I want to stay right here. I want to...stay."

Epilogue

~

Four Months Later

I now pronounce you husband and wife."

Zoe turned to Oliver and took a deep breath. "You ready for this, doc?" she whispered over the loud cheer of the crowd.

"I am so ready."

"Another kiss!" someone in the crowd yelled out.

"Are you sure?" Zoe asked. "Because you can back out, even now. I can do this alone if I need to."

"Alone? Not a chance. I'm all in, Zoe."

"It's gonna be scary sometimes."

He shook his head. "Not worried."

"We could have turbulence."

He shrugged. "A few bumps don't bother me."

"You ready to face your fears?"

He leaned forward and planted a kiss on her lips. "Remember our motto?"

"Don't let fear stop you," she replied.

"So I'm ready."

"Then we're good to go." She grinned at him, swiping back a lock of hair that had blown over her face from a much stronger than usual Gulf breeze, a reminder of just how wild this ride was about to be. She glanced over her shoulder at the crowd still clapping and calling for kisses. "You've got about five seconds to change your mind."

"Zoe, stop worrying about me and get this thing ready to fly." He heaved a sandbag and let it fall next to the basket, a fine sheen of sweat on his face from the full-out labor of inflating the snow-white balloon tethered on the beach at Barefoot Bay. "Lacey wants a million pictures for the brochure, not to mention a bride and groom who think they're about to get the ride of a lifetime. Stop worrying about me."

"Actually I'm more worried about the wind," she said. "We're right at seven knots, which means a rough ride."

She'd only had her new balloon up a few times since she'd purchased it and started taking passengers for Sylver Skies and Casa Blanca. All the trips had been smooth, including the maiden voyage when she'd taken Jocelyn and Will up after their small beachfront wedding. But today's winds would challenge the best of pilots.

With the loud cheer from the crowd on the beach, they both turned and watched about sixty people part to let Gloria and Slade glide through. The newlyweds waved, then kissed, then laughed their way across the beach, the setting sun creating a stunning backdrop of orange, blue, peach, and purple.

This should be a perfect flight...except for the damn wind.

Two photographers flanked the couple as they kissed

and walked barefoot over the sand. One cameraman was taking pictures for Gloria's album, but the other was shooting exclusively for Casa Blanca's destination wedding package that Lacey, Zoe, Jocelyn, and Tessa had spent the last four months creating.

"Look at that scene," Tessa said, carrying a tray of hors d'oeuvres that would feed the newlyweds, best man, and maid of honor once they were airborne. "You know, if this idea takes off, Casa Blanca could be booked with intimate, high-end weddings for years."

"What needs to take off is this balloon," Zoe said.

"You can do it," Oliver said quickly, his hand on her back. "Unless you don't feel okay."

"I'm fine," she said quickly, slipping away before Tessa heard the exchange. "I'm concentrating."

Around the gondola, the ground crew steadied the four-story balloon and the top-of-the-line basket that could hold up to ten people. It was no mean feat in this strong breeze.

Zoe turned to the picnic table about twenty feet away, where her very favorite weather genius tapped a tablet and then held his digital anemometer to the sky, measuring air velocity, direction, and humidity.

"What do you have, Evan?" she called.

He popped up from the table at the same time as Moonbow, the stray dog he'd found at the beach that no one ever claimed. She smiled, still in agreement with Evan that the dog was Pasha's parting gift.

Moonbow wasn't the only permanent addition to Barefoot Bay. After one month back in Chicago, Evan had pleaded with his parents to change the custody arrangement so he could live primarily with Oliver. Adele's surprising agreement had been one of the highlights of the past few months. Along with …

Zoe glanced down at her newly protruding stomach. They were going to have to make the announcement soon. There was no way to hide her secret under flowing skirts and frilly tops much longer.

Evan interrupted that thought, waving an instrument. "Fly east, Zoe. It's gusty over the Gulf."

"I plan on it, kid. Don't forget to text the velocity and humidity readings to your dad and be sure to come along with the crew when we have a landing spot, okay?"

Tessa joined them, straightening the vest of the sharp white tux she wore as the official steward of the flight. "It's showtime, folks."

Gloria and Slade reached the balloon with a wake of wedding guests and a flurry of hugs and congratulations. As Gloria gathered the skirts of her flowing white gown, Slade easily scooped her into his arms to lift her into the gondola basket, every move captured on camera.

Tessa welcomed them, getting the couple, plus the maid of honor, best man and the two cameramen situated safely while Zoe handled the piloting duties.

The crewmen directed the other guests away from the balloon, and, over the crowd, Zoe could see Lacey and Clay watching like proud parents, giving her all kinds of thumbs-ups.

When everyone was ready, Zoe fired a burner to create a brilliant balloon glow, the golden light turning the "wedding-white" balloon as bright as the sun setting behind them.

Everyone oohed and aahed as the crew let go of the lines and the Casa Blanca speakers played "Love Lifts Us Up" as the takeoff song. Zoe hummed, the satisfying hiss of her burner valve drowning out the corny but cute lyrics.

Up they floated into the wild blue yonder. And, damn, it was wild.

The gondola rocked, but they held steady, floating over the crystal-teal waters and white sands of Barefoot Bay.

"Good luck!"

"Fly safe!"

"Happy Ever After!"

The cheers rang through the air as Zoe concentrated on the most difficult part of her flight. Another mighty gust pushed them east, earning a loud gasp from the passengers but not a sound from her right-hand man.

Zoe stole a glance at Oliver, who looked nothing short of stoic. He winked at her, giving her a thrill unlike anything she'd ever gotten from ballooning.

At fifteen hundred feet she turned off the main burner and the loud hissing stopped, bathing them all in a shocking silence that was almost instantly filled with gasps of delight from the passengers.

From behind her Oliver wrapped his arms around her, and she let her head drop onto his shoulder. "My goodness, you are one calm flyer," she said.

"I'm in good hands."

"And so am I. Very, very good hands."

He squeezed her a little. "How's Junior holding up?"

"Shhh," she said, glancing over at Tessa. She was pouring champagne, but sound traveled in this silence.

"Come on, Zoe, let's tell her. She's your friend and she's going to be happy for us."

"I know but…the only thing she hates more than secrets is her BFFs getting pregnant."

"She's going to be furious you kept another one from her, then."

"I can't tell her now."

"You love to give away your secrets in the sky," he whispered.

He was right; she couldn't wait another minute. What better place than up in the clouds, warmed by the sun and—*Whoa!*

Another unexpected gust buffeted the basket, knocking everyone a little sideways.

Oliver's eyes widened. "Is that normal?"

She managed a smile and a nod, then went over to the passengers and made sure they were calm. And so was Oliver, who leaned over the side of the basket and looked straight down at the eastern side of Barefoot Bay.

"Look at that foundation," he said. "That house is going to be amazing."

She stepped to the edge of the basket to see the first wave of construction of their new home, the waterfront lot trimmed by a hundred tiny hummocks and islands and threaded with narrow, shallow canals. "That house is going to be a home," she said softly. "Our home."

"You, me, our kids, our dogs, our whole life."

"Kids? Plural?" Tessa was right next to them, surprising Zoe.

For a moment, the two women didn't speak as Zoe's stomach—and the baby inside it—took a little dive at the look on Tessa's face.

"I've been meaning to tell you."

"Really?" Tessa raised both brows. "'Cause I figured you were waiting until labor and delivery."

"You know?"

She rolled her eyes. "You might love a good secret, but your fiancé hasn't been able to wipe the smile off his face for two months."

"She wanted me to wait to tell anyone."

Tessa waved her hand. "You're off the hook. Evan spilled the lima beans."

"Evan knows?"

"You guys suck at secrets." She leaned over and pressed her cheek against Zoe's. "Congrats, my dear friend. I'm thrilled for you."

"Really?"

"Really. I love babies." She grinned. "I'm having one myself."

"*What?*" Zoe and Oliver asked the question in perfect unison.

Tessa laughed. "Not all by myself," she said. "I'm interviewing surrogates."

"A surrogate mother?" Zoe asked. "What about the father?"

"He's on his way."

The basket swayed in the wind, making Zoe grab the side. "When? Who is it?"

Tessa angled her head. "I don't know yet. But Pasha told me a long time ago he'd be here after the next blue moon."

"Are you sure she wasn't *drinking* a Blue Moon?" Zoe asked.

"And reading the beer foam?" Oliver teased.

"Joke all you want, but a lot of her predictions have come true, and you two are proof of that."

The basket listed left, then right, earning another whoop from the wedding party.

"Here's to love!" the best man called out. All the

champagne glasses shot into the air, the crystal clinking.

"To love!"

Zoe looked up at Oliver. "To love."

He kissed her. "To love."

Tessa smiled. "To the next blue moon." She scooped up the champagne bottle and made her way to the passengers to refill the empty glasses.

Zoe turned to Oliver. "What do you think?"

"I think you're the most beautiful woman in the world and I'm the luckiest guy on earth. And I'm not even scared even though we are basically suspended in midair, held by nothing but more air."

She laughed. "I meant about Tessa."

He angled his head, considering it. "I think what Pasha probably said was that love is rare and only happens once in a blue moon."

"You really don't think her predictions were true?"

"No, I don't."

"Well, I, for one, will be watching the men who come in contact with Tessa from now on."

He pulled her closer. "Hey, the only man you should be watching is the one in front of you."

She stood on her tiptoes and kissed him one more time. "I am."

"And not just once in a blue moon. Forever."

"And ever."

"You promise?" he asked. "You'll love me forever and never leave?"

She waited a moment for a voice in her head to tell her what to do.

Run, Zoe, run.

But all she heard was sweet, blissful silence. "I promise."

While all her friends have
found love, Tessa Galloway
has just about lost hope.

But a mysterious visitor to Barefoot
Bay might be just what she needs—
if his tattoos and secrets don't
scare her away first. . .

Please turn this page for a preview of

Barefoot by the Sea.

I could just walk up to a man and *ask* for sperm." Tessa picked up her bottle to punctuate her statement with a sip of cold beer but froze midway as she took in the reaction around the booth. "Guys, that was a joke."

Next to her, Jocelyn gave a thoughtful shrug and leaned in to make her point over the din of the Toasted Pelican crowd. "You never know. They love to give that stuff away."

"Absolutely," Lacey agreed from across the table, her topaz eyes lit with enthusiasm instead of humor. "Knowing your donor takes all the guess work out of it. What you see is what you get, unlike anonymous sperm."

"Spe*rrrrm*." Zoe made a disgusted face, her gaze drifting over the action in the bar. "Couldn't man's life-force have a more inviting name? You know, like 'chocolate' or 'cabernet'?"

"'Baby juice'?" Jocelyn suggested.

"'Liquid gold,'" Lacey added.

" 'Nature's protein smoothie,' " Tessa said dryly.

That made Zoe laugh, but she didn't take her eyes off the crowd. "Always thinking healthy, aren't you, Tess?"

Tessa waved her beer bottle to move the conversation along and prove that even she could have the occasional lapse in clean living.

"Let's go back to the chef problem, Lace," she said. "That's why we all stole away from the resort to talk tonight. Thanksgiving's in a few weeks, Casa Blanca is booking up, and we still haven't found the right chef. We'll worry about donors after the holidays. This is our first true season and—"

"Tess." Lacey reached across the table. "It took you a long time to find a surrogate who meets your exacting standards. You know if you don't act fast she'll be scooped up by someone else."

"I harvested my eggs." Defensiveness lifted Tessa's voice.

"Sorry, hon." Zoe tore her attention from the bar, lifting her bottle of water and giving it a shake. "That test-tube cocktail ain't got no buzz without the right mixer."

"Ugh, test tubes are so clinical," Jocelyn groaned. "I still think you should try the old-fashioned way."

Of course they'd all think she should. Her best friends were falling in bed every night with the men they loved. Lacey had a baby and Zoe's was due in six months. No doubt Jocelyn would be next.

"Listen, I tried the old-fashioned way for ten years with my ex-husband." Tessa fought to keep any bitterness out of her tone but might have failed. "And as you know, he's now the father of two. And I'm…" *Alone.* "Obviously not capable of getting pregnant by traditional methods."

"But Joss is right," Lacey insisted. "Maybe your infertility was Billy's fault."

Tessa angled her head and gave her a 'get real' look. "Tell that to his *two* children."

"There is such a thing as being inhospitable to certain sperm," Jocelyn insisted. "It's an acid and Ph balance thing."

"Please." Tessa halted the conversation with a flat hand. "Billy and I were experts on the subject of infertility. I think the conversation was the only thing that kept us together so long. Once we gave up trying, our marriage fell apart."

Zoe gave a cynical choke. "Yeah, cause it had nothing to do with him boning a twenty-two-year-old yoga instructor."

Well, there was that. Tessa studied the moon on her beer label, but Jocelyn nudged her arm. "Tess, you need to make history, not change it."

"Ah, the life coach speaks."

"The life coach is correct," Lacey said. "When was the last time you had a date? Gave a guy a chance? When was the last time you even thought about getting intimate with a *man* instead of a *test tube*?"

She smiled. "You know I like things done in a certain order."

"How long?" the others asked in unison.

"Since I found out Billy was doing more than the downward dog with a fertility goddess. So, three years at least."

They shared a suitably pitying look and Lacey leaned forward, tightening her grip on Tessa's hands. "Look at the three of us. We're living proof that love can happen when you least expect it."

Tessa gazed up at the ceiling and breathed a sigh, digging for patience. She didn't begrudge them their happiness, not one single bit. But staring all this *love* in the face every single day wasn't easy. Not to mention the fact that Casa Blanca's destination wedding business was starting to take off, and now the guests were lovestruck too.

"We just want you to be happy," Jocelyn said.

"And pregnant," Lacey added.

The din of Mimosa Key locals blowing off steam competed with an old Tom Petty song on the jukebox, but none of it was loud enough to drown out Tessa's well-meaning friends. Or the truth.

"I don't believe the guy exists who could make me happy *or* pregnant," she finally admitted.

Lacey shook her head. "You don't know that. Someone amazing could be right around the corner."

"Someone amazing *is* right around the corner," Zoe whispered, pointing across the room. "Because if that man right there can't make you happy or pregnant, then he can certainly make you scream for mercy. Probably a couple of times a night."

Jocelyn swung out of the booth to peer into the crowd. "*Whoa.* Is that a *scorpion* tattooed on his neck?"

"Lovely." Tessa took a deep drink.

Lacey popped up to look over their heads. "You mean that guy with the long hair and…wow. Those are some serious biceps. And triceps. And…" She squinted. "All ceps." She slowly dropped back in her seat. "Speaking of fertility gods…" She let out a slow whistle. "That's one hot and scary bad-ass sex god over there."

Tessa rolled her eyes again. "Great, since those are the top qualities I'm seeking in a sperm donor."

Jocelyn took another look, then turned back to face the booth, her eyes wide like she'd seen something unspeakable. "He certainly looks like he'd make a potent...protein smoothie."

Zoe's smile wavered. "And, oh wow, I think he's—"

"Enough," Tessa ordered. "I don't care if he looks like Chris Hemsworth's twin brother."

"He kinda does," Zoe said.

Tessa dug for more patience. They couldn't help it; they didn't know how hard it was to be in her position. "Guys, I was kidding, okay? I'm not going to walk up to him and say—"

"You don't have to," Zoe said softly.

Tessa closed her eyes and raised her beer bottle in the air. "Hey, scary bad-ass sex god with the long hair and deadly tattoos, can you fill 'er up with some potent liquid gold?"

Silence. Dead silence.

Slowly, Tessa opened her eyes. She felt the presence more than saw it in her peripheral vision. Something large. Something hot. Something scary and bad ass and...

"Liquid Gold. Is that a local brew?"

Oh. *Sex god* was really kind of an understatement.

In Ian's experience, they didn't usually keep the best-looking one hidden like this. Normally, females used the real beauties as bait. But this girl hadn't even gone out of her way to check him out. And that made the sweet-faced beer drinker begging for action even more appealing.

The blonde who'd been staring at him for the last ten minutes wasn't his type. The one with the wild red curls sported a shiny gold wedding band, and the other one was a little too conservative for his tastes.

But the hottie tucked into the corner was just right, looking at him with wide eyes exactly the color of the amber beer bottle she slowly lowered to the table. She wore barely a hint of makeup, so Ian could easily see her creamy complexion deepen with a flush as they held eye contact for one heartbeat past casual.

"Beer's a good choice in a place like this," he said, rattling the ice in his rocks glass. "The scotch is watered-down piss."

Surprise flickered in her eyes. Because of the curse word or had the pisswater been strong enough to bring out his accent? After all these years, he should know better than to slip and give away his British birth.

"What was that beer called again?" he asked.

"It was…a joke," she said, so softly he almost didn't hear her over the bar ruckus. "I'm…fine."

"You sure are."

The other three reacted instantly.

"We need to hit the ladies' room," one of the women said, sliding out to make room for him. "Coming, Zoe?"

The blonde scooted out too. "We'll refresh the drinks." She turned to the married one and gave a look with all the subtlety of a baseball bat. "Move it, Lacey."

"Oh yeah." She nodded and gave an equally unsubtle raised eyebrow to the woman in the corner. "Hold the booth for us, Tessa. I'm sure we'll be a while."

"We'll guard it with our lives." Ian slid right into the vacated seat next to his doe-eyed target, trapping her in the corner and getting a whiff of something flowery and clean. "Tessa. Pretty. Short for something?"

Finally she slid him a sideways look, long lashes tapering into the kind of distrustful gaze he'd been eliciting for a few years. If the tattoos, gym time, or total disregard for a haircut didn't scare them, the bike parked out front usually did.

"Just Tessa," she said as her friends disappeared into the bar, leaving laughter and chatter in their wake.

"Just Tessa," he repeated. Not to be funny, but because he'd want to remember the name tomorrow morning when he was rooting around the floor of her flat looking for his jeans. *"Apartment," dickhead, not "flat."*

"I'm John, by the way."

She hinted at a smile. "Hello, John Bytheway."

Cute. "John Brown."

"That sounds fake."

Because it is. "So tell me something about yourself, Tessa, other than the fact that you like..." He turned the beer bottle and read the label. "Belgian White Wheat Ale." Bloody Americans would buy anything they thought was from Europe.

"Blue Moon's my favorite..." She inched back. "Blue Moon," she said softly, her whole face lighting up in a way that took her from good-looking to gorgeous in the space of a second. "Maybe that's what Aunt Pasha meant."

"Who's Aunt Pasha?"

Her eyes twinkled with a secret. "A late, great...fortune teller."

He inched closer, letting his thigh press against hers and earning another sweet blush. "Did she see trouble in her crystal ball?"

"She saw...something."

"Whatever she saw, I hope it happens tonight." He gave her a slow once-over, letting a nice undercurrent of electricity buzz between them as he admired her toned arms, freckle-dusted skin, and the alluring slope of her breasts under a simple white T-shirt. This one wasn't trying too hard to get attention, and he liked that. It reminded him of—

Don't go there.

"Are you staying in Mimosa Key?" she asked.

"At the moment." For the past month, since he'd left Singapore, he'd ridden around the state of Florida, finally finding his way over a bridge to this suitably out-of-the-way island. He'd checked into the first motel he'd found and headed straight out the door for his numbing agents of choice: cheap scotch and a willing woman. He'd found one and, with a little luck, was looking at the other. "How about you?"

"I live at the resort up the road in Barefoot Bay," she said.

"You *live* on a resort?"

"I run the gardens."

That explained the sun-kissed skin and shapely shoulders.

"What do you do?" she asked.

"I don't run anything," he admitted. "I just run."

"From what?" She gave him a curious look, and he cursed himself again. What was wrong with him tonight? The scotch mustn't be watered down enough.

Instead of answering, he put his hand around the back of the booth, letting his fingers graze her shoulder, getting a quick rise of chill bumps on her arm in response.

"You're pretty," he said, happy to note that this time his standard line was actually accurate. She was very pretty, in a simple, sweet, completely real way. Another thing that reminded him of—

"You didn't answer my question."

Because I'm still fucked up. "Because you're so pretty I forgot what you asked."

She fought a smile, shaking her head in dismay.

"What do you want to know, pretty Tessa?" Not that he'd tell her anything, ever.

"Why do you have a lethal insect tattooed on your neck?"

He angled his head to let her get a real good look, remembering the unspeakably dark night when he'd gotten the ink in some hellhole off Balestier Road.

"Do you have a death wish or something?" she prompted.

"Something." He slugged the rest of his scotch. Shit, he'd better keep the small talk focused on her or his survival instinct would have him closing up shop and going home alone. "What about you?"

"Me? Well, I don't wish for death."

He stole a look at her, lost for a second in the honesty in her eyes. Damn it, sometimes the small talk wasn't enough. Maybe this meaningless chatter was a necessary evil before getting a woman on her back but for one brief instant, Ian ached for…*more*.

More information, more revelation, more than banging a babe to kill the pain for a very short while.

But John Brown couldn't have more. And Ian Browning best not forget that.

"Then what *do* you wish for?" he asked, his mouth obviously ignoring the warnings in his head.

"You want the truth?" She dropped her head back, her hair brushing his arm.

Not if she wanted truth in return. "Sure."

"The fact is, I'm wishing for a man."

He threaded his finger into her silky locks, gently turning her face toward his. "Looks like you found one."

"But I want something…specific." In her eyes, he could see the flecks of gold… and a hell of a lot more. Goodness. Understanding. *Truth*. All things he could never reciprocate.

"Whatever floats your boat, Just Tessa. I'm yours for the night." He inched back. "No promises for anything else." At least he could be *that* truthful.

He could have sworn she laughed a little as she leaned a centimeter closer. "Actually, that's perfect."

He let his lips brush hers, tasting a hint of the ale and something warm and hopeful. Sorry, but he wasn't her hope, not by a long shot. Whatever pretty Tessa wanted, she'd never get it from him.

But by the time she figured that out, he'd be long gone.

THE DISH

Where Authors Give You the Inside Scoop

♥ ♥ ♥ ♥ ♥ ♥ ♥ ♥ ♥ ♥ ♥ ♥ ♥ ♥ ♥ ♥

From the desk of Debra Webb

Dear Reader,

It's very exciting to be back again this month with RAGE, the fourth installment of the Faces of Evil series.

Writing a series can be a challenge. There are many threads related to the plots and the characters that have to be kept in line and moving forward (sometimes the characters like to go off on paths of their own!). Former Special Agent Jess Harris and Birmingham Chief of Police Dan Burnett have their hands full as usual. Murder hits close to home in this story and takes us to the next level of evil: rage. We've explored obsession, impulse, and power already and there are many more to come. The face of evil is rarely easy to spot. But Jess and Dan won't rest until they solve the case and ensure the folks of Birmingham are safe.

While I was writing this story, a new character joined the cast. I wasn't expecting a new character to appear on the page and demand some special attention, but Dr. Sylvia Baron, Jefferson County associate coroner, has a mind of her own. She stepped onto the page in her designer stilettos and her elegant business attire and told me exactly what she wanted to do. From hello Jess and Sylvia butt heads. The two keep Dan on his toes!

I hope you'll stop by www.thefacesofevil.com and visit

with me. There's a weekly briefing each Friday where I talk about what's going on in my world and with the characters as I write the next story. You can sign up as a person of interest and you might just end up a suspect!

Enjoy the story and be sure to look for *Revenge* coming in July and *Ruthless* in August!

Happy reading!

Debra Webb

♥ ♥ ♥ ♥ ♥ ♥ ♥ ♥ ♥ ♥ ♥ ♥ ♥ ♥

From the desk of Roxanne St. Claire

I packed a lot of emotional themes and intense subjects into my writer's beach bag when I penned BAREFOOT IN THE SUN, from faith and trust to life-threatening illness and life-altering secrets. The Happily Ever After is hard-won and bittersweet, but that seems to come with the Barefoot Bay territory. The heroine, Zoe Tamarin, has to overcome a tendency to run away when life goes south, and the hero, Oliver Bradbury, must learn that, despite his talents as a doctor, he can't fix everything. During their reunion romance, Zoe and Oliver grow to understand the power of a promise, the joy of a second chance, and the awesome truths told by Mother Nature.

But this is Barefoot Bay, so it can't be all heartache and healing!

In lighter moments, Oliver and Zoe play. They kiss (a lot), they laugh (this is Zoe!), they swim (some might call it skinny dipping), and occasionally Zoe whips out her deck of cards for a rockin' round of Egyptian Rat Screws (ERS).

I've mentioned Zoe's penchant for ERS in other books, and readers have written to ask about the card game. Many want to know the origin of the name, which, I have to admit, is a complete mystery to me, as the game has nothing to do with Egypt, rodents, or hardware of any kind. The secret of the name is one of many aspects of the game that reminds me of Zoe...a character who reveals in the opening scene of BAREFOOT IN THE SUN that she's not the person everyone believes she is.

Like the woman who loves to play it, Egyptian Rat Screws is fast-paced, intense, and not for the faint of heart, but I promise a good time. So grab a deck, a partner, and your most colorful curses, and I'll teach you the two-person version. ERS can also be played with more people, but I find one-on-one is the most intense...like any good romance, right?

The object of the game is simple: The winner ends up holding the whole deck. Of course, play can easily be transformed into something even wilder, such as Strip Rat Screws (Oliver's favorite) or Drinking Rat Screws, a game our four best friends, Tessa, Lacey, Jocelyn, and Zoe played a few times in college.

Before playing, the players face each other across a table and choose who goes first. Player One is selected arbitrarily—closest birthday, rock-paper-scissors, or the ever popular "least hormonal." Leading off is no advantage, so save your voice for more important arguments because there will be many. Each player gets twenty-six well-shuffled cards and *may not look at them*.

To begin, Player One flips the first card face-up on the

table. If this card is a 2 through 10, Player Two puts her first card on top of the card on the table. Again, if that card is a number card, Player Two goes again.

The action begins when either player puts down a Jack, Queen, King, or Ace. When a face card is revealed, the other player must try to "beat" it by placing another face card of equal or higher value on top of it. Depending on the face card Player One has put down, Player Two has only a certain number of tries to beat it: one for a Jack, two for a Queen, three for a King, and four for an Ace.

If Player Two can't beat the face card in her allotted number of tries, Player One gets all the cards on the table. ("Strip" ERS losers would shed one article of clothing; drinkers, take a gulp.)

If Player Two lays down another face card in her allotted tries, then Player One has the same number of tries to beat that card. (If more than two players are in the game, just keep moving around the table.) It's not uncommon for the pile to grow to five or even ten cards, which results in a constant shift of power as each play becomes more and more valuable.

That's it. Oh, except for the slap rule. And I don't mean each other. When two of the same card is laid on the pile consecutively, the first player to notice can "slap" the pile and gets to keep all the cards in it. This is why it is very important that a player lays down his or her card without looking at it.

In the case of a simultaneous slap, whoever is on the bottom gets the pile. (Hint: Remove rings and clip nails; there can be blood!)

When I step back and look at the many aspects of Zoe's character, it's no surprise ERS is her favorite card game. In many ways, this riotous game is much like Zoe herself: hilarious, unpredictable, fast, wild, addictive, and irresistible fun. Enjoy!

Roxanne St. Claire

♥ ♥ ♥ ♥ ♥ ♥ ♥ ♥ ♥ ♥ ♥ ♥ ♥ ♥ ♥ ♥ ♥

From the desk of Nina Rowan

Dear Reader,

"I want to write about Victorian robots," Fanciful Nina said as she ate another chocolate bon-bon.

"Huh?" Serious Nina looked up from alphabetizing the spice rack. "You're writing a historical romance. Not a paranormal. Not steampunk."

"But look at this," Fanciful Nina persisted, clicking on the website of the Franklin Institute. "Here's a robot...okay, an automaton, to use the historically correct term, called the Draughtsman-Writer. It was an actual invention by the eighteenth-century Swiss engineer Henri Maillardet, and it can produce four drawings and three poems in both French *and* English. Look, you can watch a video of it! How cool is that?"

"You can't just write about something because it's cool." Serious Nina arranged the paprika, parsley, and peppercorn bottles. "You have to have a reason."

"Coolness *is* a reason."

"Coolness is a reason for a teenager to wear ear cuffs. You are writing a historical romance novel. You need much more than coolness as a basis for your story. You need intense conflict, sexual attraction, danger, and agonizing goals that tear your characters apart before they overcome all obstacles and live happily ever after."

"But—"

Serious Nina frowned. "Focus and figure it out. Conflict. Emotions. Anguish. Happy ending. No robots."

"Okay, there's a war going on, right?" Fanciful Nina pushed aside her bon-bons and hauled out her research books. "Rich with possibilities for conflict and emotion. Did you know that in 1854, scientist Charles Wheatstone invented a machine that transmitted messages in cipher? It drew the attention of Baron Playfair, who thought encoded messages would be useful during the Crimean War, and they submitted the machine to the British Foreign Office. How cool is..."

"No," Serious Nina said firmly. "No cool."

"How *interesting* is that?" Fanciful Nina amended.

"May I remind you that you're writing about Sebastian Hall?" Serious Nina put a bottle of rosemary before the sage. "Sebastian is a musician, a free spirit, a gregarious, talented fellow who loves to perform and enjoy himself. He doesn't care about robots or cipher machines. His brother Darius, on the other hand..."

"But what if Sebastian has to care about a cipher machine?" Fanciful Nina reached for another bon-bon. "What if something happens that makes him lose his fun-loving attitude? Omigod, what if something happens that makes him lose his *career?*"

Serious Nina blinked. "You would make Sebastian lose his career?"

"You're the one who said 'anguish.' What if his right hand is permanently injured?"

"But . . . but Sebastian is so dreamy. So devilishly handsome. Why would you do that to him?"

"So that he's forced to find a new purpose." Fanciful Nina jumped up and started pacing. "What if Sebastian has to stop focusing on himself for once in his life in order to help someone who needs him? Like his brother? Or Clara? Or his brother *and* Clara?"

"Well . . ."

Fanciful Nina clapped her hands. "What if Darius knows something is wrong? Being a mechanical-minded fellow, he's seeking secret plans for a machine that could be used in wartime. And because encoding machines and automata often have similar mechanisms, the plans are hidden in the Museum of Automata where Clara lives. So Sebastian has to approach Clara because he promised to help Darius, only he can't tell her what he needs. And he doesn't yet know that Clara has a desperate, heart-wrenching goal of her own. And Sebastian is the only person who can help her attain it!"

Fanciful Nina raised her arms in victory. "Conflict. Anguish. Strong goals. Very hot, sexy attraction. I'll figure out the happy ending later."

Serious Nina was silent. She picked at the label of a turmeric bottle.

"What?" Fanciful Nina frowned. "It's good."

"But does Sebastian *have* to lose his career?"

"He'll find his way back to music," Fanciful Nina said reassuringly. "I promise."

"With Clara."

"Of course! Their love is so powerful that they create a

new and exhilarating future together. With lots of steamy lovemaking."

Serious Nina put the turmeric bottle back into place on the rack.

"Okay," she finally agreed. "That's cool."

Happy Reading!

Nina Rowan

♥ ♥ ♥ ♥ ♥ ♥ ♥ ♥ ♥ ♥ ♥ ♥ ♥ ♥

From the desk of Jane Graves

Dear Reader,

Our cat, Isabel, is a rescue kitty. She had it rough her first few years, but after living with her foster mom for several months, she was ready to be adopted. She was so sweet and engaging in spite of what had happened to her that we bonded instantly. Her foster mom was delighted that I was a writer, which meant someone was home all day every day to cater to Isabel's every whim. As she put it, "She hit the jackpot!"

As an animal lover, I'm always on the lookout for romance novels that feature pets. So when I was deciding what to write next, I wanted to include pets in a big way. Then I read a popular legend that revolves around pets—the Legend of the Rainbow Bridge—and I knew I'd found the basis for my new series. According to the legend, there's a spirit world tied to earth, inhabited by beloved pets who've passed to the other side. With all earthly age and disease erased, they wait in this transitional paradise for their human companions to join them. After a joyful reunion, together they cross the Rainbow Bridge to heaven.

From there, I created Rainbow Valley, a small town deep in the Texas Hill Country, which is considered to be the home of the mythical Rainbow Bridge and bills itself as the most pet-friendly town in America. The first book, COWBOY TAKE ME AWAY, revolves around the Rainbow Valley Animal Shelter, a place where animals like Isabel get a second chance to find a loving home.

As I write this, Isabel is asleep in my lap. She weighs approximately a thousand pounds these days and makes my legs fall asleep, but how can I tell her to move? We're here to make her life better than the life she knew before. I don't know if the legend is true or not. But I do know that the spirit of the legend—that of enduring love— couldn't be more appropriate for a romance novel. And I like the idea that someday, when I leave this world, she just might be waiting for me at the Rainbow Bridge.

I hope you enjoy COWBOY TAKE ME AWAY!

Happy reading!

Jane Graves

janegraves.com
Facebook.com
Twitter@janegraves